C... G...

D1179243

F/511478

UPGRADING

UPGRADING

SIMON BROOKE

ORION

First published in Great Britain in 2002 by Orion Books
an imprint of The Orion Publishing Group
Orion House, 5 Upper St Martin's Lane, London WC2H 9EA

A CIP catalogue record for this book
is available
from the British Library

ISBN (hardback) 0 75284 760 0
ISBN (trade paperback) 0 75284 761 9

Typeset by Deltatype Ltd,
Birkenhead, Merseyside
Printed and bound in Great Britain by
Clays Ltd, St Ives

To Elsie

My thanks go to my agents Kerith Biggs and Elizabeth Wright and to my editor Kirsty Fowkes.

'The rich are different from us'
F. SCOTT FITZGERALD

'They have more money'
ERNEST HEMINGWAY

'Why should I let the
toad work squat on my life?'
PHILIP LARKIN

CHAPTER ONE

I CONSIDER PRESSING THE BELL for a second
time but decide to count to ten and see what happens.

Nothing.

This is obviously a wind-up. God, how embarrassing. I
polish my shoes behind my trouser legs and, in the process,
nearly fall backwards down the steps. I steady myself on the
railings and look round discreetly to see if anyone has seen
this ridiculous manoeuvre. Fortunately they haven't.

Come on. It can't take that long to get to the door. Unless
she's on crutches. Or in a wheelchair. Or she's 105 but with
the mind and libido of a twenty-year-old. What the hell am I
doing?

It's still warm outside and the last rays of the sun are
playing gently on the back of my neck. The smell of my hair
gel begins to blend with my Chanel Gentleman's Cologne.
Oh, Christ! Perhaps it's all a bit too much – less is more in
these situations. She'll probably think I'm a poof. Probably
thinks we all are. The smell will probably put her off. She'll
be totally freaked by the whole thing and say 'Er, listen, I've
been thinking. Thanks but no thanks. Hope you understand.'
Course I do. Don't blame you. I've got dressed up, spent
seven quid on a taxi because I was terrified of being late and
all for nothing. Course I understand.

Oh, come on.

I do a quick nose and fly check and push my tie up again.

Another ten seconds and I'm out of here. Forget this ever
happened. Ring Jonathan when I get home and tell him.

Call it thirty seconds.

I've decided to be conservative in my dress and go for dark
grey trousers, blue blazer (without gold buttons – that would
be too much), a pale blue shirt and a dark maroon spotted tie.

Forget it. I'll just wander casually back along the road.

Suddenly the door is opened by a woman with a mass of

thick, back-combed hair. She has a drink in one hand and a phone in the other, the receiver clamped under her chin. She looks at me for a second through dark eye make-up while the person on the other end is talking and then she walks back down the hallway leaving the door open.

That's it. I'm definitely out of here.

Oh, Christ! What if she rings Jonathan and complains? I follow her in. The house smells of her perfume and her dog. I hear it barking madly at the back of the house and wonder whether it's on its way out to savage me and prevent its mistress from making a fool of herself with a younger man but then the noise stops.

We go into what people living round here would call a drawing room. Bookcases either side of a huge fireplace. A portrait of a woman above it. I do a double-take – is it her? No, the woman looks slightly different. Mother? Sister? I sit down on a hard leather Chesterfield settee. In front of me is a very seventies brass and smoked-glass coffee table. I look around the room. It's an odd mixture of posh and naff: an antique wooden sideboard with silver picture frames and candlesticks next to a plastic garden chair stacked up with old copies of *Tatler* and *Harpers & Queen*. Across the room is a highly polished grand piano and underneath it a dog basket littered with chewed toys. I look back, not wanting to seem nosy.

She is still on the phone. The person on the other end is giving her some strong advice.

'OK, OK', she says. 'Look, I must go, Mummy. OK, OK. I must go but I'll see you at Susie's. Yup, lots of love. Bye.'

She puts the receiver down and starts on at me. She looks like an actress – strong cheekbones and a large, sensual mouth. Have I seen her somewhere before? One of those three-part mini series on ITV, perhaps? The ones my mum watches and then says, 'How silly. I was really only waiting for the news.' Her face is lined with tension and her eyes dart around the room. The small wrinkles round her mouth are like streams flowing into a large dark lake. I realize I'm staring.

'I just want to talk, OK? Just talk.' She shrugs her shoulders and I nod, not sure what to say. She is obviously quite pissed already. 'I *don't* want anything else, OK? I don't

2

even want to *know* what kind of things you get up to with some of the women you see. I just want to talk, OK? I just want to go out and have a drink and a chat and leave it at that.'

'I know, you told me.' She looks at me blankly. 'You said when we spoke on the phone, earlier.'

'Exactly,' she says quickly. She told me that she was very embarrassed about doing this and she had never done this kind of thing before but she'd read about this service in the papers and suddenly thought this evening that it might be a good thing to check it out or 'give it a whirl', as she had put it. So here we are – me and Diana. On a date.

She flops onto the sofa, kicks off her shoes and runs her hands through her hair, staring at the ceiling. She looks tired but psyched about something. I get the feeling she spends a lot of time like this. 'I just want to relax a bit, go to a nice restaurant and have a night off. You do understand, don't you, er, Andrew? It is Andrew, isn't it? I'm sure you understand what I'm saying. We're not talking at cross purposes, are we?' She avoids looking me in the eye or, for that matter, having a conversation with me. I put it down to shyness. Or coke. Or madness.

'No,' I say. 'I know what you mean. That's fine with me.' Is that right? I wish I felt as confident as I sound.

She gets up and is off again. 'I've never done this sort of thing before. I don't know what kind of women usually do this. Probably sad old things,' she laughs nervously, a deep, forced, humourless laugh that shakes her shoulders. 'I expect you're gasping for a drink. God knows, I could do with another.'

I ask for a Scotch because that is what she is drinking and she puts it down in front of me, spilling it slightly on the coffee table. Then she looks at me again.

'You're a bit young, I must say. I would have thought they'd have sent someone older.' I'm about to say something – God know's what – when she starts again. 'Look, I'm going to get changed. There's the phone – you book somewhere. I don't know where, I really don't care. Where do people eat these days? We used to go to the Mirabelle. Is that still going?' She walks out without waiting for a reply.

I turn round and pick up the phone. I ring directory

enquiries and ask for the Mirabelle. Thank God they've got a table for two in half an hour. Perhaps I'll tell her that it was tricky but I know the maître d'. Would she believe that? Unlikely. Anyway, the Mirabelle. Should be fun. Except that I've got to entertain her for two hours. Think of something witty to say. Like what? Oh, fuck! Never mind. Better than sitting at home watching telly.

'This place has changed,' she says as she sits down. I suppose I should have known where she'd like to go from the extensive database of restaurants filed in my brain.

'When were you last here?' I ask her, suddenly realizing that this is not a tactful question.

Sure enough she looks at me for a moment and then says: 'Probably before you were born.'

I try and think of something charming to say like, 'Oh, I can't believe that', but I'm not quick enough off the mark so I have to let that one go rather ungallantly.

'Well, this is all looks delicious, doesn't it?' she says, holding the menu at a distance.

'Yeah—'

'What on earth is arugula? You see it everywhere these days, don't you? Is it a type of fish?'

'I think it's rocket, isn't it? Type of salad or something?' I say, glad to be able to explain it to her as if I know a lot about food and restaurants and what to eat.

'Oh, good. I love fish. I can never be bothered to cook at home. It's hardly worth it for one, is it? Do you live on your own? Well, I suppose you must in your line of work. I just live on toast and Marmite unless I'm having lunch with someone . . .'

I nod and smile. Well, if nothing else happens, at least I got here.

We have quite a giggle even though I can't really follow a word she says – something about her husband having an affair with some 'Euro trash totty' he met when he was working in Frankfurt but she isn't that bothered – two months after they had got married, she took up with a painter they had employed.

'What? While he was painting your house?' I ask. She looks surprised.

4

'He was painting my portrait.'

She also tells me about her mother having something done to her conservatory in Herefordshire as well, I think. She drinks two bottles of red wine on her own. I give up when I begin to feel my lips go numb. I have to stay sober for obvious reasons. I make her laugh a bit towards the end of the evening and we are almost the last to leave.

Outside I successfully hail a cab (thank God!) and we go back to hers.

'That was fun,' says Diana, as if to confirm it. She flops down on the settee and I stand for a moment, wondering whether I should make some sort of move on her. I know this isn't necessarily part of the deal and I can't say it feels right, but somehow I feel I should offer it.

So I wonder whether to sit next to her, which would mean twisting my neck round to talk to her but would be better for the Next Move, or whether to sit opposite her, which would make conversation easier but would mean I would have to cross the room at the appropriate time should the situation arise.

'Yeah,' I say as casually as any man caught in this dreadful dilemma can. Fortunately she gets up and walks over to the drinks cabinet.

'Now, how about another whisky?'

'Thanks,' I say, still standing. 'I mean brandy would be great'.

'Sit down,' she says and gestures to an armchair. Phew. That's that decided, then. I think.

As she chatters away about a holiday she had a few years ago in Mustique or somewhere like that where there was absolutely nothing to do but fortunately a girl she was at school with had the hut next to hers, I find myself waiting anxiously for some indication in her manner that she wants something else, whatever that might be. But – thank God – just before midnight she yawns and says she has to get up early the next day to walk the dog. She signs the credit card slip once she has found her glasses, slips me ten quid for my cab home and says we should do it again some time. I ring Jonathan when I get home and he sounds very pleased.

But then he always does.

That was the first one I did, I think. I can't remember now. It all seems a long time ago.

As usual, I'm the last one in at work. Sami, who sits opposite me, is already on the phone. She winks and smiles. I give her an exaggerated, goofy 'Hi'. She giggles. I hang up my jacket and cast an eye over the no-hopers I share an office with. They too have taken the bait. 'Media Sales' said a siren voice from the Media, Creative and Marketing bit of the *Guardian*. 'Move into advertising. Starting salary up to £25k+. If you're a self-starter with a good telephone manner and work well under pressure in a small team then Media Sales is for you. Clock-watchers should not apply.'

Oh, and neither should anyone with any sense.

But we all fell for it – the prospect of entering the promised land of advertising and the media and working in an office in Soho with those settees in the shape of giant lips and ultra thin plasma screens showing our latest surreally artistic adverts for bottled beer or aftershave to wowed clients.

Personally I have to say that it was the salary that caught my eye – oh, of course it was. This is the kind of job you do when it finally sinks in that you aren't bright enough or sufficiently driven to go into the front line of the Law or the City and mint it, but you do want to earn some decent money. Anyway, it's like my dad said: 'Everyone has to sell to someone.' Good, eh? I think he read it in a book.

In our office, on the second floor, Sloaney girls mix with young lads from the North who are still attached to their mum's apron strings via a pay phone in the draughty hall of their bedsit block and a saver return ticket on a Friday night from Euston or King's Cross.

There are twenty or so of us non-clock-watching, self-starters on the phone eight hours day, flogging 3cm-high spaces in a national newspaper's classified pages to people renting out holiday apartments or promising to improve your memory in six weeks or your money back – provided you can remember when you started the course.

There is an older guy (someone told me he was a disillusioned teacher – as if teachers were ever anything else) who started last week. Apparently he was once on *Countdown*. He is so enthusiastic that he still shouts 'Sale!' when he persuades someone to sign on the dotted line as we were all instructed to do on the training course.

'Wanker,' I mutter, just loud enough for him to hear. He turns round and I smile sweetly. What's he going to do about it? Put me in detention?

CHAPTER TWO

I FIRST MET JONATHAN after I read an article about him in the *Evening Standard*. 'Out placed' from an advertising agency, he had used his golden two fingers or whatever they called it to start an agency ('escort agency' would be too vulgar, he explained) supplying eligible young gentlemen to women of all ages looking for someone to escort them to the theatre or to dinner.

There was a large picture of him – a reasonably good-looking thirty-year-old, with a pleasant smile, ex-public school, ex-Oxbridge and now ex-ad agency. A female friend of his had been complaining that it was impossible to find a decent bloke to accompany her for social or work events.

Jonathan had connected this with the fact that a lot of his friends would have welcomed a bit of extra pocket money for doing no more than taking a woman out on a date. After all, if you can do something you like and get paid for it, what could be better? grinned Jonathan.

So he decided to fill what he saw as a gap in the market place. I would have thought that if there was a gap in the market this was because there was no demand, but then what did I know? I was still poor. Jonathan's faith in the enterprise culture and the free market had led him to found Men About Town.

He went on to explain that clients so far included high-powered female executives who just wanted a relaxing evening out after work, girls who were 'between boyfriends' and women whose husbands were just too busy to pay them much attention. I read more:

> But what about sex, surely that issue must arise? Smiling coyly, Jonathan explains that his escorts offer nothing more than companionship – anything beyond that is not really part of the service.

papers on his desk to make it clear he wasn't even going to countenance twenty-nine. Somehow I didn't blame him.

'Twenty-six,' I bid. He looked at me again. 'All right, twenty-four. Really.'

'Yeah, that's possible,' said Jonathan kindly.

'I am . . . really.'

'All right, I believe you,' he laughed. 'You're probably a bit young for my team but what the heck. I'm sure we'll find you some work. You're a good-looking bloke.' I felt myself blushing. 'No, I've got to say it. That's the business I'm in. You look Italian, you know, with your dark hair, brown eyes. No? Just wondered. You wouldn't believe the monsters I've had in here since that piece appeared.' We both laughed this time. 'What about sex?'

'Sorry?'

'Sex. What if these women want sex?'

'Er, yeah, I'm up for that. Oh, yeah, huh, why not?'

Jonathan shook his head and smiled. 'You are *so not* up for that.'

'Yeah, I am, I mean if they want to—'

'Don't worry, they won't. Well, ninety per cent of them won't, anyway. Our clients just want to talk and feel appreciated. They want a bit of flirtation and they want to be made to feel beautiful. Someone to open a door for them and get the bill. Sex really *is* out of the question, I wasn't just saying that for the *Standard*, you know'.

'Oh, OK,' I said casually. Christ! That was quite a relief, actually. What if we got to that stage and things, you know, didn't quite work out? Not that that's ever happened in the past, of course, but this is a different thing altogether. Would they want their money back? But Jonathan was talking again.

'Right, admin,' he said, shuffling some papers around on his desk. 'I'll need some photos if you've got them.'

'Yep, I can get those,' I said. I decided to give him a few snaps we had taken for an internal promotion thing at the office.

'Great. Now let me see: hair? Dark brown. Eyes? Brown?'

'Er, yep,' I said, looking away from him for some reason.

'OK, height? You're what, six two?' I nodded. 'Good height, they don't like men too tall. You keep in shape, obviously.' Oh, Christ, the sex thing again. I suddenly panicked that he was going to ask me to take my clothes off or something. He laughed. 'Don't worry, it's just that a beer gut and drooping shoulders don't look too good, you know.' I smiled, feeling a bit of a fool for appearing so obviously horror-struck by something so innocent and obvious.

'OK, payment. You fill in their credit card details on this slip and then ask them to sign it.' I nodded. 'It's a duplicate, see.' Jonathan nimbly rubbed the two sheets apart with his thumb and forefinger. 'You give them the bottom copy for their records and give me the top one. Just pop it in the post the next day, should be all right. You'll usually get your money about a few weeks after you did the job minus a few of my expenses but you'll soon pay those off.'

'Sure,' I said. Anyway, the forms seemed easier than the paperwork we have to fill in at work when one of our clients actually buys a slot in the paper, I thought, so I should be able to do that bit right even if I do order red wine with fish and drink the finger bowl.

'I take twenty per cent commission and most of our clients pay about £200.' I do a quick calculation – £160. Worth having.

'I presume you don't have a girlfriend at the moment.'

'No,' I said, too quickly again. 'I mean I have had one, had a few, that is. I went out with a girl for over two years at university but then she started going out with someone else.'

Oh, shit, I don't want to start thinking about Helen again now, but I find myself remembering that ridiculous conversation while she was planning to come back from France. My sugggesting I meet her at the airport and her explaining that, don't worry, she would take a taxi with Didier, who was this guy she had met while she was out there and she was really sorry, she had been going to try and tell me this before but it had all happened so quickly.

A simple chat about logistics that had changed my whole life, it seemed.

'Oh, sorry,' said Jonathan, looking away, realizing what a can of emotional worms he had inadvertantly opened.

'I've been out with a couple of other girls in London since but nothing serious,' I said helpfully.

'Don't worry,' said Jonathan, apparently embarrassed for

the first time in our conversation. 'It just, you know, makes things easier.'

I signed a piece of paper, took some of the credit card slips and left, having agreed to be available at home the following evening if he needed me.

So that's it, I thought, as I made my way back through the darkening streets to my own flat. I was going to escort women to dinner, to the theatre, to parties, to drinks at the Savoy and make witty conversation with them. I'd have to make sure I'd read reviews of all the latest films, of course. Read a few books. Read the papers so I'd know about current affairs. Read *Hello!* Well, perhaps not.

And sex? Well, if it happens, it happens. As Jonathan said, that's not really part of the service.

Just as I was pondering this point, a bloke in a pinstriped suit came striding round the corner carrying an evil-smelling curry in a plastic bag and yelling into his mobile. 'I know, I know, I thought someone had already done it. I'm sorry, I'll have it all on your desk by eight tomorrow morning . . .'

Call me an escort, call me a gigolo, but going out to smart restaurants to make interesting conversation and getting paid for it had to be better than that guy's evening.

CHAPTER THREE

TWO DAYS AFTER MY FIRST DATE, which Jonathan rings to congratulate me on, I throw my Sainsbury's bags down on the floor in the hall and pick through the post – as usual it's just for the mysterious, faceless past tenants of this hole. Who is this C K Hampson who's always being chased to take out a personal loan? And where the hell has Davina Highton-Brown gone without telling Reader's Digest Prize Draw of her whereabouts?

I shout 'Hi' and Vinny shouts back. I look into the living room where he is watching telly in Couch Position A (sitting hunched over what my mum would call an 'occasional table' eating something from a foil container). Later he will be in Couch Position B (lying down and farting).

'Jesus, what a smell. What the hell are you eating?'

'Chicken tikka lasagne with Thai dumplings. Want some?' he asks with mock enthusiasm.

'Urgh. What are you watching?'

'Foreign film.'

'Bit intellectual for you.'

'Yeah, but there's a strong chance of a bit of tit later on.'

'Oh, OK. Give us a shout.'

'I don't think you'll be around, though, your friend Jonathan rang just before you came in. Looks like another job, stud.'

My heart leaps.

'When did he ring?'

'I told you, just before you came in,' says Vinny with his mouth full, and adds in a remarkably accurate imitation of Jonathan's impeccable, strangled Home Counties vowels: 'Have him call me as soon as he gets home.'

I ring Jonathan and he snaps, 'Where have you been?'

'Er, work. Can't give up my day job yet.' What was supposed to be friendly sounds sarcastic.

'What about your mobile? It's off.'

'We have a rule about switching them off in the office and I haven't turned it on again—'

'She's very impatient, quite rude, actually,' says Jonathan, ignoring me. 'Thing is, I sold you hard to her and then I couldn't get hold of you. Bit embarrassing. I was going to try one of the older guys but she definitely wants someone your age.' He pauses. 'Sorry, mate. Bloody clients! Let me call her again and I'll come back to you.' He hangs up.

I start to put my shopping away, telling myself that I'll probably be at home this evening after all. The phone rings again and I drop a pack of cherry tomatoes which explodes like a cluster bomb on the floor. Jonathan starts talking immediately, 'Chat her up a bit. She should be all right. Just a bit pissed off at being kept waiting. Started asking me what kind of outfit I'm running here. Fucking nerve. Anyway, give her a call.' He gives me the number.

I put the phone down and close the kitchen door. Taking a deep breath I dial the number. It is engaged. Fuck! That's it. Two hundred quid out of the window. She's organizing something else. Jonathan will be furious. Fucked up on only my second date.

I pick a cherry tomato off the floor and try once more. Engaged again. I switch on the oven to convince myself that I really have given up and am ready for an evening in with Chris Tarrant and Vinny's gut-wrenching flatulence. Then I try again and it rings only once before it is answered. A slightly husky American voice says, 'Yes?'

'Hello. It's Andrew from the agency,' I say too quickly. Cool or what?

There is a pause and then the voice says, 'Ah! Hello, Andrew from the agency. About time too!'

'Sorry, I've been out.'

'So that asshole of a boss of yours said.'

I laugh nervously.

'Well, look, Andrew – you're English, right?'

'Yep.'

'OK. Look, Andrew, the thing is I just want to go out tonight and relax a little.'

'Sure,' I say, glad to get onto familiar territory.

'I've had one holy shit of a day and I just need to unwind, OK?'

'OK.'

'I'm going to make a reservation for about nine o'clock so you had better be here by eight-thirty at the latest.'

'Great.'

'OK.' She hangs up. I'm about to call a mini cab when I realize that I don't know where I am going.

I press redial. 'Yes?'

'Hi,' I snigger ridiculously. 'Er, where are you?'

'I'm at home.'

I laugh again. 'Yeah, of course, but where *is* home? The agency didn't give me your address,' I start explaining but suddenly she has said it and I've missed it. 'Sorry? I didn't catch that.'

She sighs and repeats an address in Belgravia with exaggerated clarity, adding, 'Now hurry up.'

It takes me less than five minutes to get ready but the cab is late and I am just abusing the guy at the car company when the door bell goes.

'I won't wait up, my little studling,' sniggers Vinny, now in Couch Position B.

The taxi drops me at the entrance to a quiet mews near Eaton Square. Her house is painted white and pink. There are blue flowers in the immaculate little window boxes. A Wendy house probably worth over a few of million pounds of real money. I push the bell and a moment later a tiny South American woman in a pink and white striped uniform opens the door suspiciously.

'Hi, I've come to see—' Who have I come to see? What's her fucking name? Jonathan was in such a panic he never told me. 'Er, the lady who lives here. An American lady.' But the maid jerks her head knowingly and opens the door wider to let me in. Inside, the house smells of scented candles and flowers. It is mostly cream and white with a few touches of gold. On little tables and along the mantelpiece are silver-framed photographs sprouting like mushrooms on a forest floor. There is a huge crystal vase overflowing with white lilies on a glass coffee table. The settees around it are piled high with fat cream and gold cushions. I notice that, like my first client's living room, the chairs face each other rather than the telly like in normal people's living rooms. This is how posh people must do it. The South American girl is saying something to me.

'Sorry?'

She gives a small laugh. 'I say, would you like drink something?'

'Er, yeah. I'll have a Scotch with ice,' I say, remembering that it seemed to work with my first date.

She moves over to what looks like a bookcase but the books are false and behind them is an array of bottles and cellophane-thin cut crystal glasses with gold rims. She makes my drink while I look round again and sit down, trying to mount a cushion in a dignified and manly way. She gives me my Scotch and I say, 'Thank you.' She looks at me for a moment and then her big mouth breaks into a wide grin and she turns round and almost runs out of the room.

I take a mouthful of Scotch to calm my nerves and carry on looking around, taking in this opulence. Then I hear someone coming downstairs. I stand up and turn to see a tall slim woman in a simple, mustard-coloured dress walk into the room. She is fiddling with an earring so I can't see her face properly as she eyes me up and down but she has a tan and an enormous wave of perfectly sculpted dark blonde hair.

'Got a drink, then?' she says.

'Yes, thank you,' I say like a well behaved seven-year-old staying at a friend's house for tea. Hang on, is she being saracastic?

I'm just about to ask what she wants when she says, 'Fix me a Manhattan, will you?'

A *what?* Oh shit! What's that?

'On second thoughts make it a vodka tonic. Oh! These goddamn earrings. You need surgery to get them in.'

Deciding that earrings are women's things and best left to her I poke around in the drinks cabinet and make her drink, adding lots of ice because I know Americans like it that way. When I turn round she has won her battle with the earrings and is looking me up and down again. She has a sharp, lined face but it's still very pretty – slim nose, large dark eyes and a full-lipped, sensual mouth. She must have been gorgeous twenty years ago. Perhaps thirty. She takes the drink from me, still checking me out.

17

'Chin-chin.' She wanders off around the room, moving a photograph frame imperceptibly and touching her earring again with her fingers. 'You said you're English, right?'

'Yeah, that's right.' I try a smile but I'm too nervous. My face sort of cracks.

'You don't look English.' She sounds like she thinks she's being cheated.

'I'll take that as a compliment.'

She ignores my pathetic joke.

'From London?'

'Near it, do you know Reading?' I say and immediately realize that she obviously doesn't know anywhere outside SW1.

'Reading? Never heard of it. Where is it?'

'Sort of west of London.'

'What's your last name?'

'Collins. Sorry, I've just realized I don't know yours.'

'I'm Marion,' she says quickly. Is she annoyed by my impertinence? She moves over to one of the settees and sits down, folding one leg up behind the other on the cushion and stirring the ice in her drink with a long, slim finger. 'So, Mr Andrew Collins of Reading, siddown. What do you feel like doing tonight?'

'I don't mind, it's up to you.'

She pauses, still looking at me. Is she smiling?

'I hope you like Italian.'

'Love it,' I say, beginning to feel a bit more confident.

'You love it. That's good. We're going to a little restaurant in Knightsbridge called Scarafinos. Do you know it?'

'Ermm . . .' OK, any decent Man About Town would know it, know the manager and know which is the best table and be able to get it if she wanted it. I don't. I can't. OK, I'm crap.

I'm about to say something like 'I think so' when she says, 'Obviously not.'

I decide to go on the front foot with this one.

'I'm sure it's great. There are *so* many restaurants in London, you can't know them all.'

She puts her head on one side.

'No. That's true.' She looks at me for a moment. 'Perhaps

you'd prefer to go somewhere else. What's your favourite restaurant in this neighbourhood?'

Oh, fuck. My mind goes blank. Quick, quick. Along Knightsbridge – it's all a blur. King's Road, erm. Pizza Hut. Yep, just her sort of place. She has already picked up the phone. 'I'll cancel Scarafino's if you want and we can go someplace else.'

'No, no. Scarafino's is fine with me.'

'Good.' We look at each other for a moment '*I* like it.'

'Where are you from in the States?' I say, my voice shaking slightly as nerves suddenly grip me. She ignores me.

'Been doing this for long, Andrew?' My stomach begins to tighten. This is not how it's supposed to be. I'm supposed to have charmed her, made her laugh, listed a variety of smart restaurants within a few minutes' drive and persuaded the receptionist at the one she has chosen that since it's me, yes, they *do* have a table. Instead . . . well, I think I'll just go home. I hold her stare a moment and decide to brazen it out. After all, I've got nothing to lose – except £200 and any remaining shred of dignity.

'Not long. In fact, you're only the second woman . . . client . . . I've seen.' Obviously impressed by my candour, she nods slowly.

'Good. Lucky me.'

I smile. Then I find myself pushing it further and saying, 'What about you? Do you do this often?'

Now it's her turn to be slightly wrong-footed but, of course, she regains her composure almost immediately. She looks away for a moment as she puts her drink down.

'No,' she says slowly. 'No, I don't. It's just that all my friends are out of town or busy tonight and someone gave me Jonathan's number. Back home in New York I've engaged a couple of . . . *walkers*, as we call them in the States, and I find them, I find it very relaxing. It's a great way to unwind after a tiring day. When you have money but limited time you can spend it on things like this. I mean it's quite natural to spend it in this way.'

She looks at me as if to say *touché*. She has acquitted herself very nicely.

'Makes sense,' I say. I wonder whether to ask if she always likes her *walkers* to be twenty, thirty years younger than her but I decide that really would be pushing it a bit. She stands and takes a final slip of her vodka tonic.

'Drink up, Andrew, I think the car is here.'

A huge black BMW is sitting outside. A chauffeur opens the door for her and she gets in without saying a word. He comes round to open my door but I have done it anyway so I say 'Sorry'. He smiles. Then he gets in as well.

'It's Scarafino's,' murmurs Marion, looking at her lips in her compact.

'Yes, madam,' says the guy who I realize is just a bit older than me. It only takes a few minutes, which is a shame really, because riding in that huge, soft air-conditioned car is pure sex. Driving it would be even better.

The manager at the restaurant is delighted to see Marion and bows for some reason. She acts as if it is the least he can do, as if he's promised her something and let her down.

'How are you, Mario?' she asks.

'Oh, no so badder, you know whe' you get my age.'

'Mario is a grandfather and still working,' Marion tells me, as if nothing could bore her more.

'Oh, congratulations,' is all I can think of to say. 'Congratulations'? What the hell am I on about? Fortunately they ignore this weird comment and as a young girl takes her coat from her Marion says, 'Mario, this is Mr Coleman. Coleman? Is that right?'

'Collins. Hello, nice to meet you.'

'Good evening, welcome,' says Mario, warmly. We shake hands firmly. I am obviously the only one who is embarrassed. The waiter, who has been standing behind the maître d' takes us to a little table in the corner of the room which must be one of the best in the restaurant. Probably 'her table'. The place is kitted out in royal blue with white chairs and a black and white tiled floor. I begin to feel scruffy – my clothes are quite smart, I suppose, but they sort of look like they have been worn before. Everyone else looks like theirs have just been taken off the rack. Or hand-made earlier that day. Also, unlike me, everyone else looks tanned and foreign.

And rich.

'What would you like to drink?' Marion asks as she looks across the restaurant. I look back to see another waiter, standing by our table nervously.

'Scotch with ice?' I suggest to him.

'A Manhattan,' says Marion. 'Mario knows how I like it.'

The waiter disappears and there is a pause. I begin to feel quite proud to be in this smart restaurant with a beautiful older woman. And she is beautiful with her large eyes, flawless skin and that look of contemptuous elegance. Just then she finishes scanning the room and suddenly I panic that I am not earning my money. She does look beautiful – but bored.

'You said you'd had a really bad day?' Oh good start, fuckwit! I'm sure she'll want to relive it all over dinner.

'Did I? When?'

I panic again. 'When we were talking . . . before?'

'Oh, yes. Just the usual bunch of assholes fucking things up.'

'Oh, dear.' Pathetic! I start to dig my thumbnail into my hand under the table as a punishment for being such a fool.

I try again. 'How long have you been in London?'

'Erm, let me see. Oh, a few years,' she says, looking bored rigid.

'I went to New York the year before last. It was . . . great.'

'It's OK.' She takes her drink out of the waiter's hand and tests it while while he looks on terrified. It seems to measure up. Then she says, 'What will you eat, Andrew?'

I am actually quite hungry. She suggests I have *tagliarini alla crema* with slivers of white truffle because I have never had it before and then steak because a young man of my age needs red meat. She has 'just a salad' followed by 'this shrimp thing'.

'Nice restaurant,' I say, trying to sound grateful, enthusiastic, impressed with her choice.

'Well, it's convenient,' says Marion.

'Sure,' I say, knowingly. Yes, well, it's not that nice, is it, actually? I pick up a black olive from a little bowl the waiter has given us but manage to lose control of it at the last minute and it completely disappears off the face of the earth. 'What's your, er, favourite, erm . . . restaurant . . . ?' Where the hell is it? I'm relieved to see that I haven't smeared olive oil down my tie or left a dark, greasy mark on the brilliant white, starched tablecloth but where the hell is the little

21

fucker? 'Er, in New York?' I finish, discreetly continuing my search.

Marion breaks a bread stick slowly.

'I often go to the Four Seasons for lunch. I quite like Le Cirque. They do good seafood,' she says. She pauses and then narrows her eyes slightly as she peers across at my jacket. 'It's actually gone down your sleeve.' She smiles gently. 'Now, what are the chances of that?'

We talk about London and the weather and a bit about politics, for some reason. I make all the running to begin with, thinking that I'd better try and earn my fee after my disastrous performance with the olive. She looks uninterested for most of the time and only takes any interest in me when she is taking the piss: asking about media sales, about Reading, about my 'roommate', about my work as a 'gigolo'. She asks whether I have a girlfriend and looks unsurprised when I say 'No'.

'Had one before?'

'Yeah, a few.' I'm just a bit insulted.

'Oh, I wasn't suggesting you were a virgin,' she smiles. There is a pause. That sex thing again. I'm trying to think of something clever to say that implies in an understated way that I'm actually highly proficient horizontally.

Instead all I say is, 'No.'

She insists I have some pudding and orders me *zabaglione*, which she helps herself to a couple of times, sticking her licked spoon back into the warm, sweet, alcoholic mucus and occasionally pushing mine gently but firmly out of the way. But then she refuses to eat any more and just watches me finish it.

I find myself wondering how old she is. She must be fifty. Mind you, my mum is fifty-something and she doesn't look as good as Marion. On the other hand, my mum is not rich and exotic. People in Belgravia don't necessarily age less than people from Reading, just differently. She becomes quite flirtatious and laughs unexpectedly a few times, asking me to say what I look for in girls and telling me that I am quite good looking, really. 'Nice teeth,' she says, 'for an English guy,' and dabs her immaculate mouth with an immaculate starched napkin.

By the time we leave at eleven-thirty I feel that I have

entertained her a bit and probably performed quite well, once I relaxed. The air outside is warmer than the air-conditioned restaurant but there is a bit of a breeze.

She takes my arm in her hands and says, 'Shall I send the car away? We can walk from here.'

'OK.'

'Goodnight,' she says apparently to no one and then from across the street I see the headlights of the BMW flash an acknowledgment before it moves off. She puts her head on my shoulder. Christ, I am making progress here suddenly. Progress towards what, though? I'm not on my way back from the pub with a twenty-year-old. We walk along in silence for a while and I'm wondering whether we'll end up having sex. Does she want to? Do I want to? Could I? Fifty? If her body is as good as her face then . . . yeah, why not? I'm just hoping she can't read my thoughts in some way when I see a small group coming towards us. They are talking and laughing loudly.

'Irena,' calls Marion.

'Marion, daaaarling,' says a woman in a heavy foreign accent. She and Marion miss kiss and then ask each other how they are and reply 'Good' in unison.

'Irena, this is Mr Andrew Collins. Andrew this is my best friend, Irena.'

'Pleased to meet you.' She holds out a hand and at the last moment I decide to kiss it rather than shake it. I do the same with an older American lady standing next to her. The women laugh.

'He's charming,' says the older woman to Marion. I shake hands with Irena's boyfriend who has an unnecessarily long Italian name and with the American woman's husband whose name is Moose (or is it Mousse?) for some reason. While Irena and Marion chat the rest of us look on, laughing and agreeing like an appreciative audience.

Finally Irena says, 'Vill heff larnch next veek.' She smiles girlishly as she says goodbye to me.

'Sweet girl,' says Marion as we walk away. 'Thick as pig shit. She is doing the old "I live just for my kids number" at the moment because her first husband wants to get custody. Since she got dumped by him she has had to make her own living. I mean she's taken up with that slimy gigolo Bernardo, but he has no money, not serious money, anyway, so last month or something she launched her own range of cosmetics. You know, the kind of things office girls wear. Staten Island secretaries. What do you have here? Girls from Reading or something? Anyway, it's called "Irena". And now her public relations people want her to call herself just Irena, not Irena Trountz, you know, to push the perfume. So every time she signs a visitor's book or a credit card slip she has to put a little TM after her name.'

'Really?'

'Oh God, *kidding*!'

As we walk up to the front door it is opened by the South American girl who is now in a dark green uniform. I wonder if she has a different one for each time of the day, or seasons of the year or just Marion's moods.

'Any messages, Anna Maria?' Marion asks her, throwing her Chanel bag down on the settee. Anna Maria hands her some little cards which Marion flicks through and hands back to her then she disappears.

'I'm going to have a brandy,' says Marion, walking over to the drinks cabinet.

'Great,' I say. My heart is suddenly racing. This is it. She is on for it after all. I've been watching her more closely since we came back. She does have a pretty good figure and the food and wine have made me feel relaxed. I realize that I'm entering the hinterland of horniness. She might be older but she *is* gorgeous. She clatters around in the drinks cabinet and then comes back with one glass and an envelope the same colour as the cards with the disregarded telephone messages.

'Here you are,' she says giving me the signed credit card slip. 'I really enjoyed it.' Enjoyed it? I haven't given it to you yet. 'I'll call you again,' she says, kissing me on the cheek. 'Make sure the door's closed properly when you leave,' she adds, looking down at a magazine, before picking it up and walking towards the stairs.

CHAPTER FOUR

VINNY YANKS MY ARM to one side and tries to get his foot between my legs.

'Piss . . . off,' I hiss, sweat gathering on my forehead but he just laughs and elbows his way in front of me. I fall across the work units and he lands on top of me, sending an empty wine bottle and a pile of magazines slithering onto the floor. We both pause in anguished silence for a moment but the wine bottle doesn't break on the lino so I grab the back of Vinny's neck and then yank him away by his arm. He gasps but doesn't let go. Instead he finally manages to get in between my legs, lifts his foot and gives a good kick. There is a satisfying splat as the ball hits the far wall of the kitchen.

'Y-e-e-e-s. Two one, two one, two one,' he sings above the roar of the imaginary crowd and performs a mini lap of victory round the room. I wait a moment before kicking it back into play. There is more banging from downstairs and this time a shout of protest. Vinny pulls down the corners of his mouth and winces. Then we both laugh.

'Sorry,' I shout half-heartedly. Seeing Vinny still listening intently, I take my chance and boot the ball down the other end of the room. My aim is perfect – it hits the window frame. A couple of inches either way and it would have crashed straight through – again. That's the key to Indoor One Aside Footy: precise ball control.

'Bastard. I wasn't ready,' says Vinny.

'Well you should have been, mate.' He looks despondently at me and begins to walk away. But I know this one, so I move up field and get ready in defence. Sure enough, he has turned the ball round with his toe and is lining it up to score again. Except that I'm in the way. He smashes into me and tries to barge past.

'Since when did this turn into rugby?' I ask.

'Since I got bored of football,' he says, picking up the ball.

We both have an equal grip on it and so I push my shoulder into his chest. We struggle for a moment and suddenly Vinny stops moving and gives a faint cry. The colour has drained from his face. His body goes limp. He swallows with difficulty and then lets out a breath. I release the ball and look at him intensely.

'What's the matter?' But before I've even finished the sentence he has rushed forward and placed the ball on the 'touch line' at the bottom of the far wall.

'Bastard,' I say, trying to get it back again. The phone rings. Still panting I crawl over to the table and answer it.

'Andrew?'

'Yeah?' I gasp, between breaths.

'You all right?'

'Yeah, sorry, I've been playing football.' I turn round and see Vinny trying to spin the ball on his head. It immediately slips off onto the draining board and takes a couple of saucepans and the colander with it. There is more banging from downstairs. We both yell with laughter.

'Listen, she wants to see you again,' says the voice from the phone. I sit down and wave at Vinny to shut up. 'She likes you, mate,' says Jonathan, half proud, half jealous. 'When did you first see her? Two nights ago?'

'Er, yeah, that's right. Tuesday.'

'OK. Look, give her a ring now, she's at home. Well done, superstar.' I can almost hear him wink down the phone. He gives me Marion's number again and once I've got Vinny out of the kitchen I ring her. She asks if I'm free for lunch the next day.

'Sure,' I say excitedly. Wrong answer. There is a pause.

'Don't you want to check your schedule?' she asks.

'What?'

'To make sure you're free then.'

'Er, I know I'm free,' I say. 'Just had a cancellation, actually.' Beautiful. But she laughs. 'Lucky me. Why don't you come to mine for a quarter of one.'

I leave the office at 12.25pm – as late as I can. Friday is supposed to be a quiet day in our office but somehow it never is.

'Where are you off to?' asks Sami, crossly.

'Colonic irrigation.'

'Urgh, Andrew, you are gross.'

'That's why you love me.'

Sami's expression changes. 'If you're going down there can you see if they've got a packet from me, I'm expecting something,' she says seriously. Either she has gone mad or Debbie, our martyr of a boss, is standing behind me. I assume it's the latter.

'Yes, of course,' I say looking cross-eyed at Sami. I turn round and sure enough Debbie is handing out some memos. I smile meekly and piss off.

It's grey and stormy outside but a cab comes along almost immediately and I manage to grab it just before two senior suits from upstairs. Probably not a good career move but frankly, I really don't care at the moment.

The cab gets to Marion's in ten minutes and shortly after that I am sitting in the BMW with her. She is wearing a dark-blue Chanel suit and carrying a Prada handbag.

'Good morning at the office, dear?' she enquires sweetly. This makes me laugh. 'Lovely.'

'I don't know how you do it. Sitting in a dreary room with all those dreary people, waiting to get fired.'

I don't know whether to agree so she'll pity me and feel the urge to take me away from all this etc. etc. or to show some youthful pride and defend my dead-end job and my dead-end life. In the end I just say, 'Neither do I.'

Which is probably nearer the truth.

The car sweeps up to Ciccone's in Mayfair. In one move the driver leaps out and puts up an umbrella against the unrelenting rain. A split second later he is opening the door to Marion. She seems mildly irritated – perhaps he wasn't quick enough or perhaps there was too big a gap between umbrella and car. The driver leads her to the door and comes round to pick me up. But, feeling slightly embarrassed about sitting there like an old woman, I've already set off before he arrives. We walk into each other like last night and this time both apologize gruffly.

When I get into the restaurant, soaked, the maître d' is sympathizing with Marion about the awful British weather. He is immaculately dressed in a heavy pinstripe, double-breasted suit and salmon-pink Hermès tie. He has whipped off the horn-rimmed half-glasses which he was using to read the *Herald Tribune* and is now giving her his full attention.

'Angelo, this is Mr Collins,' she gestures towards me. Immediately Mr Ciccone gives a slight bow and shakes my hand. I wonder if he is amused and intrigued by my presence but, of course, he doesn't give anything away.

'Your table is waiting, signora,' he smiles and leads us into the restaurant. It is plush, spacious and silent. It smells of money. As we sit down I glance around quickly. There are a few suits talking quietly or nodding with interest, a beautiful dark-haired girl eating in silence with an enormous grey-haired woman and two old dowagers both obviously slightly deaf, attacking huge Italian ice creams with furious concentration, as if they were performing brain surgery on their worst bridge enemies.

A waiter asks if we would like anything to drink, his heavy Italian accent bulldozing through the English consonants. Marion orders a glass of champagne and so I do too. Then she looks at the menu, her brow furrowed more in contempt that concentration.

'You should have the calves' liver,' she says.

It seems like a reasonable idea, so I nod.

'No, wait, it comes with that awful polenta shit – you know, like corn meal mush?'

'Oh, OK.' Feeling brave, I suggest spinach and ricotta ravioli and then *osso bucco*. She thinks for a minute and then agrees. Immediately an older waiter appears and takes our order, nodding approvingly.

Marion is searching for something inside her tiny handbag so I look around the room again. Some of the suits are now looking at pieces of paper. I can overhear the others on a table next to us. Two English businessmen are listening to a German colleague. He is telling them in clear but heavily accented English about how he can drive to his apartment in a leisure complex near Kitzbhul on a Friday night if he leaves the office at about 3p.m. and he can ski and then drive back late on Sunday night, having had a weekend of skiing and winter sports which is like having a holiday and if anything urgent happens over the weekend he has a fax and email in the apartment and so he need never be out of touch with the office. The English guys, bored out of their palm pilots, nod, smile and raise their eyebrows with feigned interest and enthusiasm. They're obviously trying to sell to him.

Marion, still searching in her bag, is talking to me.

'Sorry?'

'What was it you said you did again at your office?'

'I sell advertising space in a newspaper.'

'Is that good?' she asks, still ferreting in her bag.

'Erm . . . well . . .' I say to the bag.

'I mean, good prospects?' she asks, finally re-emerging.

'It could lead to other things.'

'That figures, most things could lead to other things. I meant is the salary good – but obviously not otherwise you wouldn't be working for your friend.' She grins wickedly.

'Jonathan? No, exactly.'

'Did you go to school?' she asks, making a bridge of her fingers and resting her chin on it. Fortunately I realize that she is talking about college.

'Yes, I did Business Studies at Warwick . . . University.'

Marion says, 'Well, that sounds useful.'

'I suppose it could be.'

'Mind you, I think men learn about business in the real world, not cooped up in some school room. My father went to Harvard and they taught him things but he always said the best classes were the ones on Wall Street.' I nod, just like the suits on the next table. 'He said he got to be CEO of his firm by what he learned in the job not in class.' She smiles. 'I think you'll find the same.'

'Probably,' I say, drunk with flattery. Not only is she referring to me as a 'man' and comparing me to her father but suggesting that I could become CEO which, as everyone knows, means 'boss' in American. 'Did you grow up in New York?' I ask. Pleased to have this opening question, Marion watches the waiter serving her salad with theatrical skill and then begins her life story.

She was born, the eldest of four, in Manhattan, in a quiet street just off Park Avenue in the east eighties. Her father worked on Wall Street while her mother devoted her time to the children. Her two brothers went to Harvard and then Westpoint and have now followed in her father's footsteps, working for investment banks. Her sister married a highly respected doctor and lives just a few blocks from her mother.

They have two little daughters, the sweetest things you've ever seen, one of whom is named after Marion.

She, however, has not been so lucky in marriage. Her first husband was considered a great catch in New York society at the time. Edward Gordon was from an old Connecticut family which owned land all over the States and Canada and had interests in everything from oil and minerals to sugar and cotton. Their wedding at St Patrick's on Fifth Avenue was the happiest day of her life and all the society magazines were full of it. People stood on both sides of Fifth Avenue to watch and wish the young couple well.

They moved into a large apartment on Park Avenue and began the rhythm of their married life: the office for him, lunches, bridge and fund-raising events for her. Parties, dinners and balls for both in the evening. She was happier than she ever thought possible, she says, biting a bread stick.

But after a few months she noticed a change in Edward. He seemed preoccupied, irritable, secretive. One day she called him at the office to suggest they dip out of the party they were supposed to be going to that evening and have dinner, just the two of them, at home. She would have the cook prepare his favourite food. But his private line rang unanswered all afternoon. Finally his secretary picked up and explained that Edward was in a meeting. Marion didn't mention it to him but when she called a few days later, the same thing happened again. In fact, every time she tried to call him at the office he wasn't there and his secretary couldn't or wouldn't tell her when he would return. She didn't want to challenge him, not wanting to cause a scene.

'And, I suppose, not wanting to learn anything nasty,' she explains, running her finger around the rim of her champagne glass.

After this had been going on for some weeks she confided in her mother who told her not to worry, there was probably some rational explanation.

But she *did* worry and she became ill with it. When he asked her what the matter was the only thing she could say for some reason was that she was pregnant. She waited anxiously for his reaction. But he just poured himself a drink, apparently completely uninterested in the news. 'Aren't you pleased?' she asked. 'We'll be late for dinner,' was his reply.

So one morning, she took a taxi down town to Wall Street and sat at a table in a diner opposite her husband's office. She waited there all morning drinking coffee. 'If he makes you that unhappy, he ain't worth it,' said the waitress at one point. Marion was just wondering whether she ought to forget the whole thing when she saw Edward walk quickly out of the office building. She got up and left too, her heart thumping all the more because of all the caffeine inside her.

He hailed a cab and got in. She looked around for one but there was none to be seen. Suddenly, across the road she saw that an old man had flagged down another cab. She dashed through the traffic and begged him to let her take it – it was a matter of life or death. Obviously concerned for this distraught young woman, he let her. She thanked him and asked the driver to follow Edward's cab which, fortunately, was stuck at the lights.

They went up town until they came to 40th Street. There his cab dropped him off on a corner where he looked around quickly before setting off down the street. Her cab followed him along a bit further as he walked along quickly until he went into a shabby hotel. She got out and paid the cab and was just wondering what to do next when she saw one of her best friends slip into the hotel entrance as well. What would she be doing in a dive like this? Marion did not hang around to do any more detective work. She went home and waited quietly for him to return that evening.

Just then our main course arrives and Marion smiles weakly at the waiter in gratitude. He is slightly surprised but mutters 'Prego' and leaves us.

When Edward did return he was obviously drunk. Marion told him what she had seen and they had an enormous fight. He did not bother to deny it. How could he? She respected him for that at least. He said he did not know how it had started or why. He promised to end it immediately and never see the woman again. Marion was so desperate to keep him that she took him at his word. After a few weeks things were almost back to normal. In fact she was beginning to forget the whole affair when inside the pocket of a suit she found a receipt for a hotel room. That was enough!

She confronted him with it but he simply told her to leave him alone. He took a bottle of whisky from the side board and stayed in the guest room that night. And so it continued until he hardly bothered to hide his liaisons. Sometimes when she answered the phone someone at the other end would hang up. Once the caller even asked if she would have him call Julie but would say no more than that. Some nights he would come home in the early hours or occasionally not at all. Finally she could stand it no more and they were divorced two days short of their second wedding anniversary. At the end of it she just rolls her eyeballs, looks at me and shrugs her shoulders as if to say, 'What can you do?'

'I'm very sorry,' is all I can think of to say.

'My mother was distraught but I had no alternative,' she says, putting her fork down on her almost untouched veal escalope and wiping the corners of her mouth with a napkin.

'And did you marry again?'

'I did, yes,' she says, slowly. The waiter takes our plates. 'He was much older than me, Andrew. I think I wanted some security, some stability.' I nod, understandingly. 'He was originally South American but had lived in New York for many years. He was a kind man and we had a beautiful home in Sutton Place and another in the Hamptons. Life was very good to us and I can't complain but he soon developed a terrible insecurity and became obsessively jealous. It was simply dreadful.'

She squeezes my hand. 'Andrew, I could not *look* at another man, be it in a restaurant, at a party, even at the theatre without him flying into a rage. I think on reflection that a man of his age with a pretty young wife begins to feel that he has something he cannot control as easily as he controls money and employees, objects and possessions. I was like a bird in a gilded cage, I couldn't go out on my own, I wasn't allowed friends or interests. After a few years of this I felt I was going crazy. He wanted to put me in therapy, but the point was I would never get better while he was standing over me, trying to control me like, like a puppet master.' I nod again, realizing what a good listener I must be. Then I look down very discreetly at my watch. Shit! It's two forty-five. Debbie will already have clocked that I'm not there. The Tube! I popped into town to do some shopping and there was a delay on the Tube. That'll do. Back to Marion.

She divorced husband number two and became a free

woman, which is what she is today. 'I choose my friends, where I want to live, how I want to use my time and I am beholden to no one, you see? No one.'

'Very good idea,' I say, assuming we won't have pudding which, given the time, is probably a good thing. While we wait for the bill she signs my credit card slip for Jonathan without any embarrassment and then adds: 'You'd better give me your numbers. We don't need to trouble Jonathan any more, I don't think, need we?'

I think about it for a moment. Freelance. Well, Jonathan introduced us, which is what the agency is all about but we can't keep going back to him every time we want to meet, can we? OK, so I won't get paid his £200 or whatever for the next time we meet but there could be greater rewards here than the occasional cheque. You've got to look at the bigger picture, I decide.

'Up to you,' says Marion, obviously slightly annoyed that I haven't responded immediately.

'Sorry, of course, here you are,' I say and give her both my numbers – home, work and mobile – what the hell?

'I can still make it worth your while financially,' she says, reading my thoughts as she puts her tiny gold notebook back into her handbag. 'I don't want you to be out of pocket because of me.'

'No, I mean, yeah, don't worry.'

'Why are you English so coy when it comes to talking about money?' She laughs disapprovingly. 'If you're going to be a gigolo you'd better get used to it.'

Is it just me or did she say that rather loudly? Two people at the table next to us suddenly stiffen and half-turn round.

We leave at a quarter-past three. I'm now so late back it's ridiculous but somehow, after this lunch and the promise of a few more, I just don't care. As we walk outside the rain has stopped. I thank Marion.

'You're very welcome,' she says coolly, her nose in her bag again.

'Do you need some money for a cab?'

'Erm . . .' I realize that I had better get used to this. Besides, I have one fiver in my wallet which won't quite get me back to the office so I say: 'Well, that would be very nice,' and immediately, without saying anything, she hands me a ⁕

twenty. She offers me both cheeks which I kiss, feeling her super soft skin under my lips and smelling her perfume.

She says: 'I may call you this evening, I don't know what my schedule looks like yet.' She adjusts my tie for me and then smiles. 'You never know, though, I might get a cancellation.'

'Sure,' I say with what is supposed to be cool enthusiasm but comes across as puppy-like excitement.

CHAPTER FIVE

MARION DOESN'T CALL ME that evening so I spend it watching TV with Vinny and thinking about her and this new business, if that's what it is, that I seem to have got myself into. I keep thinking about that brief, business-like kiss on the cheeks as we left the restaurant. I remember her perfume and how different it smells from any perfume I've smelled on my mum, in the office and even on Helen.

I've been wondering what it would be like to go out with someone like her, someone so exotic, exciting, so much older, so rich and just so very, very different from anyone I've ever met before. What is she doing tonight? I doubt she's watching telly like me – do the seriously rich watch television? Probably something to do with finance or luxury travel on cable. More likely she is out at a dinner party with other rich people. Maids serving, champagne flowing, heavy silver cutlery clattering on thin china plates, cars waiting outside with chauffeurs sitting on bonnets gossiping, ready to leap up and open doors for the rich people who will shortly sweep out of the party and silently get into their cars to go home.

I've been thinking as well about Marion and me going places together, other posh restaurants, smart shops, casinos, hotels. Places I've never been before and would never get to even see the inside of as a mere Media Sales Executive from Reading.

I've also been imagining what it would be like to go to bed with her. Smell her strange, different perfume again as I rub my face through her hair and feel those long, slim arms around my neck. Feel the woman with the Belgravia house, two ex-husbands and the BMW Seven Series lie back and give in to me.

'How's it going?' says Vinny as we watch *Emmerdale*.

'What?' I ask over my Marks & Spencer stir-fried salmon with courgettes and Mediterranean peppers.

'Your new job,' says Vinny. 'Mr Lurrrve For Sale.'

'All right,' I say after a while. I'm not really sure that I want to discuss it with him.

'Well?' He looks at me. I look back at the screen where two women are holding mugs of coffee and talking across a kitchen table. Then he switches off the telly and stares expectantly at me, controller in hand.

'I was watching that.'

'So? Answer my question.'

'It's going very well indeed, thank you for asking. Now can you put *Emmerdale* back on.'

'Details, please.'

I laugh, exasperated. 'Oh, all right, for fuck's sake. Yes, I have met some interesting women. No, I have not kebabbed them. Yes, I have earned some money . . . well, a bit . . . not that I've actually got it yet. No, they have not kidnapped me and dragged me off to an exotic love nest on a tiny island off the coast of Mustique, which is why I am sitting here, eating this muck and trying to watch *Emmerdale*. Now will you put the bloody thing back on again?'

Vinny looks at me sceptically for a moment.

'Mmmm,' he says, a smile playing over his lips.

I shrug my shoulders and gesture towards the TV screen.

On Monday she rings me at work to tell me, all in one breath, that we are going to a ball that night at Claridges – do I have a dinner jacket? I say 'No'. She tuts and says she can't believe it. I say I am very sorry but I just don't have much reason to wear them. I wonder if she'll offer to buy me one but she just tells me to get one and be at hers by 7.30 p.m.

I nip out at lunchtime and try a few hire shops in the West End until I find something that doesn't make me look too much like a night club bouncer or Jimmy Tarbuck at a Royal Variety Performance. As I walk into the building, Ted, the mad security guard, strikes up a conversation with me as he often does.

'You see that? Cor, bloody hell.'

I laugh. There is no point asking Ted what he is on about – you only get dragged further into it. It's like sinking sand. The best thing to do is not to struggle so I laugh knowingly.

'I tell you, I thought I needed my eyes testing,' he adds,

shaking his head and rocking on the balls of his feet. Fortunately the lift arrives. I laugh again and mutter something about new glasses as I get into it. I press the third-floor button and then jab frenziedly at the 'Close Doors' button. Ted starts to tut and turns round to look out across the empty lobby for the next four hours or so, which is probably why he is so bonkers.

I try to sneak my dinner suit into the office but Sami sees it through an irritating little clear plastic window in the bag and asks, 'Oooh, where are you off to tonight?'

'Er, nowhere,' I say quietly.

'Quite formal at home are you, then?' says Andy, a Scouse comedian who has recently joined what is laughably called 'the team'. 'Always black tie and canapés for *EastEnders?*'

'Oh, sod off,' I tell him, not unkindly. Just at that moment Debbie storms out of her office, sees me with the bag and looks up at the clock on the wall. She had not bothered to say anything about my late return on Wednesday but I know she noticed it. 'Oh shit,' I say softly and sit down. Sami is leaning across her desk, her face lit up with innocent wonder.

'Are you going somewhere exciting tonight?'

I love Sami. She had been here three months when I arrived. She is just so good. Her parents came across from Uganda when Idi Amin threw the Asians out of the country just before she was born. They don't speak a word of English – the first time I saw Sami talking to her mother on the phone I thought she'd gone mad. It was like she had turned into another person in front of my eyes. Then she put the phone down and said, 'Christ! Parents! Who'd have 'em?'

She works in the family shop on Saturday and Sunday and looks after her grandmother most evenings. She's got millions of A-levels and O-levels and she always empties the dregs of her plastic coffee cup in the Ladies instead of just chucking if in the bin half-full and watching it leak onto the floor like I do. She's so virtuous that I should hate her but actually, like I said, I love her.

'Oh, Andrew, where are you going? Tell meeee,' she begs now in her little girl's voice. I laugh.

'Oh, God. Look, it's just a ball.' Wrong answer.

'A *ball*! How exciting.'

A few other people look across, including Debbie, who

clearly thinks I am trying to make myself and my new exciting social life the centre of attention, whereas nothing could be further from the truth.

'Don't tell everyone,' I say.

'I won't,' she says, missing my sarcasm. 'Where is it? Who are you going with?'

'It's at Claridges.'

'The hotel?'

'No, the pub,' I explain.

Sami pulls a face and then asks again, 'Who are you going with?'

'Er, I'm just going with a friend.' What else can I say? Girlfriend? No. Partner? Definitely not. Lover? Older woman? Benefactor?

'Ah, waiter!' says Vinny from Couch Position B in front of the telly.

'You can sod off. Is this thing straight?' I ask, fiddling with my bow tie.

'Left hand down a bit,' he offers, squinting at me. I try and do what he says.

'Why the hell did I let you talk me into getting a real one? That ready-tied thing would have been so much easier,' I moan. Vinny said I looked like a footballer off to Stringfellows when I appeared with a neat little pre-tied bow tie five minutes earlier.

'Yes, but are you a ready-tied bow-tie person?' asks Vinny with deep sincerity. I think I know what he means. 'Oh, Christ. Here, let me have a go.' He hauls himself off the settee, which I do appreciate – other than a naked Jennifer Lopez or a serious housefire, there isn't much that will persuade Vinny to leave his sofa. He fiddles with the tie, grimacing with concentration and then stands back to admire his handiwork. 'There. That's better. You know you could have borrowed my pistachio-and salmon-pink-spotted number – genuine Crolla circa 1983. Quite a style icon.'

'Either that or the revolving one.'

'Great conversation piece.'

'Yeah, but what kind of conversation?'

'Where is it tonight, then?' he asks but I smile enigmatically and slip out of the door without answering him.

It is nearing the end of the month and the suit cost a fortune, considering that it was just for one night – the bastards must have known I was desperate – but I can't get the bus to Marion's so I invest in a mini cab. Sixty-five pounds outlay so far. Sitting in the furry seat of an old Nissan Cherry I realize the bus might have been more stylish. The driver looks me up and down out of the corner of his eye and asks where to.

'Eaton Terrace Mews,' I say. He drives in silence and I begin to wonder how much this guy will earn for driving all night and putting up with drunken abuse while his wife lies in bed at home wondering whether tonight's the night she'll get the call from the casualty department or a visit from the police. I feel like a stuffed shirt, a Sloaney pratt sitting next to him.

So I am glad to get out at Marion's. Anna Maria answers the door and giggles.

'Good eebning, Mr Andrew,' she says.

I say, 'Good evening, Anna Maria, what do you think?'

Before she can say anything Marion's voice calls down, 'Anna Maria, fix Mr Andrew a drink. I'll be right there.'

She pours me a glass of ice-cold champagne and I sit down on a tiny chair and fidget with my tie again. Then I get up because I must look ridiculous perched on this piece of dolls-house furniture. I find another chair with its back to the stairs. This means that I can listen for her approaching and can spin round dramatically. After about half an hour I hear her coming down the stairs. I turn round and shoot her a cool, narrow-eyed James Bond look which she completely ignores.

She does look great – a simple black dress with a thin gold chain and a small diamond broach. I whistle, almost accidentally, and she tuts, 'Don't *do* that, it's vulgar.' But she can't help smiling. Since we're both loosening up I wonder whether to kiss her but decide to play it safe. I'm still her escort, her walker, after all, well technically, anyway. Besides, she actually looks too good to kiss, like I might break something or mess something up.

She looks at me for a moment with her big dark eyes, almost embarrassed, and then stands back and checks her lips in the mirror over the fireplace.

'Let me look at you,' she says. 'Not bad.' Then she sighs. 'We'll need to get you a proper one, though.'

'OK, thank you,' I say, not sure how to react to this offer. It does sound like a very good idea, though.

Moving through the Park Lane traffic up towards Upper Brook Street I begin to feel that this is what it's all about. A family in a Volvo turn to look at us as we draw along side them at the lights. It makes me think of our trips up to London when we were children: shopping at Hamley's (one present each to a value of ten pounds, according to my mum), sightseeing at Madame Tussauds or the Tower of London, sometimes a film at the Odeon, Leicester Square and then tea at Fortnum & Mason or McDonalds – both were equally exciting somehow back then. My sister liked the milk shake at Fortnum's but I preferred the ones at McDonald's and besides you could dip your chips in when Mum and Dad weren't looking.

I sensed my mum's unease in town and her general disapproval of everything around her, which she saw as dirty, expensive, noisy and foreign. 'You never hear another English voice in London these days,' she would say – still says. My dad still wears his discomfort like a badge bearing the inscription 'I'm from Berkshire where we still do things properly'. God, I just wanted to get away from them and disappear into the crowd, integrate myself into London. I wanted to exchange my self-consciously up-in-London-for-the-day clothes for what the hip Londoners were wearing.

When we reach the hotel a doorman opens Marion's door and I leap out of my side and nip round to meet her on the pavement. For once the chauffeur sits tight. Got you, you bastard. We join the throng of dinner suits and evening gowns in the lobby. Marion is frowning, looking round for people she knows.

'What's this do for?' I ask her when I catch up.

'It's a charity thing,' she says, still looking round.

'Which charity?'

'How should I know? Some charity.'

We deposit our coats and go further in. Finally an old couple appear through the crowd and Marion says 'Hello.'

They exchange a few 'How are you's' and then Marion introduces us. They are old friends from New York.

We meet other old friends of Marion's. Handshakes and names and 'Nice to meet you's' merge into one another as Marion advances through the crowds, like a whale sucking in the waves of people and filtering out the plankton she feels it worth acknowledging.

I quickly learn that my place is just behind her left shoulder. We encounter another older woman with a younger man, a tall dark-haired guy. The two ladies kiss, and we men shake hands very firmly with each other. As the two ladies talk animatedly above the hubbub we watch them. It is something of a relief to see another couple in a similar configuration but it's also a bit unnerving. I can't help making comparisons. He is good-looking, but better looking than me? She is obviously rich, but richer than Marion? She clearly enjoys being on his arm, is Marion as pleased to be seen with me?

After a while I feel a prickling of sweat around my hairline. It *is* hot in here but more than that I am feeling increasingly uncomfortable, increasingly under pressure. I realize that I am here for one thing and one thing only and everybody we say hello to knows the score. We meet an Arab guy with his pretty, dark-haired daughter. It would probably be more normal if she were my date not this woman old enough to be my mother. The dark-haired girl ignores me.

Suddenly I need to get away, not just from the noise and the crowd but from this weird situation. While Marion is listening intently to some old dear describe a party in Venice given by another old dear, I whisper to her that I am going to the loo, I won't be long. She nods which, I realize, means that she is giving me permission as much as showing that she has heard me.

I push my way through people who are each paying a fortune to stand in rush hour Tube-like overcrowding, and slip into the tranquillity of the gents. As the door closes behind me the cool air and the gurgling of the cistern and the squirting of water in the urinals make the room feel like some enchanted spa. The feeling of relief is short-lived as I realize that there is someone else in here with me. I turn round quickly and see the tall guy who was with one of Marion's friends.

He is leaning up against the far wall, smoking. He looks me up and down for a moment and then offers me a cigarette, which I take.

'This is about the only place you can get away from them,' he says, tapping ash into the sink.

'From . . . ?'

'Them.'

'Oh, yeah.'

He is certainly good-looking but, in the hard fluorescent light, older than I thought at first. Early thirties, maybe. His dinner jacket is actually slightly shiny. I am not sure if I'm talking to a rival or learning from an expert. He takes a long drag and puffs out smoke rings.

'She behaving?' he asks after a moment.

'Behaving? Oh, yeah.' I don't want to sound too enthusiastic so I add, 'She's OK.'

'How long have you two been together?'

'Oh, not long,' I say vaguely. What was his name? Mark, I think. He takes a little pill box out of his jacket pocket.

'Do you . . . ?' I think about it for a moment but he laughs when he sees me hesitate. 'Please yourself.' He taps a bit onto the back of his hand and snorts it quickly. Mark, I realize, is in another league. If I'm at the lowest rung of this weird ladder, just thrilled about getting to Claridges and knocking back a couple of glasses of champagne, Mark is sitting at the top of it, looking round, elegantly bored and blasé. I realize that I haven't been this keen to impress someone since I was at school.

But then Mark says, 'You know it's a fucking mug's game.'

'Is it?' I look at him in the mirror.

He laughs. 'You haven't been doing it long, have you?' he asks, scratching something off the sleeve of his jacket.

'Er, no. Not very long,' I say casually, wondering whether I should be honest if he does ask me.

'Mind you, it beats working for a living,' is all he says.

'I know,' I add, glad to hear him sound at least slightly positive.

He sniffs and then looks at me in the mirror for a moment. 'Just one word of advice, young man. Make sure there's more give than take on their part and make sure that the give is in cash wherever possible.' He turns to look in the mirror. 'Like the song says, "Get that ice or else no dice!"'

He checks his tie, runs his hands through his thick, dark hair and wipes his nose quickly with a finger. 'OK? Shall we join the ladies?'

I had a feeling that I had been to Claridges before that night. The next day, at work, it came to me. I hadn't been there myself but, in an alcove in their living room, my mum and dad have a large ornamental brandy glass. For years they've been putting into it boxes of matches from hotels, boats and restaurants. If you dig down deep into the little envelopes and boxes you can find matches from the Canberra, the Negresco, the Moulin Rouge or the Ritz. Once when I was young I reached up and took one off the top. It was from Claridges where my mum and dad had attended some industry awards ceremony. It was a Sunday afternoon and there was nothing else to do so I took the box out into the garden and lit every match, watching it burnt down as low as I could bear the pain.

My mum was furious. Looking back, it wasn't just the fact that I could have set light to myself that upset her so much. The thing was that now she would have to wait until they went to Claridges again before she could get another one and that might not be for years to come. These silly little cardboard boxes were her only connection with a world of glamour and wealth, proof that they had been to these places, that in their own little way they had made it.

Fortunately I don't have to dance with Marion, something that had caused me huge anxiety and even prompted me to tiptoe around my bedroom, arms held aloft in an imaginary embrace, because she announces immediately after dinner that we are leaving. On the way out, we pass Mark and date. The women kiss and the old dear spends so much time telling Marion to take care of herself that you'd think she was going up the Congo with a backpack, not returning to Belgravia in a car.

Mark kisses Marion's hand and then says something that makes both women laugh but I can't catch above the noise.

He shakes my hand firmly and says 'Seeyaround', like he doesn't care whether he will or not.

'Thank God that's over,' says Marion as we get back into the car.

'Didn't you enjoy it?'

'No! Did you? Things I do for charity. I'll get my reward somewhere, I suppose.'

Although she hasn't said anything to the driver, I discover that we are going back to hers. She hardly speaks as we set off through Hyde Park Corner and Belgrave Square. I suddenly feel that I should be saying something. I'm not being paid for tonight, I suppose, but I am being paid *for* so I should still entertain. Or, at least, break this huge, overwhelming silence.

Just then the driver overtakes a coach aggressively and we pass a bus. A couple of the passengers look down at us.

We *are* on for sex, aren't we, Marion? I give her a sideways glance. There is tension in the air that has nothing to do with exhaustion after the non-stop chat and introductions of the last few hours or the state of the late-night traffic. She is clutching her evening bag as if it were a life jacket.

We arrive at hers and Marion mutters good night to the driver. She lets us into the house. The lights are on and it seems more comfortable, more inviting than when we left it. She asks me something.

'Mmm?' I say, raising my eyebrows quizzically.

She rolls her eyes unnecessarily, like 'don't make this even more awkward for me'.

'I said, do you want a drink?'

I look at her. We are standing very close. She suddenly seems very small, very vulnerable. I shake my head. Then I cup her face in my hands and kiss her. She accepts my tongue and I hear her moan slightly. She puts her arms round me and pulls me nearer. Then I pull away and begin to move down to her neck, enjoying the softness of her skin, the mixture of smells: that expensive perfume plus alcohol and someone's cigarette smoke. She gasps again and starts to push my jacket off my shoulders. I bite her neck gently, messing up her immaculate hair. She gasps again and I realize I've done the right thing. Whatever our relationship is, and at the moment, I really don't care how you'd categorize it, this just feels good. I can't rationalize now, partly because I've never been in this situation before but mainly because I'm thinking with my dick.

I begin to get an erection and push my groin into her as I kiss her neck further. She mutters something. I move round and begin to kiss the top of her breasts above her dress. I wish someone could see this: her beautiful dress being crushed and pulled, my smart dinner jacket, my mouth caressing her smooth, tanned breasts, me grinding into her, the effect I'm having on her, a man young enough to be her son.

She pushes my head away from her and then leads me upstairs. Once in her bedroom, she begins to unbutton my shirt. Thank God I got a real bow tie, not a false one. Good old Vinny, he talked me into it. He may be from Birmingham but he's got style. What the hell am I thinking about Vinny for? Quickly I get back to matters in hand and reach round to the zip of her dress. It slides down and I finish taking off my shirt. Marion looks up at me again. Her body is in incredibly good nick for a woman of her age – whatever that is. I bend down and kiss her again. She reaches round and takes off her bra. Her breasts are small and round and well shaped with large, dark nipples. She pulls my head towards her and I kiss them.

Then I quickly slide off her panties and she kicks off her shoes. This must look like some high-class porn movie – like the ones in hotels when they invite you 'to join us after hours for the finest in adult entertainment' and you're terrified in case, by accident, you do and it shows up on your bill the next day. Stop it! Concentrate! I pull off my shoes and yank off my trousers, socks and undies, nearly falling over in the process. Not very cool, that bit. She steadies me and we check out each other's bodies with that look of breathless curiosity and lust the way you do on first sex.

Then I gently lower her onto the bed, kiss her some more and push my way into her. I close my eyes and hope that I'm not going to come. Oh, God, please not now. Any other time but now. I think about Vinny again – this time picking his toenails – and it does the trick.

With the second thrust she looks at me with huge, almost frightened eyes. I am just about to ask if she is all right when she grabs my head, runs her hands through my hair and kisses me so hard I think my mouth's going to bleed. Then, breathing erratically, almost like a frightened animal she reaches down to my arse and pulls me into her again. I obey willingly.

When she comes she groans and gasps, pulling hard at my hair. My own orgasm is quite muted by comparison. Afterwards I move off her and roll over, sweating, sticky and smelling of her perfume. I turn towards her. She pushes my matted hair away from my forehead and looks seriously at me.

'Good boy,' she whispers. Then, before I can say anything, she gets up and goes to the bathroom. I hear the shower start. I follow her into the bathroom. I'm reminded of doing it at university. With Helen. The single bed, a duvet brought from home, incongruous in a study bedroom. We'd put music on to hide the noise. Afterwards there would be a cup of Happy Shopper tea with blobby UHT milk. Not this time.

I open the door of the shower slightly. Marion turns to look at me. I pull the door open further and reach in to kiss her. She kisses me quickly, slightly stiffly, then looks down and says:

'Go downstairs and get me a drink will you, hon? A brandy.'

I want to get into the shower with her. Splash around, talk to her, make love again but I put a towel round me and tiptoe downstairs.

When I come upstairs again, Marion is wrapped in a huge white bathrobe with gold trimmings.

'Have a shower,' she says, taking her drink.

'No, I'm fine, thanks.'

'Have a shower. You're all sticky.'

'I know.' I reach inside the bathrobe but she smiles and pushes me away.

'Have a shower.' All right, all right.

I have a very quick shower, dry myself roughly and feel another erection coming on. I begin to massage and kiss her neck as she sits at the dressing table, applying moisturizer.

'Get into bed,' she whispers. 'I'm just coming.'

I do as she says and lie down, hands behind my head, watching her.

'Why you staring?'

'Looking at you.'

She smiles mysteriously and goes back into the bathroom.

I feel Marion get into bed and reach over to put my arm round her. She kisses my hand and then wraps it around me.

It's the sun flooding in through the windows that wakes me up. Marion is nowhere to be seen. For a moment I think I must have dreamt last night.

'Marion?' My voice creaks. I lie back again. No, I didn't dream it. Then I get up and walk to the bathroom. My morning hard-on relents a bit and I have a pee and look round to the bathroom door.

There, just as I knew it would be, is another white fluffy bathrobe. I put it on, discover it fits perfectly and go downstairs.

Marion is sipping coffee and reading a serious-looking typed letter. She is already dressed and made up.

'Hiya,' I say and go to kiss her. She moves her mouth away slightly and I make contact with her cheek.

'You're not shaved.'

'So what?'

'Besides, I don't want the servants to see.'

'For God's sake,' I laugh.

'Look at your hair,' she says, disconcertingly like my mum does.

I turn and catch sight of myself in the mirror above the fireplace. My thick, dark curly hair looks like someone has tried to give me a beehive but given up halfway through. Vinny's bloody hair gel.

'Oh, sorry.' Deciding that Marion obviously likes things to be smart and elegant at all times, even the morning after the night before, I go back upstairs and splash some cold water on my unruly barnet. Unfortunately this has the effect of bringing me back to something like reality. I go to find my dress shirt and trousers, which have been neatly folded and placed on a chair. My DJ is on a hanger behind the door. My watch is lying on top of my trousers. 8.40 a.m. Fuck! I rip off the bathrobe and begin to chuck my clothes on.

I take the stairs two at a time.

'Marion, I'm really late for work. I'll have to go.'

'What? Already?'

'Yeah, I'm supposed to be there at nine. I didn't notice the time. I've got to go home and put my work suit on.'

'OK.' She offers a cheek. I'm too panicked to aim for her lips. I give her a quick peck. Then I fumble around to check that I've got my house keys. I'll also need a taxi.

'Marion, I—'

'Don't worry,' she says, still looking at her letter. 'The driver should be outside. He can take you on to work.'

'Oh, OK. Thanks. Bye, then.'

I stand there for a moment. A car. That'll be nice. Then it occurs to me. Of course, I've been dumped. I've given her what she wanted, now I've been dumped. Fuck' em and forget' em. Never very nice, not even when there is a chauffeur-driven car chucked in by way of consolation.

Marion looks up from her paper and says, 'I'll give you a call later at the office. I want to take you shopping.' She looks down at my suit. 'Get you some new clothes.' Oh! phew – not dumped then! The idea of her buying me clothes stops me in my tracks for a moment. What kind of clothes? Can I choose them? Which shops? If you eat at Ciccones and Claridges you can't shop at Blazer and Next. The idea thrills me suddenly. Perhaps I'll get paid for tonight with a little something from Bond Street. I feel the lapel of my rented DJ absent-mindedly before coming round to more pressing issues – like getting to work before Debbie fires me.

'Great, um, see you later,' I gasp.

'OK, honey.' She rubs my arm gently and then picks some dust off my sleeve.

Sure enough, the car is waiting. The driver says nothing, just opens the door and lets me in. I ask if we can go to Fulham please. He nods and sets off. As we move slowly along the King's Road I slide down in the seat so that people can't see that I'm still wearing my dinner suit.

By the time we get as a far as Fulham Broadway it's already past nine. I ask the driver to hang on and take me to work.

'Er, come in for a cup of tea or something while you wait.'

He looks as if this is the stupidest thing he's ever heard and then says, 'Thank you, sir, but I'd better look after the car.'

'OK, I'll be five minutes.'

I belt into the house, have a quick and dangerous shave, throw on the only ironed work shirt I can find and then run out of the door still tying my tie. We set off again and I reach for the mobile phone. I'm just about to ask the driver for permission to use it and then I realize that it's Marion's phone, not his, and she won't mind. He takes no notice as I grab the handset and dial Sami's direct line.

'Good morning. Classified. Samira speaking.'

'Hi, it's me.'

Her tone changes, 'Andrew! For goodness' sake, where are you?'

'I'm on my way, I got a bit held up'.

'You're hopeless. Debbie's already asked where you are.'

'Oh, shit.'

'When will you be in?'

'About twenty minutes. Listen, will you do me a favour? Just grab some papers, photocopy them and meet me in reception in fifteen minutes.'

'Oh, OK.'

'You're a star.'

'And you're a-a retrograde.'

I laugh. 'Sami, where do you get them from? See you in a minute.'

Of course it takes longer than I had hoped and it's nearly ten by the time I get to the office. Sure enough, Sami is waiting, lurking behind a potted plant, in reception.

'Ooooh, blimey, all right for some,' says Ted from behind his desk. 'I was saying to young Sami, here, all right for some. Wasn't I, Sami? Their very own welcoming committee.' I smile at Ted. Oh, not now, you mad old wanker.

'Here you go,' says Sami, thrusting a pile of papers at me. 'You go first, I said I had to go to Accounts about something.'

'Brilliant. Thanks, Sami.' The idea, of course, is that I walk upstairs and pretend that I've actually been in the building since before nine photocopying down in the basement and delivering things around other departments. Debbie has missed me, that's all. See?

'Tell her the copier kept getting stuck, that's why you were so long.'

'Good thinking.'

Sami presses the lift button. 'Why *are* you so late? And whose car was that? Of course! Last night!'

'Oh, don't ask.'

There is a ping and the lift doors open. We throw ourselves in – just as someone else is coming out. I get an eyefull of expensive pinstripe suit and the impact sends my papers flying into the air. Under the snowfall of A4 I see that I have hit Ken Wheatley, the dreary yet remarkably smug director of finance.

'Oh, Christ, sorry,' I gasp. He regains his balance and looks at the papers floating down around us.

'Someone's in a hurry,' he mutters with the quick wit you'd expect of senior paperpusher.

'Bit of a rush on upstairs,' says Sami quietly.

'I see,' says Wheatley. He picks up a couple of pieces while I get the rest.

'There you are,' he says, handing them to Sami very slowly and looking her in the eye. She says nothing but lets him past and then gets in the lift. I follow.

I spend most of the day drifting off, thinking about Marion, our night together, our very enjoyable sex, her house, her champagne, her car. I find myself visualizing the way she pouts, her soft lips, the way she opens her eyes wide when she is surprised or amused by something I've said. I smile to myself as I think about her strange questions, her interest in my ordinary life. I'm probably as alien to her as she is to me. Am I falling for her? I've almost forgotten what's that like.

But, shuffling my papers around my desk, as I'm paid to do, I realize that perhaps I am.

CHAPTER SIX

HARVEY NICHOLS SHIMMERS in the heat like a mirage over the Knightsbridge traffic as thousands of horsepower throb and fume impotently. I look across at Marion, who is sitting next to me on the back seat. She is furious. I touch her hand and she looks round quickly. I smile and her face softens slightly.

'Can you believe this fucking traffic?' she hisses.

'There's not much I can do, madam,' mutters the driver. Marion says nothing. His neck looks very exposed, for a moment I wonder if Marion is about to leap forward and rip a chunk out of it like a lion at a gazelle. I'm sure she doesn't mean to take it out on us, it's probably just her frustration at being kept from consuming.

'We could get out and walk,' I suggest and immediately realize that this is not an option.

'Just what the fuck do these people think they're doing?' she snaps. 'And look at all these fucking buses. They should keep buses out of town.'

After a couple of lurches and a little rolling forward up to the bumper of the car in front, we get within a hundred yards or so and Marion decides we can walk.

'Try and park as near as you can, like Reading or someplace and I'll call you when I want you,' she tells the driver.

We get out and head for Sloane Street. Walking quickly past a couple of shops, she suddenly looks in the window of one, mutters something and ducks inside with me following closely behind. The arctic air-conditioning hits me like a cold shower. A heavy, dark-haired woman in black moves forward and says in a thick foreign accent, 'May I help you?' It sounds as if she is guarding her territory rather than offering any assistance.

Without looking at her, Marion counters with, 'I don't

know yet' and begins to look at the only rack of clothes in the shop. I find a chair by the front door under a blast of cold air and sit down.

Marion called me on Sunday night and asked if I wanted to go shopping on Monday. She didn't specifically say she would be buying anything for me, but why else would she invite me? I was actually quite nervous about this. The last woman who took me shopping for clothes was my mum when I needed a new school blazer. And that wasn't a very pleasant experience, needless to say. Will it be easier with Marion? Or will I get bored and look like a berk hanging round rails of women's clothes? Or like a shop window dummy as she holds things against me and says, 'That's *so you*!'

Even more unnerving is the situation at the office. I've told them that a water pipe had burst in the roof (they do have pipes in the roof, don't they?) and that during the night I've been up and down stairs with buckets and the plumber hadn't turned up so now I was waiting for another plumber but the place was absolutely soaked and didn't know whether it would ever be the same again. I tried to make it sound funny, you know, sort of farcical, with me at one o'clock in the morning drenched and covered in plaster, but the little turd who picked up the phone when I rang – new guy, I don't know his name – didn't laugh and just said, 'OK, I'll tell Debbie.'

When I got to Marion's she let me kiss her quickly on the lips and then told me I was late. I began to apologize but the door bell rang again and she just told me to sit down.

Anna Maria introduced a camp little bloke with a white T-shirt and a Tintin quiff who turned out to be a flower consultant. ('Do you know what this room says to me?' he hissed in a South London whine. 'It says classic opulence combined with a lightness of touch.' Marion looked round her living room and said, 'Three hundred pounds max and nothing that leaves pollen stains on my clothes.') Then she sent him away and gave Anna Maria a list of things to do while I waited patiently in the corner of the room flicking through French *Vogue*.

We move on to Prada and then down a bit to Gucci. Marion sends the women in Gucci scurrying to find some jacket she'd rung up about earlier in the morning. Finally one of them is deputized to say very apologetically that they can't find the jacket in question. Marion's eyes narrow and she gives the women a long look.

'Well, when I speak to Miuccia next week I'll ask *her* about it,' she says. The woman looks confused and even more terrified but Marion turns and walks out with me following as fast as I can without looking too much like a lap dog. I probably ought to practise this – even a man having clothes bought for him by an older woman must have some dignity.

'Prada has really gone off,' she says, irritably.

I look back at the shop, just to make sure I'm right and then say, 'That was Gucci.'

'Pardon me?' she says, making for the zebra crossing.

'I said that was Gucci, not Prada.'

Marion turns and stares for a moment, then looks along to Prada.

'These cheap stores all look the same. Gucci, eh? Well, I'll certainly give Tom Ford a piece of my mind when I see him next. Copying Prada like that.'

We go into Armani and I linger over some rather nice navy blue jackets. Marion seems not to notice so I try one on. It fits perfectly. I wonder about the etiquette here: do I ask? Or just drop hints? £350. Bloody hell – I've never bought any clothes in my life for that amount of money. I walk around a bit, hoping Marion will see me. One of the assistants, a young Italian guy, comes over to me.

'Hey, that looks really good on you,' he says.

'Thanks,' I say, wondering where Marion is. He watches me as I walk around in it a bit more. 'What's it made of?' I'm really beginning to like this thing. Will she buy it? Should I try and persuade her? *How* do I try and persuade her?

'It's all cotton,' says the guy, checking the label of another jacket on the rack to make sure. 'Why don't you try the trousers?'

Finally I see Marion at the other end of the shop checking out some dresses. Would it be too presumptuous to put on the trousers too?

'OK,' I say. 'Marion, what do you think?'

She looks up distracted. 'You can't wear navy blue in the summer.'

'Can't I?' I mumble. What about later? The assistant looks at her and then at me, obviously wondering for a moment what is going on here.

Marion looks at me again, more closely this time, but then she says, 'We'll get you some summer suits. Take that off. Let's go. I'm getting a headache.'

The assistant helps me off with it, saying nothing. Yes, I would have liked to earn you some commission too, mate, but the lady with the cash is obviously not bothered – either that or I'm just not very good at this sort of thing.

We leave and Marion stomps off to another shop. There is one rail of black clothes in the middle of the shop. The rest is white limestone. A Japanese girl steps forward as Marion works her way down one end of the rack and I mooch around by the front door, enjoying the air conditioning.

'Hi, can I help you?' says the assistant in a tiny voice. Marion ignores her so she turns to me.

'Just looking, thanks,' I say smiling. She smiles back, a fixed, bored smile. Suddenly I decide that I need some fresh air. I tell Marion that I am just stepping outside.

'Oh, OK,' she says. 'But don't go far, I don't want to be here too long.' I see the assistant exchange a glance with her colleague – offended or relieved?

Despite the heat it feels good to get outside. Two Japanese girls with Chanel bags walk past me, as if they were carrying Sainsbury's plastic carriers. I walk down the street and then turn into Knightsbridge. People on the top decks of the buses gaze down at me or point things out to their uncomprehending children. I tell myself that this is better than work. It is ten to three on a Monday afternoon. Normally the street is out of bounds to ordinary working people like me at this time of day. What, I wonder, are all these people doing? Don't they have jobs to go to?

As I look across to the Hyde Park Hotel I see a tall, dark-haired guy in a leather jacket and jeans walk out of the front door and slowly down the steps. He stops to light a cigarette and as he takes a drag, he looks up and sees me. After a moment's recognition he smiles, waves and hops across the street, playing matador with the cars. It's Mark from the Claridges do.

'Hey!' He shakes my hand firmly. 'How are you?'

'I'm OK. How are you?'

'Good. You have fun the other night?'

'Erm, not really.'

''Orrible, wasn't it? I really hate that place. Still, you got her to Knightsbridgge, then?'

I got *her*? He obviously doesn't know Marion.

'She wanted to do some shopping.'

'For you?' he says, as much suggesting as asking.

I remember my clumsy attempt to interest Marion in an Armani jacket for me. What must that assistant have thought? A kept man? Well, they probably get them all the time but I'm just a rather crap example of the species.

'Yeah, yeah, we've just been to Armani,' I say casually.

'Very nice,' he says looking around for a bag.

I consider making up some story about the chauffeur taking it or yelling 'oh my god, it's been micked', but then decide to come clean.

'She didn't like the jacket I tried.'

Mark laughs at my pathetic failure. I realize he would probably have had half the shop if he wanted it.

'You've got to lead them to it subtley. Embarrass her into it. She wants you to look good because it makes her look good, right? So you make sure you look scruffy until she buys you something new and then wear it a few times and then find something else old and scruffy so that she has to buy you something else new. No problem.'

'If you say so.'

'Tried Harvey Nics?'

I shake my head.

'Take her to the men's department downstairs. Clown around a bit. Pick up some stuff. Ask her what she thinks, what she likes. You're here to entertain her, don't forget.' I laugh but he says, 'No, really, you've got to lead her by the nose but make her think she's in charge.'

'Easier said than done,' I say, but nod.

I ask what he's been doing at the Hyde Park Hotel. He glances down the street and then looks down at the pavement, tapping some imaginary ash off his cigarette.

'Oh, yeah. Just visiting someone. Another American,' he says, looking past me at the shop windows and then taking another drag.

'Americans your speciality?' I ask.

'Not really. It's just that there are a lot of them around at the moment – always are in the summer. Anyway, it's so easy to give them that English gentleman bullshit. I tell them I play cricket and they say things like "Mmm, I'd really like to see you in all that white gear." They love it. All that shit. Then I mention I went to Eton, that my family's lived in the same house for four hundred years, stuff like that. I've usually turned into Hugh Grant after half an hour.'

I laugh. 'They believe it?'

'Yeah, 'cause they want to.'

'Perhaps I should try it.'

'Works a treat. I tell them that I'm reduced to selling my body because my dissolute father gambled away my inheritance.' We both laugh at this one.

'You must read a lot of Mills & Boon.'

'Research,' he says with mock seriousness. We laugh again. 'Just invent yourself a history, the posher and sadder the better. They all go for it: Americans, Arabs, South Africans, the Hong Kong lot. South Americans really dig it for some reason.' We laugh at the absurdity of it. Then Mark says, 'Oh-oh, I think you're wanted.'

Marion is standing by the open door of the car, looking across at me meaningfully.

'I've got to go.' I wish I could think of something else to say to him.

He smiles, sadly I notice, and says, 'See you around.'

Marion gets into the car – no chance of leading her off to Harvey Nics now.

'Who was that?'

'Mark, you know, he was with your friend at the ball the other night.'

She ignores my answer. 'That shop is just so gross. That's the trouble with London these days – no one has any taste any more. All the English are running around trying to sell their asses to anyone with a platinum card'.

She looks at herself in her compact and tells the driver to take us home. No shopping for me today, obviously. Maybe next time. I'll just have to invest a few more hours on these little shopping trips. Anyway, she might give me some cash for taking her out this afternoon.

We go to Aspinalls that night and I have rather too much champagne. Marion introduces me to some people, including a couple who both have exactly the same colour hair and we play roulette a bit. It's actually very easy. I put some chips on the red panel a few times and it comes up once or twice and then have a go on the black and the same thing happens again.

'He's good, your friend,' says someone Marion hasn't introduced me to.

'He's my lucky charm,' says Marion, pinching my cheek. We all laugh. I catch her eye for a moment and she looks away quickly. Is she blushing beneath her expertly applied make-up? A woman with a tray comes along, smiling as if she is in on the joke and asks whether we'd like something to drink later at the bar. I say 'champagne' and then look at Marion, wondering if I've stepped out of line.

'Good idea, bring a bottle of the Laurent Perrier. After all, we're on a winning streak, aren't we? Put it over there, we'll be done in a minute.' At just before two Marion cashes in our chips and, as we wait in the lobby for our car, she pushes four £50 notes into my top pocket. More than I would have earned if we'd been doing it through Jonathan with his twenty per cent commission – just for taking a phone call from her and making another to me. I see what Marion meant: we can safely cut him out of this little equation.

'Thank you,' I say and kiss her lightly on the lips, partly so that other people around us can see.

When I wake up the next morning with Marion already in the shower I find them lying on the bedside table next to my keys and feel very decadent. Is this what it's all about? I wonder.

The first thing I see when I open the door of the office later that morning is Debbie. Or rather her eyes: narrowed with fury. She is standing over a new girl's desk, giving her some pieces of paper. I know that all around her, they are wondering how long this one will last, whether she will hit her target and be lucky enough to stay, whether it is worth getting to know her. By the time I have taken off my jacket Debbie has finished with the new girl and is saying, 'Can I have a word with you in my office, Andrew?'

I can tell she is really pissed off because she is using my name. I suppose I'll have to explain why I wasn't in the office yesterday morning and also why I was late this morning. It was actually because the chauffeur was late getting to Marion's to pick me up because of trafffic in the King's Road but I can hardly say that.

'Sure,' I say casually and step in.

'Close the door.' It's getting worse. 'Where did you sneak off to yesterday?'

'Yesterday? I didn't sneak off. Like I said, we had a leak at the flat and I called the plumber. Didn't you get the message? It was a disaster, there was water everywhere . . .'

'Oh, I see. It's just that Robin took a call on your phone at eleven-forty from a woman asking where you were because you were supposed to be at hers at eleven-thirty.'

Oh fuck! My mind goes blank. What the hell is the matter with Marion? Has she no sense?

'No, no. *She* was supposed to be at *mine* at eleven-thirty, you know, for the plumbing . . . and things . . . ' I mutter something about plumbers being useless. Debbie's dad is probably a plumber.

She pauses and raises her eyebrows, sceptically, 'Your plumber is an American woman?'

'No, she's just the secretary, you know, who answers the phone.'

There is another pause and Debbie shakes her head slowly and then says, 'Don't let it happen again.'

'Oh, don't worry. I think they've fixed it,' I say and immediately regret it. Debbie looks down at her desk and I realize that the interview is over. I leave feeling furious with myself or her or Marion for making me feel so stupid.

Sitting at my desk doodling angrily, I decide that the only consolation is that in the end Debbie is the stupid one. Yes, of course she is good at her job and well respected by the corporate squirrels that infest this place, but so what? She's got a job that she hates and it's taken over her whole life. She's got a miserable little flat, which gobbles up all her income and probably suffers from negative equity as well as rising damp and rampant Ikea. She spends most of her income on DIY stuff which is what she does all weekend and the rest on River Island suits for work. I mean, what is the point of living like that? She's got the spending power of a Tesco check-out girl and the stress and the workaholic lifestyle of a chief executive. It's the worst of both worlds!

Thinking about Debbie makes me more determined than ever to get something better than this. And I've got a new plan now. I was playing with those lovely crisp £50 notes on the way into work in the chaffeur-driven car this morning and it occured to me that there is plenty more where these came from.

Every evening at my mum and dad's, it's the same: both of them sitting in front of the telly, my mum knitting or flicking through a magazine and kidding herself she isn't watching, my dad tutting at the news or complaining how whatever he's watching is a waste of the licence fee and how much is this guy getting paid, anyway?

Sometimes when I was still at school, when there was nothing worth watching or I couldn't face my homework, I would leave my parents sitting in front of the set, drift upstairs and, for want of something better to do, sit on my father's side of the bed and flick through his self-help books. If he ever looked in and saw me reading he would join me, pulling one out of the stack and finding some chapter that he thought was particularly relevant. He referred to them by their authors, square-jawed, slick-haired Americans with button-down shirts whose weird names were followed by a string of qualifications from the University of God Knows Where.

'If you're thinking of going into advertising you ought to read Gierson,' he would say, running his finger down the ever-increasing pile. They all had titles and subtitles like: *Close that Deal – How to Make Them Say Yes* or *Busting The Block – Taking On The Corporation And Winning*. Each one was such a hard sell that one title was not enough. There were new ones he'd picked up in the discount bookshop and dog-eared old friends that he turned to for comfort every night, reading the patronizing, reassuring advice. Don't worry, bud, leave it to us – we'll look after you. In my dad's case, reading them and repeating their simplistic, cocksure advice like a mantra was a substitute for actually doing any of the things they advised.

Not that it was that easy to work out what they were advising you to do and whether it would be relevant to the purchasing department of a tool hire company based in Slough. 'It always seems to me like they're generally in favour of virtue,' mused my mum one day.

The central theme of one of his favourites was: Live Each Day at the Office As If It Was Your Last! 'There are two types of worker in every corporation,' boomed the blurb on the back above the price in dollars. 'The Doers and the Done-tos. Have you ever noticed how your boss and his boss are both a world apart from the geek sitting at the desk next to you? 'Course you have. And what's the difference? Your Boss is a Doer and the geek is a Done-to. So, how do you get to be a Doer? Simple.' (It always was.) 'Live every day in the office like it's your last. Like you don't mind getting fired this very afternoon.'

I don't mind getting fired in the very next ten minutes but apparently if you could wait until this afternoon, the way to act was to: 'Devise and implement operational programs that *you* want regardless of budgeting prerequisites!' and 'In meetings initiate multi-directional interfaces regardless of hierarchical command criteria!' Eh? Lots of exclamation marks and quotes from Done-tos who had managed to become Doers followed to back this up. What it boiled down to was: be a rebel, cut a swathe and you'll be promoted.

I've tried being a rebel, living as if I didn't mind getting fired whenever convenient. But the way I've done it is to come into the office late every morning, to leave early and to spend half an hour going to the coffee shop down the road where a pretty Italian girl flirts with me and her crazy old father whips up cappuccino like a deranged magician, rather than be a good boy and use the coffee machine by the loo where a thin trail of instant stuff pees into a flimsy plastic cup like a long overdue oil change. And funnily enough, it's done me absolutely no good whatsoever.

Neither has it helped my dad. None of the books have helped him. I think they just hold out the promise. Like those women in that play we once saw at school, who are always crapping on about pissing off to Moscow, knowing that they will never get round to it. My dad finds refuge in his self-help books, knowing that some day he will find the perfect solution to his life and rise up, a Doer not a Done-to! One day, dad, one day. Before you retire, perhaps.

CHAPTER SEVEN

WHEN I GET HOME FROM WORK THAT
EVENING Marion has left a message on my answerphone:
'Andrew, it's Marion. I'm having a little dinner party
tomorrow night and I would very much like for you to come.'

I've just opened the fridge to get out a Rolling Rock when
Vinny crashes through the kitchen door, talking to a tall
black guy he introduces as Malc.

'Don't mind if I do, squire,' says Vinny, peering round me
into the fridge. 'Malc?'

'Chismate,' says Malc, sitting down at the kitchen table.

'You'd like a beer, is that what you're saying?' I ask Vinny.

'When you're ready,' Vinny smiles innocently. 'You could
bloody die of thirst in here,' he says to Malc.

'You'll die of something else in a minute, shit for brains,' I
tell him.

'Andrew works in the media so he's good with words,' says
Vinny to Malc, who laughs politely. I find myself smiling too.
God, he's infuriating!

'And Vinny works in graphic design so he's good with er
. . . let me think . . . oh, absolutely nothing,' I explain.

'Malc's a graphic designer too,' says Vinny triumphantly.

'Don't worry about it, mate,' says Malc quickly. 'My dad
thinks it's something to do with coloured pencils.'

'Sorry, mate,' I say, handing Malc a beer. 'It's just that
Vinny's not a particularly good advert for your profession.'

Vinny has mock hysterics and then plays his ace: 'And
Andrew's a part-time gigolo,' he explains to Malc.

'Oh, right,' says Malc. 'It's you, is it?'

I finish choking on my beer.

'You bastard,' I say to Vinny, then to Malc, 'What he
means is . . . I sometimes . . . escort . . .' This sounds even
worse than Vinny's description.

'Do go on,' says Vinny.

'Hang on,' says Malc. 'You get *paid* to go out with women.'

I think about it for a moment. Malc looks impressed.

'Yeah,' I say, glad to hear him put it so attractively, so acceptably. 'Yeah, that's about it.'

We kick the football around a bit, idly working out how Indoor One Aside Footy could be adapted to accommodate a third player. Then we give up and decide to watch telly instead. Vinny suggests we get a pizza or some dope from a friend of Malc's. In the end we opt for a pizza because we're all quite hungry so we have a whip-round, Vinny and I poking around on dressing tables and mantelpieces for some change and negotiating who puts in what. Then Vinny sets off up the road to get it.

The mention of money makes me think of Jonathan. From what I remember him saying, I should be elligible for a cheque by next Monday for my first job for him with the mad woman. The thought of getting my hands on the dosh makes me feel pretty good – better than waiting for that little payment slip at the end of the month. That usual joke with Lucy from accounts that she has missed a nought off the end here. Ha, ha!

I promised Marion that I would be first to arrive at her party and I am, feeling decidedly shabby in my Blazer jacket, button-down-collar shirt with its slightly frayed cuffs and Chinos which have seen better days. I'm following Mark's advice: I have the air of faded grandeur you'd expect of an aristocratic son of a purchasing manager from Reading.

Oh, and I'm also sick with nerves.

Anna Maria opens the door with a smirk.

'Hiya,' I say and she giggles and looks down at the floor. 'How are you?' She giggles again, still looking at the floor. 'Where is she?' I ask, trying a different tack. The room is full of the smell of flowers. On the glass coffee table is the habitual cloud of white lilies.

'Madam is upstairs,' says Anna Maria and half-runs back into the kitchen, laughing. I seem to be a bit of a hit here – if she had a few million to chuck about I'd be well ahead in my new career plan.

I help myself to a drink and go upstairs. My first instinct is to shout 'hello' but then I decide that we must know each other well enough by now. I walk into the bedroom and Marion sees me in her dressing-table mirror. Without turning round she says, 'Hello' girlishly and smiles.

I say nothing. I walk over to her and kiss her neck very slowly. She gasps slightly, closes her eyes and lifts her head. Something about this room, this house, makes me feel as if I am in a movie. Being with Marion gives me a buzz that I never had with Helen, even when we first started going out. She was more like a comfortable pair of jeans whereas Marion is an Armani suit and every time I see her it's like the first time I'm trying it on.

Then I go and sit in a chair in the corner of the room while she puts on her make-up. She does it quickly and confidently, pausing every few seconds to pout or look sideways to check the effect. Her blonde hair is already neatly sculpted into its classic wave and she is brushing powder onto her elegant cheekbones. She puts her hand on brushes and pencils without having to look round for them. Then she examines her face from every angle, opening her huge dark eyes wider every now and then.

It's funny, I've never really watched a woman get ready. Helen hardly ever wore make-up except when we went to a wedding and she kept applying lipstick nervously during the service and asking me if it was smudged.

I could never have sat and watched my mum put her make-up on. I suppose for her, powdering her face and applying a bit of lipstick is a private, furtive thing. If people notice that she is wearing it and compliment her she gets embarrassed and says, 'Well, I thought I'd better make the effort.' Either that or she laughs with embarrassment and tells them, 'Oh, shut up!'

I never saw any of my other girlfriends get ready to go out. They probably didn't have the confidence to let a man observe this secret female ritual. One of the first, Cathy, suddenly appeared at my house on a Satuday night with dark lines around her eyes.

'Are you all right? You look ill,' I said.

'No, I'm just wearing a bit of make-up' she explained as if

it were the obvious alternative explanation for her appearance. My older sister sometimes wore it when she went out with her friends. I still remember the sound of a hairdryer over the babble of Radio One and the sharp sting of Clearasil on the landing outside her room that hit you like a sisterly slap in the face.

Finally Marion stands up, smoothes down her dress and turns to look approvingly in the mirror at herself in profile. Then she looks round and smiles at me. The kind of inviting smile that fills a room, the kind of smile that must have caught the eye of her ex-husbands and ex-lovers. And trapped them.

'Whaddya think?'

'Delicious.'

She walks over to where I am sitting and I put my arms round her hips while she buries my face in her stomach and plays with my hair. Then she pulls back, looks at me and says disappointedly, 'We'll have to get you a new shirt. Look at this, Andrew, you can't meet people dressed like this.' One of her long, tapering fingers touches my neck and suddenly I imagine them wrapped round my dick again. I pull her to me and start kissing her. She resists at first, but then gives in, begins to run her hands through my hair as she pushes her tongue harder into my mouth. I begin to manoeuvre her towards the bed but she pulls away.

'I've got people coming.'

'I'll say.'

'Oh, look, I'm all smudged.' Then she giggles. 'Andrew, you're such a naughty boy.'

'I know,' I find myself whispering.

She goes back to her dressing table and repairs the damage. Pouting and licking those lips of hers. Then she stands up again and looks at me.

'We should get you a suit, maybe. A really good suit, the kind you can wear to lunch and for shopping.'

'OK,' I say coolly.

Marion leads the way downstairs. Anna Maria is opening the door to a tall, dark-haired woman dressed in black.

'Marion, my darling, how are you?' says the woman in a thick Middle-Eastern accent, rushing in to meet her. She holds Marion's hands in hers and they triple kiss.

65

'Good, thanks,' says Marion, smiling gently. Still holding her hands, the woman studies her for a moment and then says urgently, 'You're looking well, that's the main thing.'

'Daria, this is Andrew Collins.' I stick my hand out but by this time the woman has very quickly nodded in my direction and is looking back at Marion anxiously. I let my hand drop slowly.

Daria is already getting up my nose. I decide I'd better make the effort, though. God knows how.

Fortunately, the door bell rings again and I go to open it before Anna Maria can get there. Two young guys stop talking and look up at me. I think for a moment that they must be at the wrong house. Both are in 501s and DMs, one has a tight, white T-shirt and cut-off denim jacket, the other just a tartan waistcoat covered with buckles and clips, a sort of post-punk Gaultier effort.

'Is Marion in?' asks the waistcoat in a French accent.

'Er, yeah, come in.' I gesture them into the house.

'I am Jean-Charles,' he says, 'and this is Philippe.' I give them both a firm, arm's-length handshake and take them into the living room. Somehow I didn't think Marion's friends would look like they collected glasses in a gay bar.

'Hello, boys,' calls Marion from the settee.

They walk over and kiss her.

'Jean-Charles and Philippe work at my health club,' Marion says. Daria is sitting next to her, staring at her intently. The boys get an even quicker acknowledgement from her than I did. One of them makes a face to the other who tries not to laugh. I ask them if they would like a drink. They both have Absolut and cranberry juice.

Daria is saying something to Marion. 'I saw Judy last week in New York. She is looking very old.'

'She should sue her plastic surgeon then,' says Marion to the boys who are now standing by the fireplace, gazing adoringly at her and wishing Daria would fuck off. They giggle again.

'Marion,' says one of them, 'you never come to see us anymore at the club.'

'No, I know, I'm just too busy. I have other things to keep me occupied at the moment.' She looks across at me, they follow her gaze.

'And to give you exercise,' says the one in the T-shirt. They laugh and so does Marion. I don't like the tone of this conversation. I'm beginning to feel like a strippergram. I laugh too, but slowly. Unfortunately, instead of sounding threatening and masculine, I just sound a bit thick, like I'm slow getting the joke.

'I'm going to Cap Ferrat next week,' says Daria, eyes wide. 'You should come. It will do you good. I am staying at a beautiful little hotel. Very exclusive. Exquisite service. Anouska had her breakdown there.'

'Mmm, why not? Would you like that, Andrew?' Marion asks, flirting jointly with me and the French guys.

'Wouldn't mind,' I say.

Daria looks horrified, she obviously hadn't banked on this.

'Do you like France?' asks Jean Charles or Philippe.

'Yeah, it's OK.'

'I am from the south, do you know Marseilles?' says the other.

'Oh, right,' I say and go over to the drinks cabinet to get some more champagne. Perhaps I can be promoted from strippergram to barman. I refill Marion and Daria who are having a conversation, or what passes for one with Daria. The door bell rings again and Anna Maria shoots out of the kitchen swallowing something quickly and wiping her mouth with the back of her hand.

A tall, middle-aged bloke comes into the room, enjoying a quiet, private joke with Anna Maria. He is immaculately dressed in a double-breasted suit with a ridiculously loud pinstripe and a watch chain in the lapel.

'Sorry, I came straight from work, hellishly busy, no time to change. I feel horribly underdressed,' he tells everyone. His bouffant grey hair has a definite tinge of blue. When he introduces himself to me as Christopher Maurice-Jackson he gives me a handshake with his fingers only and I am sure he is wearing eyeliner. He triple kisses Marion and Daria.

'Hello,' he says quickly to the boys. He takes a glass of champagne from me, gasps, 'Oh, lifesaver!' and then throws himself down in a chair, undoes his jacket and crosses his long, thin legs. His city brogues are the shiniest shoes I have ever seen. Why aren't mine like that? Possibly because mine come from Saxone, I've had them for two years and I've never polished them.

Another guest arrives, a young pretty Arab girl and a tall, lanky young guy with a quite a tough face and what my hairdresser, Lisa, calls a 'Paul Newman crop' when she tried to sell it to me. It actually looks pretty good on him. The Arab girl is dressed in a complicated beige outfit and he is wearing a starched a dark blue blazer, a white granddad shirt and a thin gold chain under it. They are both in their late twenties.

The girl, Farrah, triple kisses each person while everyone else watches, which takes some time. Her boyfriend, David, follows her, just shaking hands or nodding.

'So you're Andrew,' says Farrah when she gets to me. She stands very close and touches my arm. 'I've heard so much about you.' I smile graciously and say something slightly funny. Farrah laughs and says to Marion, 'Oh Marion, he's charming.'

Anna Maria is hovering. I let her do the drinks this time because she obviously wants to.

'Oh, what shall I have? David, what do you think?' says Farrah, obviously glad still to be the centre of attention.

'I'll have a Bud,' says David in a strong Geordie accent.

'Now I can't drink champagne, my hairdresser says nothing fizzy, it makes my hair brittle.'

'White wine?' I suggest.

'So acidic,' says Farrah, staring at the drinks cabinet. 'Oh, Marion, what do you think?'

'The boys are drinking Absolut and cranberry juice,' says Marion, breaking off from Daria. I am about to point out that this is acidic as well, but then realize that if Anna Maria doesn't get Farrah something to drink soon we'll never eat.

'A vodka,' says Farrah triumphantly. 'Yes, why not? A vodka please, with ice and lemon.'

Immediately Anna Maria sets about making it for her and Farrah, clearly not wanting to lose the momentum she has built up turns round and asks, 'So what have we all been up to today?'

It is a completely unanswerable question, mainly because no one has done anything, and it is clearly just an excuse for her to tell us about her day, which she does. 'Marion, I went to Joe's for lunch today with Vincente. David joined us for coffee after.' Farrah squeezes David's hand as they sit together on a settee; she is pert and upright, he is sitting back with legs open wide and face set in an uninterested, slightly aggressive way. 'Anna Maria, I spent this morning throwing out old clothes I never wear and I found a couple of dresses that would be perfect for you. David, don't you think those two dresses would look great on Anna Maria?' David nods unconvincingly, obviously not over-exercised on the subject of dresses.

She prattles on. Marion mildly amused, Daria fuming, Christopher Maurice-Jackson listening politely and the boys smirking quietly. David is taking us in one by one. 'Us'? I mean the others.

After a while, I notice that Christopher Maurice-Jackson has moved away from everyone else. He is standing, legs apart, arms loosely folded with one hand touching his chin. He stares intently at a section of wall beside the kitchen door as if it were the most important thing in the world.

'Marion,' he says, measuring the space in mid-air with his hands.

She looks across.

'I have an exquisite Beidermier table that would fit in here beautifully. The proportions are right, the width is right and it would give this room a little lift, a touch of—'

'Yeah, like I really need some more furniture,' says Marion, finishing her champagne. 'Three houses full and then some.' *Three houses?* I'm intrigued. Christopher Maurice-Jackson pauses for a moment. 'Just a thought,' he says, pained. Turning back to the group he sees me smiling and begins to scowl. 'You ought to get rid of something, then,' he suggests, still looking at me.

Marion gets up. 'Let's eat,' she says. 'I'm starved.' She squeezes my neck gently as she walks past me to the table. She allocates places quickly. We sit down, no one particularly pleased to be next to anyone else. I have Farrah and David on one side, which isn't bad, and Marion on the other.

Daria, who has managed to put herself the far side of Marion, gives a little laugh and touches Marion's hand.

'We played such an amusing game at Marina's the other night,' she says, laughing again at something that just cannot be that funny. The two French guys start laughing as well but this makes her nervous so she stops and eyes them suspiciously, then she continues, 'We played a game where you have to say who from history you would invite to your ideal dinner party.'

'Not you, that's for sure,' one of the French guys whispers to the other.

'Who would you invite, Marion? I wanted Marilyn Monroe, Mozart, Einstein, Peter the Great, Tutankhamun, and Keats. Imagine the conversation!'

'Yeah, great, except they wouldn't be able to understand each other,' sniggers one of the French guys. I smile too at this.

'Marina always knows such great games,' says Farrah, trying to smooth over the embarrassment.

Anna Maria and another South American girl I have not seen before bring in plates of Parma ham and figs. We eat with Marion's huge, heavy, silver cutlery. I look round the table. Marion, who I notice only has figs, eats slowly using only her fork while listening passively to Daria. She gives me a slow, subtle wink which makes me feel ten times better. Farrah is telling David something. The French boys have their heads down low over their plates and shovel in their food ravenously, throwing in lots of bread. I realize that I have one thing in common with them: we have to try and eat as much as possible tonight because it's free food. Christopher Maurice-Jackson takes a tiny mouthful, puts his elbows on the table and forms a roof with his fingers as he chews.

My mother always asks for small portions of everything. 'Just a little bit for me, please. Ooh! Far too much, someone else better have this one.' I remember one Sunday lunchtime at my grandparents. My grandfather had had his first stroke and was 'not quite himself', as everyone put it. I didn't know quite who he was now but whoever it was, he wasn't very nice. He had never been very affectionate or even very friendly towards his grandchildren. Me and Grandpa never went fishing together and he didn't have a mysterious shed at the bottom of the garden full of weird, dangerous things like stuffed fish and hacksaws.

He had a car, well, a series of cars, I suppose, over the

years. Always very nice ones – Mercedes, Jaguars and I think he was one of the first people where they lived to have a BMW. When we went over for Sunday lunch, as we did every Sunday, he would wash his car all morning and spend the afternoon waxing it, polishing it and hoovering the inside, occasionally shooting me and my sister a suspicious glance as we played on the lawn or in the driveway. At the time we thought it was the one good thing about Grandpa that he left us to do whatever we wanted and play anywhere as long as we kept away from the car. Looking back, it's a bit sinister really that he didn't mind us messing about in the road or with the lawn mower, just as long as we didn't damage his precious bloody motor.

God, I hated that house. It was a mean little 1950s bungalow on an estate about three-quarters of an hour's drive from us. It always smelled stale and musty. My grandparents' huge, ugly old furniture was crammed into it, ridiculously out of proportion, hopelessly out of place. Doors wouldn't open properly because there wasn't room. Wherever you stood, you were in the way of something or someone. It was cold and empty and at the same time stifling and overcrowded. When we arrived Grandma would check us over, trying to hide her disappointment and we would kiss her very quickly on the cheek. I think she had seen Prince Charles do something similar to the Queen when he was young. Grandpa would pass through as quickly as he could. He died before I could tell him, 'I know how you feel. I don't want to be here either.'

Their stuff had been brought back from India where they had 'stayed on', as my grandmother called it. I realize now that she hoped to give the impression that they had been part of the colonial service or that they were old army types. In fact, my grandfather had worked for an electronics company out there until, as with the colonials they always pretended to be, the Indians decided that they could do it better themselves and needed no more help from the British.

This particular lunchtime we sat in their dining room as usual, their large, grim dresser casting a menacing shadow over me and my sister as we ate Grandma's thick, tasteless food and struggled with her huge, unwieldy bone-handled cutlery in silence. Our parents' polite conversation was stretched like worn lace across the table, ready to break at any moment. In the end it was broken by my grandfather or, at least, the person he became after his stroke.

My grandma graciously offered my mother some pudding, guests first, of course, making it clear that Mum would never really be family. As always, my mother smiled weakly and said, 'Oh, just a bit for me, please.' This is what she had said when offered the roast lamb and the packet oxtail soup before it. It was what she said to everything. Just a little bit, just a little one, don't bother about me, I'll make do with this. No, really.

Grandpa stood up (at first I thought he was going to the loo) and shouted at her: 'Oh, for Christ's sake, woman, have some more. There's bloody heaps of it. Take as much as you want.'

Then he sat down calmly and waited for Grandma to pass him his. My mum was horrified. She turned her eyes away from him and obediently handed her plate back to Grandma who spooned some more thin, evaporated milk rice pudding onto it and then served the rest of us. It was actually quite frightening but I also wanted to laugh. What was really so funny was to hear Grandpa say 'bloody'. We ate in silence and fled soon after, leaving the old bugger vacuuming angrily under his rear passenger seat.

In the car on the way home my mother took a tattered paper tissue from the sleeve of her cardigan and began to sob. My dad quickly put his arm round her during a straight stretch of road and muttered something about Grandpa not meaning it, not being himself.

'Oh, I know he can't help it,' my mother sniffled, 'old people get like that, especially after what has happened to him. It just took me by surprise, that's all. It was a bit of shock, I'm not used to being shouted at like that.'

David is talking to me across Farrah.

'Sorry?' I say.

'I was just asking what line of business you're in.'

What line of business? Pissing about in an office and skiving off to watch a rich woman shop.

'I'm in media sales,' I say instead, trying to make it sound like a serious, heavyweight profession.

'Space,' says David.

'Er, yeah.'

'Friend of mine did that for two years. Then he went into media *buying*. You know, gamekeeper turned poacher. He's making a packet, huge basic plus commission, must be on £120K by now.'

'Who's that?' Farrah asks sweetly.

'Rob,' David says quickly to her. 'And he does consultancy work now as well. I wouldn't be surprised if he sets up on his own soon.'

'Great,' I say without enthusiasm. 'What about you? What do you do?'

It sounds really aimless and studenty, as if I'm expecting him to say that he is travelling a bit before starting teacher training.

'At the moment I've got a number of projects on the go,' he says, swallowing, obviously glad I've asked. 'I deal in old cars. Not vintage ones, you know, not London to Brighton crap but sporty little numbers from the fifties – Aston Martins, Panthers and the like. There's an incredible market for them down here. My dad and my brother pick them up for next to nothing up in the North East, we drive them down, I've got a couple of lads who check them over and do them up and then we flog 'em. Amazing what they go for.'

'Brilliant.' Part of me is, I'm afraid to say, genuinely impressed but mainly I'm amazed, as usual, at how easy it all sounds.

'They're such beautiful cars,' says Farrah with an almost pained look on her face. 'And my brother in New York is going to help him import American ones as well – Buicks, Cadillacs and stuff.'

David cuts her off, 'Also me and my mate are opening a club in South London next month and we're going to use these cars to ferry the VIP guests to and fro. Emma Bunton and that bloke from *EastEnders* – what's his name? – are doing the opening night. I'll get you and Marion on the guest list. You can use the VIP suite.'

'Oh, right, thanks.' Yeah, thanks, but somehow I *don't* think so, you flash tosser. Emma Bunton and *EastEnders*! That's the kind of thing that would impress most of the people in my office but I think I can aim higher than that now. I look round at Marion who is listening to the French boys and grinning. I stare harder but she doesn't see me. David has more.

'Then me and this mate of mine from the army are going to start opening clubs in Europe, Ibiza and places. There are no licensing laws or any of that shit and some of those clubs are huge—'

Then he is telling me that he can get me some Versace stuff, seconds, dead cheap, all sizes when I realize that the one consolation that comes with this wanker, other than that my girlfriend is richer than his, is that, with a bit of luck, he might be in prison by this time next year.

Anna Maria and the other girl clear away our plates. We move onto the next course and I realize what it is that's so strange about Marion's parties: when her friends talk, no one actually connects with what anyone else says. Sometimes their comments are sort of related but there is no interaction, no reply. People just politely wait for a pause and then stick their oar in. It is as if they are in competition with each other, trying to dominate the conversation.

'New York was terribly hot last week. We hardly went outside. To the opera once and to a party at Vanora Fielding's.'

'The only city I visit in the summer is London. I would never go to New York during July or August.'

'But you must have been to Judy's new apartment there?'

'If you want to see Judy you *have* to go to New York. She never comes here, she hates Paris and London. I just think she hates Europe altogether.'

'We went to an amazing club in Paris last weekend – go-go dancers, boys and girls. You'll never guess who we met there. Peter Katzberg. Oh, you remember Peter Katzberg, you must do. Can you imagine it? Darling Peter in this crazy club?'

'Peter Katzberg decorated Petronella Bywater's first home. You must know it, off Cadogan Square. Petronella hated it so much she sold it immediately and stayed with her parents in Venice until she found somewhere else. That cute kid, what was his name? Kevin? He picked up the search fee – £10,000, so the woman he used to live with told me.'

'Veronica del Luzio has a new apartment in Cadogan

Square on three floors, which I am *dying* to get my hands on. Di-vine!'

'Veronica's always moving. I saw her in La La last month and I said what are you doing here? She said "real estate".'

'She buys apartments the way most women buy handbags.'

'I'm going to buy another apartment, somewhere near here. I hate my apartment.'

'You shouldn't buy in London. The economy here's going down the tubes. The rich people will get the hell out and then where will London be? You know what the British are like, they just sit there waiting for someone to give them some money. Then they look at you like *they've* done *you* a favour.'

And so it goes on, people, cities, sex, money, good times, clothes, personal recommendations and utter condemnations. But all of them could be sitting at home talking to thin air.

By eleven-thirty we have finished our ice cream and coffee and I am feeling tired and slightly pissed. David has tried to sell Christopher Maurice-Jackson some of his half-price Versace crap. Now Christopher Maurice-Jackson is trying to sell Marion a chaise longue or something. She is picking some bits of fluff off her skirt and saying 'Uh, huh' in a quiet, non-committal way.

David is talking to the other French guy. 'I do ten reps for biceps every other day but I never do me abs. No, never, don't have to.'

'Tell us about the Marines,' he says, 'that must have been fun.'

'Well, they certainly look after you. I learned to ski, to snorkel ... ' Then he starts showing how you fall on the ground correctly after a parachute jump so that you don't hurt yourself. Farrah looks on and asks questions helpfully. Well, it could be useful next time she has to bail out of Harvey Nics in a hurry.

When the two French guys leave to catch the last Tube back to Brixton the others make a move as well. Daria's almost tearful farewell makes it appear like she is leaving a wake except that Marion hardly looks like a grieving widow. I find myself promising to call David for some reason. Ostrich farming, I think. Farrah makes me promise to look after Marion. Isn't it supposed to be the other way around?

Christopher Maurice-Jackson tells Marion that they will 'do lunch' next week and then gives me such a frosty goodbye that I can't help laughing as soon as the door is closed.

Marion flops down into a chair and asks for another drop of champagne. 'It's all gone,' I say, picking up the most recent of the bottles. Just then Anna Maria comes out of the kitchen with a tray to clear the table.

'Open another bottle of champagne, will you,' Marion tells her.

I sit down next to her and she puts her head on my shoulder.

'Well, do you like my friends?'

'Yeah,' I say, 'they're fun.'

There is a pause.

'They bore me to death,' says Marion and we both burst out laughing.

I stay over again that night. We don't wait for the champagne but go upstairs where I unzip Marion's dress and let it fall to the ground. She stands there for a moment in just her bra, panties and high shoes, looking up at me wide-eyed. Then I kiss her breasts and pull her towards me roughly. She gasps, almost like she's indignant, and I push her down onto the bed.

CHAPTER EIGHT

THIS TIME I REMEMBER to set the alarm. Marion is not pleased: 'It'll wake me up too.' I apologize but explain that I really need to be in time for work once in a while. I could also point out that she is usually up before me anyway but I don't want to make things worse. She sulks a bit and then goes off to have a shower. I can't decide whether it's a little bit insulting that she wants to wash me off her before she goes to sleep. I've always enjoyed falling asleep, slightly sweaty and sticky.

The next morning, Thursday, I look hopefully out of the window just to see if the car is there again. It isn't.

'You'll have to take a cab home. Chris isn't coming by until later,' says Marion's sleepy voice from behind me.

'Oh, OK,' I say, trying not to sound too disappointed.

'Get my purse from the dressing table and I'll give you some cash.' She slips off her eye pads, opens her bag and hands me a twenty as I try to see how much else she's got in there. 'I'm going out with a girlfriend tonight,' she says, turning over again. 'But I'll call you this afternoon at your office.' I kiss her goodbye and she slips her eye pads back on.

If she had given me just a bit more money I could have kept the taxi waiting while I got dressed and used it go on to work and been on time. But she didn't and, just for a change, I'm not.

I fall into a light, tense sleep in the taxi on the way home and so I feel particularly crap when we finally get to the flat. On the way to work I get a large cappuccino and two slices of toast and marmalade from the café near the office in the hope that this injection of caffeine and sugar will keep me going until lunchtime. It also makes me even later.

I sit down at my desk with my breakfast and go cross-eyed

at Sami, who is already on the phone, by way of a hello. She giggles and then waves me away crossly. I take a gulp of creamy, hot, sweet cappuccino followed by a bite of butter-drenched toast. I savour it for a moment and then, looking back at Sami, I open my mouth. She winces and then looks away.

Then I pick up my phone and dial 9. But instead of ringing a client, I find myself dialling Jonathan's number. On the second ring he picks up.

'Oh, hi, Jonathan? It's me, Andrew.'

'Hello, mate,' he says as if I was his best friend ever.

'Hi. Erm, I was just ringing to see whether I could pick up a cheque from you.'

'Oh-oh. Chasing me up, eh?' laughs Jonathan. Is that funny? I laugh anyway.

'Well, no, I just wondered—'

'Andrew, it'll be a couple of weeks or so.'

'Oh, right, sure.' Then I say quickly, 'Well, listen, I'm around if you get any other calls.'

'Fine. No problem. Listen, gotta go, other phone's ringing. Cheers, mate.' He hangs up.

'Bye,' I say.

God, I'm glad Marion and I have cut him out of our little arrangement. I suddenly feel like quite an entrepreneur. I start to make a cold call from a list Debbie gave me yesterday, determined to sell this bastard some space in the paper whatever it takes.

By mid-afternoon my eyes are heavy and I'm beginning to drift off.

'Andrew? Andrew, are you all right?' asks Sami.

'Yeah, I'm fine,' I say, closing my eyes for one gorgeous moment and breathing deeply.

'Ah, ha. Been burning the candle at both ends,' says Sami, pleased with this phrase.

'Yeah, I have. I'm going to get a coffee. Do you want anything?'

'No, thanks, I've had a strawberry yoghurt,' says Sami, as if it were an alternative.

'Sami, you're so good.'

'Andrew, you're so bad.'

I get up and walk into Debbie, which is rather embarrassing. We avoid each other's gaze and I mutter something about going to get a coffee and being right back.

I go out to the vending machine by the lifts and watch the machine as it buzzes and gurgles. The temp from Reception comes out from another door and checks me out while she waits for a lift. I'm so tired that I end up giving her a convincingly cool reaction. When the lift arrives she holds my gaze until the doors close. Funny how hot you can look when you feel like shit.

Suddenly the door to our office swings open and Maria puts her head out. I've always had a soft spot for Maria, a dark-haired thirty-something, because of what you might describe as her direct manner.

'Christ,' she once said to me in the back of a taxi after a very rare excursion to see a client. 'I've got such an itchy vag today.'

'Oh, how . . . I mean . . . that must be . . .'

She fidgeted a bit more while I kept my eyes dead ahead and then she said, 'Oh, for God's sake. I'm not asking you to scratch it for me, I'm just saying.'

If you ever wanted advice on anything from personal finance to what tie to wear with what shirt, Maria will give it to you, without hesitation. She will break off a phone conversation with a client to tell one of the girls to chuck her boyfriend and find another.

'*There* you are,' she says. 'Some American woman on your phone. Bloody rude, wouldn't leave a message, insisted on speaking to you. You're a dark horse, Andrew, and no mistake. I want the full story when you've finished. Oooh, I'm dying for a fag, I haven't had one since Friday. You haven't got one, have you?'

'No,' I laugh. 'Sorry.'

I leave Maria hunting for ciggies and go back to my desk, taking the long route round the office to avoid Debbie, who is talking to someone.

'Where were you?' says Marion.

'Just outside the office having a coffee.'

'Do you wanna go shopping?'

'When?' I ask.

'Now, silly boy.'

'Marion, it's the middle of the afternoon. I can't just get up and leave.'

'Why not? Just tell them you have a doctor's appointment or something.'

I laugh. 'I don't think they'd believe me.'

'Such a shame. I've just been to Bond Street and they have such nice jackets in Ralph Lauren this season.'

Oh, God, it's tempting. I look around the office for a moment. Phones are ringing, the place is buzzing and Debbie is talking to someone across the room. No, I can't, it would be madness.

'Why not Saturday?'

'Oh no, I've done Bond Street for one week and besides I'd like us to do something at the weekend.'

'OK.' Sounds promising.

'I thought we might go to Paris. Would you like that?'

'God, yeah.'

'OK, I'll call the airline and make some reservations. We can do better shopping in Paris than here. We'll go Saturday morning and come back Monday.'

'Great,' I say with feeling. Paris this weekend would be brilliant. Coming back on Monday would be catastrophic but I can't think about that now.

'Listen, I'm out tonight but I'll call you later.'

'OK. Love you,' I say, getting slightly over-excited by the thought of our little trip but she has clicked off.

When I put my key in the lock I find that the front door isn't chubb-locked as well. Another evening in with Vinny. We usually have a laugh with One Aside Indoor Footy or just taking the piss out of the crap that's on telly but why doesn't he ever go out? The boy really should get a social life. I let myself in and drop my stuff in the hall.

Suddenly a girl's voice shouts, 'About bloody time and all. I could've made them quicker. You're missing it.' She is sitting cross-legged in front of the telly, reddy brown hair in a bob, boot-cut jeans, bare feet and a huge white T-shirt with a sort of Warhol print on it. She looks at me as if *I've* just walked into *her* sitting room. 'Oh. Hi. Sorry. I thought you were Vinny.'

'I'm not, I'm Andrew, his flatmate.'

'Hello, I'm Jane,' she says in a gentle Liverpool accent.

She looks at the teapot and mugs in front of her and then says, 'Like a cup of tea? You can have Vinny's mug. He was supposed to be getting me some chocky bickies but I think he's left the country.'

'Thanks.'

I throw my jacket on the settee and sit down. She pours me a cup and says, 'I hope you like it strong. I can't abide weak tea.' *Abide* Who says abide?

'Love strong tea,' I say, determined not to be intimidated by this sensible, tea-making intruder. 'Is that our teapot?'

'Yes. Why? Do you mind me using it?'

'No, 'course not. I just didn't know we had one.'

'Yes, it did take quite a bit of cleaning,' she says, looking at it critically. At that moment Vinny comes in with the biscuits.

'Right, what mouth-watering smorgasbord of broadcast entertainment awaits us tonight?' he asks, collapsing on the settee dangerously near my jacket. He bowls a packet of milk chocolate digestives across the floor to Jane. 'Oh, sorry. Jane, Andrew. Andrew, Jane.'

'We've done that one,' says Jane, handing me my tea purposefully.

We spend quite a pleasant evening, drinking tea, followed by a couple of glasses of whisky each while we watch TV and take the piss out of it. When the news comes on Jane tuts at a government minister and says, 'Christ, slimy bastard' under her breath. Later in the programme, when there are scenes of sea birds wallowing helplessly in crude oil I remark that it is probably a good thing because otherwise they just crap on your windscreen. Vinny grunts in agreement. Jane shoots me a look, wondering whether I am serious. I smile back but she is still not sure. Keep them guessing.

At eleven, after we've finished watching a wildlife programme about the Australian bush by night, Jane gets up from her cross-legged position on the floor, yawns, stretches and asks, 'Time for another brew?'

Slumped across the settee Vinny and I reach for our mugs and hand them to her.

'So I'm making it, am I?'

'Woman's work,' explains Vinny kindly.

Jane laughs sarcastically.

'And you did a great job with our teapot,' I add.

'Was that our teapot?' asks Vinny. 'Blimey, I didn't know we had one.'

'Jane cleaned it for us.'

'Right, one of you had better give me a hand,' says Jane, putting the mugs back on the tray. I get up – just a bit too quickly. 'No, Vinny, you can help me. Andrew can stay here, he looks knackered.'

I worry that Vinny will tell Jane about my new 'job'. He doesn't, apparently, but probably not because he realizes it will embarrass me, I think he's just forgotten or he simply can't believe that I have actually gone and done it. Not that it's any of her business but somehow I don't think she'd approve. She would either condemn it as a form of prostitution or fall about laughing at the thought of a 'gigolo', a moustachioed smoothie in a smoking jacket. 'Well, hell-eau!'

I think the latter would be more painful. In fact other than my little conversation with Malc about my new role, I realize I don't want anyone else to know about it. How would I explain it to Sami? Sami, who thinks not putting the lid back on a pen is pretty decadent. What on earth would Debbie say? *Saint* Debbie. 'Hi, Mum, guess what?' I don't think so.

It's dawning on me that I'm about to devote a huge amount of time and effort to something that, depending on which way you look at it, is either laughable or disgusting. Taking a quick sideways glance at Jane, who has her feet curled up underneath her on the settee, and then looking down into my half-empty cup while she and Vinny watch the telly, I decide to keep this a secret. They'll laugh on the other side of their faces when I'm off that office treadmill and not relying on a monthly financial fix.

After we've finished our tea the phone rings and I go into the kitchen to answer it. It is Marion to ask what I am doing. I know she likes to hear that without her my life is a drab, impoverished grind so I am tempted to say something about clubbing together for a take-away but I think that's pushing it a bit. She tells me that she has booked us on a flight for Paris on Saturday morning and coming back Monday morning. I hope I sound pleased without being too desperately keen.

It's only when I put the phone down that I remember that I'll need another morning off work.

Jane brings the cups back into the kitchen while I'm considering how exactly to phrase this hopeless request. She shoots me a look. A disapproving look. I'm just standing here, minding my own business in my own kitchen, for God's sake.

She begins to fill the washing-up bowl, squirting detergent in from a height and rolling up her sleeves. I get the feeling a point is being made here.

'I'll do that if you want,' I say, as much to break the silence. She looks across at me quizzically. 'I said I'll wash the mugs up.' Now she looks at me as if I've offered to wipe her nose for her or wash her knickers.

'No, I'll do it,' she says. Too tired to move, I find myself watching her. After a moment she looks across at me. I look back at her, holding her stare. Her smooth white skin is slightly flushed by the hot water. 'Can't imagine you washing up.'

'Why not?'

She doesn't answer. I ask again but I know the answer.

'Oh, just too cool,' she says, turning to look at me and rolling her shoulder almost imperceptibly. I smile at this seductress with soapy hands.

She stays over that night. She has Vinny's bed and he sleeps on the settee. The next morning she has gone by the time we are up. While we rush round, ironing shirts, gulping at mugs of stewed tea, scraping margarine onto charcoal toast, I ask Vinny about her.

'She's just a mate,' he says over babble of the radio. 'Did the same course at uni, she doesn't know if she wants to be a graphic designer after all, though.'

'You schtump her?' I ask.

Sitting at the table in his boxer shorts, Sergeant Bilko T-shirt and thick, saggy black socks, Vinny chases some stray Rice Krispies round his bowl then he thinks about my question for a moment. 'Come on, mate,' I say. 'It can't be that difficult to remember, it's not like there's a whole harem of conquests to think through, is there?'

'There's a few, locked away in this card-index memory,' says Vinny, tapping the side of his head. He scratches under his arm and smells his fingers distractedly. 'I was actually thinking what it would be like to schtump her.'

'Nice tits.'

'True.'

We both sit and think about them. I look at my watch.

'Christ, I'd better get a move on. She got a boyfriend, then?'

'She *did* have one.'

'Are they still together?'

'Nah, they split up after finals. He was supposed to be revising with this other girl in their tutor group but between you and me, I think some of the revising was, you know, done in a horizontal position.'

I laugh at the thought of horizontal revising. Poor Jane. I know how she must have felt. That realization that you've made a fool of yourself, that you were so wrong.

'What was he like, this bloke?' I ask Vinny. Why do I care? I'm strangely pleased by the reply, though.

'Good-looking bastard. She seems to go for smoothies.' He gives me a slow, sly smile.

'Don't know what you mean by that. What does she do now?'

'She works in Paperchase in Tottenham Court Road or something.'

'Yeah, paper planes you mean?' Vinny scrapes something from under the nail of his big toe which is sticking through one sock. 'She's taking a year off, you know, before she moves out of the slip road of studentdom and into the fast lane of middle management. Nice girl, though.'

'Oh, yeah,' I say casually, examining my hand-in-work with the iron-razor sharp creases in all the wrong places.

'You interested, then?' asks Vinny leeringly.

'Oh, no. Well, I don't know.'

'Of course, you're a professional now,' he sniggers.

'*Don't* tell her about that, for fuck's sake. Oh, you haven't, have you?'

'No, I'd forgotten about it, actually.' He thinks for a moment and then adds 'Just don't mix business and pleasure, that's all. Now, I think you've done enough damage to that shirt, give us the iron.'

On the bus to work I am thinking desperately how to ask

Debbie for more time off. By the time my stop has come I am convinced it is my right and she cannot stop me.

'Hiya,' I say, putting my head round the door of her office. It is separated from the rest of us by glass partitioning. There are also Venetian blinds that can be closed when Debbie is sacking someone. In fact I suggested to her one day that she should just write on them 'Another one bites the dust.' It would certainly serve to motivate the rest of us 'self-starters'. She laughed. She used to laugh a lot at the things I said, way back when I first arrived. I was the class favourite. One of the girls told me that Debbie spent ten minutes in the ladies' loo talking about me and wondering whether I was available. Debbie sacked her the following week.

This morning Debbie just looks up at me and says 'Hiya' wearily and then goes back to some spreadsheets on her desk.

'I'm just going to take Monday morning off it that's OK,' I say quickly.

Her eyes move off the spreadsheet but stay fixed on her desk.

There is a pause.

'Let's see how it goes,' she says coldly.

'OK. It would just be the morning,' I say and go back to my own desk.

Sami is just sticking a yellow Post-it on my phone.

'This guy wants a repeat for next week,' she says, pulling her incredibly long dark hair away from her face. 'And a discount.'

I look at the name and number on the paper, which mean nothing to me, and throw them in the bin.

'Well, he can shove it up his bum.'

'*Andrew*. You can't do that. You're so rude.'

I laugh. '*Sami*, you're so polite.'

'I know,' she smiles.

And so it continues – the daft, amiable banter ping-ponging between us all day long. The feigned lunacy that is the only way to stay sane in an office. We should get one of those signs 'You don't have to work here but . . .' Oh, never mind.

By Friday, I am feeling as excited as a kid. I haven't been to Paris for years and even then it was a student expedition with Helen and another couple on such a tight budget that we had to sneak one of the girls into the hotel at night and have sandwiches for every meal apart from the last night when we went for the 55F menu at a little restaurant with aluminium cutlery and tables topped with chipped, yellow formica.

I first met Helen when I carried her books home from the library. It was in the third week of her first term at university, I'd already been there a year. Sweet, isn't it? It was a cloudless, sunny day but with long, autumnal shadows and a cool breeze blowing across campus. She was walking back from the library through campus and I was strolling over to the Union to meet some friends for a lunchtime drink. I saw this girl staggering along: her arms were struggling to contain a pile of books and she was stopping repeatedly, grappling with one old hardback after another to prevent them from escaping. But her face was completely calm.

'Thank you,' she said when I made my offer. I was surprised by her cool acceptance. I had expected her to laugh and look embarrassed or to say, 'Oh, don't worry, thanks,' but she just handed over some of the books and we set off to her hall of residence.

I asked her about where she came from (South London), what she was studying (French) and how she was getting on (very well, because she had covered some of the course work at A-level). I offered my own CV and she asked some questions about it.

'That was a real help, thank you again,' she said, closing the door to her room in my face.

Does Helen sound boring? There was never a dull moment with her. She arranged for us to go backpacking, we went to the theatre, she suggested books for me to read and then interrogated me on them. She showed me her Tina Turner collection one day. I was amazed. Then she did an impression. It was really incredibly accurate – the voice, the shuddering dance across the stage. It became our running joke. She'd do it in that post-coital silliness at four o'clock in the morning or a Sunday afternoon.

That was the thing about Helen – with her pale skin, her big dark eyes and her long straight hair, she looked the picture of serenity but you never quite knew exactly what she was thinking or what was going to come next.

'This is crap,' she said quietly to the owner of a hotel in the Cotswolds when we splashed out for a weekend to celebrate our second anniversary with some money her parents had given us. He looked astonished – so did I, even after two years of knowing her.

'Sorry?'

'I said this room is crap. You think because we're students that you can give us the smallest, noisiest, most horrible room in the place and we won't notice.'

The guy tried to protest but Helen continued, forcefully, eloquently.

'Our money's as good as anyone else's. Can you show me which other rooms you've got, please.'

And he did. And we got a huge room overlooking the lake.

'Better,' smiled Helen proudly, as she sat on the bed, arms stretched out behind her, legs crossed, a big toe tickling the carpet.

I sit at my desk virtuously until most people have left. I ignore someone who says 'see you on Monday' and when I do leave, at six-thirty, I don't say goodbye to Debbie in case I remind her of our little conversation the other day.

At home I gulp down a cup of tea and quickly throw some stuff into a sports bag. The clothes and the bag look scruffy but I remember what Mark said: perhaps she'll be so embarrassed by the state of my stuff she'll buy me something new.

I head off to Marion's, shouting, 'Have a good weekend' to Vinny.

'You off somewhere this weekend?' he says, opening a bottle of Rolling Rock. He is wearing his oldest, baggiest combats, a khaki T-shirt with a big red star in the middle and tatty Nike trainers.

'Yep, Paris. Where are you off to?'

'This new club in Clerkenwell, the Laundry Room. Hang on a minute, Paris? Fucking hell!'

'Work, mate.'

Vinny looks confused, then his face brightens. 'Oh, *that* work. Christ, you're doing well. What's the number of that agency again?'

I laugh and slam the front door behind me.

Over dinner in the tiny garden of a restaurant in Chelsea, Marion mentions that our flight back on Monday isn't until four in the afternoon.

'Why so late?' I ask, slightly more urgently than I had intended.

Marion looks up from her rocket and parmesan salad. 'I wanted to make the most of our time there. Is that OK?'

'Oh, yes, of course, sure.' I carry on eating.

Oh, God! OK, so we have more time in Paris, which will be great but I could have just about done a half-day in the office, which might have appeased Debbie a bit. Debbie, the office and, in particular, what Tuesday morning holds in store for me, have been on my mind all evening.

CHAPTER NINE

AS SHE SIGNS IN AT THE RITZ, Marion fires a list of questions at the guy behind the desk. He handles it well, I think, answering 'yes, of co'se' or 'no problem, madame' to everything she asks him.

Apparently satisfied, but obviously annoyed that she has found no excuse to reject the suite they have given us, Marion turns away from the desk – the signal that she is ready to go upstairs.

Two porters struggle with her Louis Vuitton luggage while I pick up my tatty sports bag. Immediately a third guy, my age perhaps, takes it from me anxiously.

'OK,' I say, giving it up. 'Thank you.'

The five of us walk down the hallway – all thick blue rugs and gilt doorframes. I glance in at a lounge on the left where people are sitting at small tables. I'm struck by how many of them look just as amazed to be here as me. Yes, guys, you're really at the Ritz in Paris – except that you're probably paying for it yourselves. A couple walking down the stairs stare at Marion so I walk on quickly to be next to her.

'It's not a *bad* hotel,' she confides.

'Mmm,' I say mildly.

'For Europe.'

In the lift I am suddenly overcome with excitement. My stomach begins to tingle and my hands shake very slightly. I have made it! Even if she dumps me tomorrow I have stayed in a suite at the Ritz in Paris.

I try to look as bored and as mildly annoyed as Marion does. I realize that the little guy holding my bag is looking at me out of the corner of his eye, through one of the mirrored walls of the lift. You may well stare, mate. Just look and wander. Who am I? What is the deal? How have I done it? Luck? Hard work?

Our suite is every bit as vast and luxurious as I had hoped.

I wander round slowly, poking at some things, looking in others, trying switches and just absorbing the fact that it's all ours. It's bigger than my entire flat at home. Meanwhile the porters scurry round, arranging the flowers, opening doors, double-checking that everyone is ready and unpacking Marion's cases.

'I'll do it,' I say quickly to the guy who picks up my holdall. That would really give the game away. One look at my Gap T-shirts, St Michael boxers and Next trousers bundled into the bag along with my ancient, toothpaste-smeared Manchester United sponge bag would blow my cover completely.

Marion pours two glasses of Perrier and gives me one, ruffling my hair and squeezing my shoulder lightly.

'I think this'll do,' she says, taking a drink and looking round the room. I nod and put my hand over hers. The porters have finished and look at her expectantly. She picks up her bag from the coffee table and looks inside.

'I don't have many Euros yet,' she says. 'I hope this is OK.' I try to see the note she gives one of them but I can't. He seems very pleased with it, anyway. They bow and slip out of the room, the little guy who carried my bag giving me a final look.

Marion goes into the bedroom. I take the opportunity to look round the living room then go next door, check out the huge white marble bathroom with its telephone, fruit bowl, flowers, white fluffy towels and bathrobes and little baskets of toiletries with the hotel's gold crest on them. I've been in lots of hotel bedrooms one way and another. Minimal comfort, portion-controlled guest-as-a-necessary-evil hotels. But this one is different. It stretches out before me, revelling in its own luxury and confident that it can fulfil my every desire, challenging me not to be impressed, not to fall in love with it and the fantasy world it is offering. Drunk with delight at this new experience, I go into the bedroom and bounce onto the bed where Marion is lying with her eyes closed. Enough cool sophistication – that was for the staff. Now I am just an excited kid.

I lean over, hold her gently and kiss her. She runs a long, red, nail-polished finger down my cheek and smiles wearily.

'You should rest some.'

'Oh, OK.' I say, still hyped.

She laughs. 'You're funny.'

'So are you,' I say, kissing her again. I lie down next to her for a minute but it's no good – 'resting some' is the last thing I can do. I prop myself up on one elbow and look down at her, again. She opens her eyes.

'*Now* what?'

'Thank you,' I find myself saying. And I do mean it. She might have slightly more available cash than absolutely anybody I've ever met but she has taken me to Paris and this kind of trip can't be cheap and I do appreciate that. My airline ticket cost over £400 and this suite must be a couple of grand per night. Helen used to give me books or CDs at Christmas and birthdays. We'd always have a limit of £15 to make things fair. That seems like a million years ago.

Marion's eyes run over my face. 'You're welcome. I know you haven't had the opportunity to travel much, I know that.' Haven't I? Oh, OK. I'm about to point out that even people from Reading do go abroad sometimes, albeit not usually to five-star hotels, but I decide this sounds ungrateful so I say what I think she wants to hear.

'No.'

'Travel will develop your horizons. You'll never see anything of the world from that office window.'

'You're right.' Well, she is, I suppose, but I'm just glad no one else can hear this ridiculous conversation. Look, she's taken me to Paris, so agreeing with her is the least I can do. It's just good manners.

'I want you to see something of life,' she says solemnly. 'There's a great big world out there and there is so much to learn. It will be a great education for you.'

'I hope so,' I say truthfully.

She lies on the bed while I watch Eurosport and MTV on the telly in the living room. Some guy speaking American English with a German accent is jigging up and down and trying to convince us he's having a good time while he introduces the next act: a Danish heavy metal band called DStrukt. I put my feet up on the settee, take a swig of beer, throw some peanuts up in the air and try and catch them in my mouth. Then I start on the chocolates they have left us.

After a while I get bored and decide to venture out – after all, the hotel may be great but we are in Paris, aren't we?

Seems a shame to waste it. I tiptoe into the bedroom to see if Marion is awake. She is still lying motionless on the bed, arms held rigidly by her sides. She must be asleep. I'll write a note – besides, I won't be long, just a walk around, buy a postcard or two. Just as I close the door she asks, 'What are you doing?'

'Er, I was just going to go out.'

'We'll have to get ready for dinner soon. I don't think you have time.' Oh, come on – it'll only take me a minute to change – if I bother to change at all.

'Just for a quick walk.'

'OK. There's money in my purse – just go down to the lobby and change it. Get me a magazine and some aspirin.'

'Oh, all right.'

I take thirty Euros from the wad in her handbag, guessing at how much is there altogether and slip out. The corridor is silent, airless and dimly lit. The carpet is thick and the silence almost suffocating. I wonder what is going on behind these other doors. Other people lying in the bath, on the bed, with prostitutes, reading glossy magazines full of things they can buy without checking their bank accounts. Relaxing. Doing the things rich people do. I buy American *Vogue* and Anadin Extra for her and a *Vogue Hommes* for me plus some funky 'Hollywood' chewing gum which I can show off with at home.

Then I go outside for a walk around and it hits me that I am in Paris. Yippee! I am in bloody Paris! So far I could have been anywhere – the plane, the hotel and the car in between them have been just nondescript international luxury – the same as London. Funny how rich people, even the ones who travel a lot, pay to make sure they only have minimum contact with any of the places they visit. On the other hand, perhaps that's the point of business-class travel and five-star hotels.

But now I really am in Paris and as I look around I see Paris and people wandering about being French; doing ordinary things with that serious, stylish intensity. A young man, my age, carrying some fairy-tale boxes of patisserie home with him, another frowning and slouched at a café table, reflecting on his wasted life or considering the meaning of it all. Two young professional women walking quickly down the street towards me, dressed to kill, smoking seriously and locked in an indignant, passionate debate.

I wander along the rue de Rivoli for a while, breathing in the atmosphere, letting it sink in that I have got this far and then I turn off and walk slowly past the Palais Royale, along the Rue St Honoré back to the hotel, stopping off on the way to buy some tiny strawberries because they look so good in their little wicker baskets.

Lying in the bath, I can hear Marion in the other room on the phone to a friend.

'Oh, poor you,' she is saying. 'Oh you poor, poor thing. That is *so* unfair.' I can tell that the news is cheering her greatly, even before she puts her head round the bathroom door to check up on me and smile. Then she rolls her eyes and goes back into the living room, continuing her sympathetic noises.

I lie back under the sweet-smelling, frothy blanket and close my eyes. I cannot remember ever using bath foam before. Limited budget, limited time, limited imagination. I don't know. Like most things before I met Marion. I massage my dick a bit until I get a lazy, half hard-on. Then I take a gulp of champagne, pop a couple of tiny, sweet strawberries into my mouth and begin to laugh at the whole ridiculous, fucking thing.

We eat at a restaurant on the Left Bank where, of course, the maître d' welcomes Marion like an old friend and she seems only mildly displeased to see him. He gives us a table in the corner and we order vodka and tonics while we decide what to eat. Putting on her glasses Marion looks down at the huge gold-embossed menus.

'I'm just going to have seafood,' she says. 'Some oysters to start with and then maybe some lobster. You should have this veal thing, it's their specialty. Here, third one down.'

I look over at her menu to see what she is pointing at and notice that, unlike mine, it has the prices. And what prices.

The waiters probably assume that this woman is taking her nephew or godson out for a special dinner. Perhaps they think I'm working in Paris or studying here.

Or perhaps I'm not the first young man Marion has brought here.

I suppose the food is good. And there is plenty of business – white gloves, lots of extra cutlery, people filling your glass after you've taken a single sip – all the kind of things that Marion likes.

During the main course Marion asks how I can spend all my day on the phone trying to sell things alongside all those other people. I explain tragically that I have to because I've got to pay the rent. This leads onto how can you live in Fulham. She drove through it once and it was full of people being sick all over Fulham Broadway. I admit that it can be a bit rough on Saturday night.

'This was a Tuesday morning,' she says.

She goes on about do I want to spend my life renting a little flat in Fulham? I should get on the property ladder. Real estate is the thing. 'Buy land – they ain't making it anymore,' as some friend of her father used to say.

'You've never invited me to your place,' she says, taking a sip of wine.

'Sorry?' I say, horrified.

She laughs at my reaction. 'I said I've never been to your apartment.'

Apartment? I wonder for a moment what kind of place Marion thinks I live in.

'Would you really want to?'

'Sure, I'd love to come and meet your roommate.'

'Really?' I gasp in horror.

'Why not?' she says in an innocent, slightly hurt tone.

'He's usually out – being sick on the Broadway,' I explain sadly.

After dinner we walk a bit and then take a taxi back to the hotel. The sex is good – we are both warmed and relaxed by the wine and the rich food. As we lie in bed, Marion's head on my chest, she asks what I would like to do the next day. The thought hasn't occurred to me, today has been so amazing. I tell her that. I would quite like to go shopping and get some new clothes but I don't tell her that. Meanwhile, she has reached down and found my dick again.

'Andrew, will you do something for me?'

'Er, yes, what is it?'

'I don't know why the British don't do it immediately like the Americans.'

'Do what?' I ask.

'In America, it's automatic with all male babies.'

I don't want to admit to myself that I think I know what she is talking about. Is she being serious?

'D-do what?' I ask again looking down at her awkwardly to see if her face gives anything away.

'Oh, you know, get circumcised.'

'What?' I move up sharply and her head falls away from my chest. She looks surprised and then props herself up on one elbow. I can see her face properly now, she isn't joking.

'It's much cleaner, more aesthetically pleasing—'

'Marion, you are kidding, aren't you?'

'No. What's the big deal? Both my husbands were. All American men are. You'll find it the most natural thing in the world. It's much more comfortable.'

'How would you know?'

'It's obvious,' she says lightly.

'Are you serious? You really think I'm going to- to . . . cut a bit of my dick off just because you'd prefer it.' I move further away from her in the vast bed and find that my hand has automatically moved over my willy. Poor bugger: it's got me this far, to Paris, in this hotel. I feel I owe it something.

'Well, it's up to you,' she says, idly rearranging her hair. 'But if you really cared, you'd—'

'What?' I gasp, getting out of bed. 'Marion, I can't believe you're saying this. I've lived twenty-four years with it like this, I'm not changing it now. Anyway, do you have any idea how painful it would be at my age?'

'It wouldn't last long and you'd soon feel the benefit.'

I look down at my dick which looks even more shrivelled and miserable than it usually does after sex. Marion shrugs her shoulders and then gets up and goes to the bathroom. As soon as she has gone and the bed has become neutral territory I get into it again. I begin to realize that this is the deal. Yes, you can travel to Paris and stay in a suite in one of the most beautiful hotels in the world. Yes, you can eat in the one of the famous restaurants and you can probably have some presents into the bargain but in return you have to lose a little bit of your manhood – literally.

Marion comes back and immediately I go into bathroom. As I brush my teeth I look at myself in the mirror and realize that I'll have to play for time – she can't mean it really. I have a quick piss and then go back and get into bed next to her. Staring up to the heavily moulded ceiling I say, 'I'll make some enquiries when we get back to London.'

'Good boy,' she says, turning slightly to face me.

I roll over and try to go to sleep.

On Sunday we get up late, have breakfast in the room and then go for a walk around the Marais which is the bit of Paris I know best. I'm glad to be able to take the initiative for once. Marion says it's beautiful but complains about the shops and when we find a little brasserie and have steak frites for lunch she says it's too small and noisy. Never mind.

Monday night, after a day of shopping – for Marion – we arrive back at hers. I am interested to see that it's just as depressing for the rich to get back from a trip as ordinary people. The house feels cold and empty and so do I.

Marion goes upstairs to change and I decide to make a cup of tea. While the kettle boils I switch on the TV and watch the end of news and the weather. Tuesday will be a typical grey, rainy June day. Then I click onto MTV and watch some Israeli boy band. The thought of work depresses me so much I feel like I've been punched in the stomach.

Marion calls from the living room, 'Andrew, would you come here a minute.' She sounds formal and serious. I wonder for a moment if she is going to 'chuck' me. I haven't been 'chucked' for years. Not since Helen. Well, at least I got Paris. And the opportunity to keep my foreskin.

'Yes?' I say, as I come into the room.

'Come here.' She holds up a watch. 'Do you know what this is?'

'It's a watch, isn't it?' Oh my God! Oh my God! I hope I don't sound too obvious.

'It's a Rolex. Twenty-two carat gold. And I want you to have it. That watch you have on at the moment is just disgusting. Get rid of it. I want you to wear this, OK?'

'OK.' I feel a bit dizzy. This is it. Get that ice or else no dice.

Mark would be proud of me. Hang on, I can't wear it to

work, someone is bound to notice. So what if they do? Why not? Five-star hotel in Paris, Rolex watch. What did *you* do this weekend, guys? Sainsbury's and the pub? This is what it's all about, after all. 'It's beautiful,' I say.

'It is a beautiful timepiece,' she says and puts it back in its box which is on the table next to her and *then takes it back upstairs with her*. What the fuck is she doing? Where is she going? Can't I wear it? What do you mean? Why are you taking it away from me? 'You can wear it next week when we go to Aspinalls for dinner,' she says casually from upstairs.

At least I think that's what she says. I can't hear properly because my head is in my hands.

The next morning I walk quickly into the office, sit down at my desk without taking off my jacket, pick up the phone and dial the number of a client. Any client. I wait and, of course, there is no answer. The ringing tone is beginning to hypnotize me and my mind is wandering off when I hear Debbie's voice behind me asking Sami to ask me to come into her office when I have finished on the phone. Debbie knows that I am not speaking to anyone and I can hear her perfectly well but it is part of her prickly, artificial politeness never to interrupt anyone on the phone. That is the thing about Debbie: you don't actually dislike her for anything in particular. It's just the fact she's Debbie.

There is no need for Sami to repeat Debbie's request. I've had enough of this ringing tone anyway, so I put the phone down and follow her into her office. As soon as I sit down I realize that this is a mistake, I should have taken a moment to think and get my story straight.

'Where were you yesterday?' she asks, pressing some aspirins out of a foil pack.

'I was away,' I say defiantly.

She throws the aspirins into her mouth and takes a sip of coffee. 'Yes, I know that. You were supposed to be here.'

I decide to go on the attack a bit. 'No I wasn't, I had the day off, remember?'

'You *didn't* have the day off,' she says, obviously trying to control her temper.

I know I am beaten but I try anyway. 'I did. Remember, I said last week—'

'I said we'd see how it goes. I never said yes and you know it.'

'Oh, come on, Debbie, I thought—'

'Come on nothing, Andrew. If I'd said yes, Claire would have marked it on the sheet and it would all have been done properly. I'm giving you another warning.'

Oh fuck it, I've lost. Better just to end this whole thing quickly.

'Well, I'm sorry. I obviously misunderstood.' I turn to leave.

'Andrew,' she says quietly. She bites her lip. 'What's the matter with you these days? Look, is there anything wrong? Anything I should know about?'

What can I say? I can't tell her the truth, I don't want to lie to her again and I'll be buggered if I'm going to apologise any more. She's had one 'sorry'. We stand in silence. She breaks it.

'You used to be good – one of our best sales people. You saved our skin on more than one occasion.' I stare at the floor, wishing she'd just shut up and let me go, wishing that what she is saying wasn't true. 'Remember that supplement they suddenly dropped on us? *How* many pages did we have to fill?' It was four and a half but I'm not going to remind her. 'You worked *so* hard and you really pulled the whole team together. I was really grateful.'

You were also nearly in tears one night, I think. I know that if I say anything now it will make things better between us but somehow I just can't. She waits a second and then her mood changes.

'OK. Don't let it happen again. That's a warning. An official warning. I've had enough.' She picks up the phone.

As I get back to my desk I decide that this isn't working out quite as smoothly as I had first thought. Paris was great – apart from Marion moaning about the lack of shops and posh restaurants in the Marais. How can anyone not like the oldest, quaintest, most beautiful part of Paris?

But now I've come back to this dump and a bollocking from a woman who can't see further than the end of a balance sheet.

My phone starts to ring but I don't answer it. I look up at the dust dancing around in a beam of sunlight. It shows the dirt on the windows. Don't they ever wash those bloody things? Why bother, we're only Classified.

What's the fun in living it up in Paris with a beautiful rich woman and then coming back to this?

I've got to escape. I need more income to do that, which means I need to meet more women like Marion, women who will spend their money on me. After all, if they've got the money just sitting there and I make them happy, so what? I mean, they wouldn't spend it on me if they didn't want to! I'm not blackmailing them or mugging them. It's just a sensible, convenient commercial arrangement. Mutually beneficial.

Does that sound immoral? Who said there was anything moral about media sales? None of us in this crappy little office is selling two-centimetre, one-column-width advertising space to people with holiday villas to rent and six-week language courses to flog because we think it will make the world a better place, we're doing it to earn twenty grand a year plus commission if we reach our targets. I can't really see anything particularly noble about that. If I'd asked about the vocational or ethical element of the job at the interview, somehow I don't think I'd have got it.

Women like Marion obviously have plenty of money – all I want is just a little bit. A little bit from her and a few others, women that Jonathan or even Mark could introduce me to and it'll soon grow. Give it five or six years, by the time I'm thirty I'll have a nice little nest egg and fuck off media sales, fuck off advertising, fuck off career plan, fuck off ever having to work in an office ever again.

I'll be young, rich and free or die in the attempt, I decide, as the tea trolley clatters into the office.

A few minutes later Sami comes back to her desk and sees me staring into space.

'All right?' she asks, her huge brown eyes wide with concern at the bollocking I've just had from Debbie. She looks so sweet that I can't help but laugh sadly.

'Yeah, fine.'

'Shall we have a drink at lunchtime?' she asks.

I suppose Sami proves that you can be hard-working and

virtuous and nice rather than hard-working and virtuous and horrible, like Debbie.

'Yes,' I say. 'Yes, let's do that.'

Sami and I leave the office at 1 p.m., carefully explaining to our colleagues that we are just nipping out and we will be back by 2 p.m. We give up on the lift and walk downstairs in silence. We get to reception almost in a trance. Ted starts to say something but we just carry on walking.

We find a quiet corner of the pub and I get a Coke for Sami and a Scotch for me. I really need a drink.

'Cheers,' I say.

'Cheers,' says Sami just as miserably. We both take a drink and put our glasses down with extra care – Sami because she always does, me because I just don't feel I can do anything properly at the moment.

'Oh, fuck,' I say.

'Oh, Andrew, don't worry.'

'I'm going to get sacked, aren't I, at this rate?'

'No, you won't. Just keep your head down for a few days. Debbie still likes you.'

'Think so?' This makes me feel slightly better. For all the bollockings she's been giving me, Debbie must still quite fancy me. At least a bit.

'Yeah, otherwise you'd have been sacked ages ago.'

'Oh, thanks,' I say, unflattered.

'Well, it's true, Andrew.' Sami smiles.

'You're probably right. Oh, God.'

She touches my arm. 'What's going on?'

'Nothing.'

'Course there is, I *know* you. You're always tired and late for work these days. Where were you yesterday?'

'Paris.'

'Paris?'

'Yeah, it's the capital of France.'

'Andrew.'

'Oh, sorry, Sami, I'm just . . . I dunno.'

'Who did you go with? That American woman who keeps ringing up?'

'Yeah.'

'Is she your girlfriend?' Girlfriend? What a weird thought. Is she? I look across the pub and then at Sami.

'Sort of, we're . . . you know.'

'What? I mean, is she nice?'

I laugh. Sami's questions! 'Nice' is an even stranger way to describe Marion than 'girlfriend'.

'Yeah, she is quite nice.'

'Well, where did you meet? How long have you been going out together?'

'Oh, a few weeks.'

'That's great. Can I meet her, then?'

'Oh, yeah, why not?' Only 165 good reasons why not. 'When you get a boyfriend we could go out in a foursome.' Sami gives me a stare that takes me by surprise. 'If you wanted to, that is.' She looks embarrassed suddenly and smiles.

'And did you have a good time? In Paris, I mean.'

I have to think about it for a moment. Paris has sort of faded from my memory since I got back to the office.

'Yeah, yeah, it was lovely. You know: cafés, delicious food, Place de la Concorde, that view down to the Arc de Triomphe. All that sort of Paris stuff.'

'I've never been,' says Sami without embarrassment.

'Haven't you? You're kidding. I'll take you. We'll go one weekend.' Sami laughs, slightly embarrassed now. 'No, it'd be fun, go on.'

'OK,' she says, taking a sip of her coke. 'I went to Rome once with school. That was fun. We bought a bottle of wine and drank it in the youth hostel. My friend Kelly was sick in my rucksack.'

I laugh. 'Oh, gross.'

'Oh, it was. She couldn't find anything else to throw up in. I was really sick too but I managed to get to the loo down the hall in time.'

'Sami, you're so good,' I tell her for the thousandth time. 'Is that why you don't drink alcohol? I thought it was, you know, because you're a Muslim.'

'Don't be daft. I *do* drink alcohol. Didn't you notice me drinking the punch at the Christmas party?'

'Were you?'

'Yeah, 'course. I had a can of lager and then two glasses of punch.'

'Wild,' I say.

'Aren't I?' She is thoughtful. I vaguely remember the tense, dull Christmas party.

'Ken Wheatley gave you a glass of champagne which was only for senior management and you said—'

'I don't like champagne very much,' she says quickly. She takes another sip of coke. 'But I like white wine. Really. Must say, though, since Kelly filled my rucksack in Rome I've never really been able to eat lasagne.'

That night, just before 2 a.m., which makes it Wednesday, I suppose, but I'm slightly losing track of the days now, I get out of a taxi and walk up the path past the bins and the nettles and crisp bags to the front door of a small house in Clapham. I had gone home after dinner at Marion's because I didn't have any spare clothes at hers and also because I knew that somehow, whatever time I set the alarm for, or however fast I shot out of the house I would end up being late yet again. And that would be once too often.

As I was just nodding off, the phone rang. It was Jonathan with a job.

'Bit late,' I said, half-joking.

He laughed as if this was terribly funny actually and then said briskly, 'Look, I won't bullshit you, this is a sensitive one but I think you're just right for it.'

'Oh, OK,' I said unconvinced.

'Thing is, Andrew, when she called she was upset and vulnerable and so I just thought you'd be the right person to talk to her. You know? I mean I've got older guys on the team but you seemed perfect for her – young and a good listener.'

'Yeah, I see what you mean.' I know when I'm being charmed but there is a possibility Jonathan actually means this. Besides the money would be useful so here I am.

'Shit!' Three door bells.

I don't believe this. In the taxi on the way over I kept reminding myself that it was supposed to be rich women at casinos not sad girls in Clapham that are my 'target market'. My plan was to be setting off to an address in Chelsea again or even Knightsbridge or somewhere in time for dinner. Not some miserable little street in South London in the early hours. At least the sex thing is very unlikely to arise here so I won't feel guilty about cheating on Marion.

In the meantime, though, I really need this money. And if Jonathan gives me some crap about credit card companies not being ready to pay, like I said, I'll just pop round to his little place in Fulham and take the money – after I've folded up his Habitat director's chair and shoved it up his arse. Not an ideal way to get paid but I'm desperate.

Desperate and knackered.

Oh God, I'm knackered. Anyway, concentrate. The top bell has two names on it so that's out. I take a guess at the other two and end up pressing the bottom one. I hear a buzz just the other side of the front door.

After a few minutes it is opened by a girl with quite a bit of metal face furniture and long blonde hair half-covering her eyes. She looks swollen with sleep and not quite with it. I am just about to apologize, assuming that I have got the wrong button and woken her up when she says, 'Er, from the agency?'

I nod and half-smile and she lets me in.

'Andrew,' I say, squeezing past her.

'Erren,' she says. The place stinks of pot and a gently maturing dustbin. This is going to be even worse than I suspected. 'I'm really sorry about the mess,' she mutters in a little girl voice. 'My brother was staying for a few days and he, like, wrecked the place. I can't believe it. Look.' As if to prove it she opens the door of the living room where a glass coffee table is shattered. Next to it is a guitar with some of the strings hanging off it and a tinfoil takeaway food container, the remains of a scruffy spliff and some cigarette ends on a dinner plate.

She thinks for a moment and then says, 'Perhaps we'll use the kitchen, yeah?' The hallway is a mixture of half-converted flat and post-party carnage. We edge past some pine shelves leaning against a wall and go into the kitchen. I nearly trip over something and look down to see two empty plastic cider bottles. The kitchen is tiny and misshapen – hacked out of a broom cupboard or something when the place was one house. A smell hits me from a pile of plates in the sink and the overflowing bin. She looks around as if trying to decide what to do next. 'What do you want to drink? There's Scotch or cider or here's some beer.' I'm not keen. Then she moves a cardboard box out of the way of the fridge and takes out a very expensive-looking bottle of white wine with a yellow convenience store price label on it. 'We could have this.' I open it while she rinses two dirty glasses under the tap.

I pour the wine into the wet, smeary glasses while she lights a cigarette, takes a deep drag and looks across at me through her red, empty eyes.

'I hope you don't mind,' she says.

At first I think she is talking about the cigarette smoke hanging in the air between us. It's the best smell in the room, so I say, 'No, not at all.' But I realize that she is talking about my coming all the way over to Clapham at two o'clock in the morning.

'I just needed someone to talk to, you know.'

'Oh sure,' I say easily. But I am beginning to feel nervous about the fact that she is standing between me and the door especially with those pieces of glass on the living-room floor.

I suddenly realize that I haven't called the agency to say that I've arrived and that everything is OK. I ask to use the phone. She looks at me blankly for a moment and then says, 'Oh, yeah, sorry' and points to it. Thank God it's safely fixed onto the wall – if it was anywhere else we'd never find it.

I wake up Jonathan. He says 'good' and asks if she's paid – it was going to be a cheque, wasn't it? I hesitate and look across at the girl who is now staring into her glass, a strand of hair in her mouth. How can I ask her to write me a cheque? I tell Jonathan everything is fine. He asks if I am sure. I say 'yes' again.

He says 'OK. Have fun!' and hangs up. *Fun?* I sit down at the table again and I'm trying to think of something to say to the girl when I notice that she is blinking back tears. 'I've had this, like, massive row with my Dad. He's such an arsehole, you know what I'm saying?'

I nod and try to smile.

'He just rings up and says you'd better come over for Sunday lunch this weekend. Last week he just shouts "get over here now", because he's had a row with my mum or something. "Get over here or I'll stop your money." But, like, why should I? You know what I'm saying?'

'No, it's up to you, isn't it?'

She looks across at me for a moment. Have I said the wrong thing? 'Yeah, it's up to me.' Her mind wanders for a moment. 'I just hate him. I really hate him.'

'Sure.'

'He doesn't get on with any of us. I've got this boyfriend slash, you see—'

She stops for a moment.

'Sorry?' I seem to be losing it. Or is she?

'Sorry?' she says.

'Sorry, you were saying you've got a boyfriend slash something.'

'Yeah.'

I laugh irritably. 'Boyfriend slash what? You mean boyfriend slash best friend or something?'

She looks at me again. 'No, that's my boyfriend's name – Slash. He's in a band.'

'Oh, right.'

We both look down at our wine and then she says, 'Look, I'm sorry I just want to be with someone tonight. I hope that's OK. I just don't want to be on my own.'

'Sure.'

She sniffs, takes a long drag and begins to tell me about her brother who has just come back from travelling and has been staying in the flat with his mate.

'What a mess,' she says at last. 'My dad'll go mental when he sees it, yeah?'

'Not surprised. I mean, will he?'

'Yeah, mental.'

There is another pause and she drifts off again, obviously thinking about her old man. I decide I'd better try and earn my money.

'What does he do?'

'Who?'

'Your dad.'

'What does he *do*?'

'For a living.'

'Oh, erm, office furniture.' She mentions a brand name and I nod because it sort of rings a bell. I put my hands down into my lap and look down at my watch discreetly. Twenty to three.

'He's South African,' she adds, as if that explains everything.

'Oh, right. When did he come over here?'

'In the fifties. "I had twenty quid in cash, a half-full suitcase and the address of my mother's aunt in Ealing," she says in a convincingly rough South African accent.

I laugh. 'Very good. The accent, I mean.'

She looks at me and then smiles for a moment. Amusement? Pride? Either way I'm just glad I've made her smile.

'It should be. I've heard it a million times.' She flicks her ash into the ashtray. 'He used to clean Tube tunnels.'

'Clean tube tunnels?'

'Yep. Bet you didn't know anybody did that. They need to clear away litter, all the fluff from people's clothes and shit. Could cause a fire.'

'What a crap job.' Not like media sales.

She laughs. 'He wanted a job that was so fucking horrible he wouldn't end up doing it for the rest of his life.'

'Then what did he do?'

'He met a man in a pub in Kilburn. He wanted to shift some stolen office furniture. So he bought it off this guy for a tenner or something and hasn't looked back.' She takes a sip of wine. 'Hasn't looked back since.'

'He must have shifted a lot of office furniture.'

'Tons of it. He's five foot nothing but he's built like a fucking fire hydrant.' She takes another mouthful of wine and tops up our glasses, slopping it on the table. 'He used to stack it up to the ceiling of this warehouse in Southwark. He had to cover it with plastic sheets because of the damp running down the walls and the rain coming in through the roof. Then he'd put on a suit and visit all these offices around the City flogging it.'

'Made a lot of money?'

She sniffs. 'Fucking minted it.'

'Sounds so easy.' She ignores me. 'Then what?'

'He decided he wanted a wife, yeah? The best money could buy. Started moving in the posh circles, you know? Ascot, Henley.' Sounds good to me. 'Load of fucking wankers. That's when he met my mum.'

'Really? She's . . . ?'

'Posh? Yeah, fucking posh. Went to Benenden? You know?

The public school? Used to go out with a lord. She showed me the cutting from *Tatler* or wherever. Pretty too. You know? Not like movie-star looks but beautiful cheekbones. Doll-like.'

'What did *her* mum and dad think about her marrying—?'

'Some rough-arsed foreigner with a chip on his shoulder the size of a plank? What do you think? They didn't speak to her for twenty years,' she says matter of factly.

'Fucking hell.'

She sniffs, flicks more ash off her cigarette. 'Yeah, well, you gonna sulk, you may as well do it properly. I remember when they came to stay once. I knew something was going on because my mum was behaving weirdly. Kept rowing with my dad, well, even more than usual. Dressed us up one day in our best clothes. I said, "Are we going to a party?".' She laughs again. This must be good therapy. Now I'm earning my money – if I ever actually get paid. 'A party! My mum looked like she was going to be sick. She told us to go and sit down in the living room and watch children's telly or something. Half an hour later she brought this old couple to meet us. He had a really disgusting red nose, I remember that. She said "This is Grannie and Grandpa."'

'What did you say?'

She shrugs her shoulders like it's an irrelevant question. '"Hello" or something. Went back to watching telly. I'd never met my dad's parents so I didn't really have a clue about grandparents. I thought it was like getting a new teacher at school or a new nanny or cleaning lady. Big deal.'

We both look down at our wine. She has nearly finished her glass. I pour some more. She murmurs, 'Cheers.'

'I hope you don't mind me going on like this,' she says, staring me in the eyes.

'No, 'course not. It's what I'm . . .' – paid for? – '. . . here for.'

'Sorry, it's just that I've got to go and see them this weekend and they'll be at each other's throats the whole fucking time.'

'Where do they live?'

'Surrey. My dad had it built. The locals call it Dynasty Towers.'

'Tasteful.'

'Very. The evenings are the worst. He gets so drunk. Starts telling my mum about how she thinks she is so grand because of the way she talks and the way she holds her knife and because she wanted the children to do French exchanges, piano lessons and go to university, you know all that shit. He always ends up up telling her she thinks she is so grand but she owes everything, *everything* to him, from the clothes she stands up in to, I don't know, the car she uses whenever she tries to leave him. Then he'll start on us – how we owe everything to him, including life itself. We think that because we've gone to posh schools and mixed with the right people that we're better than him now but we should never forget who put them there in the first place, blah, blah.'

While she is talking a thought occurs to me. There are two sorts of people who have money, serious money, I mean. Some people inherit it, which leaves them soft and rotten and pathetic so they turn to drugs and act like life has done them a terrible disservice. Then there are people who make it and that turns them hard and angry – too mean to spend it themselves and too bitter to give it to anyone else, like Paul Getty installing pay phones in his homes.

For both these kinds of people, money is a terrible affliction. It makes a disgusting, ugly mess of their lives. I, on the other hand, offer another option, a third way: I would be a perfect balance, I could spend it so well. My whole lifestyle – clothes, houses, cars, holidays, parties, whatever – would all be in the best possible taste. I would be the prime example of how to live and spend. A human advertisement for gracious living. I would become a sort of wealth performance artist. All I need is someone (and somehow I'm beginning to think it's not going to be Marion) to provide me with the raw materials – the cash to prove it and I'll be well away.

I come back to her as she is telling me about a family holiday in Barbados where her dad held her brother's head under water, nearly drowning him, while the other holiday-makers on the beach watched in horror and nearly said something to someone.

After she has been talking for a while, I look down and say 'Oh God' sympathetically. I scratch the back of my left hand and discreetly look at my watch. It is nearly three forty-five. I've got work tomorrow. I'll give it till four and then I'll go.

Suddenly I wake up with a hot, sharp pain down in my neck. My cheek is stuck to the table and my left arm has gone to sleep. As gently as I can, I peel my face off the sticky not-so-scrubbed pine surface and drag myself up, wincing in pain. Every muscle in my body is pinched tight. I stretch and shiver and breath deeply. I feel faint for a moment.

The girl is still asleep opposite me. I blink and roll my eyes and feel the pain from my neck move up into my head. I am tortured from a weird, unnatural sleep full of sad, violent dreams. The girl is out for the count, snoring gently, her eyes more red and swollen than ever, her mouth slightly open. How often does she end up doing this? Falling asleep pissed after crying and damning her father to people she doesn't know? I look around for something to put over her shoulders but I can't find anything.

I decide to make for the door. The fresh morning air revives me slightly. All around curtains are closed. I look at my watch, it's six-twenty. I suddenly realize that I haven't got a cheque from her. I can't wake her.

But I really need that money. I have to give £50 commission to Jonathan anyway. If I get the cheque I will be a hundred and fifty quid better off (minus taxi fares). If I don't, I will be fifty worse off (plus taxi fares).

I've got to do it.

I walk back into the house, deciding that brisk and business-like is the best approach. Nothing to be embarrassed about, it's just a commercial arrangement, after all.

She is still out cold. Oh, shit. I can't do this. I groan and breath out heavily, half-hoping it will wake her up. I just can't do this. I walk out again into the hall and consider for a moment. The wreckage looks even uglier in the daylight through the curtains. And the stink is worse. My stink. I've contributed to this, I'm part of it now.

I realize I am standing on a broken CD. How weird, I've never seen a broken CD before. I didn't know you *could* break them.

Oh fuck! That's it. I didn't come here in the middle of the night to listen to this pathetic girl's stories and pay fifty quid (plus cab fares) for the privilege. Fuck it, you've got to be tough in this business.

I march back into the kitchen and cough loudly where the

combined smell of rotting rubbish, booze, stale cigarettes and sleep almost makes me retch. She stirs slightly, but that's it.

'Excuse me.' Nothing. I say it again louder. She stirs slightly and then looks up at me, squinting, trying to focus.

'Sorry to wake you, but, er, I've got to go and, er, you know.'

She sniffs and frowns, obviously trying to remember who I am and what happened last night.

'I'll need a cheque,' I say quickly.

'Hey? Oh, yeah, right.' She straightens up, pushes her hair back and looks around her. She begins a pathetic attempt to find her cheque book while I stand, hands in pockets, casually looking out of the kitchen window. After a few minutes I suggest that it might be in her bedroom. Or the living room. Or under that pile of magazines over there. Oh, shit – this is hopeless. In the end I stumble around the flat, swearing softly and throwing things left and right, looking for anything that she could use to pay me – credit card, cashpoint card, anything.

Finally I find a couple of credit cards behind a pizza flyer on the mantelpiece. I choose the one with the latest expiry date and fill in my credit card slip. I put £200 on and ask her to sign it which she does in silence with big childish letters. The chances of it going through all right are minimal but by now I don't care.

She looks up at me through bloodshot eyes as she hands back the slip.

'I, er . . .' I mumble, folding it and putting it in my back pocket. 'Well, it was nice to, er . . . I hope it's not too bad this weekend, you know, with your dad.'

'Mmmm, no,' she says and sniffs.

I say, 'Thanks, bye.'

It's nearly seven as I head for the Tube.

It takes me days to get over my night of hell with Erren and her father. I notice that we do actually have some of his swivel chairs in our office but there is no one I can talk about it to even if I'd wanted to. They're the really cheap, uncomfortable ones that everyone pushes around to other desks and only the people who are last into the office in the morning – like me – end up sitting on.

*

Jonathan rings me the following evening as I'm tearing off to go to Marion's and thanks me for the job I did the previous night.

'I knew you were right for it. I'm concious that things have been quite quiet recently for you,' he says, a note of concern in his voice.

'Yeah, I know, I've been quite busy with work,' I say, although why I'm offering him an excuse I don't know.

'I thought that American woman might want to you see again.'

'Er, yeah, funny that. Mind you, I think she said she was going back to the States for a while so perhaps she's just not around,' I say confidently. This obviously sounds plausible to Jonathan.

'Probably, most of our clients are international,' he says. 'Anyway, well done, mate.' He laughs. 'They're not all like that, promise. I tell you what, next really glamorous, high-rolling job that comes in is yours.'

'Sure, I just wondered about—'

'There is one woman I was talking to who's going to Rome for business next week,' he says. 'Hates travelling alone. Just wants someone to carry her bag at the airport, sort of thing, take her to dinner while she's there. I'll put you forward for that.'

'Great.' I've never been to Rome. 'But what about—'

'Business class and five-star hotel, of course. Separate rooms, just so there's no misunderstanding . . . well, er, unless you wanted there to be but I'll leave that up to you.' We laugh. 'All right, bud, well done. Speak soon. Bye.'

'That cheque in the post?' I find myself half shouting at last.

'Oh, God, yeah. Sent it the day we spoke. Hasn't it arrived yet? Bloody post office.'

My mum rings me later that afternoon at work and after checking for twenty minutes that I have the time to talk to her (by which time I don't) she tells me that she and my dad will be in London the following Saturday. The daughter of a friend of theirs is getting married.

'It's only a registry office do but they're having drinks afterwards,' she says. 'Nice of them to invite us.' I hear my dad, who is already home at five-thirty mutter something in the background. 'Nothing's *wrong* with a registry office, I just think churches are nicer, you know with the flowers and the music. You wouldn't get married in a registry office, would you?'

'Er, I hadn't really thought about it, Mum.' I know she is thinking about Helen and the plans she was half-making for us.

'Oh, no, I'm not pressuring you, plenty of time for all that. Sorry? All *right*. Your father says to hurry up, as usual. We'll be round about six or seven if that's OK.'

'Great, see you then,' I say, watching the TV with the sound down.

'If you're not going out that night.'

'No, don't worry.'

'Don't want to cramp your style.'

I laugh. 'Don't worry, you're not cramping my style. See you on Saturday.'

When they arrive my mum's face is slightly rosy with drink and my dad has loosened his tie.

'It *was* a *lovely* dress, wasn't it, Derek?' says my mum. My dad has now switched the TV on and is slumped in front of it. He grunts. 'I think her auntie made it. Which one was her auntie? The tall lady?' My dad is even less interested in guessing the identities of this girl's relatives than he is about her dress. My mum gives me a look and rolls her eyes. 'We were just going to have something to eat and then get the train back. Do you want to come? I don't want to get in the way of your plans.'

'Honestly, you're not. I'd love to,' I say, looking at my mum and realizing that I haven't seen her for nearly two months. 'Where do you want to go? That pasta place round the corner?'

'That's a good idea. Do you think they'll be able to fit us in? I know what these London restaurants are like. You have to book weeks in advance.' I laugh at the idea of the little Italian round the corner with its wipe-clean tablecloths and wax-strung Chianti bottle candle holders being booked up. Just then there is a thump outside in the hall and Vinny arrives.

'All right, Mrs C, Mr C,' he says, stifling a burp.

'Hello, Vincent, I mean Vinny,' says my mum. I don't know why, but she adores Vinny. She's obviously slightly surprised by it herself but there you go. I think it is partly his dress sense. 'I can't believe he's going out like that,' she whispers after they meet every time.

'Nice to see you up in town tonight,' says Vinny, just slightly taking the piss, as always.

'A wedding,' explains my mum. 'Only a registry office but it was very nice.'

'Oh, right,' says Vinny. 'I went to a registry office do last month. Beautiful choral music.'

'Oh, lovely,' says my mum.

'They slightly ruined the effect when the clerk turned it off with a stereo remote control.'

'Oooh, dear.' My mum laughs in spite of herself. My dad smiles in our direction, out of politeness.

'The continuing secularization of our society,' observes Vinny.

'Mmmm, yes,' says my mum. 'She did have a *lovely* dress though.'

Vinny can't come out with us, despite my mum's invitation, because he is going to a party in Stockwell.

'Isn't that near Brixton?' says my mum. 'Bit rough round there, isn't it? Oh, do be careful, Vincent. Don't talk to any strangers.'

'That's slightly the idea of going to a party, isn't it?' says Vinny, frowning in amusement. My mum looks confused and then laughs.

'Well, make sure they're *nice* strangers,' she says.

'That's definitely the idea of going to a party,' adds Vinny, giving her a wink. She laughs again, even more confused but sure it's probably the right thing to do.

Much as I love her, my mum always drives me mad in restaurants. This particular evening she runs through her repertoire of irritating habits: she asks me what everything means and then, when I tell her, she says, 'Do you think so? What do you think Derek?' When my dad says he'll have spaghetti bolognaise she says, 'Oh, no. I was going to have that, I'd better have something else.'

'Have what you like,' says my dad. 'It doesn't matter.'

'I know but I just . . . oh, look, ravioli with *lobster*. Do you think it's fresh lobster? That's my favourite, I think I'll have that. Now, are we having a starter?'

She starts telling me about my sister Rachel and her awful husband but then falls silent when the waitress approaches, as if she's been caught talking in class.

'Hi,' says the waitress to me.

'Hi, how are you?' I ask. OK, showing off a bit.

'Very well. Your friend not here?'

'No, gone to a party,' I say.

'Oooh, party,' says the girl.

'I've got the address if you want.'

She laughs. 'No, no. When I finish I am very, very tired.'

'Shame,' I say, tutting. 'That's why we came in tonight – give you the address. He'll be really disappointed.' She laughs again, flipping open her pad.

'I'll have the ravioli,' says my mum stiffly when it's her turn to order.

When the waitress is gone she says, 'They all know you here,' half-disapproving, half-proud.

'So that's where your money goes,' says my Dad in mock disapproval, shaking his head and folding his arms.

When we leave my dad thumps me on the shoulder and says, 'Proud of you, son.' I give a sort of goofy smile and look down at my shoes. My mum kisses me then looks at me as if she is going to say something. They turn and walk back to the Tube station. I watch them for a while. They suddenly look very small.

CHAPTER TEN

'I WANT YOU TO MEET SOME PEOPLE,' Marion says, the following evening, holding her champagne glass in both hands. 'A lot of my friends have been asking about you and I'd like very much for you to meet with them so I'm throwing a little party tomorrow night.'

'Throwing a party' – I like that.

'OK,' I say, from the settee opposite her. Anna Maria pours me some more champagne and puts down another bowl of nuts. Frankly I'd rather spend an evening with a bunch of Mastermind contestants than Marion's freak-show friends but it will make her happy and anyway, I might meet some other potential cash cows. Unfortunate phrase, that.

'You haven't had a chance to meet many interesting people in your life, I know,' she says. 'It will be a chance for you to meet some of the upper classes.'

'Can I come?' says Vinny, later, when I tell him about the party for some reason. The One Aside Indoor football league has come to a temporary halt after a written warning from the landlord (inspired, no doubt, by Mr Anal Axe Murderer from downstairs) and a chunk of plaster that fell out of the wall after a spectacular header by Vinny.

'No, mate,' I explain, handing him a beer and taking a swig from mine. 'Not enough savoir-faire.'

'Oh, OK,' says Vinny. 'Fair enough. You, on the other hand—?'

'I, on the other hand, am oozing it from every pore.'

'Right.'

'You wouldn't get past the door with those trousers.' Vinny looks down at his ultra baggy cords, the crotch around his knees. 'Do they pay graphic designers to dress like clowns?'

'Yes,' says Vinny.

'Oh, actually, I suppose they do, don't they?'

'It's because I'm artistic, mate.'

'Well, your artistic, saggy-arsed trousers won't get you within a million miles of this glittering soirée.'

'Oh, well,' sighs Vinny. 'I'll just stay at home with *Changing Rooms* and a takeaway.' There is a pause.

'Lucky bugger,' I say, taking another swig.

'Ha,' says Vinny with feeling.

Thrilled as I am with the prospect of meeting the upper classes, I don't want to be there when everybody arrives so on the day of the party I take the opportunity to earn some brownie points at work by staying late. Sod's law means that there is absolutely no reason to that day. The office is completely dead. Probably because it is a Friday in July. In fact when she leaves, Debbie gives me a look of suspicion rather than gratitude or encouragement. I end up ringing a few friends but put off seeing them because, as I explain, 'I'm rather tied up at the moment.'

Yeah – with a noose round my neck.

I get back home at nearly eight, ready to get changed. I'm wearing my best work suit, which is pale grey, single-breasted, three-buttoned and a pale blue shirt which I bought specially for the occasion. Yes, that's right. *I* bought. Not quite the way I'd planned it but never mind – I do look pretty good, I have to admit. Cool, understated and, because it's all new (or near enough), rich. I've even applied a splash of some of the horrible aftershave she bought me in duty free at Charles de Gaulle.

As I walk downstairs, practising my cool, debonair look, the door buzzer sounds. I pick up the entry phone and shout, 'Hello?'

'Hi, Vinny, it's Jane.'

'Oh, Jane,' I say unnecessarily. I've been thinking about that cute little turn of the head when she was doing the washing up and I've been looking forward to seeing her again but I wasn't expecting her to be here now, this soon. Why the hell didn't Vinny warn me she was coming over?

'Hello?' she shouts.

'Well, are you going to let her in, you dork?' says Vinny from behind me.

'Yeah, sure.' I press the door button, open our front door and a few moments later she appears, stomping up the stairs.

'Oh, hello, Andrew. Was that you? I thought it was Vinny.'

'Oh, sorry, I wasn't expecting you.'

She is wearing a pale pink T-shirt and a dark blue cardigan, buttoned up to her bust. She's even prettier than I remembered her from the first time. She smiles. But it's a smile of kindness more than interest. Perhaps I was wrong. Arrogant bastard. Perhaps she doesn't like me that way at all.

'You look very smart,' she says, again less out of conviction and more simply to break the silence, it seems.

'Thank you. So do you. I like your . . .' I realize I'm about to say 'breasts' but I manage to catch myself. 'Your cardigan. It's very nice.'

She looks slightly surprised. 'Oh, thank you. It's just from a shop at home.' She laughs. 'So, you off out?'

'Yeah, I'm going to a . . . thing.' I don't want her to see me like this, dressed up like Roger Moore.

'A *thing*?' she says with a sort of mocking indulgence.

'He means a party,' says Vinny. 'They're inviting him because of his sparkling conversation.'

'Yes, a party, I mean.' Oh fuck! What's the matter with me? I want to make it clear to her that I would rather spend time here with her, even with Vinny.

'In Belgravia,' he explains. Shut up, you twat, you're only making this worse.

'Very nice,' says Jane, quietly. She pats the bottle of cheap white wine she is holding. 'Well, have a good time. Vinny and I'll probably still be watching telly and making our own version of sparkling conversation when you get back.'

'Yeah, brilliant. Well, perhaps I'll see you, then.'

'OK,' she says. There is another pause, as I try and think of something interesting to say. What words would explain my bizarre, tongue-tied behaviour, justify my current poncy garb and make her realize that basically I'm quite a nice bloke?

I feel Vinny squeezing past me. 'Listen,' he says. 'I know her name's not on the list but are you going to get out of the way and let her in?'

'Oh fuck, fuck, fuck,' I mutter as I trudge downstairs to the front door. 'Oh, Christ!'

I realize that our football-suppressing downstairs neighbour is staring at me, his key poised by the lock. 'Oh, shit!' I tell him.

Marion greets me as if I was the caterer, reminds me I am late and then turns round to talk to someone else. Fair enough. I take a glass of champagne from a tray and knock it back partly to give me Dutch courage for this ghastly event and partly to obliterate the awful memory of my bizarre performance in front of Jane.

I pick up another glass and wander around a bit, trying to looking bored and aloof but it occurs to me after a while that in fact I just look a bit dim like I don't know the point of the party. I start desperately looking for someone I know. Luckily, by the time I look around the room again it is half full of people. Everyone seems to be looking past everyone else, probably to see who they could or should be talking to. Just then Farrah says 'Hi'. We double kiss and she introduces me to some smooth-looking guy who is dressed in a tweedy jacket and a pink Brooks Brothers button-down collar shirt. All wrong but he does look rich. We shake hands. For some stupid reason I say, 'Where's David?'

Farrah gives me a look of what I realize is discreet panic. 'He couldn't come.' No, of course he couldn't. Not with his replacement here. Perhaps he's in prison, after all. That thought, together with the one and a half glasses of champagne I've just downed, cheers me no end. I knock back the remainder.

'Farrah, you look great,' I gush.

'Oh, Andrew, you're the sweetest ever. I could just eat you. I've just been to see my crystal therapist.'

'Your crystal therapist? What does he do?'

Farrah licks her lips in concentration and begins to explain.

'They apply different types of crystal to every bodily orifice and these crystals draw the impurities out of your body and replace them with positive energy.'

I laugh. By now I don't really care and I've had *two* glasses of champagne on an empty stomach.

'What? You pay someone to shove a crystal up your—'

'Andrew!' It's Marion who has come up behind me like the Belgravia Secret Police. When I turn round I notice that she does look very good indeed – diamond earrings and a simple white dress.

'You look great,' I say, giving her a quick kiss on the lips. This is going to be my standard line for this evening, I decide. I'm sure one of my Dad's books advises it: 'Try greeting every new acquaintance or prospective co-worker with a positive, opening expression of your feelings.'

'Thank you. Now, get yourself another drink. There are a lot of people here tonight that I really want you to meet.'

'Hey, you look great,' I say to Anna Maria as I grab another glass.

I'm actually really pleased to see her but Marion hisses irritably, 'Don't talk to the staff like that. Andrew, you have so much to learn.' She looks round at Anna Maria who is moving off through the crowd, tray in hand, more mystified by my comment, I think, than flattered.

Marion leads me into the centre of the room. For one awful moment I think she is going to make some sort of announcement but luckily a man leaves the group he is with and walks over to us. His aftershave arrives before he does and it burns my nostrils.

'Channing,' says Marion.

'Marion,' he says. 'We were just talking about Sonia Kaletsky. You heard she told everyone she wanted a small wedding. Well, apparently she got such a small wedding there wasn't even a groom.' We all laugh.

After a few seconds Marion has done enough laughing and she says, 'Chan*ning*. Look, Channing, this is Andrew.'

'Hi,' says Channing. He is small, dark and tanned with viciously gelled short hair. He's wearing a black and yellow Versace check jacket with dark blue jeans and black bikers' boots which reach up to his knees. We shake hands. His hand is soft, plump, hairy and heavily ringed. It lingers a little too long in mine.

'Channing is my best friend from New York,' says Marion, careful to add this geographical qualification. I've learnt that Marion has 'best friends in London', 'best friends from California', 'best friends for shopping', 'best oldest friend' etc. Everyone can be Marion's best friend as long as it's in their own particular category. I'm probably her 'best media sales friend'. Or 'best friend for imposing circumcision on'.

'Very nice,' says Channing. I sort of hope he means 'very nice to meet you' but I'm sure he doesn't.

Then he completely ignores me and starts telling Marion about somebody they know from New York who sold his apartment to someone else they know from New York and what the person who bought the apartment said about it and what they were going to do with it or something.

While I am looking around the room a girl comes to join the three of us. She is tanned with long blonde hair and a face that would be pretty if wasn't just a bit too sporty. She is also wearing dark blue jeans and on huge white shirt, undone so that I can see her bra and the top of full, freckled breasts. Her gold chains and bracelets look really good against her tan. She holds her glass in both hands in front of her. Looking up at me, in her gold and white, she looks like an altar boy, offering me the blood of Christ.

She laughs enthusiastically with Marion and Channing. She doesn't know what they are talking about and so her guffaws make me laugh and soon we are laughing at each other laughing. Marion and Channing become uneasy about the amount of laughing going on and so Marion drags me away just as the girl is putting out her hand and saying, 'Louise.'

'Hi. You look—' But Marion has pointed me in the direction of some people sitting on the settee.

'God, that girl's dumb,' she spits. 'She says she's into photography but I can't believe she knows one end of a camera from the other. At least not like she knows one end of a photographer from the other. Here, I want you to meet Toby Erskine-Crumb. Toby works in the City of London,' she says as if he were the only one who did.

'Well, that's what I do when I'm not drinking there,' laughs Toby, offering a hand. 'Hello.'

'Hello, Toby,' I say. 'Oh, fuck off, Toby,' I think. Marion whisks me off again. My head is spinning with champagne and this whirlwind tour of her friends.

At another settee she introduces me to a tiny little lady clutching her glass as if her life depended on it. In front of her is a sea of cannibalized canapés – each half-bitten through or gnawed at. Like most of Marion's friends, her face has that surprised, shiny look, probably because most of it is now gathered up behind her ears.

'Davina, I want you to meet Andrew.'

The lady's face cracks as far as it can into a smile.

'Hoi,' she says in a thick Manhattan drawl. I bow slightly and take her hand, which she obviously appreciates. In fact the only reason I am bowing is because she is so tiny. Marion leaves me squeezing onto the settee next to Davina, presumably because it is less likely I will get off with her than with Louise. As soon as I sit down Davina is off.

'Do you know Marion's problem?'

Is this going to be a joke? I shake my head, getting ready to laugh if I'm required to do so. 'Marion's *problem*?'

Davina waves a liver-spotted hand at me and draws me in closer. 'She's working class. She's blue collar and she hates it.'

I am not sure what my reaction is supposed to be. In some ways Marion is so strange that I wouldn't be surprised if she was created in a test tube or constructed by the inventor of Barbie on an off-day. On the other hand, that little speech she gave me at lunch a couple of weeks ago suggested that she was more blue blood than blue collar.

'That's why she always acts so grand,' hisses Davina from beside me, almost making me jump.

'Does she?'

Davina rolls her eyes, a rather risky manoeuvre given the number of nips and tucks there probably are around them. 'Marion acts more grand than anyone I know. Your Queen could learn something from her.' Davina takes a long slurp of champagne. 'And that's why she always surrounds herself with pretty things. You, sugar, are a case in point.'

'Am I?' I really only ask to break the tension and move the conversation on a bit. She looks at me as if I'm the stupidest thing that she has ever come into contact with.

'Course you are. You must know that. But I bet she hasn't told you.' She takes a prawn and cream cheese pastry thing, removes the prawn, scoops out the cream cheese, sucks it off her fingernail and then squashes the prawn back in the pastry and puts it back down in front of her. Then she spends some time running her tongue round the inside of her mouth to clear it of cheese. I watch repulsed, fascinated, suddenly feeling stone-cold sober.

She looks round the room with her hard little eyes and starts to tell me a story. 'Marion's father sold furniture out of a big warehouse in Brooklyn. I mean, it was supposed to be a store and her mother had pretensions about it being, you know, Bergdorf Goodman or something but the point is her mother never went there. The only people visited Marion's father's store were people who had been to the fancy stores and realized that they couldn't afford the fancy prices. They would sneak into that place, *praying* that their friends and neighbours wouldn't see them there, see where they had ended up just trying to save a few bucks when they wanted a new sofa or a chair or something. And the reason why Marion's mother had pretensions about it was like I said, because she never went there. Oh no, she sat in that house in Scarsdale and took tea and spoke to her friends on the telephone. All very nice, all very proper. Wishing her husband was a society doctor or a big shot lawyer or something.'

'I thought her father worked on Wall Street,' I say. Davina cackles, boy am I ever stupid! Anna Maria comes back again with the champagne. Davina swipes another glass. I smile at Anna Maria and help myself as well. She beams back, unaware that her mistress is being ripped apart and her guts left out for carrion on the sun-scorched hill tops of Manhattan society. On the other hand, if she did know, would she care?

Davina is off again, half-finishing her glass in a single slurp. She ignores my contribution – obviously I am too dumb to bother with.

'And do you know why she has no children?'

Oh Christ! I hope this is not going to be too gynaecological. Women's things always make me feel slightly sick. I want Davina to stop but at the same time I desperately want to hear more. Thing is, I know that Marion will be able to tell with one quick glance at my innocent face that I know all.

I look around the room quickly to check that she isn't looking. Nowhere to be seen. Probably upstairs adjusting something.

'Well *do* you know?' Davina punches my arm.

'No,' I gasp, in some pain.

It is the answer Davina is looking for. She raises her painted eyebrows slightly and looks shocked. 'She doesn't want the competition.'

'Competition?'

'Sure. She doesn't want to have to compete with anyone. What if she had a daughter and what if the daughter was pretty and popular? What if she outshone Marion? What then? Or worse still—' Davina stares even more fiercely – 'but what if she didn't? What if Marion had a kid that was plain and boring — you know, mousy hair, bottle-bottom glasses and braces like a railway siding. OK, she could have a little surgery. Oh sure, a little cutting and tweaking here and there, we've all had it but if you ain't got the raw materials in the first place, bone structure and all, not even the best surgeon in the world can do anything and don't tell me he can.

'No, she doesn't want the competition so she figures it's much better to use surrogates. Surrogate children. Like you. Choose them, parade them around like a poodle and then, if they fail to impress, or, if they impress too much you can always ditch 'em and get another. Oh, yes,' she says, shaking her head, 'Marion has had plenty of those.'

Nice to hear.

'Of course, I don't suppose you've heard about the husbands.' She doesn't wait for an answer. 'Now, I must confess, I did like the first. You couldn't help liking Edward. A bit dumb, a bit of a bore but basically a nice guy. What he did have going for him, though, was potential. You know? Potential. And that's what Marion liked about him, his potential. He was potentially very rich. His father had made a fortune as an oil broker, well, he was a broker in anything. He was the complete opposite of Edward – a devious little scheister. Which is not necessarily a bad thing, in business. But the problem was that he hated Marion. God, he hated her.' Davina takes another great slurp of champagne and, for some reason, hands me her empty glass. I look around for a passing tray and then put it down between us. There is a pause while Davina's intense stare draws over another waitress with more champagne.

'*Hated* her, absolutely hated her.'

'Why?'

'Why?' She takes another gulp. 'He thought she was stuck up and had airs and graces. But cheap all the same. Which is what she is. But what Edward's father really hated about her was that he thought she was a gold-digger. And she thought he was rude and vulgar and rough as a stevedore's ass, which he was. What really got him, though, was when Marion tried to ban him from the wedding. She figured she needed *her* father, who was not exactly smooth as a kid glove, to give her away but she sure as hell didn't need Edward's.'

'This was the wedding at Saint Patrick's Cathedral?' I say, hoping this will earn me some credibility. Wrong. Davina looks at me in disbelief.

'Saint Patrick's? Saint Patrick's Fifth Avenue? Not exactly, sugar. They couldn't exactly afford that. It could have been their local church, but Marion figured that didn't look none too good so she broke her family's heart and found a hotel. Sure, it was a pretty hotel but Fifth Avenue it was not. Anyway, however pretty the goddamn hotel is, if the atmosphere is ugly, the wedding is ugly.'

'Ugly atmosphere?' I ask a little unnecessarily.

'They needed Henry Kissinger to negotiate the table plan.'

'How long did the marriage last?'

'Oh, a couple of years and then she realized that he was going no place and didn't have a nickel to scratch his ass with and so she dumped him.'

'I thought he, er, committed adultery,' I say, trying not to sound too suburban about it. I needn't have bothered.

'He never got chance. She beat him to it. But one thing's for sure, if he had of, she'd have been juggling his balls.'

'So who was Marion's second husband?' I mention her name in the hope that we have been talking at cross purposes and this is not Marion I have been hearing about. She takes a long breath. 'He had more going for him than Edward. At least, he did till Marion got hold of him. He was rich, good-looking and had a sort of savoir-faire, know what I mean? Josef. He was Colombian. They gave the best parties.' She looks disparagingly around her. 'Their apartment in New York was *so* beautiful it had a swimming-pool in the dining room. Models, actors, fashion designers. Drinking, fucking, snorting coke off each other. God, it was beautiful.'

'Beautiful,' I say, trying to imagine this little splosh 'n' nosh love nest.

'And then they had the apartment on Ipanema Beach.'

'Sounds lovely.'

'Honey, it was,' says Davina, looking up at me longingly.

'It was beautiful. And she used it to very good effect. She met her third husband there.'

'Third? I thought there were only two.'

'There were four altogether. Plus a little snacking in between meals, you know what I'm saying.'

'So who was the third?'

'Henry somebody. He was an English lord. Looked a bit like you, sugar, only a bit older.'

'What was he like?'

'Boring, boring, boring. I think someone must have told him to go to Rio to loosen up a bit, you know? Learn to have a good time.'

'Did he?'

'Oh, sure, he learned to take off his tie on the beach. Rio is where Marion developed her taste for younger men. Unfortunately so did lordie.'

'He left Marion for a younger man?'

'Some beach bum.'

'Oh, God. And then she married someone else?'

'Yep. Lordie was boring and, fatally, not as rich as Marion first thought. He had this cold, draughty old pile miles from anywhere in the English countryside which didn't appeal. Ten bedrooms and only two bathrooms. Not only that, it seemed almost everything the family owned would go in tax when his father checked out. So then she met Carlos. He was probably the best of the lot: nasty, ruthless but great fun to be with. And he was the richest. Used to sleep with a Smith & Wesson under his pillow at night. What a guy!'

'Sounds like quite a character.'

'Oh, he was. They gave even better parties than when she was with Josef.' Her face hardens. 'The only bad thing was that she met that bitchy little fag Channing there and they've been together ever since. Marion says he's more faithful than a husband.'

'I met him just now.'

Davina is staring across the room at Channing, hatred screwing up her face as much as her surgery will allow.

Intrigued, I ask, 'You've crossed swords in the past, then?' 'Crossed swords'? I sound like my dad.

'I'd like to cross his fat neck with a sword,' says Davina. Just then Marion appears.

'Marion!' I gasp.

'Are you guys having fun?' she says.

Before I can think of something to say and say it innocently, Davina says, 'Beautiful party, Marion', and smiles warmly. I do the same except that I must look like a grinning idiot. Marion looks at us both for a moment and then touches my arm. I get up and she tells me there are some other people she wants me to meet.

'See you later,' I say to Davina. She just smiles knowingly.

'Was Davina boring you to death?' asks Marion.

'Oh no,' I say casually. 'Just chatting.'

'She's getting on a bit. Sometimes I think she's losing it – too many heated rollers when she was young. I only invite her to things out of pity.'

Just after one o'clock people start to leave and within a few minutes the room is empty. Some woman with heavy eye make-up comes up to me and says: 'Andrew, there you are. We never got a chance to talk all evening.'

'No,' I say. 'We'll have to do it next time.' By which time I might have worked out who she is and thought of something to say to her. Everyone triple kisses Marion and thanks her so much you'd have thought she'd saved their lives.

When we are alone together I put my arms round Marion and look into her eyes. 'Nice party,' I say softly.

'Thanks. I throw better ones in New York but there's just no room in London.' She kisses me on the lips and runs her hand through my hair. 'Let's go to bed.'

I look at her carefully for a moment, wondering if what Davina said was true. 'I'm just going for a quick walk to clear my head,' I say, already thinking about the hangover I'm going to have the next morning.

'Oh, must you?'

'Just quickly.'

I wonder out into the mews trying to avoid any last guests in case they think I have been chucked by Marion. At the gateway I take a deep breath and stretch my arms above my head and bring one of them down on Louise, the Australian girl.

'Oh, sorry, I didn't see you standing there,' I say, wondering what she is doing lurking around by the gatepost.

'No problem,' she says. There is a pause. 'Hi.'

'Hi,' I say, remembering what she is like at conversation. There is a pause. 'Could you see me home?'

'Er, well . . .'

'Look, here's a cab.'

Before I can say anything more she has rushed over the street and thrown herself at a taxi which stops just inches before it makes contact with her. She turns and yells across to me to come on. I run over as well and get in.

'Where do you live?' I ask, trying to make it sound like a casual opening line of conversation rather than a panicked enquiry about where the hell we are going.

'Kensington High Street,' she says and suddenly yells with laughter. 'It's not far.'

Louise leads me along a silent, empty corridor of her block in West Kensington. The whole place has probably not changed much since the seventies – Hessian wallpaper, brown swirly carpets, groovy orange lightshades, some of them slightly melted. She is giggling and breathing heavily. Suddenly she throws herself against a front door and says, 'Home sweet home.'

'OK,' I say, hopelessly. 'Well, good night then.'

'No,' she squeals in protest, and lets us both in, flinging the door wide open and rushing over to switch on a small table lamp. The room is empty apart from a large scruffy sofa bed. Everything else is lying on the floor: the phone, some magazines, a CD player and CDs, clothes and a horribly ugly, terminally ill house plant.

'Look, Louise, I must be getting back.'

'One quick coffee,' she says, so I close the door behind us and walk round the flat while she goes into the tiny kitchenette. I look down on the headlights of the traffic moving slowly below us and open one of the creaky metal-framed windows for a moment to get some air but the noise is deafening so I close it again. She asks what I want to drink.

'Whatever,' I say, moving over to the dividing unit. I can guess what is in her fridge: a few cans of beer and diet coke, a bottle of champagne and perhaps some cottage cheese (probably with smoked salmon or prawns), well past the sell-by date. What's called a 'tart's fridge'. On the wall is a notice board with cards for a mini-cab service, a Pizza Hut discount leaflet and a flyer for a club I have never heard of, although Vinny probably has.

Louise leaps up from the behind the counter with a bottle of champagne in one hand and two glasses in the other. 'Look what I found,' she says and collapses laughing on the floor.

'I'd love to but I'd better not,' I say.

She pouts. 'You've been drinking all night. Why stop now? Just one.'

'Well—'

'A nightcap.'

'Oh, well, thank you,' I say. 'But just one glass'.

'OK,' she says as the champagne cork shoots off and hits the polystyrene ceiling tiles. 'Wow! That's what I love about champagne.' I can't help laughing at her delight. I sit down on a squashy leather settee and say 'Nice place' for some stupid reason.

'No, it's not,' she says. 'It's a shit hole but at least it's quite central and doesn't cost anything.'

'Why's that?' I ask. Not very cool but I genuinely want to know. There is supposed to be no free lunch but somehow I begin to suspect that everyone else is queuing up with their trays ahead of me.

'Oh,' she winks. 'An arrangement.' Then she howls with laughter again and falls over, almost doing the splits. I help her recover. Suddenly she is serious.

'Ow! Oh, no, I think I've done something to my leg.'

'Ah you all right?'

She puts her arm round my shoulder and I lead her over to the settee and help her sit down, me beside her. She is squeezing her inner thigh and wincing slightly. She gets up and walks round, stretching it.

'That's better.' Then she comes back and stands over me, one hand on her hip, the other still on her inner thigh, legs apart: 'Finish your drink.'

I open my mouth to say something but she tuts and takes the glass out of my hand. Then she straddles me and starts kissing me deep and hard. She tastes of booze and ciggies. I try to resist, pushing away.

'Lou . . . ise,' I hiss through squashed lips but she ignores me. Her tongue explores my mouth and her hands run through my hair. She pulls at my ears, at first gently then so hard it almost hurts but the force of her tongue and the gentle rubbing of her crotch against mine take my mind off it. Suddenly she gets up, unbuttons her shirt and takes it and her bra off. She looks at me as she touches her breasts.

'Louise, for God's sake I—'

'Shut up.'

I feel my dick pressing against my underpants and a second later she has released it and is sliding my trousers down. I try to stop her but she bats my hand away. She works at my dick with her mouth. She is serious, determined, driven. I close my eyes and let my head fall back slightly. I'll give her two minutes then I'll stop, really. Two minutes. Well, perhaps five.

Oh, what the fuck! I put my hand on the top of her head and run my fingers through her hair. Then suddenly she stops and is gone. A second later she is walking back from the bedroom, tearing at a tiny package. Skilfully she forces a condom down over my cock in a split second and slips off her jeans, eyeing it hungrily.

'Shall we go to the bedroom?' I ask, my heart pounding, but she mutters something about it being a mess and then climbs on to my legs and eases herself down onto me, moaning softly. I gasp as the feeling washes over me. For a second I think I am about to come but I pause for a moment, think of Vinny in his dressing gown and I'm OK. Louise begins to move up and down. Slowly I reach out to touch her left breast. She grabs my hands and forces them onto both breasts, pressing hard. I crane up and take one in my mouth.

For what seems like hours we destroy the remaining springs in the settee, knock over a glass, bang my head against the wall countless times, rip the buttons off my new shirt, oh God, my brand new shirt and rub my legs raw against the zip of my fly.

Then suddenly she begins to move faster and starts gasping, 'Ow, ow, ow.' Suddenly I feel myself coming as well. She slows her rhythm and I wait. For a moment I don't think I'll do it after all and I have to push myself into her harder. As a result, my orgasm is extra good. I shout out with the pleasure and exquisite pain.

'Hey! A screamer,' says Louise. She rolls down onto the floor panting and pushing her long blonde hair away from her face and her damp forehead. I laugh and catch my breath. She sits up, looks at me for a moment and laughs again. 'Ooh, animal!' Before I can stop her she gently but firmly pulls the condom off my dick and goes into the bathroom to throw it away.

Meanwhile, I'm trying to put my clothes back together. Sweaty and still weak, I manage to do up my fly and belt but decide that my shirt is a bit of dead loss and so I just tuck it in as best as I can. Fuck, what a mess. What a waste, too.

The toilet flushes and she comes back from the bathroom still naked. She has a beautiful, bronzed, athletic body which I wish I'd had time to get to know a bit better. Funny to have sex and then check out her bod afterwards. She laughs, kisses me lightly on the lips and collects the glasses to refill them.

'Er, no thanks,' I say. 'I must be getting back.'

'Oh, no worries then,' says Louise. 'You can get a cab out in the street – dead easy.'

In my state of post-coital exhaustion and sogginess I suddenly feel guilty about Marion – and more than a little nervous about what she'll do if she finds out what I've been up to. That was a hell of a long breath of fresh air. I'll have to get undressed downstairs or something. I'll have to take the suit to the dry cleaners and buy a new shirt tomorrow.

'It'll be OK,' says Louise, knocking back half a glass of champagne in one mouthful and eyeing it disdainfully.

'I suppose so,' I mutter, guilt and embarrassment really kicking in now.

'Hey, cheer up, mate, I wasn't *that* bad, was I?'

'No. I mean, you were very good. I enjoyed it,' I say, but somehow it doesn't sound very complimentary, more like I'm saying goodbye to a prostitute and somehow I don't like thinking about prostitution at the moment.

'Well, what's the matter then?' She looks at me suspiciously. 'You in a relationship at the moment? That it?'

'Yes,' I say quietly.

'Don't tell me she was there – at the party?' says Louise, more intrigued than troubled.

'Yes,' I tell her. 'It was *her* party.'

'Christ,' giggles Louise. 'I didn't even know whose party it was. Who was she?'

'Marion.'

'Marion,' she says pensively. 'Oh, *her*. That old American

woman with the blonde hair? Looked like she'd got a poker up her ass all night?'

'Yes. I mean, no, she doesn't look . . . like that.' I feel indignant on Marion's behalf (guilt again) but I suppose that is how she must appear to the rest of the world.

'Christ, I'm thirsty tonight,' she says, sticking her head into the fridge. 'You and her together, then?'

'Yes, we are,' I say in a very English sort of way.

'Kinky. She's old enough to be your mother.'

'I like mature women,' I say even more stiffly. Louise comes over to me, opening a diet Coke. She looks me in the face.

'Course you do, mate. Why not? I like older men – especially if they've got a bit of cash.' She takes a swig of Coke and waits a moment for my reaction. 'She should see you all right. That house must be worth a couple of mill. Hey, you might get a flat like this, play your cards right. You're a good-looking boy, not bad where it counts.' She makes a playful grab for my crotch and I immediately pull away. She laughs.

'Why did you bring me back here?' I ask slowly.

She looks surprised by the question.

'Because I just fancied someone my own age, I suppose.' She fiddles with the tab on her Coke can. 'And because you were the best-looking straight guy at that party. I thought if I didn't get you someone else would.' She looks up at me leeringly. 'Bit of a trophy fuck, I suppose. You should be flattered.'

I sort of am. But then I'm also just a commodity, a piece of meat. It's becoming quite a familiar sensation.

Louise walks away.

'G'night, mate. Make sure the door's closed behind you.'

As I walk out into the warm night air fatigue catches up with me. My feelings of shame about Marion are mingled with a sense of unease. Presumably Louise produces that little performance on a regular basis for whoever pays for her flat.

And perhaps that's it. For all Jonathan's grinning, charming bullshit about his escorts offering nothing more than companionship and anything beyond that not really being part of the service, perhaps if you really want a nice flat rent free, clothes bought for you and enough pocket money to do your own thing you've got to fuck for it.

CHAPTER ELEVEN

I PUT MY KEY INTO THE LOCK and creep in. The house is half in darkness and still smells of the party. I take off my jacket and undo my trousers. The zip is totally buggered and the material around it creased and pulled out of shape. Marion must never see this, I tell my shadowy face in the mirror. Then it occurs to me that even if she does ever buy me a suit it'll only be to replace this one and I'll end up just breaking even. The shirt isn't as bad as I first thought – I've lost three buttons but I can easily ask Anna Maria if she'll sew them on again and not tell Madam. My tie is so tightly knotted I don't think I'll ever get it undone but with a bit of luck Marion will be so embarrassed she'll buy me another one as Mark suggested. God, at this stage even a new tie would be nice.

I take my shoes off and creep upstairs. Needless to say, Marion is still awake when I tiptoe into the bedroom.

'Where the hell have you been?' she asks quietly, without moving.

'Er, just seeing Louise home,' I say lightly.

'Oh, yeah?'

'Yeah, she, er, she was a bit nervous about going home on her own at night.'

'*She* was nervous? I would have thought that most of the men in West London had more reason to be nervous,' whispers Marion venomously. I begin to take my underpants off and discover that my dick is stuck to the material. I pull it off as gently as I can but can't help gasping in pain. 'Now what?' says the voice from the bed.

'Nothing. Just going to brush my teeth.'

'There's some mouthwash in there too.'

The next day, Saturday, Marion has gone out by the time I wake up. Her side of the bed is just a vast, empty expanse of rumpled retribution. Oh, Christ, I've done it now.

An hour later while I'm eating the Rice Krispies, which I've finally persuaded Anna Maria to buy by writing it out for her, my mobile rings and I answer it. I hear a muffled voice at the other end saying she wants a change from white lilies, they're such a cliché.

'Hello?' I say, realizing that it is Marion. She's rung me and then got carried away bollocking someone. Probably, just practising for me. 'Hello-o-o-o?' I say again.

Anna Maria, pouring more coffee for me, looks enquiringly.

'Madam,' I say. She rolls her eyes and walks off. This makes me laugh.

'Some of those cute pink and purple ones,' says the muffled voice irritably. 'The ones you said came from somewhere.'

I try again. 'Hello, Marion?'

'Andrew?' says Marion.

'Hi,' I say nervously.

'I'm just buying some flowers.'

'So I heard.'

Marion ignores me and says, 'I need to talk to you. Meet me in Joe's in half an hour.'

'But I'm not dressed, yet. Make it an hour.'

'Not those,' screeches a voice from the other end of the phone. 'Some fresh ones – those look like they've been under an elephant's ass for a month.' Then, 'Andrew, it's nearly eleven. Really! Have you just got up? OK, I'll just come home.' She rings off.

I put the phone down. That's it – I'm going to be chucked. And I deserve it. Bloody Louise. Fucking Louise, more like. I do feel bad about Marion. I was never once unfaithful to Helen from the time we started going out in her first term at university to the time she dumped me when she was coming back from France. Four years and not once.

I had offers.

That party, in a flat off campus when Helen had gone home for the weekend to see her parents. The girl in the doorway of the kitchen. Slightly pissed, face flushed, breasts heaving, under the thin fabric of her dress, leaning back against the doorframe. Laughing, saying things like, 'You're so horrible to me, I hate you.' The kind of things girls say when they really fancy you. The smell of her warm body and perfume. I was tempted. I took another swig of warm lager and looked at her lips as she ran her tongue over them, waiting for me to make a move.

I did make a move. I muttered, 'Better go. Got an essay to do tomorrow,' and staggered off home.

Marion is walking through the door as I come downstairs, freshly showered and shaved. She is wearing sunglasses. A bad sign. Chris is following her, trying to manipulate the biggest bunch of flowers I've ever seen through the front door. I'm guessing they're not for me.

'Hi,' I say as brightly as I can.

'Hello, darling,' she says.

There is a silence as she puts her bag down and helps herself to a glass of Perrier from the drinks cabinet so I say, 'What are you doing for lunch today?'

She says quietly, 'I have a luncheon engagement with an old friend but Anna Maria will fix you something.' She looks across at the driver. 'Chris, just leave those flowers on the settee and wait a moment, I need to go out again.' He nods and obeys. She takes a sip of water.

Oh, Marion, please get this over with. Just tell me we're finished and let me get my stuff and get back to normality.

'OK,' I say quietly.

'Sit down.' She pats the cushion of the settee next to her. I sit down. She doesn't take off her sunglasses. 'I just wanted to check something,' she says, looking straight ahead at the far wall. 'You didn't sleep with Louise last night, did you?'

I'm suddenly very much aware of Chris, the driver, being in the same room with us. He is staring out of the window, having laid the flowers down on the settee. I don't know what to say but somehow my mouth has started without me.

'Louise? No. I – I just saw her home, like I said.'

'She didn't make a pass you?'

The idea that Louise, drunk and giggly, would drag me back to her flat *without* trying it on just doesn't sound convincing so I say, 'Well, she did, sort of but I, er, resisted,' I stammer. I *resisted*? What am I on about? Suddenly I'm the virtuous heroine in a Victorian melodrama. Why is it Marion makes me say such weird things?

134

'Good.' She squeezes my leg affectionately. 'Good boy. I really can't stand cheaters. You know, after Edward.'

She looks round, touches my cheek and stares into my eyes. I look for hers but all I can see is my shameless, lying face reflected back at me from the huge black lenses.

Yes, all right, I lied. I had a one-night stand and now I've lied about it. I am a pathetic little piece of shit, I admit it. But I've never been unfaithful before, that's the point. My mates were straying all the time. I provided my friend Ben with an alibi half a dozen times but I was always completely faithful to Helen – and look what I got for it. I'm twenty-four and it's about time I did what most blokes my age having been doing for years: having great, mindless sex whenever they feel like it.

Besides, from what Davina said at the party, Marion's been lying to me for the three weeks since we met, which is kind of hurtful in its own way. Unless Davina really was just bonkers. Anyway, Marion and I really does feel like a fling, not like we're going out properly. How could we go out together in the usual sense? We're hardly likely to get married. And I know from what Davina says of her past that Marion's no angel.

'I want you to wear that Rolex,' she says suddenly.

Oh, God. Why now?

She reaches round to the table next to the settee, opens a drawer and takes it out. She opens the box elegantly and there it is, gleaming in the sunlight – Swiss-made, accurate to a few seconds a year, waterproof, twenty-two carat guilt, I mean, gold.

Now I do feel like shit. She hands it to me and I put it on while she watches.

It does look good, though.

'Thank you,' I say, kissing her on the lips.

'I know it's difficult for you dating an older woman. It's difficult for me with a younger man. I've never done it before, either,' she says, taking my hand. 'And I know that the world of luxury you've been thrown into takes some getting used to but if a relationship is worth having, it's worth working at.'

'Yes, I know,' I say, overwhelmed by this sudden outburst of emotion. What is she saying? I thought she thought we were just having fun.

'I want you to wear the Rolex tonight.'

'Sure,' I say quietly. 'Where are we going?'

'Well, I'm going to a dinner party,' she says, closing the box and putting it back in her handbag. 'But you're having dinner with Channing.'

'What?'

'I said to Channing you'd have dinner with with him.'

'Without you?'

'Like I said, I'm going to another dinner party.'

'What? Go *out* with him? Oh, Marion.' I knew this was too good to be true.

'Just have dinner with him.'

'What? With that old poof?'

Does Chris snigger from across the room?

'What's a "poof"?'

'Poof. Fag.'

'Don't call him that,' says Marion, closing her handbag with a resounding snap. 'Channing is one of my best and dearest friends. I am sure if you get to know him, he'll become one of yours too.'

I get up and begin to pace the room. '*Un*likely.'

'Andrew. It's an invitation to dinner. You should be flattered,' she says, getting up.

'Flattered? He just wants to-to—'

'To get to know you?'

'To get my trousers off.'

Chris is definitely stifling a giggle now but I don't care.

'Andrew, don't be ridiculous. He knows you are my lover.' She pauses. 'He knows you would never be unfaithful to me.'

Ooops. I try another tack. 'Oh, Marion, come on—'

'And I'm sure you won't object to some free dinner.' A bit below the belt, that. I sigh deeply.

'Oh, OK, then. If it'll make you happy.'

'Good. I've said you'll be there at eight.'

Strangely enough, when I get home to get changed, Vinny is lying on the settee watching TV. He has the phone carefully wedged between his face and a cushion.

'So? What was she like?' he says, raising his eyebrows in welcome at me. 'Yeah? Yeah? Ah, rampant nymphomania – I've always admired that in a woman.'

Oh! God. Normality. How I miss it.

I walk along the tiny Chelsea street where Channing lives, counting down the numbers on the toy houses until I come to his. I'm wearing my blue blazer and a pair of very ordinary grey trousers that I haven't worn for ages. Catching my reflection in the window of the tube train I decide it's probably some desire to want to appear as wholesome and clean-cut as possible. Except that the stripey tie makes me look like a schoolboy.

Since I started in this business, getting dressed has become something of minefield. The idea was that I'd acquire a wardrobe full of gear and enjoy choosing what to put on everyday. Instead I've got the same stuff plus quite a few other bits *I've* had to buy myself. My credit card bill is probably affecting the balance-of-payments deficit. Deciding what I should wear each evening occupies my mind from lunchtime onwards. It's just lucky that I haven't got anything more important to think about.

Lying in the bath, earlier in the evening, I tried to look on the bright side. I might find out something more about Marion. Perhaps she really has been just lying to me and I've believed it all, like a fool. Perhaps she is not as rich as she says, or perhaps she just invented her entire past because she thought it would impress me.

Or perhaps Marion wants to get something more on me. Find out whether I *did* do it with Louise. Discover my true intentions, check that I'm not just a paid escort on the make – which I'm not, of course.

Or perhaps Channing hopes I am, that I'll go out with anyone who pays, that I'll do anything for money. Is that why he is so keen to have dinner with me? Oh no, I hope not. I feel slightly sick at the thought of it. Anyway, it's not going to happen. Funnily enough, it's not even the physical act, it's the seediness of it. Look on the bright side though, I might meet some new people – female ones, that is – who might help me out financially if, when, Marion dumps me.

At least, as Marion so kindly pointed out, I'll get a free dinner.

I watch him for a moment through the front window, phone clamped under his chin, spinning around the room adjusting the invitations on the mantelpiece, shoving a new CD in the machine, throwing glossy magazines into a pile in the corner. I am just considering how likely it would sound that I had forgotten the address and the phone number and so I had not been able to meet up after all, when Channing turns and sees me. Still on the phone, he raises his eyebrows and shouts over his shoulder at someone.

As I walk up the few steps to the front door it is opened by the maid, a dour, wrinkled little South American woman, probably aged well beyond her years. How did I know he'd have a South American maid? Inside the house dance music is belting out of the CD player.

'G'd evening,' I say.

She looks at me mournfully and I realize that she has obviously never had a good evening in her life. Her days are probably pretty grim as well. She lets me in and walks back down the hallway.

Suddenly a tiny dog appears, yapping around my feet. I wait until the maid has turned her back and is disappearing downstairs again and then try and kick it away. Obviously thinking this is a game, the little bastard comes back for more. I turn to it and start mouthing 'Stay' and holding up my hand. It leaps up at my finger, snapping and snarling, its diamond collar glinting in the light of the chandeliers. I yank my finger out of the way and hold my whole hand up. Now it thinks I am doing some kind of dance and so it gets even more excited. Still backing off, I walk straight into Channing who has obviously been wondering how it could take anyone so long to travel the three yards from the front door to the living room. Still on the phone he rolls his eyes and shrieks, 'Coco! Bad dog!' Coco runs off happily.

Channing finishes his call and puts the phone back. He looks me up and down, smiles coquettishly and asks what I would like to drink. For some reason I say beer, which he does not have, so I settle on Scotch with ice but without water. He has a vodka martini. Then he gestures me to take a seat. Like Marion's house, there is nowhere to sit comfortably, you can either perch on a tiny, hard doll's-house chair or collapse into a cotton-wool settee. I go for the perch option and immediately feel ridiculous. He, of course, knows which is the only sensible seat in the room and takes it.

We sit facing each other for a moment like one of us is going to draw and shoot and then, still smiling, he says, 'Well, I'm so glad you could make it.'

'So am I,' I lie.

'Nice of Marion to let you out of her sight for an evening,' he smirks.

'Oh, she does from time to time,' I say blandly.

'Marion usually keeps her boys on a short leash.'

'Perhaps I'm not one of her boys, then,' I say coolly. He laughs loudly and sweeps off to refill his glass. Grimacing with discomfort, I take the opportunity to swap seats onto the soft settee and sit bolt upright, my hands on my knees. He sits down again and smiles broadly. God, I wish he wouldn't do that. I'm beginning to recognize expensive dentistry when I see it.

'So, you from London originally?' he asks. Oh, Christ, we're not going to go through all this, are we? On the other hand, at least it is quite a safe topic so we do the whole thing and then move on to him.

He is originally from Georgia but had moved to New York City when he was about eighteen to escape his small-town parents and their small-town ideas. He worked in a clothes shop or 'couturier', as he calls it, on Fifth Avenue and ended up living with the owner. He then did the same thing with an interior designer, a night club manager and finally, an antiques dealer, where he learnt his trade. But he had got bored with New York and then went to Rio where he had some wild years and met Marion. Now he is giving London a shot.

Lucky London.

And it's OK. A bit quiet and a really early town, you just cannot eat anywhere decent after midnight except Joe Allen's but it will do him for a while. I agree and say that it is a bugger that the Tube finishes at midnight. He laughs and I realize that he has probably never been on the Tube in his life.

Then he announces that we had better go or we will miss our reservation and he dashes off to get ready. I suddenly feel a lot more relaxed – partly at the thought of a short break from him and partly at the thought of some nice food somewhere.

I leap out of the horrible settee and have a good stretch,

discovering that I can nearly touch the ceiling. I help myself to another drink and wander around the room, tripping up on a huge leopard skin rug. There is a lot of leopard skin now I that I come to notice it. His friend Irena, he tells me later, gave him the idea – she has a whole room decorated in leopard skin. 'Most of it real,' he says enthusiastically.

All over the little tables and the huge mantelpiece are hundreds of picture frames. He is in most of the pictures: with Joan Collins, with Fergie, with Princess Diana (ignoring him in a receiving line), with Elizabeth Taylor, with models, male and female, and other people with lots of blond, blow-dried hair, with some other old queen in a black tie, on a white sandy beach with a young guy who is laughing, underneath a flowery umbrella drinking long drinks with a lady in sunglasses and a big hat. More and more pictures of him and his friends in party mode, glamourous and fun, tanned and blond and blowed-dried and beautiful. Yes, I've got the message, Channing: you're a glamorous, attractive person with lots of glamorous, attractive friends and life is just fab. No dreary suburban lifestyle, no bored wife or fat kids staring at the box and demanding to be fed.

A shriek of 'Coco! Bad dog!' and a waft of Georgio of Beverly Hills aftershave announce his return. I quickly pick up a picture and pretend to glance at it casually. Channing appears behind me wearing a huge coat with fur collars despite the heat. He takes the photograph out of my hand. It is of him and a young guy at a black-tie do.

'Nice guy. Real shame,' he says and hands it back to me. 'Come on, you know San Lorenzo, you're not *pronto, pronto* you losa that *tavola*.'

His black Merc drops us off outside San Lorenzo and some waiting papparazi relax as they see it is no one famous.

'It's such a relief coming here with somebody nobody's ever heard of for a change,' says Channing, gathering his coat around himself and leading the way into the restaurant.

The maître d' feigns delight to see Mr Charisse and sizes me up in the split second it takes for him to arrange for a girl to take Channing's coat.

We are shown to what I suppose is a reasonably good table. I look around for celebrities. Lots of pony tails, more blond blow-dried hair and honey tans. Lots of older guys, some with blue blazers, some just with white shirts. Thick dark hair, flecked with grey erupts from unbuttoned shirt fronts or sweeps down from neatly turned back cuffs. Big, thick, hairy hands, big, thick gold jewellery are everywhere. Bits of Versace splashed here and there. Except on me, of course.

'My God, look at that shirt,' says Channing, shaking out his napkin.

'Where?'

'To your left. It looks like a cat fight between a beach towel and a roll of psychedelic wallpaper.'

I look round and see what I think he is talking about. I laugh politely. Then I look back and realize I can't see the difference between it and his. He is looking at me taking the place in.

'I can't believe that Marion has never brought you here before,' he says, biting the end off a bread stick and chewing furiously.

'Erm, I don't think she has,' I say, as if it is difficult to keep track of all the places we go to.

'It's best for lunch, of course, but I can go for it any time,' he says, looking past me and smiling at someone. A waiter comes over.

'Can I get you gentlemen some drinks?'

'I'll have a vodka martini. What you will have? Scotch?'

'Er, yes, please.'

'OK.' The waiter smiles knowingly. I realize that he probably thinks we are 'together'. God! Marion, why are doing this to me?

'Cute, huh?'

I realize that while I'm thinking, I've been watching the waiter walk off. I decide to ignore this comment and look at the menu. Channing consults his with the same bored, weary look that Marion reserves for menus.

'I should have something light, I guess I'll just have the grilled sea bass,' he sighs, finishing the last of the bread sticks with a flick of the wrist. 'You should have their linguine. To *die* for.'

'I'll have the steak,' I say firmly.

We order from the same waiter and to my horror I find myself blushing deeply. Channing smiles and starts talking;

he compares British boys (smelly, bad teeth) to Brazilians and Americans. He tells me about how awful Concorde is (so cramped you can't swing a hair dryer), what his house in Brazil was like and how you could gaze down onto Ipanema beach and choose whatever you wanted.

'Well, why don't you fuck off back there, then,' I find myself thinking but I decide to be polite and just eat some bread and sit and listen. Besides, behind his head I spot a very pretty blonde girl, French or something, who is with what looks like her grandparents. She notices me look at her and looks back, then, the second time, she half-smiles and looks away as the old lady says something to her.

Channing does not seem to notice. Our first course arrives and he carries on, pausing every now and then for a reaction. He makes various references to my sex life with Marion and hints that I am just one of many worthless young men she has got herself mixed up with over the years he has known her but I just let it go.

'She's an incredibly attractive woman – you should think yourself very lucky,' he says.

'I do,' I say quickly.

'I've never known her take such a liking to one of her escorts.' I'm beginning to hate that word. Someone at a nearby table turns round. 'Do many of your clients see you as much as Marion?'

'I don't have *clients*, I just met Marion and we started going out,' I say.

'Going *out*?'

'Yes.' Channing smiles and concentrates on his food. 'What's wrong with that?'

'Nothing.' I watch Channing eating for a second.

'Has she seen many es—I mean, people like me, of my age.'

'Sorry? People of your age? No. I mean, she has paid guys to take her out to dinner a couple of times in New York. Quite a few young actors who haven't had a break yet or models. You know. Why not? She's a rich woman. She has the money.'

'I see.'

'I've introduced her to a few as well. She likes young people. So do I – that's what keeps us young and there arc always young people around who'll accept a free dinner.'

Like tonight, I think, but I don't say it. He looks enquiring at me but I still say nothing so he adds, 'I must say, though, you're certainly the youngest yet.'

'I see. How old is she?'

Channing looks shocked. 'You never ask a woman that question.'

'I'm not asking a woman, I'm asking you.'

'I can't tell.'

'Go on, I won't say you've told me,' I say, enjoying making the running for a change.

'No, I mean I can't tell, she hides it very well.'

'Oh, I see.'

We both eat in silence for a moment. Then I ask, 'How many husbands has Marion had?'

'You mean how many has she married, or how many has she, you know, *had*.' He raises his eyebrows wickedly.

'Let's start with married.'

'Oh, I don't know. I think it's two.'

'Two? Not three?'

'Two is not three, that's true.'

'Very clever. All rich, though?'

'Well, of course. Is there another kind? Why do you wanna know? Feeling a little *insecure?*'

'No.' I pay some attention to my food. Channing is obviously not going to play ball.

'That's probably why she likes you,' he says, obviously trying to regain the initiative.

I look up from my plate. Having got the reaction he wants, he immediately looks down at his.

'How do you mean?'

'Mmm?'

'I said, "How do you mean?"'

'Well, you're different. Young, unsophisticated, fresh.' He pauses. 'You're kinda naive, proud but without a cent to scratch your ass with.'

I take another mouthful of food and chew it thoughtfully.

'Go on,' I say, although I'm not sure I want him to. This is fascinating but distinctly unnerving.

'Let me see,' says Channing, clearly sensing my discomfort and relishing it. 'You're a bit like ... a blank canvas, someone for her to develop, to mould. There is something

143

about your gauche immaturity that she finds, what's the word? Refreshing.' He purses his lips and opens his eyes wide, in an exaggerated version of something I've seen Marion do so often. 'Besides, you're so British. She likes that.'

'British?' I spit.

'Oh, you know. Quiet, reserved. Kinda macho in an understated way.' Just in case I might possibly think he is paying me a compliment, he sniggers slightly.

'I see.' I think perhaps I do.

I notice that the blonde girl is looking again. I smile at her and so Channing seizes his moment to take charge of the conversation.

'Seen someone you know?' he says loudly, with sarcastic excitement. 'Someone from Fulham make it over here? Where? I want to see, let's go say hello.' He is almost shouting by now.

'Oh, shut up,' I groan.

'Well, hoi there, how are *you*?' hisses a strangled voice from above us. It is not exactly loud but somehow theatrical enough for most of the nearby tables to turn and look. This guy certainly knows how to 'project'. He is short and very slim with a dark tan and immaculate, shiny dark hair and long, dark eyelashes. Eyeliner again. He wears dark blue jeans with black velvet slippers, a crisp white shirt and a loud red tie. His aftershave begins a fight with Channing's.

'*He*llo,' he says seriously, extending a hand. He is also American. I stand up for some reason and tower over him clumsily, drawing even more attention to us. I notice that his suspiciously single-tone hair is scraped over a bald patch on top.

'Hi,' I say.

'Oh, sweet,' says Channing.

We both look at him.

'You stood up. I love that – so well behaved. Friend of Marion's,' says Channing to the other guy.

'Oh, OK,' says the guy, smiling to Channing.

'Who are you with?' asked Channing, looking to see the guy's table.

'Oh, just Carolyn, Lauren and a bunch of fashion people,' yawns the guy. They talk some more, the other guy saying, 'And so I said to Carolyn, Judy would not say a thing like that, I know Judy, she is my best friend and she would not say a thing like that.' I look across the room at the girl with blonde hair. She is absorbed by something the old lady was telling her. I realize that she has probably decided that she has made a mistake, and that I bat for the other side, and am just a prick tease or a fanny tease, or whatever girls call it.

Finally our main course arrives so the guy says goodbye and goes back to his own table, stopping for a bit of glad-handing on the way.

'Dear old Auntie David,' sighs Channing, 'she's such a dizzy queen.' I nod in agreement, which makes Channing laugh. 'Don't you think?' he asks. Whatever you say, mate.

As we get up to leave, just before midnight, I realize that I am actually pretty pissed but I am still aware of being observed by the waiters, the girl who gives Channing his coat, and the door man. I quite enjoy this experience when I'm with Marion, people guessing what the score is, but with Channing it is just plain embarrassing.

We step outside. While the car moves down the street towards us, Channing notices two girls in the street examine a lipstick, and then each use it, puckering their lips up at each other.

'Don't share lipsticks, girls, you could catch gonorrhoea,' he tells them as he gets into the car. They look at each other in disbelief and then burst out laughing. I just can't think of anything to say so I smile meekly as if to endorse Channing's unusual healthcare advice and then follow him into the car as soon as I can.

The journey back to his house is quite uneventful apart from Channing opening his window when we stop at traffic lights and shouting 'Cute ass' at a policeman.

'Nightcap?' he asks, dropping his coat on the settee back at his place.

'No thanks, I'd better be going in a minute,' I say, suddenly overcome with tiredness and alcohol.

'No problem,' he says, pouring himself one. 'Siddown.'

'Don't mind if I do,' I say groggily.

What happens next is something of a blur. I slump down on the settee and put my feet up on the arm. Not the best of manners, Marion would have been furious, but she isn't there, is she? I am just thinking I should drag myself up and make a move when I feel a strange stirring in my crotch which is, well, not all of my own making. I open my eyes, Channing is standing over me, a drink in one hand, the other very gently unzipping my fly.

'Oh, get *off*,' I groan, more in irritation than in shock. I push his hand away and swing my legs round to get up. My head is swimming and I can hardly even guide it into my hands. I nearly stab myself in the eye with my thumb. How much *have* I drunk this evening?

'Just trying to find out exactly what Marion does see in you,' smiles Channing, walking back across the room. 'It's certainly not your conversation.'

'I've – I've got to go,' I say, getting up.

'Wasn't that part of the deal tonight?' I hear him say.

'No,' I say, feeling that I should make something more of it, be a bit angry and threaten to punch him or something, except that I just can't be bothered. Let alone aim. Why the hell had I lain down on the settee in the first place? I can't really blame him for getting the wrong idea.

'Oh, I'm sorry, but quite a few of Marion's other boys have been, you know, more than happy to oblige.'

'Well, I'm not.'

'Never mind. It's just a little game Marion and I have.'

'A little game?' I ask, putting my head between my legs for a moment.

'Oh, you know, share and share alike. Brother and sister.' He knocks back his drink and goes to get another.

'You're disgusting.'

He laughs. 'Oh don't be so upset. Let's face it, if I offered you enough money, you'd do it.'

'Oh, fuck *off*.'

He laughs again. 'Oh, Andrew,' he says quietly, 'where do you get off with this high and mighty stuff? What have I offended? Your honour? Your machismo? Your great British pride? Come on, you're sleeping with Marion to get what you can out of her. I don't have any quarrel with that. I've done the same thing myself,' he says, pausing for effect. 'That's what people do when they are young. You see all this luxury, this . . . opulence—' he gestures round the room – 'and you want a piece of it. OK, that's understandable, but don't get so upset and give me all that English gentleman bullshit when someone comes on to you. I don't really fancy you anyway,' he says putting his head on one side and looking me up and down again, 'quite nice buns but I prefer shorter hair and bigger tits.'

Pleased with this final comment he turns to get another drink.

'Thanks,' I say, not sure whether to be angry or not. I can't be bothered to come up with a witty put-down.

'I've really enjoyed this evening,' he says with wide-eyed sincerity, leaning against the fireplace. 'The driver will take you home if you want.'

'Don't worry, I'll walk.'

'No problem,' says Channing graciously. 'Oh, here.' He reaches into his jacket, takes out a Louis Vuitton wallet, opens it and pulls out a note, snapping it in his fingers to check that there is just one. It's a fifty. 'Go on. Take it. For your taxi.' We both know I don't need fifty to get home and that no cab driver would even change one.

I look at it for a moment, planning a proud, defiant gesture but I'm too tired and drunk – and poor. So, like a man in a dream, I reach out and take it.

I walk quite a long way to try and clear my head. Did I take that money for letting him take me to dinner or just for a taxi home? Or because he's got lots of it and I haven't any and it seems only fair? Or did I take it because I let him have a quick grope? I think what he enjoyed about touching me up was less to do with sexual gratification and more to do with just casually insulting me. I shudder at the thought and turn to look at my reflection in a shop window. My face, a ghostly apparition amongst the expensive black suits on display, appears older and thinner than it did a few weeks ago.

Or did I just take that fifty because I'm used to taking cash from people now without even thinking about it?

CHAPTER TWELVE

I DON'T RING MARION on Sunday, just to make the point but when I get back from buying the papers and some bread there's a message from her on the machine telling me that she is unable to see me tonight because some old friends are in town and she has arranged to take them to Wiltons in Jermyn Street. She will call me tomorrow.

She sounds like she is talking to an idiot.

Perhaps she is.

I am actually quite relieved. Rolex aside (and it now seems to smell of Channing's aftershave, like my hair and all my clothes), I'm pretty pissed off with her at the moment. I'm also absolutely knackered: the prospect of a quiet evening in on my own without meeting new people, going to new places and having to rise to the challenge of yet more artificial social intercourse is very welcome. Having mooched around all day, at about six I go and take a cold Rolling Rock out of the fridge, find the controller down the side of the settee and put the telly on.

It's not just my exhausting social life – the tension in the office has worn me out too. Avoiding Debbie, judging her mood whenever I have to talk to her, thinking up skives for the next few days and rehearsing my arguments for the rows we're going to have is more tiring than working.

It's not even like I've got much cash to show for it. It's all very well having Marion pay for everything and I am grateful to her, but it means that she's always involved and always calling the shots. The idea was for me to have money to spend as I want to. Being Marion's lap dog is harder than working for a living.

Making a mental note to ring Jonathan first thing Monday morning, I am almost nodding off in front of the early evening news, when I hear Vinny's key in the lock.

'All right?' says Vinny, falling into the living room.

'Hiya,' I say unenthusiastically and sink further down into the armchair – not difficult since it only has one spring left. Never one to take a hint, he ploughs on. 'What's this?' he asks, gawping at the telly, hands on hips.

'Nothing,' I say and switch over. Upstairs the loo flushes and a moment later, Jane bursts in.

'Oh, hiya,' she says, slightly surprised to see me.

'Hi,' I say, sitting up a bit. 'How are you?'

'Fine. How are you?'

'I'm all right.' I wonder whether to stand up then decide against it. She looks at Vinny so I look back at the telly. Vinny starts to say something about what we're watching so I switch over again.

'Shall I give them a call, then?' asks Jane excitedly.

'Yeah, the phone's in the kitchen,' says Vinny, collapsing onto the settee and staring at the box. Jane is still buzzing for some reason.

'All right then, Libby, Vicky, Seth . . . Paul?'

'OK,' says Vinny. Jane leaps out of the room, saying she'll put the kettle on.

'What's happening?' I mutter.

'Er, we're off to the pub. Wanna come?'

I think about it for a moment. It would be good to see Jane again but I'm just not in the mood. 'No thanks.'

But somehow I end up coming with them.

The others arrive pretty quickly after Jane has summoned them, and so the six of us – me, Jane, Vinny, a grungy student called Seth who introduces himself as a musician, his drabby girlfriend Libby, and Vicky, a rather sexy Australian, walk to the pub in a ragged crocodile. Once inside Jane grabs a table in a corner by the cigarette machine. Five of us slide round onto the bench seat and Vinny finds a stool. It's a while since I've been in a pub. I savour the warm, musty smell for a moment. The thick fog of voices and thump of music from the jukebox is punctuated by electronic squawks and bleeps from the games machines and the till. Two fat blokes in T-shirts and tracksuit bottoms leaning over the bar look round contemptuously at us but then return to their half-drunk pints and carry on mumbling irritably at each other. It feels good to be doing something ordinary, something familiar.

Jane puts her hands on the table, and looks round, making a joke about a Ouija board. We all laugh. Then she starts talking finance. I have forgotten the financial negotiations involved at the start of a group pub visit on a limited budget. Jane has elected herself chairperson of the board. There is a discussion about rounds or a kitty. We vote on it with me abstaining. The kitty proposal is passed by the board but Jane is not pleased.

'You haven't voted,' she says accusingly.

'That's because, I don't mind what we do,' I say.

'Loadsa dosh,' says Vinny, 'he'll just put it on his Gold Amex.'

They laugh and I have mock hysterics. Actually, I am seized with panic that Vinny will tell her about Marion and my new 'job'. I shoot him a look. He smiles goofily – is the bastard just playing with me? God, I'll foul him so badly in the next round of Indoor One A Side Footy.

'Right,' says Jane, 'five quid each should see us through. Everyone give me five quid.' People obey, unzipping leather jackets and pulling notes from the back pockets of their jeans. There is some discussion between Libby and Seth and finally she puts a tenner into the middle of the table, explaining that this is for both of them. Jane takes it matter of factly but I notice her exchange a little look with Vicky.

It occurs to me that that's the fun of going out with a group of people you don't know, it's like eavesdropping on a conversation on a bus – you get the entertainment and intrigue without any of the obligations that come with having to contribute. There is no need to get involved in tensions and disputes since Vicky and Jane are obviously full of righteous indignation that Seth the slob was taking Libby, who seems a bit wet, for a ride.

I lift my bum off the seat a bit and feel in my jeans for the notes I stuffed into them as we went out. I take out a fiver and chuck it onto the table with the rest. Except that it isn't a fiver. It's a fifty. The one Channing gave me. Jane picks it up slowly just to check and then puts it back disdainfully. The others look on amazed. Vinny breaks the silence. 'See?' he laughs. 'Drinks on you tonight, Andrew, mine's a pint – of Bollinger, that is.'

'Sorry,' I say, embarrassed, and snatch it back. 'Here, I've got a ten if you've got change, Jane.'

'Never seen one of those come out of the cashpoint,' she says quietly as she gives me my change.

'Oh, Andrew doesn't use the cashpoint,' says Vinny.

'OK, Vinny,' I say quietly. But that makes it worse. I realize I should have let him run on until everyone got bored with him as they undoubtedly would. Jane and Vicky go up to the bar with our order. I know they are talking about me because out of the corner of my eye I see Vicky look round at me. To change the subject I ask Seth about his band.

'Yeah,' he says, nodding. His dreadlocks make him look like a burst mattress with its stuffing sticking out. There is a pause as he waits for me to interview him about it. What the hell am I doing with these people?

'What's it called?' I ask at last.

Libby, who I notice is now hugging his right arm, and wearing a T-shirt which says 'Why Should I Tidy My Room When the World is Such a Mess?', answers for him: 'It's called the Leisure Complex. They used to be called the Consumers, that was my idea, but Seth felt it sounded too *flippant.*'

'Oh, right. You don't want to sound flippant,' I say.

'Not *too* flippant, anyway,' adds Vinny for good measure. 'Oh no, people might accuse you of being, you know, jejune or something.'

'I'd hate to be thought jejune,' I say, shaking my head and playing with a beer mat.

'No,' agrees Libby, not sure whether we are taking the piss. She turns her gentle, trusting eyes on Seth for some support. He just carries on nodding, either in agreement, or to the beat of the juke box or because that's what Neanderthals do.

'What kind of music is it?' I ask.

'Erm,' says Libby, looking up at the brim of the ridiculous hat she is wearing as if trying to find the words to adequately describe Seth's output.

Seth decides he can handle this one himself. 'Mainly rock. Some might see elements of grunge or even R&B in it but we don't want to be labelled.'

'No,' says Libby gratefully.

'Oooof, you don't want to be labelled,' says Vinny, as if it's a problem he's frequently suffered from in his career.

'Oh, no,' I add, 'I *hate* being labelled.'

'Detest it,' says Vinny with feeling. Libby looks at us both for a moment.

'Where have you played?' I ask. Seth gives it some thought. Libby also looks quizzical, taking her cue from him after a quick, sideways glance.

'Well, er, Christ, it's not easy in London at the moment. My drummer's got a contact at the Dublin Castle so we're hoping something'll turn up there but, er, you know it's difficult. We gigged at North London Poly last month, that was OK.'

'They have a battle of the bands, once a month,' explains Libby sweetly. Seth stiffens slightly and Libby realizes that she has rather given the game away on that one.

'Do you do birthdays and bar mitzvahs and the like?' asks Vinny.

Fortunately at that moment the girls come back with our drinks. Pints all round. I would have preferred a Bud or a Scotch but after the fifty-pound-note episode I decide to play it safe and try to fit in. Even then I haven't got it quite right: they have bitter, I have lager. Suddenly I have a longing for ice-cold champagne served in one of Marion's heavy cut crystal glasses.

In his usual gloomy, deadpan way, Vinny tells a story about being in the kitchenette at work and reaching up to the cupboard for the coffee jar and accidentally grabbing this fierce old bag's tit or 'ample bosom', as he describes it on the third retelling. Vicky and Jane are in hysterics. But I don't think that it is just Vinny's story that is making them giggle so helplessly, that's just an alibi for a private girly joke.

After a while Jane suggests we check out the jukebox. I volunteer to go with her. We squeeze out and cross the crowded, smoky bar to the machine. A bloke in a blue blazer knocks into me and then gives me a scornful look by way of apology.

'Hope you don't mind the pub,' she says above the noise.

'*Mind* it? Why should I? It's fine.'

'I thought it might be a bit of a come-down for you. I'm sure you're used to something slightly more upmarket.'

'Not at all,' I mutter, wondering how much she knows then ask, 'Has the board allocated resources for this little extra, then?'

'Heh?'

'Have you budgeted for the jukebox?'

'No, I haven't, actually. Give us some money,' she says, leading the way.

'Oh, OK,' I say.

'And it doesn't take fifty pound notes, I don't think.'

'Ha, ha.' Better to make a joke of it. She consults the list. I find two pound coins and she takes them silently.

'Now, what would you like?' she muses.

'I don't mind, what are you into?'

'Well . . .' she says, still looking down the list, beginning to frown with concentration and then disappointment that nothing leaps out at her.

'Let me guess,' I say, 'nothing too mainstream, too commercial.'

'Well, not BoyzOne, I don't think.'

'And not Abba.'

'Wrong! I like Abba, actually.'

'Oh, that's interesting.'

'And what about you? Something nice and safe and yuppie. Have they got any Dire Straits, I wonder—' I laugh indignantly and try to interrupt but she carries on '– or Enya.'

'Wrong on both counts.'

'What do you like, then?'

I consult the list. 'Erm. Brand New Heavies?'

She pulls a face and mulls it over. 'A bit self-consciously trendy. I don't quite believe that.'

'Don't, then. Look, here's one for you – Radiohead.' I point to it on the list and immediately my Rolex peeks from under my sleeve, its face catching a stray spotlight. Jane doesn't notice – or at least pretends she doesn't.

'Not bad. A bit over-exposed now, though. Even my mum's read about them in the *Daily Mail*. I bet they've got some of those old early eighties dance tracks for you – Cool and the Gang or, er, oh look, Randy Crawford. Perfect for dancing with the secretaries from work on a Friday night when they've dragged you off to a club.' She begins to sway about, rolling her eyes and smiling insanely. I can't help laughing.

'Well, you can't like Madonna,' I say. 'What about the Cranberries? I can see you *almost* dancing to them at the Students' Union.'

'Ha, ha. I do like Madonna, actually. She's such a strong woman, a post-feminist role model.'

'Right on, sister.' She gives me a sarcastic smile.

'What's that?' she says, pushing my hand gently away. I feel a slight thrill as we touch but if Jane does too she doesn't give anything away.

'Blimey, Morrissey,' I say. 'A bit before your time.'

'No, quite like him, actually. Even though I don't know what "before your time" means, you patronizing bastard. How old are you?'

I think about it for a moment and I realize that, actually, I don't have to lie this time.

'Twenty-four – and you?'

'Twenty-two. There's nothing in it.' Still looking down the list, she hesitates for a moment as we both realize what that sounds like. 'No, I used to listen to my older sister's tapes all the time.'

'Why do you work in Paperchase?' Why did I ask that? She looks slightly surprised and turns back to the jukebox.

'Why not? It's quite fun. It pays the rent. Besides, I don't know what I want to do yet. I might go travelling next month.'

'Where to?'

'Probably South America. One of my friends from university is teaching English as a foreign language in Buenos Aires.'

'That'd be fun – the Paris of the Southern Hemisphere.'

'Sorry?'

'That's what they call Buenos Aires – the Paris of the Southern Hemisphere.'

'Oh, right. Well, I haven't actually done any research about it yet, like I said – I'm still thinking,' she says slightly irritably. What did I do? Did it sound like I was showing off? 'Here, let's have the Eurythmics, I love them. My sisters used to play them all the time.' She consults the chart and presses the code. 'Why do you sell space?'

'Media sales?'

'Media sales, then. S'cuse me.' She pulls a face.

'Oh, fuck knows. It's a job. I wanted to get into advertising. Once upon a time. I suppose I just fell in to it. My mum and dad think it's a good thing.' I don't dare tell her that it was the promised salary which caught my eye first. There is a pause as we both look through the remaining songs. I wonder again what Vinny has told her. I suggest our final track and she casually agrees. We get back to the table.

I turn to say something to Vinny but he is talking very intently to Libby. 'You see most people think you start with the big things and then move up to the smaller ones, you know – your croutons, corn, grated cheese, bacon bits, whatever. I might even include kidney beans in that.' He thinks for a moment. 'Yes, kidney beans too. But in fact you *start* with these because they provide you with a good solid foundation. Then you can add the larger pieces. Myself I'd go for tomatoes, cucumber, whatever. Then you can balance the really big pieces like lettuce leaves on top.' Libby looks at him the way most people look at their financial advisers after they've been urged to put a bit more aside for a pension.

'Vinny knows what he's talking about,' I say to Libby. 'He can pile it up a foot high at Pizza Hut.'

'I've been banned from the salad bar in three branches in Central London,' says Vinny proudly. Vicky looks at us both in amazement and then at Jane.

When my choice comes on the jukebox it's not what I thought it was. It's a muzacky soul track and I feel embarrassed about requesting it. It's such a responsibility choosing these things.

We leave the pub at closing time – our kitty runs out quite a bit earlier so we spend the last three quarters of an hour or so smoking a couple of furtive joints courtesy of Vicky and absent-mindedly tearing up beer mats while we talk – or the others talk and I watch, wondering what Vicky and Jane have been talking about. Libby, who works at the DSS in Neasden, tells us about a man who completely lost it and leapt over the counter to attack the bloke who was talking to him.

'That's terrible,' says Jane. 'What happened?'

'Oh, well, he was suspended.'

'What? Because a claimant attacked him?' demands Vicky.

'No,' says Libby in her little girl's voice, 'he was working for the DSS. The guy he *attacked* was a claimant. He was, you know, really getting on his nerves.' Vinny and I laugh. Libby looks bemused and Vicky mutters, 'Jesus.' I think she is talking about Libby.

Somehow a round-the-table quiz starts. We start with the first record everyone has bought, and then the worst record. Mine is 'Eye of the Tiger'. Everyone laughs, including me. Confession must be good for the soul.

'That *is* bad,' says Jane.

'What was yours?' I ask.

'Probably "The Final Countdown".' We all laugh again and I catch Jane's eye for a moment. She looks away.

After that, the conversation is slow and full of long-running in-jokes, so I don't say much. But when we get up I find the thick, warm atmosphere of the pub and the long evening of slow boozing has left me pleasantly mellowed.

Outside, Vinny and I wish Seth good luck with the band and then he, Vicky and Libby set off for the Tube station and the three of us walk back to ours. I am glad that our farewell consists of waves and shouts of 'Cheers'. I don't even mind Vicky winking and miming a telephone receiver at Jane. Kissing Marion's friends goodbye is always so exhausting – even if you can remember who does single kisses, who does double kisses (usually a safe bet) and who triple kisses, it still takes forever to say goodbye and then if you have done all yours you still have to wait, an awkward spectator, while everyone else finishes their elaborate choreography of hand-shakes and kisses. I am sure that is why evenings with Marion's friends seem neverending.

We walk back in silence and I notice that Jane has put her arm through Vinny's in a sisterly sort of way. We stop for a takeaway curry. Jane has a vegetable thing, I have a chicken bhuna and Vinny has his usual, which he doesn't even have to ask for now because they recognise him as soon as he walks in. He describes it as a Chernobyl vindaloo. Then he makes his usual joke about nuclear 'phal' out and burps violently.

'Vinny!' says Jane.

'Fucking animal,' I add.

We eat them in the kitchen at Jane's insistence, saying little as we realize how hungry we are and then we retire to the living room with mugs of tea to see if there is anything on telly. At about half-past eleven Vinny yawns and says 'night'.

'Goodnight' say Jane and I in unison. Embarrassing. It only emphasizes the fact that there are just the two of us now, sitting in a darkness broken only by the flickering light of the TV.

We stare at the box where two alternative comedians discuss wanking and zits with a studio audience of thirty-somethings who are obviously wondering why they splashed out on a babysitter for this rubbish. Eyes fixed on the picture, slightly embarrassed, we half-laugh every now and then. If we're not laughing why are we watching? And if we don't watch, what else do we do? I find myself wishing Vinny was still here.

''Scuse me a minute,' I say and leap up off the settee. I dash upstairs to find Vinny, who is in the bathroom brushing his teeth.

'Vinny,' I whisper urgently, half-closing the door behind me.

'Ussh?' he says, through a mouthful of toothbrush and froth.

'What have you told Jane about me?'

'Usshing,' he says, looking alarmed.

'What? Didn't tell her about my, you know, other job?' I can't bring myself to say 'escort' even to Vinny.

'No.'

'Oh, good. Thanks. Did you tell her I was seeing someone else?'

He looks slightly apologetic and then removes the tooth-brush and spits out, a procedure which seems to take about half an hour.

'She wanted to know, mate. Wondered where you were going the other evening when she was just arriving.'

'Oh, OK.'

'Sorry,' he says.

'Oh, don't worry.' My mind is racing. Jane must be wondering what we're talking about. I'd better get back.

'Thanks.'

Halfway down the stairs I turn and run back.

'Ow wha'?' says Vinny, his mouth full of toothpaste again.

'Did you say how serious it was?'

He spits out once more.

'No, I just said you were seeing a woman and that's where you were off to that night, s'all.'

'OK.' I think about it. Vinny picks up the toothpaste again. 'Woman? Did you say how old she was?'

'No, 'course not, I don't know how old she is.'

'No, sure. And you didn't say where she lived?'

Vinny looks exasperated. 'No, I don't know her bloody postcode either. For Christ's sake, Jane obviously likes you. Just get back there and don't come back – I'm running out of toothpaste here. Jesus! She's a lovely girl. I'm not going to tell anyone you're playing away from home.'

'I'm *not* playing away from home, it's not that kind of relationship,' I say quickly.

No, it's not that kind of relationship. It's not going to last for ever with Marion, certainly not after what Channing said. I almost shudder at the memory of our dinner. Besides, I've already been unfaithful to her once. In fact, thinking about it, I might just cut my losses now. To be really brutal about it, it was fun while it lasted, we had a good time together. Having the Rolex is great, assuming she doesn't want it back, and Paris was brilliant but . . . well, it can't go on for ever. I know that.

I'm pretty self-conscious about being seen in restaurants with Marion – especially when she gets the menu with the prices and I don't. A normal relationship with a normal girl suddenly seems so attractive, so right. No more playing lap dog and no more evenings spent with a bunch of extras from *Dynasty*. Instead, someone I could relax and be myself with, someone I just have something in common with. Besides, after Helen, I've got some catching up to do in the snogging stakes, haven't I?

I look at Vinny, who is smiling and holding something out at me. It's a rather old packet of condoms. I laugh and dash back downstairs again without taking them.

'Sorry about that. Just had to talk to Vinny about the rent before tommorrow,' I find myself saying. God, I'm getting good at lying.

Jane just smiles and looks back at the telly.

So now, without looking away from the screen I begin to review the situation and the ways in which it might develop.

Jane will obviously have to sleep in my bed, but will I be there too or down here on the settee? At what time should I say 'I think I'll crash'? Is that what she is waiting for? If I say that will she take the hint and make it clear that she would like to be invited? Or will she just think I want to go to bed alone. I *am* sitting quite close to her, I *could* make a move now. Very discreetly I turn my eyes towards her. She is wide-eyed at the screen. Nobody could be that interested in anything on TV. She obviously isn't watching this crap.

God, she does look pretty, though. I love the way she sweeps her hair back behind her ear. She has a smooth, white forehead and a strong, intelligent mouth. Now that she has taken off her jacket and her thick pullover I can see her small, rounded breasts through her T-shirt. I am only two feet away from her on this old heap of a settee. I could just reach out and gently put my arm round behind her. I could do the old stretch and yawn routine. What the hell, let's just see what happens. Besides, you can't let a girl like Jane just slip through your fingers. The simple fact is that I do really, really like her. I've had a good time with Marion but nothing she could give me in the way of presents would be as good as spending some time with Jane.

I look round at her slowly and move forward a few inches. She turns to me, eyes wide with a look of calm expectation. I reach over and push her hair back slightly with my left hand while putting my right on her shoulder, then I move forward and kiss her lips.

Her mouth tastes of tea and sweet spices. I move further across and draw her into me, slowly taking my hand down towards her breast. As I touch it she gasps slightly and I feel her nipple harden under the T-shirt. We kiss for some time – gently but not shyly and I am pleased I made this move, especially when I feel her arm round my neck pulling me gently on to her. It goes on for some time and I begin to feel hard so I make a move for what I once overheard my sister and her friends describe as 'inside downstairs' but she gently pulls my hand away.

'Sorry,' I whisper.

She lowers her eyes and says very softly, 'I don't want to do that right now, Andrew. I mean, I like you but it's too soon.' She pauses for a moment. 'Besides, you're seeing someone else right now, aren't you?' Oh fuck. How do I answer that? Why don't I have a reply ready? I should have thought of it upstairs with Vinny. I can't deny it and I can't say yes, because it'll just look like I'm looking for a one-night stand and somehow I don't think Jane would go for that. And perhaps I don't want to go for that with Jane.

But it's too late now. I've taken too long to answer. The moment has passed. She realizes things are not as simple as she had hoped. She moves away.

'I am but it's coming to an end. It's, it's not really right . . . '

She looks at me for a moment. 'Listen, we'd better get to bed. I'll use the settee,' she says.

'No,' I say too loudly. 'I mean, I'll stay down here, you have my bed.' I can't think of what to add. I start to say something but it comes out as rubbish. She strokes my cheek and looks at me for a moment.

Then she does something to her hair and says, 'Do you need to get anything out of your room before I go to bed?'

Jane has gone again by the time I get up the next morning. I was looking forward to having breakfast with her and saying goodbye. I didn't sleep much last night, wondering where we stand, where we go from here, how our conversation seemed to her. I can't ever imagine Jane wanting to have a relationship if she thought I was already in one. If I *am* in a relationship.

In some sort of perverse, misguided effort at revenge, I ring Marion on my mobile on the way to work and wake her up.

'Well, I had the evening from hell on Saturday,' I tell her as soon as she picks up the phone.

'Why? What happened?' she croaks, still not awake at eight o'clock.

'Channing. Marion, it was awful, it was so bloody embarrassing.'

She coughs and takes a deep breath. 'Why?'

'Why?' I shout. 'Why?' Where to start? I can't really put my finger on any particular event, it's just that the whole thing was so appalling. Then I remember the weirdest bit. 'He made a pass at me.'

'Did he? Really? He is *terrible*,' she says innocently and begins to giggle. Her laughter develops into a cough. I try and decide whether she is genuinely surprised or whether she was expecting it. Or even planning it.

'Well, I'm glad you find it so funny. It was bloody awful.'

'Did he do it in the restaurant?' she says creakily.

'No, back at his flat, after dinner.' I sound even more prissy.

'You shouldn't have gone back there then.' Good point.

'I shouldn't have gone to dinner with him in the first place.'

'I hope you declined his kind offer.'

She is beginning to annoy me now so I say, 'He told me that it wasn't that unusual because you sometimes . . .' I'm begining to wish I hadn't started this conversation '. . . you shared lovers.'

'Shared?'

'Yeah, sometimes your . . . boys, as he called them . . . would, you know . . . with him.'

She seems a bit taken aback but a second later she has regained her composure.

'Oh, Channing. He'll say *anything* to shock.'

'He certainly was embarrassing.'

'You're not going to up and leave me and make a little love nest with him, are you?' she says more kindly.

'I'm tempted to,' I say sulkily. This isn't going anywhere, she obviously doesn't feel any guilt whatsoever. Not a very Marion emotion, I suppose. I just look like a silly, strait-laced Englishman.

She laughs again and says, 'Never mind. Look, you'd better hurry up and get to the office before you get fired.'

'Yeah, I suppose so.'

'Shall we go to New York this weekend?'

'What?'

'I said, shall we go to New York this weekend? Didn't you say you liked New York City?'

'God, I love it, I'd love to. Yeah, that would be brilliant.'

'Let's go Friday morning, I'll call the airline now.'

'Yeah, Friday would be great,' I say realizing that Friday would also be great for finally getting sacked.

'Call me when you get home tonight,' she says and puts the phone down.

At work I follow one of the very few useful pieces of advice I have ever read in my dad's management books. Instead of asking Debbie for Friday and Monday off, I write her a memo saying that *unless she objects*, I will be taking Friday and Monday off. Clever, eh? My violent threats against the word processor, although issued under my breath, attract the attention of Claire, Debbie's dreary secretary.

'What are you doing?' she asks irritably.

'Why won't it type there?' I moan, pointing at the screen and the uncooperative cursor which just blinks at us insolently. Claire mutters something about tabs, her fingers dance over the keys and the machine does what I want it to. She lingers a moment while I send it through to print. Then I sign it, copy it and drop it discreetly on Claire's desk, which, to my irritation, is unusually tidy today. I walk past the desk again, pick up the memo and put it into a folder on her desk so that she won't find it as quickly. I *had* thought of back-dating it by a few days until Claire saw me type it.

'I'm off to New York this weekend,' I tell Sami casually when I get back to my desk. 'Can I get you anything?'

'Wow, really?' she gasps. 'Ooh yes, I'd love, I'd love . . . what would I love?' She scratches around the bottom of her yogurt carton with a plastic spoon and licks it thoughtfully. 'Oh whatever, something nice.' I laugh and decide that if I do nothing else in NYC I will get something nice for Sami.

I must have been on the phone when the Claire dropped my memo back on my desk. As I turn round to make a note of someone's phone number I see it. At first I think it is my copy then I notice Debbie's firm, ugly handwriting along the bottom. 'Sorry,' it says, 'we're still understaffed as you know and I think you've had enough time off recently. DL.' I read it through twice. How can she have seen it so quickly? Claire must have read it on the word processor screen and warned Debbie it was coming. God that bitch! That fucking bitch! What is it to her if I take some time off work? The hours I've put in for her over the last few years!

I feel like someone has thumped me in the stomach. When will Debbie ever give me a break? It's just not fair. I am just getting up to go and see her with it when Sami reaches across the desk and catches my arm.

'Andrew, don't.' She has obviously read the note while I was on the phone. I sit down heavily.

'Why, Sami? Why? For God's sake. Why has she got it in for me these days?'

Sami shrugs her shoulders gently.

'I told you – just keep your head down,' she says. 'New York will still be there in a couple of months' time. Just hang on.'

'I can't hang on,' I say, thinking out loud.

'Oh, Andrew.'

'Oh, shut up,' I say, getting up to walk up and down the corridor a bit.

I wander into the corridor. There is a ping from the lift. People. I can't face them. I nip into a disused office and close the door quietly behind me. There is a phone so I ring Jonathan to see if I can get my money yet. I'm not holding my breath, he is obviously going to make me wait for my cash. While the phone rings I do a quick calculation and discover that it's been a month since I did my first jobs. There must be a cheque ready now. I reckon I've had a couple of hundred quid from Marion in tens, twenties and fifties. Plus Paris and the Rolex. But I need some cash. Living this lifestyle is costing me money too.

Jonathan is friendly but cool.

'Yep, let me just make sure here on my sheet. Bub-bubbub-bub-bah. No problem, I'm putting a cheque in the post to you today.'

I'm almost dumbstruck.

'Really? Oh, great. Thanks.'

'No problem. Hope you're around for the next few days because things are certainly hotting up here,' he says.

'Yeah, yes, I will be.' Hang on, what am I on about? I won't be around at all. As usual, I'll be with Marion for the next few days. Or years.

When I come back Sami is on the phone so I pass her a Post-it note: 'Sorry about that. Shall we go to that Italian café and have some lunch? Andrew X.'

She reads my note and then finishes her call and thinks about it.

'I'm sick of sandwiches,' I whisper. 'Let's have something decent.'

'Oh, Andrew.'

'Oh, Sami.' She thinks about it for a moment longer and then makes a face in gentle annoyance.

'Go on, then. If it'll cheer you up. We'll have to be very quick, though.'

I push open the door of the café and let Sami in first. We are met with clouds of warm, sweet-smelling steam, the clatter of plates and the piercing scream of the Gaggia machine. Most people are finishing up and leaving so finding a table is no problem. Two of the girls from the paper's Home and Style section are just leaving. I smile hello at one of them who I've spoken to before at a staff party. She is wearing a totally unnecessary scarf and gives me a fleeting, patronizing smile and carries on talking to her colleague:

'I'm still working on that food piece about that stall in the Farmer's Market in New York that specializes in basil.'

'Oh, yah,' says her friend, flipping her hair away from her face and adjusting her heavy, narrow, black-framed glasses. 'Isadora's piece. I saw the copy when it came in. It's like, totally amazing, that place – seventeen different types.'

'Fourteen,' the first girl corrects her as they head for the door. When I first came to London I couldn't understand how girls like this earn less than we do but have their own flats in South Kensington, fly business class to New York for a wedding and go skiing in Gstaad every year. How naive, how suburban, how middle class was I to assume that income necessarily has any connection with salary?

The café owner's daughter comes over to us and hands out two menus, typed fifty years ago and warped with damp in their smeary plastic covers.

'We'll start with a bottle of champagne,' I inform her haughtily.

'Yeah, sure,' she says in her throaty, London-Italian voice. 'We put it on ice this morning just in case you showed up.'

'Jolly good,' I say.

'You wanna watch him,' shouts her dad from over the counter. 'He order everythin', yeah? Then he stick *you* with the bill.' He laughs loudly, ignoring another customer who is trying to tell him something about the sandwich he is making for her. Sami laughs shyly and looks at me.

'That's ruined your date, hasn't it?' says the daughter,

poking my shoulder affectionately with the blunt end of her pencil.

'Sami is not my *date*,' I explain with feigned indignation. 'She's my *colleague*. I'm taking her for lunch, that's all.'

'Yeah, well hurry up and order – we're nearly sold out.'

'Lasagna?' I ask Sami.

She looks horrified. 'No, I told you—'

'Kidding,' I say, squeezing her arm across the table. I ask the Italian girl, 'Got any of your mum's spag bol left?'

'Yep, just enough for two, as it happens.'

'Spag bol?' I say to Sami. 'It's quite good here.'

'*Quite* good! Cheeky bugger,' says the girl.

'I'll have the spaghetti bolognaise then. Thank you,' says Sami, smiling nervously.

'To drink?'

I order mineral water for us both and when the girl has gone Sami whispers, 'Andrew, I haven't got enough money. Can I borrow some until—?'

'No,' I say abruptly. Sami rolls her eyes. 'This is on me.' I feel in my pocket just to check that I've still got a twenty Marion gave me.

'Andrew, don't be daft, I'll pay you back—'

'No. I told you, it doesn't matter.'

'I'll have to go to the cashpoint afterwards.' She looks at her watch. 'Actually it'd better be tonight, if that's OK.'

'Oh, shut up.'

Sami raises her eyebrows.

'Don't tell me to shut up,' she says. She waves her tiny fist at me and pulls a face. I laugh at this naked aggression, Sami-style.

'Sorry. I hate talking about money,' I say seriously. 'Please let me buy your lunch, Sami.'

The Italian girl comes back with a bottle of San Pellegrino.

'Moet & Chandon for two,' she announces, banging down the bottle of water and two small unbreakable glasses, still hot from the dishwasher.

I wink thanks at her and then carry on talking to Sami.

'Don't you ever get fed up worrying about money? You know – a fiver for this or that and then panicking about going overdrawn?'

'Everyone worries about money,' says Sami, frowning.

'No, they don't.'

'Well, millionaires might not but normal people do. Everyone I know does – once in a while, anyway.'

'Don't you ever get sick of it?'

Sami shrugs her shoulders. 'It's part of life, isn't it?'

'Is it?'

She pours us both some water and takes a delicate sip.

'Well, unless you've won the Lottery.'

'Then you wouldn't have to worry.'

'You would – what about someone scratching your Rolls Royce or your servants stealing things?'

'At least you'd be able to have a plate of spaghetti bolognaise without having to rush to the cashpoint, hoping it would let you have enough money. You could go on holiday or buy new clothes whenever you wanted without having to save up.'

'But I like saving up,' says Sami. 'It's part of the fun.'

'Really?'

'Yes. You wouldn't enjoy something if you could just buy it like that, would you?' I think about this for a moment. The girl brings us our spaghetti bolognaise and I savour the smell for a moment, before adding the dried, bright yellow, sick-smelling parmesan. 'Anyway, you're not doing badly for money, are you? Paris and now New York.'

'I just want more than this.'

'You think yourself lucky, matey,' says Sami, carefully coiling pasta round her fork. 'I just want to be able to meet the guy I'm going to marry *before* my wedding day.'

CHAPTER THIRTEEN

ON FRIDAY MORNING while Anna Maria is serving breakfast, I stare at the phone, debating whether to go through the motions of leaving a message at the office about not feeling well. I decide not to. It's too undignified, I'll take it on the chin when I get back.

Marion asks me why I'm so quiet and I explain that taking time off work is worrying me.

'Well, if you want to spend time in that dreary office of yours instead of coming to New York, you're very welcome to do so,' she says over the top of the *International Herald Tribune*.

'I don't *want* to, I'm just frightened of getting fired,' I say, moving my knife idly around the toast crumbs on my plate.

'Well, like I told you, you should broaden your horizons, think beyond those four walls.'

'It's all right for you. I—' I realize that I'm about to ask her for money, straight out. Would it work? I try it. 'I'm a bit broke, Marion, you couldn't just lend me, er, I don't know, two hundred, could you?'

She puts the paper down properly. 'Why do you need money? You can't be short.'

'Well . . .'

'I already pay for everything.' Ouch! Point taken.

'Yeah, I know, and I'm very grateful but—'

'But what?'

'Just for occasional expenses,' I find myself saying, surprised at this phrase.

'You've got your salary, too. What do you want more money for? You're not doing drugs, are you?'

The honest answer is I want more money so that I can get some freedom from her for twenty minutes or even a whole evening for a bit of normality but I can't think of a reply that

I can actually give her so I just carry on playing with my knife.

'And stop doing that, will you? It's driving me crazy!' she snaps, returning to her newspaper.

I'm back staring at the phone again.

'Are you ready, Andrew?' she says now, breaking my trance.

'Yep,' I say, deciding not to think about the office for the next few days.

'Where is your luggage?' she asks. She knows that my luggage is an old Head sports bag slumped by the front door.

'It's there.' I nod towards the door, awaiting her indignant reaction.

'Oh, really! Not that old thing again, it's so embarrassing seeing you with that piece of garbage.'

'It's all I've got,' I say crossly, knowing what she'll say in reply.

'We'll have to get you something else in New York.'

Yeah, yeah.

The car roars up the M4 to Heathrow and an hour later we're in the executive lounge where I help myself to another cup of coffee that I don't want and then catch sight of a bank of payphones. There is even a fax. Perhaps I could fax Debbie rather than having to speak to her. Next to us three Americans in comfy sweaters, Burberry raincoats, dark blue jeans and trainers read the *Wall Street Journal*, *Time* and some golfing magazine. A couple who look like they have been upgraded or won a free trip hug each other and stare at Marion who, in turn, is staring at herself rather crossly in a tiny mirror, trying to make her hair do something it doesn't want to.

After half an hour I've read most of the newspapers and the magazines don't appeal. Nobody could really want to read all this business shit, it must just be there to help people justify the fact that they are travelling business class. The headlines on the front remind me of Dad's self-help management books. I bump into a man in a suit while I mooch around the complimentary drinks buffet. He apologizes but gives me a faintly enquiring look as if to ask what I'm doing in the executive lounge, which is reserved for people like him with customized luggage labels and membership of at least nine frequent flyer programmes. I leave my cup of coffee on the counter and wander back to Marion.

'Bored?' she says.

I make a face which says, 'I'm afraid so.'

She roots in her bag, gives me a £50 note and says: 'Go shopping but be back in fifteen minutes.'

Don't worry I'm not likely to leave the country on this, I think as I wander out of the club lounge cocoon into the mind-numbing hubbub of the rest of the airport.

On the plane, as we turn left to Business Class, I cannot resist a backwards glance into the 'goat' class cabin. People look like battery hens, fidgeting already, trying to pack even more bags and bits and pieces into the overhead lockers while others start to read or stare blankly ahead – the full horror of the cramped, dry-aired, white-noise-filled, seven-hour ordeal that awaits them slowly sinking in.

'Good morning, Mr Collins, can I get you something to drink?' says our perma-delighted stewardess.

'Can I have some champagne,' I say, noticing that that is what Marion has ordered. I sit back and let the seat embrace me, shuddering slightly at the thought of those poor bastards behind us. I remember my last trip to New York with a couple of friends: stuck between a screaming, snotty two-year-old and a fat bloke who sniffed and sweated his way across the Atlantic.

'More champagne, Mr Collins?' she says, still clearly absolutely delighted to have the opportunity to serve me. It is actually a bit unnerving and makes me feel I should be paying her my full attention.

'Any more and you'll have to carry me off the plane,' I tell her.

She laughs and moves on.

'Don't speak to the stewardess like that,' hisses Marion. She turns to watch the girl who is now serving, with, apparently, even more delight, a fifty-something businessman behind me. 'Peanut-brained slut,' she adds.

After lunch has been cleared away, Marion opens a magazine and starts shaking her head disapprovingly. I am going to ask her what is wrong but then I think, sod it. Marion disapproves of most things: English plumbing and dental work, pretty girls, anything that isn't expensive and, I'm beginning to suspect, me.

I feel in the seat pocket for the Walkman and the cassettes I bought with Marion's fifty at the airport. My ears fill with music and, gazing out over the cold, clean, bright skies I feel insulated, cosy and safe for the first time in weeks. This is how I could spend the rest of my life.

The hotel room is filled with flowers. We're staying in a hotel because her house is rented out, apparently. Marion looks at one card after another not with joy but with grim satisfaction. 'Hmm,' she says to some and 'Huh!' to others.

'Well, word has certainly gotten round that we're here,' she says.

'Obviously.' I survey the foliage. 'Very nice.'

'What would you like to do?' she asks, wandering into the bedroom.

'I don't know.' I'm not sure if I feel jet-lagged or just overcome by the fact that I'm here, in New York, in this ritzy hotel. She decides we'll go for a walk down Fifth Avenue which is only five minutes away. The Upper East Side is leafy and lazy and sunny as I look down the cliff faces of the buildings narrowing down into the horizon.

'Isn't this near where you were brought up?' I ask as we walk back to the hotel in the late afternoon sun.

'Quite near,' she says quickly.

Marion arranges for us to have dinner with her friends Charles and Victoria. I would have preferred to taste a bit of the night life in Times Square or the Village or SoHo but Marion tells me that all those areas are really disgusting and are full of the kind of places that I should not be seen in, so that settles that.

Charles and Victoria live not far from the hotel and I manage to persuade Marion to let us walk there. We arrive at a block with a dark blue awning and gold lettering. The doorman, a huge black guy, smiles broadly at Marion, asks her how she is doing. He lets us into the marbled hallway and we get into a huge lift. I begin to feel sick, partly with the motion and partly with nerves. I'm in New York, for God's sake. I'm going to be fired on Monday – I should be trying to enjoy myself while I'm here.

When the lift doors open Charles and Victoria are waiting for us. He is tall and thin and she is small and almost round which is strange because I didn't think Marion knew anyone that shape – most of her female friends are so skinny you can almost see their insides working.

They both kiss Marion and ask how she is, as if she has suffered some horrible accident. Then they turn to me.

'You are Andrew,' beams Victoria.

'Yes,' I say, trying to match her enthusiasm.

'I am Victoria,' she explains in a strong South American accent and offers me a cheek. I kiss it, grateful for a moment to think what I am supposed to do next. She turns her head and I kiss the other cheek. Single kiss, double kiss, triple kiss, miss kiss. Oh, I give up. I can't remember who does what. Fortunately she starts talking as if we are old friends.

She is dressed in a black and gold Chanel-type suit and though she is not very pretty, she makes the most of what she has got, as my mum would say. Her thick black hair is scraped back and held with a huge gold slide. She has a kind smile, probably the most genuine one I've seen amongst Marion's friends.

'This is my husband, Charles,' she says.

The tall guy bows slightly and then offers a hand but extends it only a bit. I shake it and end up taking just his fingers which feel cold and soft. I am sure my dad's books have something to say about this, about Charles making me step into his territory, or something.

Victoria grabs my arm and leads me along the dark, thickly carpeted corridor to the living room. The walls are painted dark red and hung with impressionist and abstract paintings. I don't look too closely but it occurs to me that they are probably originals. Victoria explains that she and Charles know Marion originally from New York, but when Marion came to London they followed her and now, here they are, all in New York again.

'Do you like London?' I ask, glad no one else can hear this ridiculously banal question.

'Oh, it's lovely. So old,' she says as we sit down. A waiter offers me some champagne and I sit back and listen to her while she goes on about her favourite shops, the time she went to a real English pub and their visit last summer to the country.

'Where did you go?' I ask.

Her grin fixes slightly. 'The country.'

'Er, right, whereabouts?'

Still smiling wildly, she looks to the the ceiling for inspiration. 'Outside of London.'

Some other people arrive a bit later and we sit down to eat. I suddenly want to go to sleep very badly. My eyelids weigh half a ton each. I think about excusing myself and going to the loo but decide that not only is this not the done thing but I will probably fall asleep on the pot and this would be even more embarrassing.

One of the women is wittering on to us about some people I do not know and so as to appear the slightest bit interested I ask who she is talking about.

'Pardon me?' says the woman and looks across at Marion as if she is supposed to be in control of me.

'Sorry,' I say, panic whipping drowsiness away from me like a duvet on a cold morning. 'I just wondered who that woman was. I, er, think I know her.'

I look across at Marion, who is both smiling and frowning quizzically.

'Cin Kettner? Cin Kettner is the thinnest woman in New York,' announces the woman as if she were presenting a prize.

'Do you know her, Andrew?' asks Marion, carefully putting a piece of lobster in her mouth.

'Er, I, er, perhaps not,' I say, deciding not to risk some cock and bull story about knowing her sister or something. The woman carries on looking at me for a moment just to check that I have completely finished thank you very much and then carries on with her story.

Charles and Victoria arrange a car to take us the four or five blocks back to our hotel.

'What was your weird comment about Cin Kettner for?' asks Marion, amused.

I yawn. I just want to sleep, not relive that horribly embarrassing moment.

'Oh, I don't know, I just thought I'd better contribute

something to the conversation,' I say. 'I thought I was falling asleep.'

'Sorry you were so bored,' says Marion, looking out of the window.

'Oh, I wasn't,' I say, taking her hand. 'No, I was just so tired.'

'When people invite you to dinner, even if you've just flown in from another time zone, you really should make the effort,' she says, her hand, cold and lifeless. I let go of it.

'All right, I'm sorry. I was just . . .' But I'm repeating myself now.

We go to bed in near silence but when I wake up at just after seven and find Marion sleeping with her back to me I shuffle up behind her. She half-wakes up too.

'Morning,' she whispers.

I mumble something even I can't understand and then begin to bite her neck gently. She groans and lifts her head. I do it a bit more, enjoying the smell of her: sleep plus the remains of her perfume. After a moment she rolls over and looks up at me, her eyes searching my face. I stroke her cheek and then kiss her gently. We make love slowly and then I fall asleep again. When I wake the next time a waiter is wheeling in a trolley of breakfast things.

'What time is it?' I ask. The waiter, a young Hispanic guy in a crisp white jacket looks at me, wondering whether to answer. I notice him do a slight double-take. Yeah, that'll give you something to talk about downstairs, I think, lying back.

It is actually just after ten. I pull on the inevitable massive fluffy white bathrobe and knock back a glass of ice-cold, freshly squeezed orange juice.

'I hope you're hungry, honey,' says Marion, tearing off a piece of dry toast and popping it in her mouth.

'Starved,' I say, yawning and bending down to kiss her. She lifts a huge silver dome from off a plate to reveal scrambled eggs, hash browns and sausages.

'Here,' she says, handing me a cup of coffee. 'Now, hurry up or we won't have time for lunch.'

Not surprisingly, we still manage to do plenty with Marion in charge of the itinerary. We visit some shops at the top of Fifth Avenue where the staff are all delighted to see her. We go to Bloomingdales and she actually buys me some clothes. A pale grey DKNY suit, a white shirt to go with it and some trousers I would never wear but I don't dare refuse. Perhaps she took on board my remark about needing some money. Perhaps she realizes that, like Mark says, if I don't look good, she doesn't look good. As we leave the store and look for a taxi back to the hotel, I feel that my luck might just be changing.

That night we go to see an opera at the Met and in the interval a woman comes up to Marion and kisses her fondly on both cheeks.

'How are you?' she says, holding both of Marion's hands.

'Good,' says Marion. 'I'm good, thank you.'

'And this,' says the woman, 'must be Andrew.'

'Hello,' I say, extending a hand.

'Andrew, it's such a pleasure.'

'Yes,' I say. 'I mean, it's a pleasure for me too.' Can't I ever get it right? The woman turns back to Marion.

'It's so good to see you back in New York. Can we have a drink, just the three of us, before you go back to England?'

'I'd really like that,' says Marion, batting her eyelids with sincerity.

'Enjoy the second half,' says the woman, walking off.

'Who was that?' I ask.

'No idea,' says Marion, still smiling sweetly.

The next day we have brunch at a café where normally you have to book six months in advance just for coffee, according to the people at the opera the night before. They serve a mixture of Italian and native American food.

'My name is Walter,' says a very tall, improbably thin, red-haired guy as we sit down at a table beside a huge Roy Lichtenstein-style mural of an Indian chief. 'I'll be your server this morning and I'd very much like to welcome you to the Café Hueva today. If there is anything I can do to make your visit just that little bit more pleasurable please just let me know. Now, let me tell you something about the specials we can offer you. Today we have—'

'Er, Walter, honey,' says a voice. I look across the table and realize it is Marion. 'Can we have some coffee and juice and then I'll be all ears for your specials.'

Furious at having his speech interrupted, Walter hisses, 'Yes, ma'am' and waltzes off.

I start laughing and Marion looks up from unfolding her napkin at me in surprise.

'What's funny?'

'You are,' I say. She shrugs her shoulders and smiles.

I push open the door of our office and stride in, hoping I look relaxed and casual, although I feel sick with depression, jet lag and nerves. Someone has hung their jacket on my coat hanger so I carefully take it off and hang it on a peg and then put my new DKNY jacket on it. I can't believe how irritated I feel – almost violated. Working in an office makes you so petty, so territorial.

My strategy has not worked. I am not the first into the office. Well somehow when I came to set the alarm last night I compromised on that one; seven seemed beyond endurance in my jet-lagged state so I set it for seven-thirty and decided not to bother trying to be the first. But, as I look round, I realize that I am not even one of the first! It's eight-thirty and this shabby little hell hole is almost full, humming with activity.

I take my seat and Sami gives me her 'Oh, Andrew' look. I make a silly face but my heart isn't really in it. She finishes her call.

'How was New York?'

'It was great, really good fun,' I say quietly.

'I'm glad. What did you do?'

'Central Park, Fifth Avenue. We went to the Opera.'

'Wow,' says Sami gently. Then she says what I least want to hear: 'Debbie wants to see you.'

I nod gratefully and smile.

'I bought you this, by the way.' It's the Statue of Liberty in a snowstorm. I bought it at JFK on the way home. Sami looks up at me and smiles sadly.

My stomach suddenly feels light and empty. A couple of people look up discreetly from their desks and watch me go towards her office. She is on the phone telling someone to leave it with her and she'll come back to them. And I know she will. I sit down and decide that sullen apology is my best bet so I stare moodily at my shoes.

'Where have you been the last two days?' she asks quietly, looking down at her desk.

'I was ill,' I say, more in the way of a suggestion than an apology. I look away – I can't meet her eyes.

'I rang, Claire rang twice. What was the matter with you?'

'I dunno, I just felt—'

'Bullshit. I don't care where you were, Andrew, and I don't care what you were doing but you're supposed to *work* here, remember?'

'I was ill,' I mumble again.

Ignoring me, she goes on. 'It's been really busy in this office while you've been running around. Our figures have been down over the last few months and this was our chance to catch up, to turn the corner. We've had people working twelve-hour days trying to meet the targets upstairs have set us.' She stops and then adds, 'We needed you, it's just not fair on everyone else.' That hurts.

'I'm sorry.' There is a pause, my excuse is dead and buried. 'Did you meet them?' I don't know if I really care or whether I am just being polite, trying to fill the awful heavy silence. Now Debbie seems slightly surprised and irritated by my question.

'Well, we just did it but it was tough on everyone. Paul's dad's been ill and Maria had to leave on Tuesday afternoon to pick up her youngest who'd had an accident at school or something. You know, it's just not fair.' Oh God, why did I ask?

'Sorry,' I say again, getting up to leave. I've had enough, this is beginning to piss me off. I don't know who I'm angriest with: Debbie or myself.

'Hang on a minute,' she says quietly. But I know it isn't good news: this is not going to be an olive branch. 'I'm giving you another warning. I've got to.' She hands me a letter.

'Sure,' I say quietly and go.

From all round the room eyes follow me as I make my way back to my desk. Sami looks at me sadly and says, 'Sorry.'

I laugh bitterly. 'You didn't do anything. I did it.'

I pick up a piece of paper and stare at it for a few moments.

I can't bear it. I get up again and Sami says, 'Andrew?' I laugh again and tell her that I am just going to the loo.

The thick, sterile air of the corridor, enclosed for weeks by fire doors feels fresh compared to the atmosphere in the office. I push open the door of the gents; the smell of disinfectant and an echo of dripping water welcome me. An older man I don't know is finishing at the urinal. For a second I can't decide what to do next so I wash my hands, dry them for ages under the dryer and then go into one of the cubicles and close the door. I lower the seat, sit down and put my head in my hands.

I never got into trouble much at school. If I ever did, it was a sin of omission rather than commission, as my headmaster put it. Come to think of it, I never did anything much at all at school. No outrageous pranks, no leading my classmates in rebellions, nothing to make the teachers say, 'He'll come to nothing, that boy' like they do about most millionaires and successful politicians.

I was a petty criminal, not a great train robber or a serial killer. My crimes were small, white-collar ones: skiving games, spur of the moment cheating in an end-of-term test, not giving my parents my report one year. I suppose that is why I used to receive a dreary nagging rather than a fully fledged, all guns blazing bollocking, together with a caning, which I could have taken like a man while biting my lip. Nothing I could have boasted about in later years.

Just the ancient, unanswerable question: 'Why? Why did you do it, Andrew?'

'Because I wondered what it would be like, because I thought I could get away with, because I was bored, because I couldn't be bothered not to.' Which answer do you want to hear? Which will fit best and get me out of here fastest?'

I wonder what Jane would think. She wouldn't do a thing like this at Paperchase, or if she did she would have made a better job of defending herself. Sitting on the loo, scratching the roll of toilet paper slightly so that it distorts and blisters, thinking about her, I'm embarrassed.

I ring my mum and dad that evening. It's not something I do very often, not because I don't like them, it's just that I can never really think of anything to say to them on the phone. My dad answers.

'Hi, Dad, it's me.'

'Hi, there. Good to see you other night. How's things? Everything all right?'

'Fine, yeah. You?'

'Oh, mustn't grumble. We were just trying to think of the name of that French teacher of yours.'

'French teacher? You mean Mr Holden?'

'Holden! Yeah, that's the one. We saw him in Sainsbury's last Saturday. Couldn't remember his name. Anyway, I'll get your mum.' This is typical of my dad's conversation – or lack of it.

'Hello, darling,' says my mum as if I had just been plucked from shark-infested waters after two months afloat on an open raft.

'Hi, Mum.'

'Everything all right?'

'Yeah, fine. You?'

'Me? Oh, yes. Well, you know, mustn't grumble.'

There is a pause.

'We saw your old French teacher—'

'Mr Jenkins,' shouts my dad from the background.

'Yes, I know, Dad said.'

'In Sainsbury's. Last Saturday. By the fruit and veg, you know, where you come in. We didn't say anything. We couldn't remember his name.'

'We used to call him Twitch.'

'Oh, you are horrible. Why are boys so horrible? He does have that awful facial tick. Poor man. Do you have much opportunity to keep up your French?'

Oh, Mum.

'Mais, oui,' I say.

'Sorry?'

'No, not really.'

'Such a shame. You were very good. Remember when we went to Boulogne on the ferry that time—'

'Yeah. Ages ago.' I don't want my mum to mention that Helen was with us. I bought her some perfume secretly from the duty-free shop on the boat and then gave it to her as we sat on the bench in the garden that evening. I can't bear to smell it on anyone now. 'Listen, I've got to go. I'm going out tonight. I'll see you soon.'

'Yes, come down for a weekend.'

'Will do. Bye.' I turn the sound back up on the telly.

After my mum and dad I ring Marion and tell her just how much trouble I'm in at work. How much trouble she's got me into, more like. I've just got paid. My salary this month is only just over half the usual amount. I could hardly believe it when I read the computer print out. But it was right – half of what we earn is based on commission and I've not been around or not been concentrating for the last few weeks so it's hardly surprising that I've got just enough to pay the rent, cough up for my share of the bills, get a monthly travel pass and buy a sandwich at lunchtime.

I haven't always hated that place. I used to be good at selling and Debbie used to like me. But now I'm just bored and can't see a way out and what at first appeared to be the biggest amount of money anyone had ever earned (well, in comparison to a student loan, anyway) soon disappeared in no time. Back then I felt comfortably superior to that bunch of no-hopers who sat at desks around me but now I feel like I'm just not up to it. They can hold this stupid job down but it seems I can't.

Neither can I do the Marion thing properly. How come Mark can 'get that ice' and I just get – what do I get, apart from into trouble at work? I decide to tell her that I just can't carry on our life together and put in so many hours at this awful sweatshop. Perhaps she'll feel guilty and tell me just to quit that ridiculous, demeaning job and give me enough money to be able to step off the treadmill for a few weeks or months and decide what I *do* want to do with my life. I've never had a gap year and unlike the girls upstairs, those junior fashion assistants who go to the South of France for the weekend, I've never had the opportunity to do anything without paying for it with my own hard-earned money or £50 at Christmas from my parents. I just want some money so that I've got a bit of freedom to come up for air for five minutes.

Why can't Marion just go the whole hog, be done with it and just set up a comfortable trust fund for me? It would be nothing to her.

Of course, when I ring her, she is completely unsympathetic. She just suggests I get another job.

'Better still,' she says, crunching pretzels. 'Start your own business. Why be a wage slave? You'll never get rich working for some corporation. My father didn't and neither did either of my husbands.'

'That's a possibility,' I say. It is, actually.

'That's the problem with you Brits, you have no get up and go,' she adds. 'Someone pointed it out to me on Concorde last month – you go to the best schools, the best colleges and then you all go and work for some big corporation, like rats on a wheel. It's crazy. Start your own business – that's the only way to do it, Andrew.'

'I've got a degree in Business Studies. For God's sake, I should be able to do something with it, shouldn't I?' I'm quite warming to this idea. I hope she is too. But it's never quite that simple. 'I just need the capital.'

'Sell things,' she says absentmindedly. 'Sell things to rich people. Antiques, cars . . . what else? Horses. Rich people *love* horses. You should meet my friend Carla who lives in Argentina. She has a stack of horses. And those other things . . . er, cattle. Loves them.' She is distracted for a moment and then continues. 'Sell things. Sell things to rich people, they'll always be buying whatever the economy does,' she adds with a flourish.

I sometimes wonder whether Marion lives in the real world. Then I realize she doesn't – which is the whole point of her.

'Thanks, very helpful,' I say but my sarcasm is wasted on her as usual.

'It's the only way to develop yourself professionally.' I decide to go for broke – after all I've got nothing to lose.

'Marion,' I say, trying the little-boy thing. 'I've just got no money.'

'I know, you mentioned it before. We'll sort something out. Do you know where I can get one of those plug things?'

'What?'

'You know by the bed I've got a lamp and a radio and an ionizer and now I've got this humidifier. I want one of those things to plug them all in together.'

'You mean an adaptor,' I say miserably.

'What's it called?'

'An adapter.'

'Yeah, that's right – an adapter. Where can I buy one from?'

'Oh, I don't know – Peter Jones across the way from you.'

'In Sloane Square?'

'Yeah, they'll have one.'

'OK.' I hear her throw some more pretzels into her mouth and shout to Anna Maria. 'Peter Jones – that big store in Sloane Square has them, Andrew says. Oh, and take these goddamn pretzels away from me before I eat the lot.' There is a pause while she hands Anna Maria some stray pretzels and I decide for the umpteenth time to jack it in with her and find another rich woman. I'm beginning to wonder if anyone with money is as reluctant as Marion to actually give any of it out – even to their lover. I pull the telephone cable out straight, distractedly, while I ponder that must be worth one last try. I could spend my life on the phone talking column inches and discount rates, if I'm not careful. Anyway, if Mark can do it so successfully, why can't I? I just can't believe that every rich divorcee or widow can be so fucking mean and plain exhausting to go out with as Marion. She is talking again.

'Listen, honey, I'm going away this weekend to Venice to see an old, old friend. Do you want to borrow the car while I'm away?'

Do I?

'Gosh that would be great,' I say sweetly. (Gosh? When do I ever say 'Gosh?')

'That's good. I don't want that asshole racing around London in it while I'm away.'

'Sure.'

'You know he still lives with his mother? The back seat of my car is the only place he can fuck in peace and quiet.'

'Bloody hell.'

'Makes me sick just thinking about it. OK, come by any time and pick up the keys from Anna Maria. I'm going Friday. What do you want?'

'How do you mean?'

'From Venice. What do you want from Venice?'

'Oh, whatever.'

'Oh, you. I'll find you something nice.'

I have to stifle a contemptuous laugh.

Vinny arrives back with Malc just as I put the phone down. 'Evenin' all,' he says. I nod hello to Malc.

'Where have you been?' I say absentmindedly, flicking around between channels.

'Have you missed me, darling?' says Vinny.

'Been counting the seconds.'

'Jane's just on her way over,' he mutters, watching the telly. 'Christ! Hasn't this woman got a big mouth? Imagine snogging that! You could bloody fall in.'

I sit up and find myself looking down at what I'm wearing. Navy-blue polo shirt and faded 501s – neither of which seem to have anything spilt down them, strangely enough. I check that my collar isn't turned in and then mutter, 'Oh, OK.'

'OK, is that all?' he says, surprised.

'Whatever,' I say coolly.

'*Whateve-e-e-r*,' drools Vinny.

'What does that mean?'

'I saw that discreet wardrobe check.'

'What are you talking about?'

'I'm talkin' about *lurrve*!' He gives me a sideways look through narrowed eyes. 'I think you find Jane strangely . . .'

'Oh, leave it out, will you?' I say, laughing with embarrassment.

'Malc's a mate of hers,' he says, savouring this information.

'Oh, right,' I say quickly. 'So?'

'Just saying.'

'Knew her at college,' says Malc, scratching his shaved head. 'Nice girl.'

'Yeah, she is,' I say. 'And did you go out with her? Did you have sex with her? *What was it like?* Was it any good? Were *you* any good?' I ask. Well, I don't, of course, but I'd like to.

Vinny hasn't given up.

'Is that the beginnings of a blush spreading across those chiselled features?'

'Look, mate, your nose will be spreading across your features, if you don't shut up,' I tell him.

'Oooh, be like that,' says Vinny. 'Just thought Malc might be able to fill you in.'

'I don't need filling in. Now piss off'.

'OK,' says Vinny, enjoying my discomfort.

Just then the door buzzer goes. Suddenly Vinny screeches theatrically and throws his hands into the air. 'Argh! Panic. She's here and I haven't a thing to wear. Quick! Mouthwash! Cologne! Moisturizer.'

'Oh, blow it out your arse, will you.'

'Your hair's sticking out at the back,' he says seriously as he gets up to let her in. Discreetly I spit on my hand and attempt to press down the disobedient locks.

When they're not drinking lager out of smeary glasses, Vinny and Jane's idea of an evening's entertainment consists of making pancakes, I discover. Malc has gone to meet some friends in the West End so Vinny and I sit at the table and drink the cans Jane has bought while she gets to work with the pancakes: whisking up batter, carefully checking the consistency and tutting at us about the state of our frying pan. Just as I could have predicted, Jane is thorough and conscientious: flipping each yellow and brown blistering disc while balancing herself with one hand and then carefully sliding the finished product onto a plate which she keeps warming in what we discover is the upper oven.

'We've got *two* ovens?' asks Vinny, intrigued.

'Didn't you know?' says Jane disapprovingly. 'It's for cooking light meals or keeping plates warm.'

'Oooh, can't wait to drop that into conversation at the golf club,' says Vinny.

Finally Jane has used all the batter and the pile of pancakes is dripping with lemon juice and sugar. My mouth is literally watering as she puts them on the table and hands out our knives and forks.

'Deeelicious,' I say as I carefully lift one off the top.

'What are you doing?' says Jane indignantly.

'Erm, taking a pancake.' I wonder if we're supposed to say grace or whether I just appear horribly greedy which, of course, I am.

'We don't do it like that,' says Jane. 'We cut it like a cake.'

'You *idiot*,' hisses Vinny melodramatically. 'Sorry, he's just got no savoir faire,' he says to Jane but she just mutters, 'It's much better this way' and carefully serves me a syrupy, slithery portion.

We eat quickly.

'Lovely,' I say to Jane by way of apology.

'Thanks,' she says quickly, concentrating on her food. After we've finished Vinny knocks back his beer and then burps loudly.

'I see those deportment lessons are finally paying off,' I observe, helping myself to more lemony syrup from the bottom of the plate.

'Daddy'll be delighted,' says Vinny in a cut crystal accent. Jane is laughing, half-choking on her last mouthful.

'Ooops, sorry,' she says, putting her hand over her mouth and regaining her usual composure. 'You're quite funny.' I look up at Vinny, who is smiling too and then realize that Jane is talking to me.

'What? Me?'

'Yeah, that was rather witty,' she says, as if stating the obvious. 'You can be rather droll for a . . . er . . .'

'For a stuffed shirt?' I offer.

'I was going to say for a smug yuppie twat,' she says sweetly. Now it's Vinny's turn to laugh.

'I'll hold her and you hit her,' he suggests.

CHAPTER FOURTEEN

ON FRIDAY I NIP ROUND TO MARION'S after work and drive the BMW home with all the windows open and Oasis's *Wonderwall* blaring out through the warm dirty air.

Saturday morning, after a sleepless night wondering whether it has been nicked every five minutes, I show the car to Vinny because he is walking out of the door for his copy of the *Guardian* and to have the fry-up at the greasy spoon down the road that we often have together. He is not as impressed as I had been hoping he'd be.

'Porkin' hell,' he says, peering at it from every angle. 'She give you this?'

'I wish. She's just lent it to me for the weekend.'

'Mean old trout. Still, you could always sell it.'

'That's true. You wanna lift?'

'No, thanks. I think I can walk to the end of the road.'

'Go on,' I say, clicking the remote at the object of my affection.

'Frankly, I'd feel like a bit of a tit in that,' he says, kicking one of the rear wheels.

'As opposed to feeling a tit everywhere else.' It comes out less funny and more unkindly than I'd intended.

'Very witty, Damon Hill,' Vinny laughs sarcastically.

'Oh, go on, mate,' I say. I realize that I genuinely want Vinny's company more than I want to show the car off to him. 'We can drive down to the café.'

'It's only down the road.'

'Yeah, I know, but it would be a laugh.'

'What you going to have? Double egg, chips, beans and valet parking?'

I smile. 'Might do.'

He thinks about it for a moment and says quietly, 'No,

you're all right' and sets off down the road whistling. I open the car door and he turns round. 'Is this what you want?'

'Heh?'

'This. This big snazzy car.'

It's a funny thing to say and Vinny is now a good ten feet away from me so it doesn't help that this odd, unexpected comment is coming to me long distance.

'Er, yeah,' I say. 'Well, it's a bit of a laugh, isn't it?'

'Is it?' He thinks about it for a moment. Then he laughs and shrugs his shoulders. 'What you doing?'

'How do you mean?' I say, by now completely phased.

Vinny starts to walk back towards me.

'I mean, what's going on, mate? Borrowing this ridiculous motor – are you insured for it?' Am I? Christ, I never stopped to think. I suppose I am otherwise Marion wouldn't have lent it to me. On the other hand Marion's consciousness of little domestic details like motor insurance is probably pretty sketchy. 'Going to posh restaurants with a bunch of old farts. Flying all over the world like a member of a Fulham jet set.' Somehow Vinny makes it all sound like shit. My desperate, unconvincing, wannabee high life. 'How old is this woman? Where did she get her money from?' I'm about to say 'from her ex-husbands' as if to defend her and emphasize the fact that, huh, *actually*, Vinny, she is *very rich* but then I realize that this makes it all sound even worse. 'Just wondered. Cheers, mate.'

He carries on down the road. I think about joining him for a moment but instead I decide to go to Sainsbury's so that I can stock up things I can't carry home on the bus. Very sensible, except that I can't think of anything to stock up on now that I'm eating with Marion all the time so I buy some boxes of bottled beer, some crisps, a pound of grapes and six family packs of toilet rolls. I wonder whether the girl at the check out thinks I must have a really bad stomach problem to need so much bog roll – if she ever notices what she's scanning.

Driving back I pass Vinny's greasy spoon. Fucking hell, Vinny. Every Saturday morning you go that café, have the same breakfast, read the paper, come back and then just lie on the settee and watch telly. The most you might stretch to is the pub with your mates. Which makes me think about Jane. Which gives me an idea.

Our phone book has been thrown down behind the settee along with an old can of Foster's, heavy with cigarette ends. The first few hundred pages have been stuck together with a sweet-smelling yellow liquid. Fortunately the pages of Ps seem to have escaped this fate so I find the number of Paperchase in Tottenham Court Road very easily.

The first time I call Jane is on her break. I wonder whether this is a good idea after all. The pancake evening was nice, laid back. Do I want to look like I'm trying to sweep her off her feet? Well, perhaps I do. Surely the desire to drive your woman in your car, to impress her with its horsepower and to challenge other predatory males in their smaller, less powerful cars is one of man's strongest primeval urges.

Anyway, she can't object to a drive and a lift home on a sunny Saturday afternoon. I try again later and Jane says 'Hello?' slightly surprised.

'It's me, Andrew.'

'Hi.'

'Busy?'

'Sorry? Oh yeah, well it's quieter now.'

'Thanks for the pancakes the other night.'

'Oh, you're welcome. I enjoyed it.' There is a pause.

'I was wondering if you wanted a lift home?'

'A lift home?'

'Yeah, a lift in a car?'

'But you haven't got a car, have you? What are you going to do? Give me a piggy back?'

'Just wait and see.'

'OK. Hang on a minute.' I hear her telling someone that they sold out this morning but there are some more on order. She comes back. 'Er, yeah.'

'Where shall I see you?'

'Erm, let's see. In front of the shop just after six?'

'Great. See you then.'

I don't feel nearly so confident as I sound but I'm committed now. Besides, not everyone enjoys personal calls at work as much as I do. I watch *Grandstand* and eat my grapes until about half past five and then pick up my keys and step out of the house to see my baby and make sure she hasn't been keyed.

Admiring my parking, I operate the remote control from thirty feet away but nothing happens – bit optimistic, perhaps. Then I try ten feet and she's ready. I get in and am greeted by the familiar sweet smell of leather and electronics. The sun is low and it floods the car with a warm, yellow light. I sit back in the seat for a minute and then put the key in the ignition and turn it. Immediately the car growls and comes to life. Lights come on, indicator needles move up ready for action and there are small clicks and buzzes as the electronics check themselves and stand to attention. The control panel is lit up before me like my own private staff reporting for duty. Powerful, efficient, confident, awaiting my orders.

This is not like my friends' cars where everything has been pushed and pulled and jiggled while they explain, 'Sorry, it's a bit temperamental' or 'She doesn't like the cold weather'. This is not like the car my mother used to take my sister and me to school in where everything was the simplest, cheapest possible and the driver had to do all the work. A car which said, 'Well, we've had a go with the heating and the hazard lights, but now it's up to you.' In this car everything is effortless. The merest touch and everything is done for you.

I put on my Ray-Bans and check how I look in the mirror behind the sun shield. Then I take the handbreak off, move it up to 'D' and spin the wheel round with the palm of my hand.

Parking in the West End is a nightmare. Even though most of the shoppers are leaving it takes me ages to find a space which is not barred by some stupid restriction. Finally I find a little side street off Tottenham Court Road. As I get out two lads sitting on a low wall look menacingly at me. Envy? Yeah, probably. Even a couple of policemen sitting in their Ford Fiesta at the traffic lights at Charing Cross Road had done a double-take. 'What the hell is a kid like him doing in a car like that?'

But these boys are making me nervous, one watching my car, the other watching me as I walk casually back to Tottenham Court Road. I am just about to turn the corner when anxiety gets the better of me and I decide to return to the car. They are talking to each other now. I get back and wonder exactly what I am going to do – pretend I have forgotten something? This thing is such a bloody responsibility. I get in, start the engine and move off. It is 6.10 p.m. No time to park anywhere else. I drive round, back into the main road. Passing Paperchase on the other side of the road I see Jane waiting by the main entrance, dressed in a white T-shirt and long skirt, carrying a large shoulder bag. She is chewing a nail and looking round suspiciously. She looks prettier than ever.

I slow down and wave, hoping to attract her attention somehow, even though she is looking the other way. I beep the horn quickly but still she doesn't turn – unlike everyone else. I realize she doesn't even know what she is looking out for. She probably assumes it's a Renault Five or a Datsun Cherry. I beep again and shout.

Still she doesn't turn.

By now the cars in front have started to move off and a cab driver behind honks at me. I consider going round the block and coming back but it would take forever. The cab driver behind starts shouting at me to get a move on.

Jane sighs and puts her bag down between her legs and looks up again but through me. I shout again but what attracts her attention is the cab driver behind me honking again. Jane frowns and I shout again 'Jane! Here!' and wave her over. She doesn't smile but looks round at the traffic in the hope of a gap between the cars. Of course, they are moving quickly and solidly up towards Euston Road. I turn to tell the cabbie to shut up but he has realized what I am waiting for and is moaning to his passengers via his rear-view mirror. Meanwhile, some other cars behind him have decided to vent their frustration and there is an echo of horns down the street. I try to move into the next lane to let them pass but there's just not enough room. Someone starts shouting at me. Fuck! Fuck! Fuck! This is so uncool.

Jane finds a space before a bus and dashes across to get to me. I set off immediately and we travel for a moment in silence, glad not to be the centre of attention any longer.

'How are you?' I ask as casually as I can.

'OK. Whose car?'

I can't believe I haven't got an answer ready for this. 'Just a friend.'

'You must have some pretty rich friends.'

I can't think of an answer to this either. I'm fine if someone asks me in the office but Jane is a bit close to home and I realize that I don't want to lie to her so I change the subject: 'Where shall we go?'

'I don't know. You're driving,' she says, running her hands through her hair and gently moving it away from her face. Her white skin looks hot and slightly sticky.

'OK,' I say slowly, thinking about the traffic. 'We could drive up to Hampstead Heath and find a pub or something near there.'

'Sure,' she says without enthusiasm.

We crawl through the unrelenting traffic. Part of me is absorbed in driving: desperately urging lights to go green so that I can move ahead a few feet or wondering what the hell other drivers are playing at and all the time hoping more than anything else in all the world that we don't get stuck behind a bus. But part of me is aware of Jane sitting sulkily beside me – unenthusiastic, ungrateful, unimpressed. After five long, long minutes I decide to break the silence and bring the situation to a head.

'Are you all right?'

'Fine.'

Pause.

'Because I can drop you at a Tube station or a bus stop somewhere. I don't know how you usually get home but it's no trouble to me,' I say quickly, looking straight ahead. It all sounds more aggressive than I wanted it to. She looks round at me and I glance across at her quickly.

She says, 'Well, what do you want me to say, Andrew? "What a big car. I bet you've got a big penis as well"?'

'Oh! For Christ's sake,' I say, not sure how to answer her. She laughs irritably and looks across at me, raising her eyebrows quizzically.

'I'm sorry, but do I look like the kind of woman who's impressed with a big car?'

'Jesus! Of course not!' There is another pause and I decide to act hurt. 'OK, I apologize. I just thought I'd offer you a lift home and perhaps we could spend some time together this evening. You could have said no when I rang.' Either my logic or my hurt little-boy voice has the right effect.

She sighs and says, 'I'm sorry. I thought it would be fun to meet up but this doesn't feel right. Here, in this ridiculous car, that's all.' She looks around it disapprovingly and back at me. 'It's *her* car, isn't it?' she says slowly.

I'm about to say 'Whose?' but I realize that playing the innocent will only make things worse.

'Yes.' We sit at a traffic light which I realize is in fact green. She sighs. 'I can't do this.'

I look round quickly and she is running her hand over the door looking for the handle.

'Jane!'

'Sorry, Andrew.' She gets out, slams the door and walks off down the street. I see her in the rear-view mirror. I try and stop but suddenly the traffic begins to move again and immediately the frustrated rally driver in the car behind me begins to honk. There is no way I can stop and besides, even by twisting round in my seat and looking behind me I can't see her. She has just vanished. The honking starts again. The road in front of me is empty.

'Oh, fuck *offffff*!' I shout at the driver and the world in general but, of course, no one can hear me through the thick glass and the roar of the air-conditioning.

I drive back. It takes me hours. Fucking Jane. I like her so much it annoys me. But what was I thinking of? Offering her a lift in this car? I knew she wouldn't be impressed with it and it's also bloody insulting, like suggesting to your mistress that she borrow some of your wife's clothes.

'Oh, fuck.' At the inevitable red light, I take the opportunity to bang my head against the steering wheel. Outside a cyclist in a safety helmet and a Barbour, coasting to a halt at the lights, looks down at me, surprised and disapproving.

At home there is a message from Jonathan asking me to call. My cheque! It seems like small compensation after my disastrous experience with Jane but it would be better than nothing. I ring him back.

'Who? Oh, Andrew, hi mate. Sorry, it was a job for tonight but I had to give it to one of the other guys.'

'Oh, sorry about that. I just wondered, though—'

'You'll have to make yourself available a bit more if you're going to get some work.'

'Sure.' Perhaps those little wage-slave cheques from Jonathan would be easier and more reliable than trying to get something out of Marion.

While I'm getting a beer out of the fridge I realize that Jane would never in a million years understand what I want in life. In fact she would probably be really shocked. That also annoys me about Jane – she's so bloody sensible. Most men are wary of sensible women because they remind them of their primary school teachers, those patronizing Stalinists with flat shoes and sensible skirts who had an answer for everything.

What I really want is the best of both worlds: spend time with Jane and spend Marion's money. At the moment I don't seem to have either. I need to get some cash together and then I'll be in the market for a serious relationship again. But will Jane still be around?

I think about ringing Marion but then realize that she hasn't left a number or even told me which hotel she's gone to. I don't know any posh hotels in Venice so, instead, I channel-surf for a while wishing we had cable so that there were more channels I could find nothing to watch on. I realize that Vinny must be out. What's he doing out on Saturday night while I'm stuck here? I ought to just ring some of my friends, see if they're around tonight. Except that I don't seem to have any friends anymore. Did I ever? I can't remember. Sure I did. I must have. My past life all seems something of a blur since Marion.

At about ten I decide to order a curry and find a flyer for one that delivers. When it arrives three quarters of an hour later it is cold and not what I ordered. What's the matter with me? Can't I even order a curry these days?

I think about Jane. The way she scoops her hair back behind her ear. Her bossiness when she made pancakes for Vinny and me the other night. Her trendy, right-on friends that she thinks I'll hate. The way she laughs. Why is she working in Paperchase and living in Holloway or wherever the hell it was? Why can't she want more? More than just working to earn enough to pay the bills, a salary addict. Or better still, why can't she just be rich? If Jane had Marion's money, I'd be OK.

After a while I go out and look at the car again. Partly to check it is still safe, I must admit. Luckily the dodgy family opposite have not taken the wheels off it. Yet. Perhaps Vinny was right. What would happen if I sold it? Would Marion mind? I could probably get fifty grand for it. I'd be laughing. I get in and switch on the CD player. I turn it up, start the car and set off for a drive around. I go up the Fulham Road and into Chelsea, looking at people in restaurants and watching a couple leaving a party in a house while I wait for the lights to change.

The woman shouts something to the host who laughs loudly then the man puts his arm around her and they begin to walk down the pavement together. Suddenly I feel like crying. What am I doing driving around on my own on a Saturday night? I turn the CD off and head back home.

On Sunday morning while I'm out getting some milk and the papers Marion leaves a message on the machine to say that she has decided to go on to Paris. 'I've got a ton of shopping to do and my personal shopper's arriving from London to give me a hand,' she says.

Vinny surfaces at about two while I'm watching a video.

'Mornin' all,' he mutters, flopping down on the settee.

'Afternoon,' I correct him.

'Ooooh, 'scusez-moi.' He pulls the expectant, slightly pained expression that I know only too well.

'Oi, don't you dare.' But it's too late. I throw a cushion at him and waft away the toxic odour with the *Sunday Times* magazine.

'Sorry, mate. Vegetarian bangers and beefburgers have that effect on me.'

'Sounds delicious. What you do last night?'

'Barbie, mate,' he says in a terrible cod Australian accent.

'Was it good?' I ask, flicking through the channels. There is no answer so I look round at Vinny, wondering whether he's fallen asleep again. But instead he's staring mischievously at me. 'I just asked whether it was good.'

'Oh, yes,' says Vinny, still smiling demonically. 'It was good.'

'Whose was it?' I ask.

'Guess,' he says.

'Whose?' I don't like the sound of this.

'I told you – guess,' he says again, delighted at my growing unease.

'I've no idea,' I say, even though I have. 'Whose barbecue, you stinky bastard?'

'You had your chance.'

'Jane had a barbecue last night and you went.'

'Bingo!' Vinny is triumphant. 'Are we jealous?'

'No,' I say shortly. So she left me in the car and went off to a barbecue she didn't even mention.

'I think we are.' I look back at the telly. 'Well, you would have been if you'd been there.' He picks up the Appointments section and begins to scan it ostentatiously.

'What does that mean?'

'One here for you, mate – Sales Director for Durex. Both your talents rolled into one.'

'What happened?'

'Oh, Jane was having a rather in-depth conversation with some bloke from the local Friends of the Earth group. Bit of a hunk, according to the females present.'

'Liar.'

'I think it was Jane's very own rain forest he was interested in, if you get my drift.'

'Shut up.'

'OK.' He carries on scrutinizing pages of jobs that he has absolutely no interest in. I have a vision of Jane, beer in hand, looking up adoringly at some dreadlocked eco warrior.

'You kidding me?'

'Oh, Christ! Well, actually she spent most of the night trying to get away from him, but the point is, Mr Love For Sale, you'd better get in there, otherwise . . .'

'All right, all right.'

'Well I'm just saying . . .'

'Look, I don't need to ask you for advice on women,' I tell him. 'But I'll be all ears next time I need help on . . .' Vinny's particular sphere of knowledge escapes me for a moment. 'Erm . . . stupid trousers.'

'My wise counsel is at your disposal,' he says, smiling and scratching his bum energetically.

The person I *do* need to get some advice from is Mark, I decide. I ring his number that evening and get the answerphone. 'Hi, this is Mark, this is the tone, you know what to do.'

I start speaking but then Mark picks up so we arrange that I'll go over and see him after work on Monday.

His flat in Notting Hill is on the ground floor of a white stucco-fronted building. On one side a Trustafarian couple are just arriving back from a long weekend in Gloucestershire in a Merc estate, dripping children, scruffy soft toys and car blankets. On the other side there is what can only be a crack den. I buzz Mark's flat and he lets me in.

'Hello, mate,' he says, giving me a firm handshake. 'How's it going?'

He is wearing creased, very soft cotton trousers, mules and a cream, sleeveless knitted top which looks like a Dries Van Noten. It has that casually expensive look that I'd frankly give anything in the world to be able to do. It shows off Mark's elegantly muscled, honey-tanned arms which, I guess, like the rest of him, have been carefully developed for the benefit of a select, paying clientele.

The flat is huge and high-ceilinged with wooden floors, cream coloured walls and a white settee covered in a huge, white loose cover. I smile to myself as I wonder how long a white settee would last at my and Vinny's place. The ornate marble fireplace is stacked with stiff card invites and snapshots. Next to it there is a CD player and two truly huge piles of CDs. It has a look of cavalier understated elegance like Mark's arms, clothes, answer machine message – his whole life, in fact.

I sit down on the settee and he takes an easy chair. He looks at me for a moment and smiles.

'So, my little studling, how's it going?'

'Oh,' I start optimistically and then decide not to lie. 'Crap.'

Mark laughs. 'Marion not paying up, then?'

'Not a penny.'

'Anything at all?'

'Oh, a few clothes but I'm not really sure I even like them.'

'I told you, get it in cash if you can,' he says, walking round to the kitchenette. 'Clothes won't pay your rent, will they?'

'No, I suppose not. The most I get is a twenty every now and then to pay my taxi fare.'

'What do you want?' he asks getting up.

'Well, I just want enough money to enjoy myself a bit. Buy my own clothes, go on holiday, have the kind of fun you can't when you're twenty and you've got a crap job and just enough to pay the rent and go to the pub a couple of times a week. You know?' I suddenly think of Debbie. 'I want to get enough to buy a flat or even put something away so that I can start my own business one day – I've had enough of working for other people. I mean, I'm not so naive as to think that Marion will set me up for life but, you know, a few thou would help, if nothing else.'

Mark looks at me for a moment, slightly confused. 'Actually, I just mean what do you want to drink?'

'Oh, er—' Shit, how embarrassing.

'There's some good white wine,' says Mark.

'Oh, yeah, wine would be great, thanks.'

'No, that sounds very reasonable,' says Mark as he pours two glasses of perfectly chilled Orvieto. Slighty distracted by my embarrassing outburst I walk around the room a bit looking at the photographs stuck on the wall and lying on the mantelpiece: Mark in black tie, on a beach, at a restaurant with two older women and a silver-grey-haired man, at Ascot, saluting the camera with a glass of champagne: always smiling, always handsome, always good value, always working. There is one picture of him with a toddler in a sunny garden. Mark hands me my wine.

'My son. Ben.'

'Your son?'

'Yep,' he says, picking up the picture and studying it carefully. 'This was taken ages ago. He's nearly eight now.'

'Sweet kid.'

'Thanks,' says Mark, still looking at him. 'So funny. Very serious. Always frowning and asking questions. How does a plane stay up?'

'Search me. Wings?' I say, shrugging my shoulders.

He smiles.

'I had to buy him a book about it.' He looks at the photo again and then carefully puts it back, arranging it in pride of place amongst the invitations. He sits down.

'Do you see him much?' I ask, sensing he wants to talk about it.

'Once a fortnight, just for a few hours. His mum, who he lives with, got a very good deal in court. Not surprising, really, given she's a barrister.' He looks into his glass. 'Question was: should he live with his mother, who as I say, is a barrister and has a nice house in Dulwich and a husband who works in the City, or should he live with his father who's a rent boy? Tough question for the judge, eh?'

'Rent boy.' I laugh, uneasily. He shrugs his shoulders. 'I'm sorry.'

'Oh, well.' He takes a large mouthful of wine. 'Now, what are we going to do for you? I did tell you it's a mug's game.'

'Yeah, but so's working in an office for a miserable . . .' Words fail me.

'True. How is old Marion?'

'Old Marion is OK. Well, you know, mad as a hatter.'

'Most people are. She likes *you*, though.'

'Well. That's nice.'

'But, you're not getting any goodies?' sighs Mark. Am I being patronised here? Again?

'No, not really. The only thing I am going to get at this rate is the sack.'

'Oh, Marion won't sack you.'

'I meant from my day job.'

'Is that a problem? It sounds pretty crap if you don't mind me saying.'

'Oh, don't you start,' I snap.

'Just saying.'

'Oh, sorry, mate.' I look around the flat again. 'How do you know what my job is?'

'Oh, someone told me. You hear these things.'

'Do you? I don't mind you knowing, I just wondered.'

'Anyway, kiddo,' he says kindly. 'Marion giving you a hard time?'

'Always. The thing about Marion is that she always knows best. She never seems to have a moment's doubt about anything.' Or was that Jane I was thinking about? Women.

'You've got to hate where you came from and love where you're going to.'

'Heh?'

'That's what Marion said to me once.'

'Sounds like her. It's probably good advice. I wonder where Marion does come from.'

'I think she fell out of the pages of a glossy magazine like one of those perfume samples.'

Laughing at the thought, 'Probably.' I stretch my neck and look into my glass. Somehow it feels like it's been a long day already. 'What do *you* think I should do?'

'Well,' says Mark, getting up and standing by the fireplace like some Victorian father giving advice to his wayward son. 'You've got to decide what you want. Marion will probably give you a bit of cash, cufflinks, a watch, something like that. You can sell them after a while, I know a jewellers near Victoria station – great for that sort of thing. Never asks questions. Mention my name, they won't rip you off. Then Marion will get bored of you after a while—'

'I thought you said she liked me.'

'Yeah, but she'll still get bored, like your favourite Christmas present when you were a kid. Were you still playing with that in February?'

'Can't remember.'

'Course you weren't.'

'But if she really likes me won't she give me things?'

'Little bits and pieces, yes, but she's not going to shell out a huge great wad so that you can go off, do your own thing and leave her, is she? She wants to keep you on a short lead, just a little bit at a time.'

'Oh, Christ.'

Mark laughs and refills our glasses. 'Marion's not stupid, she knows a gold-digger when she sees one.'

I'm suddenly really offended by that phrase. 'I'm not a gold-digger, it's just that if they – Marion or any of her friends – have got all that money and they want to spend it on me, why shouldn't they? Anyway, what am I saying this to *you* for?'

'I know exactly what you mean. I'm just saying Marion isn't going to pay out and let you run off, she wants something for her money.'

'I do like Marion,' I say, looking into my drink. 'She's funny and she has been very kind, taking me to Paris and New York. It's just that – well, like you said, there's no long-term future in it, is there?' I remember Channing's words over dinner.

'She knows that too.'

'It's just a bit of fun. To be honest I'm just beginning to go off her a bit. She's starting to drive me mad at the moment – always picking, always complaining. And we always do what *she* wants to do.'

'But that's the deal – she's paying,' says Mark, laughing at my naivety.

'I can't do this much longer,' I mutter, almost to myself.

'Well, then what's a better bet? Let me think. You might get something off some other old dears I know. I'll introduce you, you'll have no problem. But the thing is if you really want to earn some decent money and see the world . . .'

I look up at him. 'Yeah?'

'If you really want to earn money to live on, you know, comfortably, it's going to have to be sex – with men buying.'

'What? Oh, I don't know about—' I'm startled.

'Hang on, I didn't say sex *with* men, although if you can put up with it there's always work there. No, it might mean sex with their wives or girlfriends or with a hooker while they watch or something.'

'What? Do you, you know, do a lot of that?'

'Bread and butter, mate.'

'Why do they want to watch?'

Mark rolls his eyes. 'Derr! They get turned on by it. Like having a porno movie live in their bedroom.'

'Weird.'

'It's a weird world, mate.'

I try and imagine the scene but give up when it all becomes part of a movie I saw at a friend's house when I was sixteen and the video got stuck and I panicked thinking I heard the police downstairs and we'd been raided and what would I tell my parents?

'And you don't have any problem with that?' I ask.

'No, not at all.'

'And you don't ever find that you can't, you know, get it up?'

'Hardly ever. It's quite a turn-on, really. Especially having those crisp fifties pressed into your hand afterwards.'

I nod uncertainly and look up at the ceiling. I don't want to meet his eyes. And I really don't want to hear what he's saying. I certainly don't want to hear what comes next.

'Truth is that women will buy you little presents, let you live in their house or something and give you enough cash to tide you over but it's men that actually pay up,' he says. It sounds as much as if he's confessing as giving advice. 'When I met you in Knightsbridge a few weeks ago, you didn't think it was a woman that I'd been seeing, did you?'

'Wasn't it?' I say rather unnecessarily. I look across at him; for once he looks slightly off his guard.

'You've got a lot to learn, mate.'

'That I do know. But with men?'

'It pays cash, it pays the bills,' says Mark urgently. 'Dinner with a woman might be fun but look at the balance sheet: four, five hours and a hundred, a hundred and fifty quid. Big deal. I can earn more in just one hour with . . . other clients.' He regains his composure slightly. 'Oh, don't look so shocked, you must have known it happens. It's the ultimate fantasy for them – a Hugh Grant they can actually have sex with.'

'I can't do that, sorry, I just couldn't.'

Mark laughs. 'Up to you, I'm just saying that's what makes money. Refill?'

I leave Mark to his beautiful, off-white minimalist world just after eight because he has to be somewhere by nine. I thank him and he says he'll try and introduce me to some other people. But it's been a pretty depressing conversation especially when Mark refilled my glass and admitted that not only did he get turned on by the feel of those crisp fifties – 'very flat, very smooth, just out of the bank, with that slight roughness where the print is' – but that these days he couldn't really get turned on *without* them.

CHAPTER FIFTEEN

MY CHEQUE ARRIVES FROM JONATHAN on Tuesday morning as I'm dashing out of the front door. By my calculation it should have been for £160 but it's just £23. The accompanying photocopied note just says, rather mysteriously, 'Deductions for administration: £137.' What the hell does that mean? Funnily enough I get the answer phone when I ring. I leave a message but somehow I doubt he'll call back.

Marion rings me at work in the afternoon to tell me what a crap time she's having in Paris and that she'll be back by dinner time.

'Where do you want to go tonight?'

'Don't mind, whatever you think,' I say, already lifted by the thought of good food and wine. That I *can* do. The idea of dinner in a smart restaurant sounds sort of pleasant and familiar and comforting after my conversation with Mark. I find myself visualizing, yet again, the tall, dark, handsome guy I met at Claridges in his dinner jacket and later padding round his drop-dead elegant flat, having sex with an ageing American man in a hotel bedroom. The American has a dodgy wig for some reason in my little fantasy. Is Mark enjoying this? No, impossible, surely. Participating? As little as possible, I suppose. Then picking up his clothes off the floor and getting dressed as quickly as he can. Taking a wad of cash off the old guy, telling him it had been fun and promising to see him again soon.

One thing's for sure, I might have a lot to learn about persuading women to buy me clothes and dole out cash but I'll never, never do that.

'I don't want too much,' Marion is saying.

'What?' I snap.

'I just I said I don't want to each too much, just a Caesar salad or something,' she says. 'I thought maybe just grab a bite at Le Caprice.'

'Yeah,' I say. 'Yeah, sounds great. I'll come over to yours at about seven-thirty then.' I look up and see Sami roll her eyes. 'Out again?' she mouths.

I smile but Marion is off, 'Oh, one other thing, Andrew. I think you should start thinking about moving in.' I can't quite believe I heard that. What is she talking about?

'What? With you?'

'No, with Charles and Camilla,' she sighs. 'Of course with me. It's crazy you trying to live in two places and besides I can't bear to think of you in that slum in Fulham.'

'It's not a slum,' I mutter distractedly as the whole terrible scenario opens up slowly before my eyes.

'Doing your own ironing in the kitchen is not the kind of lifestyle I want for you.' Christ! What a thought. I would never see my friends, never have any privacy, never be able to slob in front of the telly. It might improve my chances of getting more presents and even some serious income but I could probably kiss goodbye to my sanity. Besides, what could I say to my parents? They would understand that I'd moved, but to Belgravia? With an older woman? Oh my God, they might want to meet her. She might want to meet them!

'Andrew?'

'Erm . . .'

'Well, think about. It's only sensible, I'm sure you'll agree. See you at seven-thirty. Don't be late.'

She hangs up and I stare down at my desk for a minute. Perhaps this was the downside of having her fall for me that Mark was on about. He's right – again. I'll end up being a poodle, not a gigolo. And a cash-poor poodle at that.

'Everything OK?' It's Sami.

'Yeah. Fine . . . fine.'

I feel in need of another coffee – and a lot of drugs.

Thinking about it from Marion's point of view, it does make sense: she'd have me on tap. Never late for dinner, never out when she phones. Less likely to be seeing anyone else. Perfect.

Getting a cup of coffee from the disgusting machine by the lifts I decide that I can stall her for a while – say something about deposits and tenancy agreements or I can half-move in, take some clothes over in a bag and spend some nights there and some nights in Fulham. After all, I am already staying at her place two or three nights a week. I'll just increase it to four or five. On the other hand, if I gave up Fulham completely I'll save a fortune on rent. And food. And just about everything else. My salary would be all mine for spending.

But what about when I want a bit of time on my own? Or if I want to have some friends round? If Marion wasn't there it would be great: 'Come round to dinner,' I could say. But not for the old lasagna and salad off assorted Habitat and John Lewis plates courtesy of the landlord or previous tenants. No running between the kitchen and the living room to check everything is all right. No finding the pan has boiled dry and the place is filling with black smoke. No dragging it all home from Sainsbury's on the bus and getting back four minutes before the first guest arrives. Do it properly for once. Whatever I want, whenever I want, served by the maid from big china plates and solid silver cutlery. Pretty impressive, eh?

Suddenly I see Jane's face. Bloody hell. That would completely end it. As soon as she found out she'd never want to speak to me again.

I decide to put off making a decision for a bit and perhaps ask Mark for his advice.

'Move in?' he says over an early evening drink at a bar near his. I want to exorcise our last conversation, assure myself that although this guy is basically a rent boy, he is still Mark, still pretty cool. Wearing a dark suit, one button done up and an immaculate white shirt without a tie, he does look pretty cool. 'That's a big commitment.'

'Telling me.' He turns away from the bar, looks across the room and smiles devastatingly. I carry on, 'I mean it would save me rent and food money and things but talk about a bird in a gilded cage.'

'Yeah,' says Mark slowly. I turn to where he is looking and see two teenage Sloanes in polo neck pullovers giggling and whispering to each other over bottles of Michelob.

'Don't get too excited, they're probably still getting pocket money,' I tell him, turning back to the bar.

'Think so?'

'You're too old for them, mate, face it.'

Mark turns back to me and laughs. 'Oooh. You're not supposed to get this bitter for a least another couple of years.'

'Mark, I'm sorry, I just want some advice.'

He sighs, looks into his drink. 'OK. If you move in you will save a lot of money and you will increase the chance perhaps of her giving you something decent in the long term. On the other hand, she *will* keep you on a very tight lead.'

'No social life.'

'No *life*.'

'So what would you do?'

But now Mark is distracted by someone at the other end of the bar.

'Mark?' No reaction. I'm wasting my time here – again. I take another swig of beer and stand up. He stands up and catches my arm.

'Look, I'm sorry, mate,' he says.

'You just can't help it, can you?'

'No,' he says seriously. 'I can't.'

I take a deep breath. 'Sorry, I lost my rag. I just don't know what to do.'

'Hang in there,' he says without hesitation.

'Really?'

'Marion's a tough one to crack but I suppose you've invested quite a bit of time with her already.' Mark stands with his arms folded, staring down at the floor, frowning with concentration. He looks like a model advertising a suit. 'She just wants you around, not at the end of a phone line. Yeah, that's good – move in. Like I said, Marion really likes you and she'll look after you. Where did you go the other weekend? New York? Hey, why not? At least you'll travel a bit. Work at the clothes thing, like I told you.'

'Sure.'

'Oh, and in the meanwhile, I'll introduce you to some other people – less, you know, control freaky. Can't do any harm.'

I suddenly feel a strange pang of remorse for Marion. I'm moving in but with the option of dumping her in favour of someone else. Am I really such a shit? Mark senses my concern.

'It's a tough business,' he says. 'You don't think when she was with each of her husbands she didn't have her eye on the bigger chance, a better catch? You've got to grab the opportunities as they come along – all of them.'

'I suppose so.'

'Look, do you want to go to New York business class and wear that Rolex or not?'

'Yeah but do I have to—'

'If you want get some money out of these people you've got to be ruthless about it. The truth is, Andrew, that two seconds after Marion gets bored of you she'll be looking for someone else.'

'You said.'

'Exactly. Hot brick!' He looks at me. 'You don't get it, do you? The reason why Marion has all that money is that she's worked for it – rich husbands didn't rush up to her with cheque books in hand. She went out and got it.

'You want to make serious money, not just pocket money, you say? Yeah? You want more than just a couple of hundred for dinner – and you don't want to do the sex thing – if that's the case you've got to be tougher than me, more determined, more ruthless.'

Ruthless? Me? Debbie said in my last appraisal that I could be 'quite determined' but 'ruthless'? That's another story. Even if I could be as hard and money grabbing as . . . well, Marion, there is still one other little complication.

Jane.

I'm still horribly embarrassed about her reaction to my stupid stunt with the car. How would she feel if not only am I driving Marion's smart expensive car, but I'm living in her smart expensive house too?

'Look,' says Mark. 'Set yourself a deadline.' He points a finger at me thoughtfully. 'A month, say. If you still feel you're pissing about for pocket money and not a lot else, then knock it on the head. Like I said, I can introduce you to some other people.' That sounds reasonable. Somehow a time-limit makes it more bearable.

'OK.'

'Good man,' says Mark, punching me on the arm. I still can't decide, though, if I feel dirty and immoral at the end of this conversation or just a berk, a smooth operator with an unscruplous master plan or just a media sales executive from Fulham with delusions.

'Thanks, mate,' I say.

'You're welcome.'

I think about it all for a moment longer while Mark watches me digest his words. Then I look across at the girls and say to him, 'Go on, go and talk to them.'

I arrive at Marion's at just after seven-thirty. She asks where I've been, she rang me at home and the office and no one knew where I was. I tell her I was having a drink with someone. Someone she doesn't know. Then we kiss and and go upstairs. We begin to make love slowly while a warm breeze blows in through the windows. But I'm not really into it. We lie back halfway through and let the sweat on our bodies evaporate.

I can't help wondering now whether Marion was meeting someone in Paris. Someone younger, better in bed, more innocent and emollient. A blanker canvas. A cuter, blanker canvas.

'How was Paris?' I say after a while.

'It was boring.'

'Boring? How come?'

'It just was.'

'Why was it boring? Who did you see there?'

'Oh,' she says dismissively. 'Well . . . Let me see.' She takes a deep breath and looks around the room. 'I had boring things to do. I had to visit with some old friends who you would have hated and I had to get some clothes for the Fall. There's just nothing in London, I've looked.'

'OK.' She looks across at me without moving. I do the same.

'It's true. Everyone says London is great for shopping but frankly I've been appalled at the choice. It's an absolute scandal – your newspaper should do an article about it.' I think the Home and Style section already has.

'I see . . . ' What do I see? Marion has obviously had enough of this conversation.

'Fix me a drink, will you?'

Without saying anything I get up and walk over to the tiny fridge in one corner of the room. I remember my dad coming home from work one day in a foul mood. Quarrelling with my mum, picking on me and my sister. It turned out that some management consultants had advised the company to cut costs by removing the executive fridges from the offices of his level of management.

'What d'you want?' I say, opening the fridge.

'There a bottle of champagne in there?'

There is. I take it out and bring it back to the bed with two glasses. I open it and pour. We both take a sip and lie back.

'Buy me anything?' I ask.

'There's some aftershave in one of those bags,' she says, closing her eyes and squeezing the top of her nose. Aftershave. Duty free. Great. Forgot about me until the last minute. Mark is right, I've got to keep any eye out for something better.

Marion is having a dinner party. We're eating some dark brown stew. I haven't touched mine but around me the others are tucking in, talking and laughing. Anna Maria and another girl are serving salad. I know I've got to leave the room to do something but I can't remember what. Someone next to me is talking non stop and I'm dying for them to pause a moment so that I can make my excuses and get up. I know I haven't got much time. Desperately I look round in search of the door which, for some reason, is not where it usually is. To my left is Channing, who is holding a champagne glass in one hand and a fork full of food in the other. He is smiling lecherously at me and some of the stew is dripping down his chin. The person on my right who keeps talking is not a woman, as I had first thought, but Ted the security guard from work. Ted, shut up, I'm thinking. I look around to see who the hell else is here and directly opposite me is Jane.

I feel slightly sick and shivery although it's stifling in the room. Am I coming down with something? I must have fallen asleep. I close my eyes and move my head to ease my stiff neck. Suddenly I see Jane again, looking impassively at me across the dinner table.

I wonder a moment if I called out her name in my sleep. Did Marion hear me? No, she's in the shower.

Later, I have a shower myself and get dressed. While Marion is putting on her make-up I go down into the living room and open another bottle of champagne, even though we haven't finished the last one. Finally she comes down and she does look gorgeous. A pale blue dress that I haven't seen before, her hair is slightly different. She flops down, slowly crosses her long slim legs and asks me to fix her a vodka on the rocks.

'God, it's warm this evening, huh? I can't ever remember London being this warm. We should get you a lightweight suit, maybe. Something in linen. You'd look great. You've got the height, Andrew. You should be a little bolder with your choice of clothes. You're not a kid any more, you can go for a more mature approach to your apparel.'

My what? I don't say anything but hand her her drink. 'I've booked the restaurant for eight-thirty.' I nod and smile. 'What's the matter? You seem very quiet'.

'No, it's just that I was thinking about this moving-in idea.'

'Good.' She smiles kindly. 'I'll have Anna Maria and Chris go over to Fulham and pick up your stuff.'

I laugh in exasperation and sit down opposite her. 'Marion, I don't think you realize that it's quite a big deal for me.'

I know we're risking another row but I just want her to be aware of the sacrifice I'm making for her.

'You mean it's a commitment,' she says patronizingly. Despite her tone it does sound very grim, very final. I'm being committed.

'Well, perhaps it is,' I say. 'I'm just a bit nervous about it. I've never lived with a girl before. Except at college and that doesn't really count.'

Marion asks, 'Worried about what your parents and your friends will say?'

'Well, I—'

'Just tell them that you're moving in with your girlfriend.' It sounds so strange to hear her say it. Is that what we are: girlfriend and boyfriend? She gets up to put some more ice in her drink. 'When I announced that I would be marrying my second husband it was a huge step. I was terribly concerned about what people would think, but if you always worry about such things, you'll never do anything. If we are having a relationship, Andrew, it's only sensible that you live here, as much for practical reasons as for anything else. I don't want people knowing that my lover lives in Fulham.'

'Eh?'

She looks surprised and then comes to sit down next to me on the settee. 'Andrew, I have a certain reputation and certain standards to maintain. No one, for example, knows how we met.' Her face changes for a moment. 'If anyone asks, by the way, it was in Fortnum & Mason – you helped me choose some tea as a present for someone.'

'Oh, OK.' I think I am being insulted but it seems to have happened so often to me recently that I just can't tell anymore.

'We just got talking. It was Orange Pekoe.'

'Sorry?'

'The tea. It was Orange Pekoe.'

'Sure.'

There is a pause.

'Where was I?' She looks down at the floor for inspiration. 'Oh, yes. You have to remember, Andrew, that you are moving in a different circle of people now. People with expectations and a certain degree of style. They would be very surprised to find themselves in the same room with—' she shrugs her shoulders and looks up at the ceiling – 'with an office boy living in a tiny apartment in a place like Fulham.'

Apart from 'fuck off' I can't quite think how to respond. In a way it's all to the good: the more poor and pathetic I seem, the more I'll appear in need of expensive food and clothing. She seems to take my silence as agreement. 'So I'll arrange it. You can get packed up with Anna Maria and then the driver can bring your things over here. OK, now let's go eat.'

In fact we eat at Charles and Victoria's that night because they ring us in the car on the way to the restaurant and tell us that they've just got home from New York and they're dying to see us.

'Home?' I say to Marion as we execute an elegant U-turn and set off in the direction of Kensington Church Street. 'I thought they lived in New York.'

'And London,' says Marion casually, putting her phone back in her bag. As soon as she says it, I realize, of course, that I'm being naive. I still have the idea that people live in one place and, at most, have a timeshare in somewhere like Wales or Spain. But all Marion's friends seem to live in at least two or three cities around the world.

It's quite a fun evening – or at least it starts off that way. Victoria rabbits on endlessly and seems quite pleased, albeit surprised when she makes me laugh – because she *is* very funny. Marion spends some time, well a long time, actually, cursing the French and announcing that for moisturizers Paris is actually worse than London. Or is it vice versa? London is also pretty crap for a lot of things. I try to defend it but Marion gives me a look that says, What would I know, I've got no terms of reference.

Charles, whose grey-flecked, wavy hair matches his charcoal grey pinstripe suit perfectly, I notice, asks if anyone would like some charlie. He smiles at me and very gently raises a professionally plucked eyebrow above a dark, hooded eye. I say yes, don't mind if I do, mainly to annoy Marion.

'Are you sure you won't, Marion?' says Victoria, carefully putting a rolled twenty into her left nostril, her diamond-ringed little finger sticking out elegantly.

'No, thank you,' says Marion primly, 'and Andrew, I think you've had enough, you'll never sleep tonight.'

'I'll be fine,' I say, indulging again.

'Sure, until you wake up one morning and find you've only got one nostril,' she says.

Charles, Victoria and I sit back and enjoy the sensation. It blots out Marion's wifely nagging.

'That's good stuff,' says Charles, vaguely.

'Mmm,' says Victoria. She calls the maid who tops up our glasses of champagne.

'I was saying to Andrew that he should start his own business,' says Marion to Charles. I look at her, wondering if this is her revenge for my doing charlie. She ignores my expression of irritation and continues, 'I've told him that he's never going to make any money selling advertising space for some two-bit tabloid—'

'It's not a two-bit tabloid,' I tell her.

'Well, is he?' says Marion, ignoring the fact that Charles is high as a 747. 'I said he should try a little private enterprise. Get out and do something on his own.'

'Mmm,' says Charles in his usual non-committal way. Part of me hopes this will be the end of it but I would also be quite glad of Charles's input. He's absolutely loaded – of course – so how did he make it? Zapping through my coke-charged brain comes the thought that perhaps he needs an assistant or that he might have use for a sharp, presentable, enterprising . . . person.

Marion, clearly not in the least discouraged by Charles's total lack of interest, ploughs on. She keeps selling me to him, painting me out as a desperate, hard-up, no-hoper with a dead-end job and no prospects. I know I sold this story to her when we first met and it's probably true but I don't really want her to relay it to everyone.

Why doesn't she just ask me to do a jig and rattle a collecting tin at them? I'm sure we could find a stupified baby to shove in their faces while we're at it. Marion is studiously ignoring my protests and looking expectantly at Charles. Oh, for God's sake. It's one thing for Charles and Victoria to know that Marion pays for my dinner and travel but quite another to ask them to chip in.

'Marion, I don't think—'

Ever keen to pour oil on troubled water, Victoria chimes in, 'I'm sure Charles would be delighted to help. He knows lots of people in the business world.'

'Mmm,' says Charles, holding up his glass by the stem and watching the bubbles rise and burst.

We leave just after midnight and walk back home in silence. Marion knows she doesn't have to say anything more. Even more infuriatingly she is right – I can't sleep. I switch on the telly and tell her I'll be up a bit later.

'Look, I don't want you waking me up, tossing and turning all night.'

'OK,' I say, still looking at the telly. 'I'll go home.'

She waits for a while and then says, 'Just be quiet when you come up.' She turns off all the lights so that I'm left in darkness, apart from the harsh, ghostly glow of the box, and then goes up to bed.

After half an hour an idea comes to me. I decide to go back and see Charles and Victoria. I could do with some more fresh air anyway, so I pick up my keys and slip out. Without Marion giving the impression that my job at the paper consists of dragging a millstone in the basement to generate electricity for the building, I might be able to talk seriously to Charles.

'We're still on New York time,' he said as we left and

Victoria told us that we couldn't go already. 'We'll be up for ages.'

Perhaps there are other reasons for going back. I want to show that I am not just Marion's lap dog, that I am a person in my own right. Also, if I can get Victoria on her own for a moment and, though it will be difficult, get her to look at me and listen to what I am saying, I might be able ask her about Marion, the woman who hates where she came from and loves where she's going to.

I pause for a minute at the end of the street wondering how I'll introduce this subject. What *am* I doing? I consider just going back to Marion's and going to bed but I decide to go ahead. So I walk towards the house, rehearsing what I am going to say and, more importantly, how casually I'll say it. 'Thought I'd nip back for a nightcap if the offer's still on. Thanks, I'd love one. Left Marion sleeping. Yeah, bit of a night bird myself. Usually in bed by dawn. Ha ha.'

Just then I hear the growl and rattle of a cab coming down the street from the opposite direction. As it approaches Charles and Victoria's I stop dead still in the darkness between two street lamps. Two people get out and the taller one pays the driver. After a few seconds the cab moves on and the couple walk up the path and ring the bell. Charles opens the door and in the flood of light from the hall I see that the visitors are both young men: the shorter one looks Thai or something but the taller one I recognize immediately as Mark.

I walk back slowly and let myself in. I pour myself a whisky, flick on the telly and begin to watch some audience show where a blonde woman with a cockney accent is shoving a microphone in people's faces and they seem to be telling her when they've wet themselves in public. Then there is something with a hidden camera in a shop but I'm too tired to work out what the joke is supposed to be so I switch it off and go to bed.

The alarm wakes her up again. She swears and puts her head under the pillow. I lie back, looking at the ceiling for a moment, doing a systems check to see how terrible I feel. I've got a thumping head and my jaw aches as if I've been grinding my teeth all night. I take a deep breath, get up and go into the bathroom. In the bright light I look older, like Mark did that time when we met in the Gents at Claridges. Was he with Victoria or Charles last night? Or both? And where did the other guy fit it – literally – I wonder?

Suddenly going to the office and flogging column inches seems relatively easy and comfortable. I have a shave but realize I don't have time to shower. Marion has bought me a couple of new work shirts which are hanging up in my few inches of wardrobe space. I pick the blue one rather than a pink striped number which makes me look like a city trader. There are a couple of rather nice Hermès ties, too. Neither shirt nor tie go with with my suit but I don't really care.

I hack my hair down into place. Marion is now wandering around the bedroom in a huge dressing gown looking sleepy but cross.

'Morning,' I venture as I knot my tie.

'Morning,' she says, brushing her hair. 'You must feel terrible.'

I decide to humour her. 'Yeah, I do.' Actually, I do.

'You need some breakfast inside you,' she says as she leaves the room. I don't feel like breakfast and I certainly haven't got time, although the coffee and croissants smell pretty good. I put my shoes on, polish them on the back of my trousers while I adjust my tie and reach down for my watch.

It's gone.

I look around hastily as it dawns on me what has happened.

'It needs cleaning, that's all,' says Marion lightly when I ask her about it.

'It looked all right to me.'

'I think I'm more familiar with expensive timepieces than you.'

God, you love this, I think. She pours herself and then me some coffee.

'Can't stop for breakfast, I'm late already,' I say.

'But you need to eat something.'

I grab a croissant and notice that she is aiming her cheek at me. I bend down and kiss it.

She says nothing.

Somehow I know that the car won't be waiting outside for me this morning. I walk out of the mews but can't resist nipping back a few moments later just in time to see the huge BMW inching over the cobbled street from around the corner where it has been hiding.

As a dedicated clock-watcher, I miss my Rolex. I have to keep looking round at the clock on the office wall every few minutes instead. Early in the afternoon I ring Marion and tell her that I'm going to see an old mate for a drink so I won't be round tonight. I don't feel particlarly guilty after the theft of my watch and her frostiness this morning.

'Honey, won't I see you?' Her sweetness takes me aback slightly.

'Er, well, not tonight.'

'But I've booked a table at Scarafino's – just like our first date.'

'I'll see you tomorrow night, though.'

'Oh, don't leave her on her own tonight,' says my colleague Maria who seems to have magically appeared behind me, ostensibly handing out a memo.

I put my hand over the receiver and hiss 'Shut up' at her. She laughs and gives me a tragi-comic grimace.

'Who was that?' says Marion.

'Oh, no one, sorry. Look, can we go to Scarafino's tomorrow night?' There is a pause. 'Can't we?'

'OK,' says Marion briskly.

'I'll call you tonight, anyway,' I say.

'Sure,' she says. 'Have fun.'

Bloody hell, Marion. Steal my watch, take away my lift to work and then come on all luvvy duvvy. I don't believe there's any booking tonight at Scarafino's for us.

'Women!' I say to Sami.

'Men,' she snaps back.

Yes, we are bunch of shits, probably, but we can't help it, I think to myself as I leave the office early again.

Jane doesn't exactly look pleased to see me.

'I don't need a lift, thanks, anyway,' she says, walking briskly away from the Paperchase staff entrance.

'Good, because I haven't got a car,' I say, following her.

'Why not?'

'Gave it back,' I say. She can't help registering some

interest at this. Even though it was unplanned, I realize it was the right answer.

We walk on in silence for a while until she says, 'What do you want?'

'Take you for a drink.'

'Sorry, I'm running late.' We walk a bit further until she stops and says, 'Are you going to follow me home?'

I think about it. 'Perhaps.'

We walk on down the street and I'm beginning to wonder whether I should get on the Tube and go home with her, at least we would be able to talk in private. But just then she stops. She turns to look at me and already her face has softened slightly. She chews her lip for a moment while she considers the pathetic retrograde in front of her. I smile, gently wondering what I can say to give me five minutes.

'There's a bar round the corner we sometimes go to after work, it's usually pretty quiet.' She leads the way.

We order a half pint of Pimms each from a big, blonde Scandanavian girl. I have just enough money to pay for them. As we sit down at a quiet table near the window I decide to dive straight in.

'I'm sorry about that stupid stunt with the car the other day,' I say, playing with the fruit in my glass. 'I just wanted to talk to you.'

She snorts. 'Very tactful way to do it.'

'I know, it was really stupid. I wasn't trying to impress, I just thought we could spend some time together.'

'In *her* car.'

'Yeah,' I say, beaten on this. What the fuck was I thinking about? She seems to accept my complete capitulation.

'She must be pretty rich.'

'Her father gave it to her,' I hear myself saying.

'All right for some.'

'Yeah,' I smile, glad that she is sort of aligning us together on this one. Rich people, huh!

Jane takes a sip of her drink. 'Sorry, I lost my temper that day.'

'I don't blame you.'

'No, I shouldn't have stormed off, that was childish.' God, she's so sensible, so reasonable. 'I was just pissed off and tired.'

'I suppose Saturdays are always the busiest days, aren't they?' I ask, not the slightest bit interested but glad to move into a proper conversation.

'Erm,' she says, idly looking around the bar which is now filling up, 'it depends. Sometimes. I think that day was particularly bad because every customer was really complicated and foreign and also my boss was in a bad mood because she had a row with her boyfriend.'

'She shouldn't bring her love life into work with her.'

'Well, she can't help it, her boyfriend's the store manager.'

I laugh and so does she. She tells me about her manager's complicated love life and how she has to listen to her sob stories. 'She's got a husband and three kids at home in Stanmore.'

'No!'

'Yes,' says Jane, warming up to her tale. 'I said to her, "Doesn't he notice when you don't come home at night?" She said, "Well, he hasn't mentioned anything".' We both laugh again. I love the way Jane throws back her head when she laughs. For a girl who is so petite, she has a big, dirty laugh. 'Then there was this amazingly thick American woman—'

She looks at me mischievously. 'But I shouldn't be rude about Americans, should I?'

'Up to you.'

'She's American, isn't she?'

I decide to play it cool, see how much she knows – and how much she cares. 'Vinny told you that, did he?'

'Yes. I know you swore him to secrecy but Vinny's hopeless.' She looks serious for a moment. 'Don't take it out on him, will you?' I'm too busy wondering exactly how many beans Vinny has spilt. He did promise me he hadn't told her about my escort work. I would just die if Jane knew about that, I realize. But then she wouldn't be here if she did. I feel myself blushing at the thought and looking away.

I decide that I'll go so far as to tell her that I'm seeing the woman, which in Jane's feminist vocabulary probably includes 'girl' and that she does have a bit of money, hence the car but leave it at that. I won't tell her that Marion is older than me and I certainly won't tell her how we met. It occurs to me though that if Jane has interrogated Vinny about me, she must be interested.

'No, I won't take it out on him,' I smile. 'You really like Vinny, don't you?' Again, I'm glad to change the subject.

'Yeah, I do,' she says thoughtfully. 'He's so kind and I love his dry sense of humour. It's amazing, even now he can lead me on for hours before I realize what he's doing.'

'Yeah, I suppose he *is* quite funny in his own way.'

'All the girls at university adored him.'

'Really?' I think about it for a moment, decide women are too much of mystery to try and work out in one evening and ask, 'Did Vinny have any girlfriends? He never talks about them.'

She frowns thoughtfully. 'Not really. I think there was one girl he was very keen on. He always had lots of female friends. I don't think he's gay, though. I mean it wouldn't bother me if he was, I just don't think he is.'

'No,' I say and stir my drink with my straw. I realize that, having dealt with the car episode, I had better mention what I wanted to talk to her about if she hadn't stormed off; in other words what happened after our visit to the pub. 'The other night, after the pub,' I say but I realize that I don't know how to put it. 'That's actually what I wanted to talk to you about when . . .'

'Yes,' says Jane. 'We do need to talk . . . but . . . well . . . you know what I'm going to say.'

'No.'

'You do know!' Before I can think of a way to avoid mentioning Marion she says, 'There's your American.'

'We're just . . .'

'Just good friends?' Oh, we're not even that, Jane. It's a fling and not even a fun fling. Half the time I think Marion is running rings around me, laughing and plotting behind my back with her freakish friends. Demanding and suffocating one minute and cold and manipulative the next. Being with Jane feels so relaxed and uncomplicated.

But I'm painfully aware that there are things to be cleared up between us so I say, 'Sort of. Look, I'd really like to see you again.'

There is a pause. She smiles. 'OK, but if you're going out with somebody else, you've really got to sort that out first, haven't you?' Oh, Jane, you're so right. Have I ever got to sort this out.

'Well, we're not really going out, it's just a sort of . . . thing.'

'Sort of fling thing?'

Why isn't there a better word than fling? It sounds like one of us is being thrown across the room.

'It's a bit of fun.' That sounds worse so I try to explain. 'I suppose I'm sort of on the rebound after a long relationship at university.' Jane nods. 'Vinny told you about that as well, didn't he?' She nods again, unembarrassed. 'What's your job at Paperchase, interrogations?'

She laughs and then begins to pick some more wax off the candle holder on the table between us. 'So she's just a rebound . . . fling thing?'

It doesn't sound very nice.

'Well, I suppose I just decided that I should just get out more, see some girls.' I wait for some reaction to my shallow, blokish confession but Jane's too good a listener for that. She raises her eyebrows sympathetically. 'But it's going nowhere. Worse than nowhere. I'd have finished it even if I hadn't met you.'

'Well,' she says, rolling up the remainder of the wax and putting it neatly at the foot of the bottle. 'You're the only one who can do that – if you really want to, that is.'

'I do.' We both take a sip. 'I . . . ' I have to say this. 'I must say, I didn't think I was your type, though.'

Jane looks surprised.

'My type?' She laughs. 'What's my *type*?' But I want her to answer the question. 'All right, when I first met you I thought you were such a smug yuppie, that you really fancied yourself but you're actually quite funny, like I said. And . . . well, I suppose Vinny convinced me.'

'Vinny?'

'Yep, I suppose you've got Vinny to thank,' she says. 'I thought you were so smart-arsed and knew you were good looking.' For some stupid reason I feel myself blushing, so I look down at the table and play with an imaginary bit of fluff. Jane continues mercilessly. 'Well, you know you are. You can't help it. I think that's why sometimes you come across as ultra cool, sort of aloof, when people first meet you, when we first met, that night. You're just shy, I suppose. Bit self conscious.' She takes my silence as assent. 'It must be a bit of nuisance actually – girls falling for you for the most superficial reason.'

I laugh, embarrassed.

'But you fell for me for a deep, serious reason.'

'Not really. And you and Vinny are really funny together. Your football game.' Oh God, good old One A Side Indoor Footy – whatever happened to that? 'He's a huge fan of yours.'

'What?'

'He is. He really looks up to you. He loves the fact that you share that flat together. He thinks it's really cool. Oh, you know how boys hero-worship each other but you two are sweet together.'

'Perhaps I should go out with him, then.'

She rolls her eyes but she can tell I need more convincing.

'For instance, he was so grateful when you sorted out his tax thing, or something?'

'What? Oh, that.' Earlier in the year Vinny had decided the best way to deal with a demand from the Inland Revenue for some freelance work he had done was to put it behind the toaster for a few months. Then he received another official letter and got incredibly worked up about the whole thing so I sent it to my brother-in-law who knows about tax and grown-up things and he sorted it out without any charge.

'He was so relieved and so grateful,' continues Jane. God, Vinny's weird – it really was no big deal. 'I just thought that was really kind. So, despite all my reservations, Vinny won me round and made me think that if I did like you, there was actually a good reason for it. It wasn't just that you looked like you'd walked out of a glossy magazine.'

'Well, I suppose I should be grateful, then. Good old Vinny,' I say, bemused. 'To Vinny.' We clink glasses and finish our drinks. I want to kiss her again and she realizes it so she looks away.

'But like I said, it's really up to, you've got to decide.' I consider the truth of this observation, once again. I'm sure instead of 'decide' she means 'chuck her'.

'Would you like another?' I ask.

Without checking her watch she says, 'I should be making a move. I'm going out tonight.' She looks me in the eye for a moment and then reaches over and runs a finger down my cheek and over my mouth. It tickles slightly and makes me smile. I look down at my empty glass. She gets up and picks up her bag. I get up too, realizing I have half a hard-on.

'You can come if you want.'

'Sorry?'

'Tonight.'

A date? I like the idea of seeing Jane on a proper date. A few drinks, a bit of music, some food – why not? But am I ready to be introduced to the friends yet? There'll be the usual quick ring round the next morning for feedback. I suddenly feel very nervous. Jane's friends would probably hate me. I'd probably hate them.

'Erm . . .'

'Actually, you'd hate it. We're going to a pub.'

'I don't mind pubs. We went to a pub that night, *the* night.'

'Yeah and you looked like a fish out of water, mineral water.'

'Ha, ha.'

'No,' says Jane slowly. 'But you'd probably hate my friends.'

'Why?'

'You just would.' We look at each other, both realizing that the Judgement of The Friends is a bit premature.

'Here, I'll walk you as far as the Tube station at least.'

She laughs and squeezes my arm.

'Thank you,' she says.

On the way to the Tube station Jane tells me what she has against James Bond and his treatment of women.

'He is pretty sexist, I suppose, but everyone was in those days,' I say. Then, for good measure I add: 'They didn't know any better.'

'It's not just the way he treats women as a bit of totty,' says Jane enthusiastically. 'Of course, he smacks them on the bum and sends them away like the woman who's been massaging him by the pool at the beginning of *Goldfinger* or the way he slaps them around to get information out of them. It's the way women die around him.'

'Do they?'

'Yes, especially after a sexual encounter. He shags that woman in *Goldfinger* and then she is painted with gold and dies. In *From Russia with Love* he pushes the woman he is dancing with in front of an assassin's bullet to protect himself. He's always doing it.'

'Yeah, but women are always getting killed in action movies, even today.'

'No,' says Jane, exasperated. 'The thing about Bond movies is the juxtaposition of sex and death. They're just glorified snuff movies, really.' I suddenly feel slightly concerned that Jane is some kind of Bond anorak but I'm also impressed – she is the only girl I've ever met who uses words like juxtaposition without thinking about it. Her face lights up. 'Actually, it's not just sex – even with marriage,' she says. 'Look at *On Her Majesty's Secret Service*. George Lazenby and Diana Rigg tie the knot at the end and she is shot immediately after. And- and when he marries that Japanese woman in *Dr No* she gets poisoned by having stuff trickled down that thread while she and Sean Connery are lying in their matrimonial bed together.'

'Well, they couldn't have a *married* James Bond, could they?'

'Why go through the whole ceremony, then? Or he could ask her and she could say no.'

'How do you know so much about James Bond films anyway? You seen them all?'

'*Everyone's* seen them all. I just look at them more closely than most people, think about them more.'

'He is a bastard,' I mutter admiringly.

Jane looks at me for a moment. 'Yeah, he is'

CHAPTER SIXTEEN

IRONICALLY AFTER MY EXCUSE to Marion and, as it happens, very conveniently for my battle-scarred conscience, I do end up seeing an old mate that night. As I walk back down Tottenham Court Road, lost in thought about Jane and how I break it to Marion, I literally bump into a guy I was at university with.

After an initial exchange of irritable muttering we recognize each other.

'Fuckin' 'ell,' he says, by way of greeting.

'Jesus, long time no see,' I say in reply.

We end up in a pub round the corner. Pete mimes a drink.

'Oh, cheers,' I say, aware I've got hardly any money at all. 'Pint of lager.'

He gets them in. The two girls at the bar look round at me. I smile at them but then look round quickly to see where Pete is with the drinks. I wish I could do the flirting thing better.

After the usual update of common friends, a discussion about work and how crap our bosses are, shouted above the noise, we commandeer a newly vacated table in a quieter corner and he asks me about my love life. I know he never liked Helen. None of my friends did.

'You're well shot of that smug, dreary cow,' he told me once when we met for a drink just after I'd split up with her. Then he looked at me, frowning quizzically through an alcohol-fogged brain. 'You haven't married her, have you?'

On this occasion I find myself telling him all about Marion. Well, nearly all. I tell him we met when she was buying tea in Fortnum & Mason.

'And you were shoplifting,' he suggests. My casually being in Fortnum & Mason must sound a bit odd so I tell him I was buying a present for my parents.

'And she's older, and rich?'

'Very rich,' I say.

'Kin' 'ell,' says Pete, thoughtfully.

I tell him, matter of factly, a bit about our trips and the restaurants we go to. I want to reassure myself that I've been very lucky so far, that it might just be worth hanging in there.

''Kin 'ell, mate,' he says. 'You jammy bastard.' I laugh at just how incredibly wrong he is. Then he says, 'How old *is* she? And what's she like, you know, physically? It's not . . .' He mimes two grotesquely low-slung breasts.

'No, very good nick.'

'You're laughing, then.'

I am *so* not laughing. I tell him about Jane.

'So you're shagging the rich old one but you'd like to be shagging the young one.'

'Yep.'

'Does the young one know about the other one, then?'

'She knows I'm sort of seeing someone else but she doesn't know any more than that. I told her I wanted to finish it.'

'Then tell her you've finished it, see her when you want and keep the old one going on the side. Want another?' He shakes an empty glass at me, obviously abandoning the hope that I'll offer. Wish I could, Pete.

'But that's not really fair on either of them,' I say, desperately playing devil's advocate. Come up with a good answer, Pete, please.

''Kin 'ell, mate, life's *not* fair,' says Pete, getting up. I watch him push his way through to the bar, a young man in a middle-aged suit and tie, the crushing burden of life, a man's life, weighing down on his already stooped shoulders. Accepting his lot with unspoken, unthinking good grace. Poor sod.

I can't do that. I just can't.

We go for a Chinese which I manage to squeeze onto my one remaining credit card and spend a couple of happy hours reminiscing about university and discussing the meaning of life and whether you can have kids and live in London. We end up analysing areas of London in which you could conceivably afford to live, followed by towns and villages in the south east and relevant commuting distances as we try and identify some urban nirvana which will give us a half-decent lifestyle within our pathetic budgets.

Afterwards, we walk down to Cambridge Circus and part there, promising not to leave it so long next time. I manage to get a bus back home. I'd really love a taxi but financially that is out of the question as the cash machine confirms. 'Do you require another service?' it asks very helpfully, having denied me any actual cash. Yes, I'd like to order a new cheque book and get home on that.

My eyes are closing and my head is lolling against the vibrating window when, after a couple of stops two couples get on, clambering up the stairs unsteadily, the girls squealing and falling about onto the men. Once they've decided who is sitting where they continue the argument they've been having and then one of the girls says to me, "'Scuse me. Can I ask you something?'

The men start to shout her down but she persists. 'No, no, let's ask him. He's another bloke, right? OK, if you were in a relationship, yeah? And you met a girl in a bar and you really fancied her, no, no, let's just hear what he thinks, OK? And you really fancied this girl and thought you were getting somewhere with her, would you, you know, shag her and not feel, like, guilty?' The two men start arguing again but she ignores them. 'Or would you do it and tell your girlfriend and say you were really sorry?'

'It wasn't *like* that,' one of the men tells her but she keeps looking at me expectantly.

'So, do I know the girl?' I ask, still half-asleep.

'No. Never met her before.' The others stop talking.

'Well, if I didn't know her and I didn't think we'd ever meet again . . .'

'There you go,' says one of the boys triumphantly.

'No, let him finish,' says the girl, willing me to say the right thing.

'If I didn't think we'd ever meet again,' I say, thinking carefully, 'I'd go back to hers, but then when she was in the loo or making coffee or something . . .'

'Yeah?' she says, beginning to smile and half-turning to one of the boys.

'. . . I'd steal everything I could lay my hands on and get out of there.'

The house is silent when I get back. Vinny must be in bed. I was hoping he would still be up. Knackered though I am, I could do with a quick game of One A Side Indoor Footy. Instead I fall into bed and finally get to sleep after tossing and turning for what seems like hours.

Coming from someone so sensible and, well, ordinary, Pete's advice seems pretty sound. And it was good to have a drink with Jane, a normal date with a girl. Besides, I'm just going nowhere with Marion and Jane won't wait forever.

But then I remember Pete pushing his way through the crowd in the pub, his life set out before him as if he were a rat in a maze. No way out. No chance of winning. Perhaps I should just stick to my plan, even if it has been modified to involve doing something in business to make some money, as Marion and Charles and I were discussing that night. Be ruthless. Anything to avoid Pete's fate. Yeah, there'll be other girls like Jane. If Jane and I got married we'd end up living in a tiny flat until we could afford to move to a tiny house in Woking and I'd commute until I was old enough to follow her round Sainsbury's and fuck up the house, with unnecessary DIY.

Ruthless, Mark said. Ruthless or hopeless. Fuck it. I'll spend a month with Marion and if she still doesn't give me something worth having, I'll end it. After all, she'll find another bit of arm candy and I'll do something with Charles or else find someone who *will* give me that tiny bit of their enormous pile of cash that will allow me to avoid Pete's fate.

But I could never have a really relaxed evening or a boys' night out like I had with Pete, for instance, if I was living with Marion, I realize, spreading myself out under my own duvet. On the other hand, I won't get anything serious from her unless I do move in.

My thoughts are running on ahead of me, all over the place, like a yelping dog let off its lead in a park.

I am finally being pulled down into unconsciousness when the phone rings. There is nothing more unnerving than a phone echoing through the house in the middle of the night. I consider ignoring it for a moment and then decide to answer it, hoping it's not my mum or dad with bad news. More likely it's Marion ringing to tell me to come over. Or never to come over again. I stumble into the kitchen just as Vinny's door is opening.

'I'll get it,' I say to the silent darkness. I pick up the phone and whisper, 'Hello.'

'Andrew?' says a man's voice urgently.

Scared, I say, 'Yeah. Who's that?'

'It's me, Jonathan.'

'Oh, right,' I say, squinting at the clock on the cooker. Quarter to three.

'I haven't spoken to you for ages. How are you?' Jonathan says casually.

'Well, I'm asleep, since you ask.'

'Yeah, sorry about that. Listen, I've got a great job for you. Really easy and just round the corner from you in Chelsea.'

'What? Now?' I remember the sheer horror of the poor little rich girl a few weeks ago.

'Yep,' Jonathan gives a desperate little laugh. 'This is the time people feel like it.' Feel like what? Talking? I certainly don't. I fold my arms, the phone clamped under my chin and my eyes closed. I can almost sense already how awful I am going to feel tomorrow morning.

'Jonathan, I'm really sorry, I've got work tomorrow. I'm so tired—'

'Five hundred quid, Andrew,' he almost sings.

'What?'

'I said five hundred quid – and it's in cash this time. Still feeling tired?' he asks. I'm feeling dead to the world but five hundred quid is five hundred quid. In cash, too.

'Why cash?'

'Regular client, we have an arrangement.'

I think about it for a moment. 'What do I have to do?'

Jonathan's voice changes back to its old self. 'Well,' he says gently, like a careers master, 'the client's an old guy—'

'An old *guy*? Oh no—'

'Don't worry, there's a girl there too. He lives in Chelsea, just off Sloane Avenue, take you ten minutes this time of night in a cab, and the girl he's got there is called, er . . .' I can hear him check a piece of paper. 'Vivienne. And he just wants to watch you and Vivienne, you know, mess around together.'

'Mess around together?'

Jonathan's voice changes again, 'Yeah, play Scrabble! What do you think?'

Still half-asleep I take a moment to consider what he is saying. 'But when we met you said, sex wasn't—'

I hear Jonathan mutter 'Jesus' under his breath. Then he hisses, 'Who gives a fuck what I said back then? What are you? A fucking choir boy? Do you wanna earn five hundred quid tonight – cash – or not?'

I can't believe this is the same guy with the ready smile and the floppy hair I met a few weeks ago in his Fulham flat.

'OK, OK.' I think quickly, wide awake now. This is prostitution, isn't it? I'm going to be a rent boy. Like Mark. But five hundred quid. Cash. More than I have got out of Marion, more than a week's salary. Oh, what the fuck! Just mess around. I can do that. Whatever it means. Never mind, play it by ear. Can't be that bad. Despite my conversation with Mark, part of me always knew that this was coming. It's a fine line which I was never going to cross. But five hundred quid. I guess I have my price. 'What's the address?'

'Good boy,' coos Jonathan. He gives it to me, tells me to get going and rings off. I press the button down and then call a cab. I put on some clean underpants, my jeans and a T-shirt and go outside to wait for it.

After about ten minutes I notice a silver Skoda drawing up, the driver peering out to check the house number. I jerk my head at him. Who else would be hanging around outside at this time of night? The car is warm and stuffy and sweet-smelling. I'm glad of the heat because for some reason I'm shivering. I slide into the furry passenger seat and say, 'Hi.'

'Hi,' says the driver uncomfortably. I give him the address and we speed off. I'm trying to work out a story in case he asks where the hell I am going at this time of night but he just turns up the radio – some Greek station – and stares straight ahead. Above the overflowing ashtray, next to the 'No Smoking' sign are two pictures, a pretty girl taken at a party and a fuzzy picture of a baby in its cot. Around them hangs a chain with a tiny gold St Christopher.

We find the mews easily and crawl along it until we come to the right house. I push a five-pound note into his hand and say thanks. He says nothing and begins to reverse slowly over the cobbles.

I ring the door bell. There is a pause and I panic for a moment that Jonathan has given me the wrong address.

Fucking embarrassing to wake someone up at this time of night – especially around here. They'd probably ring the police, I'd get arrested and have to try and explain what I am doing. Name, address and phone number. Vinny answering the phone and wondering what the hell is going on . . .

Bolts are being drawn and the door is opened on a chain. A girl with blonde hair piled messily up high and a lot of make-up looks up at me menacingly.

'Oh, excuse me—' She slams the door in my face. Oh fuck. I turn to see if the mini cab is still here but then the door opens again, wider this time, and the girl stands back for me to enter. Despite feeling tired, ill and suddenly very nervous, I walk in, smile and say hello the way I have done before, the way I think Jonathan would expect me to.

'Didn't they tell you to leave taxi at top o' t'mews,' she snaps in a thick Yorkshire accent.

'Er, no.'

She tuts.

'Got any drugs?' she says leading me through a small white and gold marbled hallway into an even tinier kitchen. I can see that her dress is only half zipped up at the back.

'Sorry?'

'Drugs? You boys usually 'ave 'em.'

'Sorry, no one told me,' I say like a boy scout. What 'boys'?

She tuts again and opens the fridge. 'Champagne or beer or—' She peers into it, scrunching up her face which is quite pretty under all the powder. 'Or whatever you want, but if you want a Bloody Mary or owt like that you'll have to make it yourself.'

'Whatever's open.'

Without saying anything she picks up a tall, heavy glass, thrusts it into my hand and pours champagne into it until it drips over my fingers.

'Thanks,' I say, licking some of the froth off my fingers. She takes something from behind the cappuccino machine. It's an envelope. She half-pulls some fifty pounds notes out of it.

'That's your five hundred plus another two,' she says, shaking the notes in my face. 'Extra. If you do a good job.' She puts it back and makes towards a spiral staircase, slipping her stilettos off as she goes.

'Hang on a minute,' I say, finally catching my breath. 'It's you and me, right?'

She tuts and rolls her eyes. 'See this house?' She nods in the direction of the sitting room. 'Ten of 'em like this. He owns the whole bloody mews,' she hisses, as if that is supposed to explain what we are going to do. 'Just look as if you're having the fuck o' your life and don't worry about me – I'll make the right noises.'

I follow her up the tiny spiral staircase trying not to trip up or bang my head. I realize that my hand is shaking slightly on the rail. We emerge into a bedroom which covers the whole upper floor of the house. It is lined with black wood, mirrored cupboards and a thick, cream coloured shag pile carpet. The lights are on low and the place is full of shadows. I can make out an empty champagne bottle lying on the floor next to an ashtray and a handbag. Most of the room is taken up by a huge bed which is covered with a white fur bedspread. It looks as if there is a dead pig on it. In fact it is a fat bloke lying on his stomach, his head hanging over the edge.

Vivienne strokes his scraggly grey hair and then runs her hand down his hairy back to his huge fat bum which is also covered with grey hair.

'Wake up, love,' she says tenderly. 'Look what I've brought you.'

He grunts and stirs and then squints at her, taking a moment to remember who she is. Then he says, 'What have you brought me, Viv, my love?'

'A young stud,' says Viv. Hang on – that's me. I try to smile seductively but I feel more like a future son-in-law than a panting sex machine. He stares up at me. So does Viv, giving me a look of 'Oh, put your back into it.' His face is like the rest of his body, bulging, sagging and pink with wisps of grey hair. His huge bloodshot eyes struggle to focus on me and as they do so his fat fingers, with their heavy gold rings, grasp the bedcover tightly. Only a chunky gold identity bracelet shows where the fur ends and the grey hair of his forearms begins. He farts and belches and then his head drops down on to the bed again. I look at Viv for guidance.

'My love,' she says to him. The old man mumbles something. 'What did you say, my darling?'

229

He moves his head out of the furry bedcovers and and say, 'Tell him to take his clothes off.'

She looks up at me. 'Well, you heard what he said.' I freeze for a moment. Obviously I knew from the start this was going to happen from the time Jonathan first told me about the job but standing here with these two it feels even weirder than I thought it would. 'Go on,' she says again, like I'm a bit slow.

My hands tremble even more as I pull off my T-shirt. I stop at my underpants. Viv rolls her eyes. '*All* your clothes, he wants to see what you've got for me.' I take a deep breath and slip off my underpants with all the erotic finesse of a man facing an army medical. The old guy is watching me now. I feel very vulnerable, I have to stop myself from covering my dick with my hands.

'He's big,' coos the man. 'You've done well, my dear.' I'm feeling slightly sick by now.

'Ye-e-e-s,' says Vivienne. 'He's a big boy.'

'Vivienne,' says the man, like the presenter of a 1950s TV programme to a guest who brought a baby tiger cub in to show the children, 'will you show me what you do to boys like this.' Viv gets up and fixes me with a mean, sneering look. Then she kicks off her shoes, drops to her knees and takes my dick in her mouth. I gasp more with surprise than pleasure and the client looks up at me. Then Vivienne begins to make groaning noises. She starts to dig her long, sharp nails into my bum, out of spite, I think, rather than desire. I decide I'd better make an effort if I want that five hundred, no, *seven* hundred pounds. I say it to myself again. In cash. I start to moan too and move rhythmically in and out of Viv's mouth.

'Mmmm,' says Viv from down below.

'Oh y-e-a-h,' I gasp, hoping it sounds genuine. But my voice is shaking slightly.

'Oh, yes,' says the little piglet enthusiastically, as if he were endorsing a motion at the Residents' Association meeting. It's actually the least surreal conversation we have had all evening. After a while he seems to get bored.

'Vivienne?' he asks politely.

She looks round at him, still with her mouth full.

'Vivienne? What else can he do?'

She stands up. 'Shall we show him?' I look at her dumbly.

She slips off her dress, bra and panties very quickly while the piglet and I watch. When she stands naked I notice that her pubic hair is blonde with tiny black roots.

'There's a condom in the draw, stud,' she says. I pull open the drawer, take out a condom, tear open its packet with difficulty (I am sure Viv rolls her eyes at this point). For some reason I *have* got a hard on. It's as if my dick is betraying me. Shouldn't it feel revolted and appalled by this whole thing? Apparently not. I roll the condom on while they both watch. When I look up again Viv is moving onto the bed.

'You like it doggy style, don't you, Viv?' says the piglet. This time even I can tell that he means, 'I don't care how you like it, Viv, I'm paying.'

'Oh, *yes*,' murmurs Viv, moving onto all fours next to him on the bed. She pouts and inserts a long red fingernail into her mouth. 'That's the way I like it,' she gasps and I realize this is an invitation to me to get to work.

I move over towards her. But I can't do it. My dick has finally got the message. This isn't right – worse, it's just disgusting. No amount of money is worth this, in fact the idea of the money suddenly makes me feel even more dirty.

Viv looks round irritably to see why our little live show, audience of one, has stalled. I stare at the floor, trying to avoid her eyes. But Viv, obviously quick-thinking and resourceful, has nimbly backed on to me and is apparently enjoying great sex, moaning and arching her back. I stand there, numb, wondering whether it looks convincing to our client or whether he just wants it to. But then I notice that the old git has slumped forward with his eyes closed again.

'K-c-n?' Viv whispers in ecstasy. No reaction. 'Ken?' she groans again, louder this time. 'Ken?' Her tone changes to one of irritation. '*Ken?*' She reaches across and pokes him roughly. 'He's off at last,' she says. 'Thank fook for that. What's the matter wi' you, anyway, you're not fooking being paid just to stand there, you gormless twat,' she says, pulling off a false eyelash while reaching across to the ashtray for her ciggie which is now mainly ash. She takes a drag and picks some ash out of her pubes. Just then Ken wakes again and looks round at us. Instantly Viv is back in position and in ecstasy again, gasping and squealing this time. But this time I move away. I don't even want to touch her. I stand back against the wall, breathing hard. Feeling dizzy. Feeling disgusted. Trapped.

'Come back, my love,' murmurs Viv, giving me a furious look.

I just stare at her for a moment.

'What's the matter, young stud?' says Ken, also slightly pissed off that his purchase isn't doing what he bought it for.

I don't say anything – what can I say? I look at them both lying on the bed. I realize that they are almost the same colour. Pale, pink, insipid. Ugly. So very, very ugly. Like me. We're all so very ugly. I just reach down quickly and find my underpants.

''Ang on,' says Viv, getting up.

'We haven't finished yet,' says the piglet, as if I was a waiter trying to take his plate away.

I open my mouth to say something – excuse, abuse – but nothing comes out. My underpants are on at last and so is my T-shirt, distorted and wrapped around my body in my panicked haste. I throw my trainers down the spiral stairs and follow them, tripping and falling down the last few steps. Sprawled at the bottom, I pull my jeans on, and without doing them up get up again and run into the kitchen.

'Oi,' says Viv from above me. I don't look up. I reach round behind the capuccino maker for the envelope. I'm entitled to at least *some* of that money.

It's not there.

Where the fuck is it? I'm *sure* she put it back there. I ferret around quickly to see if it's somewhere else but then I hear the stairs start creaking behind me. I have one last desperate thrash around on the shelf and send glass jars of coffee and tea bags together with a full wine glass crashing onto the floor. No good, it's not fucking there. Suddenly I feel a couple of notes, two fifties, a hundred quid. Fuck it, that'll do. It'll have to.

I skid on the mess and then make a run for the door.

'He's taken money, the robbin' cunt,' I hear Viv screech behind me. This brings the old man to his feet and I hear the staircase creak as it takes his weight. I manage to slide the bolts of the front door back and throw it open before they get to the glass-embedded mess on the kitchen floor.

I run out into the mews still carrying my trainers. I sprint down the empty, darkened street towards what looks like a main road. The sound of Viv screeching pain and swearing about a cut foot reaches me but I also hear the man running behind me. He is silent. And somehow that's worse.

I keep running long after I know the man has given up. He must either be naked or wearing only a robe anyway so he can't go far. I just want to keep on. I stop and sit down on the pavement, conscious of the few people around at this time of night staring at me discreetly – intrigued but desperate not to get involved.

I quickly put my trainers on, realizing that I must have left my socks behind.

I start to walk back home.

CHAPTER SEVENTEEN

THE NEXT MORNING I LIE IN BED for a moment wondering whether I dreamt the whole of last night. A cross between a nightmare and a wet dream. Even after a long hot shower I can still smell Viv on me. I find myself wondering: do people like that have no shame? That man presumably buys sex whenever he wants, just as if he were buying dinner or a holiday. Last night he bought me. Do I have no shame, anymore? Viv and I were both prostitutes last night. And if you come from a nice middle class home and have a degree in business studies and wear a suit, what excuse do you have for doing that?

As I stare up at the ceiling, wide awake, now more awake than I've been for a long time, another thought dawns on me. What *is* the difference between me and Marion and Viv and the piglet? There is one, isn't there? There must be. Just what the fuck is it?

I turn over and hug the pillow as if a different position will produce different logic. What's really funny is that however uncomfortable and disgusted I feel, I don't feel tired this morning. It takes me a while to get used to this new sensation. Sleepy yes, but not tired. Yesterday morning I felt more knackered than when I'd hit the sack and today I should feel worse than ever but instead I feel well rested and strangely relaxed. I look around the room and notice how light it is. And it's not just lighter than normal, it's the quality of the light that is different.

Why isn't my clock radio on?

I sit up. It's very quiet. No echo of Vinny's radio downstairs, no showers on anywhere, no cars queuing up the street to get into the main road. The day has a sort of used feel, it's lost that early morning rawness and got into its stride – without me.

Oh my God!

I take a deep breath and look round at the clock radio. It's 1.23 p.m.

1.23 p.m.? How the hell could it have got so late? I haven't just overslept, I've been entombed. I leap up and look around for my clothes. Suddenly the room is moving around me. I sit down on the edge of the bed again and put my head in my hands. I feel better and then it occurs to me that I'm so late there is no real point in hurrying. I may as well take my time. I breath deeply and stretch a bit, trying to touch the ceiling. I put on a T-shirt and wander downstairs to make a cup of tea. There is some post on the mat but none of it is for me or Vinny, for that matter.

I put the kettle on and try and decide what to tell the office – I'll just have to be honest and tell them, I mean her, Debbie, that is, that I completely and utterly overslept. She's more likely to believe that than some story about unreliable plumbers or sudden illnesses.

I pour boiling water on a tea bag and watch it swell and surface for a moment. Still half asleep, I dredge it out with a spoon and flick it across the floor into the sink, where it lands with a satisfying splat, leaving a trail of dark brown spots across the floor and up the cupboard door.

I pour in some milk and stab the wet spoon into the bag of sugar. After a couple of sips I look across at the phone, sitting menacingly on the kitchen table. I hate that thing. It's like an evil envoy from the outside world. If it didn't exist I could just close the door and keep everyone out. I notice that the light is flashing on the answer machine. I wander over, just too out of it to be bothered with any of this and press 'play'. The first message is from Sami.

'Andrew? Andrew? Hello? Are you there?' There is a pause. 'Oh, Andrew? Where the hell are you? Please pick up the phone. Please.' She clicks off. She sounds so worried, so concerned that I feel a spasm around my lips, like I almost want to cry. Sorry, Sami, I wish I wasn't putting you through this.

There is a beep and it's Claire's voice.

'Andrew, it's Claire, it's, um, nearly a quarter to eleven. Obviously we're just wondering where you are and if you could make contact just to let us know that everything is all right and there is no reason to worry I'd be very grateful. I don't seem to have you booked out on annual leave today but if you could just give me a ring, that would be very helpful. Thanks. Bye.'

Oh, fuck off, you smug bitch.

There is another beep and it's Marion.

'Andrew, I called you at the office but they said you weren't there. It's a quarter after eleven. I want to make arrangements for this evening. Call me on my mobile.'

Her message just goes right through me. I just can't really think about Marion or what I'm doing this evening. I've just had enough. I take another gulp of tea, the machine beeps again and Debbie's voice comes on.

'Andrew. It's twelve-thirty. Where are you? Could you either give me a call or come into the office. Thanks,' she says evenly. There is no message from Jonathan, thank God. Presumably Viv and the pig decided that it was not worth making a fuss over £100.

I ring Sami but she's out at lunch so I tell someone I don't know that I've overslept and I'm on my way in. It sounds like it's their first day and they're so polite that I feel like adding, 'By the way, have you *any* idea how much trouble I'm in?'

I decide to have a shower and wash my hair – since I'm so incredibly late anyway, half an hour extra won't make any difference. I have a couple of pieces of toast and another cup of tea standing in the kitchen, still trying to come round properly and then set off. My suit and shirt feel odd on me, perhaps because I'm not used to putting them on halfway through the day. Needless to say, I have to wait ages for a bus and when I finally walk into the office it is gone half-past three and I don't know why I bothered.

Sami doesn't see me because she's on the phone but Claire just says lightly, 'Oh, hi. Debbie wants a word, let me just see if she's free.' Debbie is on the phone so I have an agonizing wait until she finishes her call. Sami sees me and looks up with a mixture of anger and concern. I mouth 'overslept' and she gives me a desperate look. She is just telling the person on the phone to hang on a minute when Debbie calls me in. I shrug my shoulders, smile apologetically and go into Debbie's office.

It all happened very quickly. I thought I'd just get a

bollocking as usual but when Debbie said she wanted me to resign 'for all our sakes' I didn't argue.

She was right: I had pushed it too far. I could have asked for another chance and told her quite honestly that I had genuinely overslept this time, but to tell the truth I just couldn't be bothered. I was fed up with the lying and the atmosphere and the constant strain of trying to work out new excuses for getting time off. I was fed up with rehearsing my arguments with her and trying to justify myself to her. I was fed up with constantly being on the verge of being sacked. Debbie had finally won.

I wrote a brief letter to confirm my resignation and the terms we'd agreed and put it on Debbie's desk. She looked up at me as if she was about to say something but I just walked out. I thought about apologizing for the trouble I'd caused but really I never wanted to see her again. I started clearing out my desk and then realized that there wasn't anything to clear out – I didn't actually own any of this shit and I certainly didn't want it. Sami's chin was trembling as she tried to force back tears. She looked so much like a seven-year-old being brave that I couldn't help smiling – which was probably what stopped me from crying. I touched her arm and she started to sob, then I muttered 'Sorry' and she ran out of the office. Another girl caught my eye across the room and tried to look sympathetic. That really did make me laugh. She looked slightly confused.

As I walked out of the office for the last time I heard Claire say something about my P45 being in the post. How many times had we joked about that?

I walk most of the way home. My only thought is 'Oh God, I've got to take my suit off again – I only put it on five minutes ago.' I pop into the corner shop, Knightsbridge Food & Wine, and then drop the thin, striped polythene bag of milk and orange juice in the hallway, drift into the living room and flop down in the armchair. I switch the telly on. A black and white film with Kenneth More, then a quiz show with a contestant wearing a tie and a V-neck pullover. By the end of the programme he has won £25. He seems quite pleased. Then I switch over and it is the news: pictures of women in veils wailing at the camera and later a long shot of people walking down Oxford Street.

Suddenly it's evening. I decide to go for a run. I haven't done it for ages. It'll do me good. Wake me up. Help me to think through what I should do next.

I tip the dirty laundry basket upside down and find my sweat pants. I pull on my trainers, a T-shirt from this morning and set off. At first it feels awful – legs like lead, heart racing. I've forgotten how to do it. I pass some girls on the other side of the road and I decide they must have had a laugh even though I can't hear them do it. But after a while as I get back into the old rhythm a bit more I begin to enjoy it. The sweat starts to run down my face, into my eyes, blurring my vision. The pumping of blood and the roar of my breath shut out the noise around me. Belting down the quiet streets, breathing hard and sweating, I feel completely calm, for the first time since I don't know when.

Even though I'm not as fit as the last time I ran a few months ago, I push myself hard and after I've done my old circuit, I carry on. I go back round the park into some nearby streets I've never been down before.

Finally I begin to make my way back. Gasping and wheezing. I put the key in the lock and run upstairs, collapsing on top of the clothes I'd scattered from the dirty laundry basket. The room is spinning slightly and my heart is thumping through my ribcage but I feel much better.

I have a shower and feel strangely calm and relaxed. Marion rings from the car while I am drying my hair.

'Hi, honey. You have a good time last night with your *mate*?' She articulates the word not just as an absurd piece of English slang, but as if it were totally absurd that I should have any mates at all. 'Where'd you go?' she asks reproach-fully but I don't rise to it.

'Yeah, it was fun. We just went for a few beers and a Chinese,' I say flatly.

'Sounds thrilling. Anyway, I'm on my way to Lord and Lady Caterham's for drinks but I'll be back around eight-thirty so I'll call you then and we'll go eat some place, OK?'

'Sure.'

'Hey, guess who I saw today?'

'Who?'

'I was having lunch with an old friend at Joe's Café and I bumped into Farrah. She was raving about you. So charming, so good looking, she said. Anyway she wants us to go over for dinner next week.'

'Great.'

'You sound a bit down, everything OK? Still feeling hungover from all that charlie?'

I take a deep breath and tell her. 'Marion, I got sacked from work today. I overslept and when I went in they sacked me.'

'Sacked? What does "sacked" mean? Fired?'

'Yeah.'

'Oh God! You'll need cheering up tonight.'

'Cheering up? Just a bit. What the hell am I going to do?' But she is telling the driver something about parking.

'Look, I'll call you about eight-thirty and we'll talk about it then. OK. Kisses.'

'Yeah, bye.'

I put on a rugby shirt and my oldest jeans and get a beer out of the fridge. There is another game show on telly and I realize I have started answering some of the questions so I turn over quickly. Vinny comes in.

'Evening all.' Funny thing about me and Vinny, we've lived together for very nearly a year now, seen each other naked, seen each other ill, made tea for each other, dragged each other up to bed when we've been too pissed to put one foot in front of the other but we hardly ever call each other by our first names. 'All', 'mate', 'sunny Jim', 'dog breath', even surnames, but never our first names.

'Hi,' I say.

He disappears into the kitchen and comes back a few moments later carrying a tray with a steaming polystyrene box and a bottle of beer on it.

'Don't mind, do you?' he says, holding up the bottle of beer.

'What?' It's one of mine. 'Oh, no, help yourself. What's that?' I say, looking at his food.

'Baked potato with chicken tikka,' says Vinny, clearly pleased I've asked. 'From that new place near the Tube station. £2.95. Can't be bad, can it? Stir fried beef and chilli £3.25, Thai prawns £2.95, Guacamole £2.75 – or was that the beef? Can't remember, anyway something like that.

Gastronomy from around the world gathered for your delectation, lovingly microwaved and gently laid out in an expanded polystyrene tray. I should be a copywriter not a graphic designer.'

'Brilliant.' We watch the telly a bit longer.

'So how's the prostitution going?' he asks wow-wow-wowing some hot potato. I give half a laugh. 'Well?'

'Never mind.'

Vinny pokes around in his baked potato a bit more. 'All right, how's the throbbing hub of the media world then?'

'Dunno. I got sacked today.'

He looks round at me and swallows hard. 'Bloody hell.'

I look at him. 'I overslept this morning and when I went in they sacked me.'

'Oh, shit, mate, I'd have woken you but I thought you were staying at hers.'

'Oh, it's not your fault. It was just the last straw, they'd have sacked me for something else.'

'What time did you get in to the office, then?'

'About three-thirty.' We look at each other for a moment and then burst out laughing.

'That *is* late,' points out Vinny.

'Well, I like to do these things in style.'

'Who sacked you? That sour-faced cow you're always moaning about – what's her name?'

'Debbie. Yeah. She was trying to be really nice about it as well, the bitch.'

'Bitch.'

'*Fucking* bitch.'

Somehow telling Vinny about it has brought it all home. What am I going to tell my mum and dad? How am I going to make next month's rent? Will Debbie give me some sort of reference? I'll have to speak to her about it. Arghh! It's not worth it. I'll do without. With no job, no money, no references and no way of getting together next month's rent without going cap in hand to my parents, I've now got to move in with Marion. Keeping this place on as a bolthole is no longer an option either.

'Thing is,' says Vinny. I sense a prepared speech is about to follow. 'Thing is, do you think *she* might have been the cause of it?'

'Who? Debbie?'

'No – her.'

'Oh, Marion.'

'It's just that I know it's nothing to do with me but she has caused you some trouble recently.' He pauses but I let him go on. 'I mean, tell me to mind my own, but like I said to you other day, since you've been seeing her, you've been stressed out, miserable as fuck, forgetting things . . . the Indoor One A Side Football League has gone to pot.'

'I know.'

'Your rent cheque bounced. The landlord rang yesterday, asked me to tell you,' says Vinny sadly.

'Oh fuck,' I say quietly. 'I'll sort that out.'

I look back at the telly where a blond woman in a smart, pink suit is opening and closing a washing-machine door with a look of anger and concern on her face.

'Hey,' says Vinny. 'Shall I ring Jane? We could go for a drink. The three of us. Go on, it would be a laugh.'

Oh, Jane. She'd probably find it funny or at least ironic that I'd lost my job. Mind you, at least she'd be more sympathetic than Marion. Perhaps I do want to tell her. She might even offer some helpful advice. I imagine Jane, who knows everything, telling me what to do next with my life. The thought of it makes me smile. I could get a job with her in Paperchase. Share a house at the end of a Tube line with God knows how many other people. At that moment the phone rings. I reach down and pick it up.

'Hi, it's me,' says Marion on her mobile. 'That party was a mind-bending bore so I left early but I've booked a table at Bibendum for nine. I'll send the car for you at eight-thirty OK?'

'Great, see you then.'

'Oooh. Try and cheer up, sweetie.'

'Will do.' I hang up.

'That her?' says Vinny, without looking at me.

'Yeah.'

We watch telly in silence and I get us another beer each. I realize that, in fact, they are not some cool, exotic French label as I had thought but Sainsbury's own brand. Still, Vinny won't mind.

I change into a dark suit with a dark grey shirt to match my mood and go back to the living room to wait for the car.

'See? Table by the window. I know you like being by the window,' says Marion. Do I? I really can't remember.

'So, what happened?' she says, as the waiter unfolds a napkin and puts it in her lap.

'Well, I just overslept and when I got in—'

'What do you want to drink? I'll have a vodka martini, very dry. Same for you?' Why not, perhaps I like vodka martini as well as sitting by the window.

'Yeah,' I say to the waiter, a French-looking guy with very black slicked-back hair and an under-lip goatee. A working man, not like me.

'Then we'll have some champagne. A bottle of Louise Roderer.'

She begins to sound less like she is trying to cheer me up and more like she is celebrating. 'So, you got into work and they fired you?' she asks, looking around the restaurant to see if there is any one she knows. Obviously disappointed that there isn't, she turns back to me.

'Well, I overslept.'

'I called and you weren't there.'

'I know, I didn't get in till half-past three.' This time it doesn't sound so funny.

'Well, you can't blame them, then.' Very logical.

'Marion, it wasn't just that. It was all the other time I took off work, going shopping and things with you.' Marion is silent for a moment, letting the full patheticness of this little whinge sink in.

'*My* fault? Andrew, you didn't *have* come to New York and Paris.' I sigh and look down at the table for a moment. Logical again.

'I know, I'm very grateful and I had a wonderful time but since I've been going out with you it's been just one thing after another.'

'What? Like presents, foreign trips, pocket money? Great sex? Stuff like that?' says Marion, taking an olive stone out of her mouth as if someone were about to give her a prize for finding it. 'Andrew, you *wanted* to get fired.'

'What?'

'You know you did. You kept pushing it until finally they fired you.'

'Oh, bollocks.'

'Don't say that to me. You hated it, you kept telling me how much you hated it and now you're free of it. Tomorrow is the first day of the rest of your life. That is what people kept saying to me when I left Edward.'

'It's hardly the same.'

'It's *exactly* the same. Life is what you make of it and you were never going to do anything in that crappy little office. Besides,' she says, taking my hand, 'have you ever thought of it from my position? How embarrassing it's been for me?'

'Eh?'

'Andrew, what am I supposed to tell my friends? That my lover sells advertising space at some sleazy tabloid?'

'It's not a sleazy tabloid, it's a broadsheet with the second highest ABC1 readership in the country. Oh, for God's sake, who cares now? Look Marion, the thing is I've got no money.'

'I know, I was thinking about that,' she says kindly. What did she say? Is she finally going to give me some cash? I decide to push it a little more.

'I've got rent to pay, food, all kinds of stuff.'

'Well, that won't be a problem, you'll be living with me from now on, right?' Oh, yes, of course. That'll solve everything.

'Yeah, but there are other things. I can't just live without money.' I'm just inches away from grabbing her by the lapels of her jacket and yelling at her: YOU GOT ME INTO THIS MESS, YOU MAD BITCH, NOW YOU GET ME OUT OF IT.

'I know,' she says, folding her arms on the table. 'Listen, I'm going to make some sort of arrangement for you. You'll have your own cheque book and bank account just to tide you over. Besides, you'll need to get a new suit, a more fashionable one than that awful thing you've been wearing since I met you, and some other new things.' I don't believe it. Could this be it? Could this finally be what I've been working for for all these months? At last I might get 'that ice'. Is this the deal? I've finally sold out completely, hit rock bottom, shown to myself that basically I'll do anything for money and now I'm finally getting some of it. The champagne arrives – perfect timing.

CHAPTER EIGHTEEN

I FEEL RATHER HUNGOVER when I wake up. Marion is in the bath. I can hear her splashing around gently and humming to herself. The bedroom is beginning to smell of her luxurious bath oil. I turn over, duff up the pillow a bit and then find a cool place for my feet. The upside of getting the sack is that I don't have to go to work today. I don't have to put on a suit, get that fucking Tube and suffer that Tube smell: aftershave, shampoo, stale alcohol from the night before (or this morning?) and perhaps a smothered fart from a hastily eaten breakfast.

And – this is the real relief – I don't have to worry about finding an excuse for being away from the office or what kind of welcome I can expect when I do get in there to face Debbie. I'll miss seeing Sami every day, though. But we'll keep in touch. I'll give her a ring and we'll go out for a drink or something. Or I'll take her somewhere nice for lunch with Marion's money. We'll definitely see each other. She could meet Vinny. They'd get on like a house on fire.

I get up and walk into the bathroom to see Marion. She looks up at me and smiles sweetly.

'Hi, honey.' That reminds me that we made love last night. It was pretty good too – fast and passionate, ripping our clothes off (not that I'd actually dare rip anything of Marion's but she didn't tell me to hang anything up, which is pretty devil-may-care in her book) and then slowly, like we didn't care whether we climaxed again or not. Amazing what a powerful aphrodisiac the promise of a cheque book can be. Especially when you begin to associate sex so closely with money.

'Hiya,' I say and kiss her gently on the lips. She splashes some water around her and leans back, closing her eyes.

'What are you going to do today?'

'No idea,' I say, sitting down on the loo. 'Absolutely no

idea.' She lifts her foot out of the water and puts her big toe with its perfect, pink shiny toenail up to the bath tap which is in the shape of a golden dolphin. It spews a few drops of water which drip down over her foot.

We both look at it.

'I do have nice feet, don't I?' I nod. 'I have a meeting this morning with my lawyer about my residency or something. Honestly, the amount I spend in this country, you'd think they'd be begging me to stay.' I smile. 'We could have lunch somewhere and then go to the bank and sort things out if you want.'

'Sure,' I say casually. I'm genuinely very laid back about this, partly because I can hardly believe it's happening and partly because somehow I believe it isn't. Something is bound to go wrong.

'I do want to help you, you know that,' she says, taking my hand. I smile. 'I know you haven't had all the advantages in life that I have.'

I get into the bath water after her and then have a quick shave. Anna Maria has coffee, orange juice and warm croissants waiting for me downstairs. Marion is sitting at the table, reading the *International Herald Tribune* by holding it at some distance from her and tutting. It's nearly half-past ten and I really could get used to this.

Marion sets off to her meeting at just after eleven, leaving me two twenty pound notes to tide me over until lunch. I spend the morning reading the papers and some old copies of *Vanity Fair* and watching the cable channels on her telly. I look in the fridge to see if there is anything else to eat.

Marion's fridge is so different to mine and Vinny's. Not only is it smaller and sparkling clean but all it contains is a carton of orange juice and one of semi-skimmed milk, a box of Belgian chocolates, some strawberries and some grease-proof paper with Parma ham in it.

At any one time our knackered, smeary old English Electric fridge in Fulham will harbour: two bottles of drinkable milk, one packet of cheese, a half-eaten kebab/pizza/Indian, an open tin of baked beans which has formed a buffalo hide skin on top and a lump of butter still in its sliced-up packet, dotted with toast crumbs and going transparent with age around the edges. There will also be something sinister in a jar or open tin in the back that predates history and that we will have to draw lots to remove and take straight outside and throw in the bin. Or over the wall into the garden of that ghastly Sloaney couple next door who are always having barbecues and talking loudly about good prep schools.

I polish off the strawberries, even though I'm not hungry and mooch about the house, wondering what to do next. I pick up an American magazine but then realize I've already read it. I decide to go for a walk but realize I can't find my keys so I stay at home.

I ring Sami's number at the office but it is engaged. Then I ring Paperchase in Tottenham Court Road but put the phone down before they answer because I just don't know what to say to Jane. 'Hello, you know I said I'd finish with that American woman? Well, I've moved in with her instead.'

Shit. Give it a month.

At just after twelve Marion rings from the car to tell me she'll see me at Cibo in Albermarle Street at 1.15 p.m., which certainly beats a sandwich at my desk. Poor Sami will be trying to decide whether to queue at the sandwich shop round the corner with its sweating margarine tubs of tuna and processed chicken roll or the grimly claustrophobic office canteen which opens at noon and runs out of anything worth eating at 12.01. Ice-cream scoop of Smash, anyone?

Even though I've stuffed my face all morning I'm starving by the time I arrive at the restaurant and the risotto sounds good. Marion is not there yet so the waitress brings me a copy of the *Standard* with my beer. I'm just reading about a really hip new men's shop in the Fulham Road, which I'll check out as soon as I get my money, when Marion arrives. We double kiss which seems odd since I only saw her two hours ago but never mind, that's Marion.

'Fucking lawyers,' she mutters, patting her hair into place as she sits down.

'Bad meeting?' I ask.

'Oh, you know what they're like. Telling you what you can't do, how they can't help you and then charging you the earth for it.'

'What was it about this morning? Your residency?'

She looks up at me from the menu. 'Well, mine's probably

OK because of a corporation I've set up here and because I spent quite a bit of time abroad recently but it's poor Anna Maria.'

'Anna Maria? What's the problem?'

'She was working for her own country's embassy before she came to work for me so that was all cool but apparently it's a real pain in the ass if she's working for a private individual.'

'Why?'

'Because she just can't, basically. She doesn't have a green card or a work permit or whatever it's called. As soon as the authorities catch up with her she'll have to leave and go back to Ecuador.'

'Where?'

'Ecuador, South America. It's where she's from.'

'Poor Anna Maria.'

'You can say that again. Imagine swapping Belgravia for a mud hut halfway up the Andes or wherever. Have you seen those women's skin? Like an alligator's ass.'

'That's awful.'

'Andrew, you have no idea how these people live. Moisturizers and exfoliation are a totally alien concept to them.'

'No, I meant just having to go back there. Poor Anna Maria, what a crap life. Can't she get a work permit or something?'

'Well, she could but it would take months and she'd have to leave the country while they do it for some dumb reason and I just can't live without her. Even then it would be pretty unlikely because she doesn't have a skill that's in demand or something.'

'What are you going to do?'

'Well, the only thing we can do is get her to marry a Brit.'

'Right. That way she'd get British citizenship.' Marion is looking at me again and suddenly it hits me. 'Hang on a minute. You want *me* to marry her?' Marion looks sweetly at me. 'Oh, no.'

'Andrew, it would really help.'

'Yeah, but I can't.'

'Why not?' says Marion quietly. Yet again she has asked one of those simple innocent-sounding questions which are completely unanswerable.

'Because . . . because I just can't. I'd be caught out. You probably go to jail for something like this.'

'No,' says Marion, reaching for an olive. The waiter arrives and we give our orders. I've lost my appetite slightly but I go for the risotto anyway. For once Marion doesn't tell me what I should have.

'It's so simple,' she says when the waiter has gone. 'You just go to a Registry Office and then send all your paperwork – marriage certificate, passports, birth certificate – to the Home Office naturalization department in Croydon and then they send back her passport a few weeks later lifting her residency restrictions.'

'You've worked this all out then.'

'Of course.'

'That's what you were doing at the solicitor's this morning.'

'It was one of the things we discussed.' There is another heavy silence between us then Marion says, 'Look, I'll give you five thousand pounds.' It catches me off guard slightly. Five thousand quid would be very nice.

I line up my cutlery and then slowly polish my bread knife with my napkin. I could divorce Anna Maria as soon as possible afterwards. No one need know anything about it. Apart from the police. I was reading the other day about how all the official computers in the country are secretly being connected to each other. I'd be paying for a shirt with a credit card one day when the store detective would arrest me for fraudulent marriage.

Even if I did get away with it legally, how would I tell my wife-to-be in five years time or whatever that we can't get married in that idyllic little family church because I'm actually divorced. Who from? she'd gasp, putting down the wedding list. Oh, nobody, don't worry, she didn't mean anything to me, darling – I just did it for the money. Oh, that's all right then, what about pink for the bridesmaids?

No, I can't do this.

The waiter brings our first courses and we claim them in silence. Then I say, 'Marion, I just can't.'

'OK,' she says quietly.

'Oh, for Christ's sake. Can't you find someone else? What about Mark? He'd do it.'

'Fraid not,' says Marion.

'I'm sure he would.'

'He's already married,' she says irritably, stabbing her *gamberoni* in the eye and pulling its tail off.

'*Already* married?'

'Yeah, to Arabella della Schierra's hairdresser.'

'Really?'

'Yeah – no! Wait a minute, that was last time. They divorced around Christmas. Now I think it's Victoria's manicurist. Sweet girl. From the Ukraine or someplace. Mark's made a lot of money out of that,' she adds temptingly. He's also made a lot of money out of shagging old women in front of their husbands and getting sucked off by old men in the Hyde Park Hotel. I'm still not enthusiastic. Marion is talking again. 'I think Mark normally charges £5,000, that's why I suggested it, but since it's you and I'd like to do you a favour in return what if I double that? Make it £10,000? I'll pay it into your bank account this afternoon.'

I swallow hard. *Ten thousand pounds.* That's six months' salary at a stroke, tax free. I poke at my risotto for a moment. *Ten thousand.* God, that would be useful, so useful.

'OK,' says Marion. 'I know this is a big decision for you, I certainly don't much like the idea of you marrying another woman but it wouldn't mean anything, of course, it's only for practical, legal reasons. It would be huge favour to me, honey, and I'd really appreciate it.'

What's she saying? If you really loved me, you'd marry another woman?

Then she says, 'How about I triple that – £15,000?'

My head is swimming with these figures. With £15,000 I could put down a deposit on a flat. Start a business, like we were talking about the other day. Or just bank it.

'Think about it,' says Marion, sipping her wine. 'Don't decide immediately.'

We finish the rest of lunch in an awkward silence. The risotto has filled me up and I can't be bothered to eat my fish. Marion pushes her salad round her plate and starts a story about her friend Renata in New York who found her husband in bed with a seventeen-year-old dog walker and shot him in the leg but got off because her lawyer convinced the jury that she was on some diet pills that affected her judgment. We skip pudding and coffee. Marion double kisses me again outside the restaurant.

'I thought we were going to the bank,' I say quietly, looking down at the pavement. Marion rubs the side of my arm gently.

'That's up to you,' she says earnestly. 'Remember what I said. Fifteen thousand pounds. Most boys would jump at the chance. Look, here's my lawyer's number.' She takes a card out of her bag and stuffs it into the breast pocket of my jacket. 'Call him and he'll explain all the legal stuff. It couldn't be simpler. People do it all the time. See you tonight.'

She gets into her car and I begin to walk down the street towards Piccadilly. I knew it was all too simple. Just let's slip into the bank together and I'll give you a huge wad. Fifteen thousand pounds. I'll have to think about it. Fifteen. Thousand. That's nearly a whole year's basic salary. And I'm also helping poor, long-suffering Anna Maria. Suddenly it does sound tempting.

In the Tube station I pull out Marion's lawyer's card and go to a phone to ring him but find myself dialling Sami's number. It rings for a while and I decide to tease her about not picking up after the third ring as our performance targets demand. But when someone does answer, it's not her.

'Sami?' the voice says. 'Er, hang on.' I hear the echoey squelch of a hand going over the receiver and a conversation takes place which I can't make out. 'She's not here at the moment. Can I help at all?'

'No, don't worry. Do you know when she'll be back?'

'Hang on.' Another muffled conversation and then the phone is passed to someone else.

'Can I help you?' It's that former teacher. For a moment his classroom voice freezes me in fear.

'Yeah, I just wanted to speak to Sami, but don't worry, I'll call back later.'

'I'm not sure when she'll be back. Can I ask who's calling?' What the fuck is going on?

'No, it doesn't matter.' I hang up.

I go back to Fulham and take my suit off and put on a pair of shorts even though it is not very warm today. I pick up the phone to try Sami again but then remember who I should be calling.

I dial Jonathan's number but I'm told to wait by a recorded message while my call is being transferred then amid a noise that sounds like frying fish Jonathan answers.

'Hi,' I say as brightly as possible, 'it's Andrew.'

'Hi, Andrew,' says Jonathan quickly. I wait for him to say something about the other night. But in a rather disturbing Jekyll & Hyde way he is very pleasant. 'What can I do for you?'

'It was about that cheque. It wasn't for as much as I thought it was going to be.' I wait for him to say something but there is nothing. 'What are all these deductions?'

'Administration and things. I have to take them out of your first cheque, I'm afraid,' he says, unapologetically.

'But a hundred and forty quid's worth. What costs that much?' I demand.

'Phone calls, office costs.'

'But . . . well, could you give me a breakdown?' Funnily enough the only breakdown I get is on the phone line as the frying fish reaches a crescendo and the connection goes. Quelle surprise! as Marion would say.

So I make another call.

'Lipkin, Markby, Smythe. Good afternoon,' says a woman who obviously didn't quite make it as a Radio 3 announcer.

'Can I speak to Mr Markby, please?'

'I'll put you through to his secretary.'

A woman with a warm, motherly voice answers. 'Mr Markby's office, good afternoon.'

'Can I speak to him, please?'

'Who's calling?'

'My name's Andrew Collins, I'm a friend of Marion's, she suggested I call him.' I realize I've said more than I need to. The secretary pauses for a moment just to let it sink in to us both how pathetic and seedy this sounds.

'One moment, please.'

Mr Markby is every bit as terrifying as I had feared.

'Mr Collins?'

'Hello, Mr Markby. Er, Marion, erm, suggested I call you about Anna Maria.'

'Anna Maria?'

'Her maid, you know, who might have to leave the country.'

'Oh, yes,' he says sharply.

'Well, I was thinking of, you know, helping her and I just wondered what it entailed.'

'Helping her?' Oh fuck off and give me a break.

'Yes, with her immigration problem.'

'Yes?' I'm tempted to put the phone down there and then.

'And, I, er, understood that if she were to marry a British person, man, that is, she could stay in the country.'

Mr Markby takes a deep breath.

'I'm retained by your friend, Mr Collins, so when she asked me about the law regarding this situation I naturally explained it to her.'

'Right.'

'I am sure she could explain it to you as well.'

'Oh, she has.' I decide to dive straight in, after all, it can't get any worse. 'I was just wondering if I were to marry her, would the Home Office let her stay in the country?'

'If she marries a British National she can apply to the Home Office to have the residence restrictions lifted on her passport.'

'How long would I have to stay married to her?'

There is another pause, as Mr Markby, no doubt sitting at his antique repro desk in his large, wood panelled office, silently blows a gasket.

'Mr Collins, my client asked me about this situation and she now knows the law because I have explained it to her. What she, you and the other woman you mention do about it is entirely your business.'

'Oh, yeah, but I just wondered—'

'I'm afraid, Mr Collins, since you're not a client I can't advise you any further. Good afternoon.'

'But—' Pompous old fart. Fifteen thousand quid does sound more attractive by the minute. Even he doesn't charge that per hour. I ring Mark's number to see what he thinks. I get his answer phone and ask him to ring me.

I go back to Marion's that evening and she announces that we are eating in. We have lobster and huge sweet juicy prawns ordered in from some restaurant down the road.

Unfortunately Marion's friend Daria, Goddess of Doom, joins us. She looks every bit as unhappy to see me as she was at Marion's dinner party. I smile like a simpleton and this pisses her off even more. She spends the whole evening telling Marion she looks tired and talking to her about a friend of theirs whose husband jumped into a pool on their honeymoon and died of a heart attack.

'How awful,' says Marion, cracking open a lobster claw. 'I'd have sued. Is she over it, yet?'

'Well, I saw her at a little drinks party last night and she was making light of it but I don't know,' says Daria, shaking her head sadly. 'When I looked into her eyes I could see deep, deep sadness. Her new fiancé says she cries herself to sleep every night.'

I tut sadly but it must be too loud or something because Marion and Daria suddenly look across at me. Behind them I see Anna Maria in fits of giggles.

The next morning after my coffee and croissants I set off to Jonathan's flat in Fulham to talk to him face to face, although my fist is clenched expectantly for most of the journey and by the time I arrive I'm ready to shake him warmly – by the neck.

I ring the door bell and, just as I could have predicted, there is no answer. His flat is on the ground floor so I peer into the window through the net curtains to see if he is lurking around somewhere at the back of the room but then I notice that there is no furniture in the flat. Where the hell is he? No wonder his phone was diverted to a mobile again.

He'll never tell me where he is now if I ring him and there isn't even a For Sale sign so I stare up at the house for a moment thinking about what to do next.

I go to the house next door which is so scruffy it must be owned by some old dear who will be at home at this time of day. Luckily she is. I see a figure moving about behind the rippled glass panel in the front door. A cat pushes between her legs, peers up at me and then walks back along the hallway.

'Hello?' comes a voice, itching for a fight.

'Hello,' I say, bending down to address the letter box

properly. 'I wonder if you can help me. I'm looking for Jonathan – your neighbour.'

'Who?'

'Jonathan. The young man who used to live next door to you.'

'He's moved,' says the voice.

'I know,' I say, moving closer to the letter box so that I'm almost sticking my tongue into it. I look in and see a grey puckered mouth with coarse white hairs sprouting from above it. There is a sour, meaty smell of cat food. I stand back a bit. 'I wondered if you knew where he'd moved to.'

'Up and left. Never said a word but they don't these days, do they? Removal van came last week. Parked outside. Blocked the light out of my living room. I went and complained. They told me to go to the office in the high street but I'm not going there with my leg.'

'I don't blame you,' I say, standing up. 'Thanks, anyway.'

I set off back to the high street to find the Tube. I pop into a shop to buy a paper and as I walk out again I see a sign on the building opposite for a removal company. It's a thought. I go in and luckily there is a bored, teenage girl at reception.

'Can I help you?' she says folding up a copy of the *Sun*. I switch into full-on charm mode – the kind of thing that got me the job at the newspaper and could have got me some way up the 'space' ladder if I hadn't realized quite early on that it was all a load of crap and skilfully fucked it up. I start fiddling with my ear lobe like a cross between Hugh Grant and Prince Charles and make a joke which makes her laugh. I explain that I'm desperate to get hold of an old school chum who was living nearby but he moved recently, did they have his new address by any chance? She asks for Jonathan's surname and then takes out a file. She runs her finger down a page and then says:

'I'm not really sure whether we're allowed to give out this sort of thing.'

'Oh, dear, what a shame. I really did want to get in touch.'

There is a pause and then the girl says, 'Hang on, I'll just check with the boss.' She looks round to find him but I've already read Jonathan's new address upside down.

He's moved to Cambridge Street in Pimlico, the little shit. So much for Fulham being too expensive. I take a Tube along there and find that he is now in a flat in a white stucco building. I ring the bell. Jonathan is not there, of course. Or pretending not to be. I stand back and try and work out which windows are for his flat or office. What the hell am I going to do now?

I hadn't really planned for this so I sit down on the step and begin to wait.

It feels like I've been waiting for two hours at least, pondering on my predicament, but when I look at my watch it's actually been about twenty minutes. The smell from the bins and the drains below me is getting too much.

I walk slowly upstairs. A woman in a severe business suit is arriving at the front door upstairs. She gives me a filthy look but I ask her anyway whether she has seen Jonathan. She looks down at me but just ignores me. The intercom clicks and she says, 'Hello, it's Charlotte.' The door buzzes open and walks in.

'Thanks a bunch for all your help,' I shout to the closing door. An old man walking past in a homburg stares at me.

I get back to Marion's and decide to make myself a cup of tea. Anna Maria is clearly not happy about this. Either Marion's told her that I won't marry her or she just doesn't like having her kitchen invaded.

Then I find that there isn't any tea. Not proper tea, anyway, just herbal stuff and something with a prescription label with a New York address on it.

'What the hell's this?' I ask Anna Maria. Not that I'm interested, I just want to make the point that what kind of a house is this without any tea in it?

'For madam's eyes,' says Anna Maria, pointing to her own just in case I've forgotten what they're called in English.

'Her eyes? How can she have tea for her eyes?'

'Yes, bery important doctor in New York give it to madam.'

I sniff the greeny brown leaves. They smell like a hamster's cage.

'Phwoar! Anna Maria, how can we not have any tea?' I demand. 'I just want a bloody cup of tea.' Just then the kitchen door opens and Marion comes in.

'And what on earth is going on in here?' she says, taking off her gloves.

'I just wanted a cup of tea,' I say sulkily and turn my back on her and pretend to close up the foil bag of her disgusting infusion.

'Andrew, can I have a word with you?' says Marion, putting her handbag down. We go into the living room.

'How dare you talk to my maid like that?' she asks calmly.

'Oh, Christ. I'm really sorry, I wasn't shouting at her, I just wanted a cup of tea and there was no tea in the house and I lost my temper because I've had a hell of an afternoon—' I suddenly realize where this is going, so I change tack. 'I'm really sorry, Marion. I'll go out and buy some tea from the shop. Is there anything you want?' I put my arms around her and kiss her on the mouth. I feel her relax slightly.

'Nothing for me, thank you. Andrew, I know you're not accustomed to servants and that if you're not brought up with them like I was they can take a bit of getting used to, but please don't treat them like that.'

'I wasn't. I'm sorry, I just lost my temper.'

Marion looks at the kitchen door and drops down to a whisper.

'I know Anna Maria isn't very bright. Believe me, a clever servant is a real liability – but you must be patient with her.'

'I am – normally. Anyway, she's in a really bad mood. You, er, you haven't mentioned to her about this marriage thing, have you?'

Marion is quiet for a moment. 'Well, she know's that I'm looking for someone to help her out . . . I haven't mentioned you in particular but . . .'

'But what?'

'Well, she knows that you would be an ideal candidate so she must be wondering why you don't help her.'

'Why I don't break the law for her?'

'It's not breaking the law, Andrew, I told you, there is nothing illegal about this. People do it all the time.'

'Oh, I don't want to get into that again.'

'Well, just look at it from Anna Maria's point of view. From Knightsbridge to Nowhere in twenty-four hours.'

'I spoke to your lawyer today.'

'Oh, yes?' Marion brightens slightly.

'He wasn't very helpful – he gave me a really hard time.'

'Lawyers always treat you like that until they know you. I've known Gerald for ten years so now he treats me properly. He was the one who suggested this in the first place.'

'Really? He sounded appalled to me.'

'Only because he doesn't know you.' I look at her for a moment, wondering why she always has an answer to everything.

Then I say 'I'm going to get some tea.'

'Don't go out. I've got some tea here. It helps make the whites of your eyes whiter. Look.' She pulls down her bottom lid and stares at me like a bug-eyed loony.

'Yes, but it tastes like a hamster crapped in the box,' I explain.

'Have you thought any more about Anna Maria?' says Marion over a glass of champagne that evening before we go out.

'Oh, God, Marion. I'm not sure. I'm sorry, I'll just have to think about it.'

'Fifteen thousand pounds. I can make it cash if you want,' she says, fishing some imaginary speck out of her champagne glass. I think about it for a moment. Christ, it gets more tempting every time she says it.

'Marion, I just can't. I'm sorry. Can't someone else do it?' She takes a sip of champagne and stares thoughtfully across the room for a moment.

'Oh, I'm sure I can find someone. I just wanted to give you first refusal.'

'Well, thank you.' For what, I'm not quite sure.

'Don't mention it,' she says.

She takes another sip of champagne and I have to ask her, 'Don't you feel funny about me marrying another woman?'

She looks surprised and then says brightly, 'So are you going to marry her?'

'Well, I don't know yet, but don't you feel odd about your . . . lover . . . marrying another woman?'

'But it's not a proper marriage. It's just a piece of paper, just a technical arrangement to get over this little difficulty.' She allows her words to sink in and then, pouring me more champagne, adds, 'It doesn't mean anything. As soon as the paperwork is done you can start the divorce proceedings. I'd do it myself if I could, but being a woman and an American citizen I kind of fall down on two counts.'

The gratuitous sarcasm actually undermines her appeal slightly by making it obvious that she thinks she is talking to an idiot. Obviously realizing this, she adds, 'I'm sure Mark could find me someone else and I'd pay them – not as much, of course – but I wanted to help you out financially.'

'I suppose so,' I say, taking a sip of champagne thoughtfully.

'Look, I've been thinking,' she says, leaning over and pushing my hair away from my forehead. 'I would still very much like for you do this marriage thing. It is, as I said, a great opportunity but I've got something else which might help you earn a bit of money. I know that boys from Reading who sell space don't often get the chance to make something of themselves but after our conversation over dinner with Charles and Victoria the other evening, Charles told me today that he's got a friend who's starting some businesses and he could really use some help.'

As we're driven to one of Marion's friends' houses for dinner I begin to think, why not? I've been thinking about this business thing quite seriously. With some capital from Marion and perhaps some of her friends plus Charles's contacts, this might be a runner. After all, most of Marion's friends seem to make money more easily than running it off a photocopier so there might be some trick I can learn from Charles's colleague.

If I do the marriage thing, take my fifteen thousand and get some sort of project going with Charles or one of his mates, then I'll be doing OK.

It would make it easier for me and Marion to split up. I shoot her a guilty glance. Sorry, Marion, but I can't do this much longer. With a tidy sum in the bank and my own little business venture I won't be doing badly – even Jane can't object to that.

Charles sounds slightly nonplussed when I call him the next day and remind him of his conversation with Marion about a business colleague looking for help.

'Oh, er, yes, of course. He's a young guy I know who is

working in property, at the moment. It's a growing market. I think he's looking for someone to help raise finance,' he says in his mid-Atlantic, aristocratic drawl. 'Your experience is in sales, isn't it?'

Flattered that he remembers my job, well my *former* employment, I confirm this, click into sales mode and give him a quick spiel about my talents and experience.

'Very good, very good indeed. I think you might be just what ... er ... my ... er business associate is looking for.'

CHAPTER NINETEEN

S O T H E F O L L O W I N G M O N D A Y I am up early – well, ten-thirty, pacing around the living room with a mug of tea in my hand, dividing my attention between *I Love Lucy* on the telly and the front door. I am ready for business: smart suit, new tie, shaved and groomed with free samples from some of Marion's magazines.

Charles's colleague is Ralph and he is going to introduce me to the property business. I've been reading up on the sector in the newspapers and the business magazines in the last day or so and I've reached the conclusion that the market being what it is, provided you've got the capital, you can't really fail. And Charles and Marion's friends sure have the capital.

Marion, who has gone out to have something plucked or massaged or reshaped, stroked my cheek and wished me luck before she went.

I've decided against a briefcase because I'll look like a sales rep and also because I don't want Ralph to think that I think that making money in business is about writing your name and today's date neatly across the top of a piece of paper.

Ralph finally arrives. An hour late. I get to the door before Anna Maria does. At first I think there is no one there but then, when I look round, I see him slouched against the side of the house. He is younger than I expected, his face a gruesome patchwork of bum fluff and eczema. His mousy hair looks like it has never been combed and he is wearing a pair of knackered old aviator sunglasses. He is also sporting a very old, navy blue Crombie overcoat, an Oxford cotton shirt and red corduroy jeans without a belt.

'Hi . . .' he says. I realize he's forgotten my name.

'Andrew,' I say, holding out a hand.

'Yeah, hi, Ralph.' There is an awkward pause.

'Shall we go?' I say.

'Go? Er, yeah, let's go. Er, can I just use your . . . er . . .'

'Sure, upstairs on the left.'

He stumbles into the house and upstairs. I wait an embarrassingly long time. When he finally re-emerges I wonder whether to ask if everything is OK.

'Right,' he says, rubbing his hands together.

'OK,' I say enthusiastically. 'Shall we go?'

'What? Oh, yes. OK.'

He leads the way out of the house and sets off down the mews and out into the street, then he turns round and walks back the other way. We stand there for a moment. I'm just about to ask what his car, assuming that is what he has lost, looks like.

Finally he spots a very old, dark blue Jag, which is actually pretty conspicuous amongst the immaculate Mercs and BMWs that litter the streets around Marion's. As I sit down in the cracked maroon leather seat I can smell stale cigarettes, body odour and pot. The car, something of a vintage, is a mess. Every surface is covered with papers, business cards, pages of some fragmented A-Z, cigarette packets and old Tango cans. I realize that by the time I get out, somehow, somewhere, my suit will be permanently marked.

Ralph, meanwhile, is trying to start the car, easing out the choke, tickling the accelerator and whispering, 'Come on, baby, *come on*.' Finally the old crate, aroused by his efforts, groans and roars into life.

'*Yeah*,' gasps Ralph and we move off. We turn out into the main road and a car we narrowly miss flashes its lights behind us. Ralph seems not to notice.

After we have been driving for some minutes I try to make conversation by asking, 'Where are we going, then?'

Ralph suddenly seems to notice my presence. 'Oh, right, yeah. Where do you want to go?'

'Well, you know best. Erm, I thought we were going to look at some property or something.'

'Er, OK. Let's do that.' He drives a bit more then says, 'Where do you think?'

This is beginning to piss me off. 'I thought Charles had spoken to you about this?'

'Charles?'

'Oh, Christ! Yes, Charles Montague thought you might

know of some properties that Marion and, er, I might want to invest in?'

'Oh, yeah. Of course, sorry, man. Got the picture.' He nods violently and carries on saying 'yeah' until we come to some traffic lights at which point he asks, 'I wonder which is the best way to get there?'

He lights a cigarette and begins grooving out to some imaginary music, thumping on the steering wheel. The car behind us beeps and I realize that the lights have changed.

'Er, Ralph.'

'Heh?'

The car beeps again. 'Lights,' I say, nodding up at them.

'Christ! God! Sorry!'

We lurch off and drive on a little further until he says, 'Yeah, Notting Hill. That's the place to invest. I know some beautiful little places round there.' At last we seem to be getting somewhere.

'Great,' I say enthusiastically. 'Let's go.'

We drive on in silence, me reminding him from time to time to go when the lights change to green and once or twice to stop when they are red. Ralph is still grooving out to the track going round in his brain or staring into space. At one point his mobile rings and he grabs it from the section behind the gear lever.

'Haello? Er, he's not here. No, I'm just looking after his phone. No, I don't know where he is.' He doesn't wait for an answer, just switches off the phone and throws it onto the back seat. I keep looking straight ahead.

Finally we arrive in a deserted street in W11 – council blocks on one side, white stucco terraced houses on the other. The houses have the tell-tale signs of socio-economic decline – Xpelairs at most windows and a line of doorbells at every front door. Washing hangs despondently from lines on both sides of the street. In the distance a radio plays reggae and a baby is screaming.

'Where exactly were you thinking of?' I'm hoping against hope that he has something in mind.

'Erm.' At that moment we pass a For Sale sign and he breaks violently and says, 'Well, that's something you could be thinking about.'

'You know it, do you?' I say, knowing full well he doesn't but getting pretty pissed off by now.

'Er . . . Oh, yeah. Er, look, let's stop and have a coffee, shall we?' I agree. The smell of the car and Ralph's last-minute braking is beginning to make me feel sick. We double park and go into a tiny café with sticky-back plastic on the tables and a yellowed picture of some Italian seaside town on the wall next to a sign written in felt tip offering, 'Gigs £3'.

We order cappuccinos, which I pay for. We take them to an empty table near the window and Ralph pours sugar from the shaker into his coffee for a few minutes.

He lights a cigarette and says, 'Yeah, Charles! Jesus!'

I take this to be an opening for some sort of conversation. By now, I have completely given up on finding any property or doing any business at all with this daft little turd but I decide that I might at least find out something interesting and even useful about Charles and Victoria.

'How do you know him?'

'Who?'

'Charles,' I say. 'You fuckwit,' I think.

'Oh, we just move in the same circles. We've done some business together.'

'Property?'

'All kinds of shit.'

'He seems quite an interesting guy.'

'Yeah. Wild,' says Ralph, blowing smoke out and shaking his head gently.

'Why's he wild?' I ask, deciding, sod it, let's just go for the third degree after all. If necessary I'll just put him up against the wall and hit him a bit or hold his face over the chip pan.

'Oh, he just is. Wild man. Christ!'

'How does he make his money?'

Ralph stares at me for a moment. At last I seem to have engaged him.

'He's got a number of, er, business interests.'

I nod, knowingly. Ralph sniffs, rubs his nose and mutters something about paying a visit before we go. He gets up and then from behind me I hear him being told that there isn't really a toilet but he can use the staff one out in the yard. I finish my coffee. He hasn't touched his.

When he returns, about ten minutes later, I am standing up

ready to go. He sits down again. So I do too. Then he looks at me, gets up again and says, 'Ready?' God, this is exhausting.

We step outside and I wonder whether I should just say thanks, nice meeting you, and find a Tube station. Ralph stops to light another cigarette and then starts off, shaking his head and saying, 'Yeah, wild.'

'What is?' I say irritably.

'What?' he says blankly.

'You said something was wild.'

He looks at me for a moment and then laughs and says, 'Yeah, I'll say.'

I follow, looking around for something to get me out of here: a Tube station, a phone or even a For Sale sign. I decide to make one more effort with Ralph, he must know something useful or Charles would not bother with him.

'You think this is the best place to buy, then?' I say, gazing up at the houses around us for some inspiration. No reply. When I turn to look at him, Ralph is gone. I stop and look around for a moment.

Suddenly I hear his voice, an urgent whisper this time, 'Fucking move it, will you.'

'What?' Ralph is standing in a doorway, pressed against a door, a look of stark terror on his face. At that second I am aware of someone standing very close to me, I turn round and see a young guy whose tight, ugly smiling face is almost touching mine. It is the kid standing next to him who speaks.

'Hello, Ralphie. Who's your mate, then?'

'What?' is all I manage to say before the first guy slaps me hard across the face and then thumps me in the stomach. I fall down onto the pavement and am just about to retch when I feel a boot on the side of my head, crushing my ear. It pushes me gently but powerfully onto the ground and holds me there. The pavement bites into my forehead. I suddenly find myself focusing on the really thick tread on the sole of a shoe, the stitching and the smell of plastic. I feel sick, more out of shock than the punch in the guts I've just suffered.

I can't see properly, can't breathe properly and with one ear squashed onto the pavement and one folded underneath a DM, I can't even hear properly. I'm still staring at the sole that is less than an inch away from my left eye. The other boot, I suddenly realize to my horror, is probably poised to swing into my face. But it doesn't and a second later I am aware of the pressure on my head being released and both boots moving away quickly.

I lie on the ground for what seems like hours, trying to catch my breath and work out if I dare get up. Somewhere behind me I can hear thumping and grunting. It's a bit like a fight at school only slower and heavier. And it all happens in silence: no shouting, no swearing, no cheering. Just an atmosphere of quiet concentration. I lie still. Paralysed. Looking down at the shops above my head, the pavement next to my right eye and the vast expanse of innocent blue sky next to my left.

I hear a voice say 'OK, OK' and the noise stops. My throat goes into spasm – for a second I think that they are about the start on me. Oh, Jesus! Why did I ever get involved in this? What the hell am I doing with these people? Christ, I'm sorry, I've learnt my lesson. There *is* no free lunch. Please don't let it happen and I'll forget my plan with the rich women. I don't want to be mixed up with people like this. If I'd ever known, if I'd ever had *any* idea that this is what it meant, I wouldn't have dreamt of it. Oh, please! I'm sorry, I'll go back to media sales, or accountancy or anything. I want to be safe and suburban and not beaten to mush!

But nothing happens – they're walking away. Walking. Not running. Just ambling down the street for a lunchtime pint. A job well done. Fucking *nerve*. I lie perfectly still until I am sure they have gone for good. All I can hear is Ralph coughing behind me. Then I hear a rumbling and shuffling. Help? First Aid? A stretcher? That was quick. No, it is a little old lady with her trolley. She pauses for a moment and looks down at me with mild interest. She turns her face square onto mine, she looks down my twisted, curled up body, frowns for a moment and then shuffles off.

I decide to get up. My stomach aches and my face stings. My arms and legs are trembling but otherwise I'm not hurt. When I look at Ralph I immediately feel sick and have to get down on my hands and knees to stop myself from fainting. It isn't just the blood but the thought that what had happened to him could have happened to me.

Still shaking, I walk slowly over to the doorway he is lying in.

'Are you all right?'

His face is a mess: blood, snot and spit are marbled over his nose, mouth and shirt. His left cheek and eyebrow have a deep cut in them and his lip is already beginning to swell. I begin to find myself feeling sorry for Ralph. He looks like he is in shock, poor kid. I notice for the first time how stick thin he is. I try to help him up but he is too weak and shaky.

The letter box above us rattles and I realize that someone is looking out at us.

'Help,' I say weakly but it rattles shut and I hear someone behind the door running upstairs. 'Could you call an ambulance, please?' I add pathetically.

'No,' says Ralph. He starts to get up, wincing in pain. I help him and this time, eventually he is standing, bowed like an old man. His coat is ripped and his shirt, which has footprints on it, is hanging open. He attempts to tuck it in. 'Bastards,' he murmurs. It seems so inadequate, as if they had taken his parking place. I remember his silence as they worked him over.

'Ralph, who the hell were they? Do you know them?'

'Just some . . .' He winces again in pain, holding the side of his stomach. He spits out some blood and reaches inside his mouth. Something tiny and white – a bit of tooth. We stare at it for a moment.

'Just some friends of a friend.'

'Friends? We'd better call the police.'

'No!' he shouts. 'No. There's . . . there's no need for that.' He disengages himself from my hands and leans over to pick up his sunglasses, which are miraculously still in one piece.

'Ralph, mate,' I gasp, 'shouldn't you see a doctor or something?'

'No! I'm fine, just let me get my breath back, that's all. Should have used my TA training. Too many of them.'

'What are you talking about? Who are they?'

'Never mind, it's just business. It's not always very pleasant making money.'

He lets me take him back to the café which is only fifty yards away.

The girl behind the Gaggia machine gasps and looks terrified but lets us use the staff toilet again. Ralph says he is fine and so I go back to the counter and order two more

266

cappuccinos from the girl, who is flattened against the far wall. I try to make a joke to reassure her but she is having none of it. I feel pretty disgusting in front of this quiet, hard-working, law-abiding girl with her clean counter and her sensible job. What am I doing? What am I playing at? Is this how it is going to be from now on? I put a generous measure of sugar in one cup for Ralph and begin to sip the other myself, trying to work out what to do next.

After a while Ralph re-emerges, looking cleaner but still badly beaten.

'Cheers,' he says to the girl, with well-rehearsed but very unconvincing jollity. She looks more terrified than ever by this. His left eye is already swollen shut. He limps up to where I am sitting, trying to walk as normally as possible. Watching him brings back my own pain and I feel my stomach. Bruised, but nothing broken. My ear is bleeding slightly and my cheek is burning.

'Right,' he says, trying to smile through swollen lips. I can see now where he has lost a bit of front tooth. 'There are some places a couple of blocks away from here that would be right up your street. Oh, no pun intended.' He laughs at his own joke.

I just stare in disbelief and then say slowly, 'You're going to hospital.'

'What? Oh, Jesus! I'm fine. I told you, business isn't always a tea party, you know. You can't make an omelette without breaking eggs.'

'Look,' I say, taking some money out for the coffee. 'I'm going. You'd better see a doctor or something.'

As I walk out of the door, I hear him shout, 'Come back, Anthony. I-I mean, Andrew, come back. I've got some other ideas I'd like to run past you.'

I walk down to Notting Hill station and buy a paper to read on the Tube home but it is difficult to concentrate on anything. The side of my face stings and my ear is still bleeding a bit. I can still hear that dull thump of the first kick that landed on Ralph. I'm think I'm still in shock. As a favour to Marion, Charles had obviously promised him fifty quid or the equivalent in coke if he went through the motions of giving me some business advice.

I sit on the rocking, jarring Circle Line train and am pestered by weirdoes. A variety of weirdoes: a white-haired City gent in a slightly crumpled but otherwise respectable pinstripe suit suddenly shouts at the woman next to him to stop feeding all these fucking immigrants.

She looks horrified and then giggles to her friend. 'He's another one,' shouts the old man pointing to me. A Rumanian gypsy pushes her floppy, drugged baby in my face and then offers her upturned hand, muttering something incomprehensible. At South Kensington station a blonde girl with dreadlocks and a ring through her eyebrow and her nose rattles an old McDonalds cup at me as if she hated doing it but it had to be done.

In their own way, all of these loonies and drop-outs seem to have better prospects than me, a better sales pitch. I've sold all I can sell and I haven't got much in return for it. Perhaps the most I can expect is a few more little treats from Marion until one of us gets sick of the other.

Anna Maria opens the door and says, 'Oh, Mr Andrew, your face.' I smile sadly at her. As I start to walk upstairs I hear Marion grunt and then groan. I look round to Anna Maria for some explanation but she has pissed off back to the kitchen. I go further upstairs and hear Marion breathing deeply. The bed creaks slightly and then she gasps again, 'Oh God!'

This was something I hadn't quite banked on. I suddenly feel quite hurt. OK, she might shower me with gifts by way of apology but all the same it *is* bloody insulting. The worst thing is that I had never heard her make noises quite like this when we're making love. What's his secret?

Two more steps reveal that his secret is that he is a her, weighs twenty stone, is wearing a white apron and is rubbing Marion's back aggressively with some oils that smell of eucalyptus and mint. I walk in and sit down on the chair while the masseuse carries on pummelling and Marion smiles at me dreamily.

'Oh God,' she says with faint irritation when I tell her the whole story.

'You don't sound very concerned. I could have had the shit

kicked out of me,' I say, yanking off my tie and dropping it on the floor, which I know will irritate her.

'Have you seen a doctor?' she says bossily. Then she reaches out and strokes my injured face gently. 'Poor baby.' I begin to feel slightly horny like a medieval knight back from the crusades ready to reclaim my conjugal rights.

'No, it's not serious,' I say. 'I'll go and put some TCP on it in a moment. I just got thumped in the stomach but you should have seen the state of Ralph. I think he's lost a tooth.'

'Oh no,' she gasps in horror. 'That sort of thing always makes me feel nauseous. I wish you hadn't told me that. I've got a thing about teeth – can't even have mine capped. Not that I need to.' She runs her tongue over them luxuriously. 'It made me feel quite nauseous as well. What kind of friends does Charles have?'

'I don't know. Charles has a lot of contacts and some of them probably aren't nice people. You don't always do business with people you would invite to dinner.'

'Oh, don't you start.'

'Well, I'm sorry, Andrew, but it's true. Where do you want to go for dinner, by the way? Never mind, I'll think of somewhere.' She groans as the masseuse continues her work. 'Anyway, you can have your Rolex back.'

I look up but she is facing the other way now.

'Thank you. Has it been cleaned, then?'

'Clea—?' Caught you, I think to myself with grim satisfaction. I should know, though, that there is no embarrassing Marion. 'Yes, yes, they cleaned it at the Rolex store.' She gives into her massage again for a moment and then says, 'I think you should have a good quality watch. A watch is one of the ways people evaluate you by.'

'Oh, thank you. It is beautiful.'

I find myself picking my tie up off the floor in gratitude.

'You're welcome, sweetie. We can discuss it tonight at dinner. I'll book a table at Aspinalls for eight-thirty. We'll eat outside if the weather's still good.'

At this point I can tell she is getting bored with the conversation and wants to devote herself entirely to Brune-hilda or whatever her name is.

Lying in the bath, I decide that if making money the Charles Montague way involves getting the shit kicked out of you at regular intervals, then I'd rather not bother. On the other hand, getting my beloved Rolex back (I'm wearing it now and I'll never take it off again) and the thought of eating tonight and probably tomorrow and the day after that at the kind of restaurants that people in the office can only read about in magazines, makes me reconsider my idea about chucking it all in during that state of panic with my head sandwiched between DM and paving stone. That certainly won't be a long-term plan – I did say I'd give it a month with Marion, didn't I? But I'll never go back to selling fucking ad space as long as I live.

Just as I'm trying to forget it all and enjoy the embrace of the warm bath water on my still aching body, Anna Maria's voice asking Marion something reminds me of the only alternative.

As the head waiter leads us across the restaurant to our table Marion smiles hello at a couple of people. I do too, in case I've met them. The waiter pulls back her chair to let her in and sit down. I could certainly do with some food and good wine after my experiences today. The waiter hands us menus and we order vodka martinis.

'I've got a couple of brochures back home you should maybe have a look at,' says Marion, engrossed in the menu.

'Brochures?' I say, wondering what the *brochette de fruits de mer* with saffron sauce will be like. On the other hand, the chateaubriand does sound good. Holiday brochures, I suppose. Well, that's one good thing about being fired, at least I can go on holiday whenever I want. No need to worry about Debbie giving me time off – or not, more likely. 'Brochures for what?'

'Circumcision,' says Marion. 'You said you'd do it, remember?' Oh, my God. I'd hoped she'd forgotten. The price for living with her, I suppose. How typical of Marion – no tact whatsoever. Halfway through persuading me to do one demeaning little favour for her, like marry her maid, she starts pushing another at me.

'I think we're ready to order,' I say to the waiter, who has chosen this moment to reappear.

Mark clicks his tongue when I tell him that I'm going to move in for a month as we drink lattes in the King's Road the next morning.

'You want me to talk you out of it?' he asks.

'No.' So why am I telling him?

'You want me to tell you how to deal with it?'

'Yeah. Yeah, I suppose so. Point is, I've got no money, this business thing didn't come off and I'm not going back to work in a fucking office so I've got to stay with her – at least I don't have to spend anything on food and bits and pieces. I'll give up my room in Fulham and then I'll give it a month, well, perhaps two, then I'll get out whatever happens.'

'I told you – you'll be on a short lead.'

'I know, it seems to be getting shorter every day but I can't afford anything else at the moment and she has bought me a few things recently.'

'Good,' says Mark warmly. 'Like I said: Marion wants to have you on standby at any time rather than have to ferret you out of Fulham, that's all, that's how she looks at it.'

He smiles at the waitress, who brings us our coffee. She melts. I get pissed off: come on, Mark, what do you think you're going to get out of her? We've already paid for the coffee. Well, I have.

'I did it with this mad old thing who used to be an actress. No one famous but her husband had croaked two years earlier and left her a packet,' he says. 'She had a place just outside Nice in the good old S of F. It was great. You could swim in the pool and look out across at the Med. I spent, what? four months just hanging out. Swimming, sunbathing. Met this local girl. Used to see her while Yvonne, the actress that is, was having a nap in the afternoons.'

'Sounds great.'

'It was – for a while. We'd go to parties but they were, well, you've been to Marion's dos, haven't you? Anyway, I realized that the more pre-lunch martinis she had the longer her naps became. Sometimes she woke up just in time to go to bed. But I suppose I got bored and I wasn't earning anything, you know. I thought I'd strangle her by the end of it. Eventually I nicked some money from her safe, took a taxi to the airport and came home. Was I ever glad to be back.'

'Nicked it?'

'Well, she owed me *something* for all those weeks,' says Mark casually. 'I'm not a bloody charity.'

'I was really hoping she'd set me up in my own flat somewhere,' I say almost to myself.

'No,' Mark tell me authoritatively. 'A man would do that. I used to see this German banker when I was about eighteen, nineteen or something. He paid my rent in a place just off Kensington Church Street. Flew in once a week. Couple of meetings in the City, bit of sex, early night and then back to his wife and family in Frankfurt.' That sex thing again. I'm beginning to develop a bit of a hang up about it. He finishes his coffee, although I've only just started mine and raises his eyebrows to the waitress who is only too happy to come over. He hands back his coffee cup and asks for another. 'Men want sex, you see. Pure and simple. Women want company, conversation, foreplay, cuddling, dinners – all that bollocks. God, women are a pain.' We consider the truth of this profound statement for a moment.

'She said she was embarrassed about my job and the fact that I live in Fulham.'

Mark hoots with laughter and slaps his thigh. 'She say that?' I nod. 'Good old Marion. Tactful or what?'

I take a mouthful of creamy, comforting coffee and then mention the marriage thing to him.

'Oh, yeah,' he says blandly. 'Might as well.'

'Really? You've done it, haven't you?'

'Me? Yeah. Who hasn't?'

'You married Victoria's maid or something?'

'Oh, yeah – what's her name?' He watches a girl walk past us along the road. 'It's no big deal. Most registry office marriages in London are fake anyway, I saw a thing about it on the news. They can't catch you. How much is Marion paying you? Five thousand?'

'More than that.'

'Ten?'

'Fifteen.'

'Fuckin' 'ell,' Mark gasps. 'You're doing all right. What you waiting for?'

'I'm still thinking about it.'

I decide not to mention the circumcision thing.

*

With elaborate care Vinny puts the ball away in its usual place: balanced on top of the teapot we've only ever used once, when Jane came round, but whose lid we've somehow managed to break since that occasion. My ball control has been crap tonight. It's been such a half-hearted game that we haven't even elicited any bangs of complaint from downstairs. I've been looking anxiously at my watch between shots as eight o'clock approaches.

'Do you want a beer?' I ask, opening the fridge and leaning on the door for a moment.

'Line 'em up, Barkeep.' I open a couple of cold Rolling Rocks and hand one to him. Hot and thirsty, we both drink in silence for a moment. 'You're quiet,' says Vinny. He burps. 'You're not usually like this when you've been thrashed. Who the hell do you think you are? David Beckham?' I laugh and take another swig. 'How's Mrs Robinson?'

'Who?'

'The older woman?'

'Oh, right. She's . . . I'm, er, I'm moving in with her.'

Vinny swallows a mouthful of beer quickly. 'Really?'

'Oh, right. Well, it's your . . .'

'Funeral?'

'Probably.' We both stare at our beers for a while. 'When are you moving out?'

'Well, tonight, actually.'

Vinny looks shocked. 'Tonight? Bloody hell! That was quick.'

'Yeah, I know.' Poor Vinny. I think of Jane's words. I'll miss him.

'I can't believe . . . well . . . you know.'

'Thing is, I've just got no money since I got . . . since I left my job and I don't have to pay any rent at hers—'

'Oh, God, no, mate,' says Vinny, shrugging his shoulders. 'I see what you mean. It makes sense.'

'It's the only way—'

'Oh, yeah, sure.' We look at our beers again. Vinny gets the ball again and bounces it a couple of times on the ground. 'Have you written to the landlord?'

'Yeah, I did it this afternoon.'

'Oh, right. Do you want a hand with your stuff?'

'Oh, no, don't worry. She's sending the . . . someone's

coming. He'll be here at eight. Anyway, you're going out tonight, aren't you?'

'Well, I was just going for a drink with some mates but . . .'

'Oh, well, go. Go on, don't worry.'

Vinny puts his foot on the ball. I'm trying to work out how long we've lived here. Just over eleven months.

He says, 'OK, I'd better . . .'

'Yep. I've got some packing to do.' He makes for the door and I wonder what to do next. 'I'll see you though. We'll keep in touch.'

'Oh, sure,' says Vinny, finishing his beer.

I scoop the football off the floor and spin it around in my hand. 'After all, I want revenge.'

'In your dreams, mate,' he says, staring at the ball.

'I'll be back for fry-ups on Saturday,' I say, though I don't know how.

'I should hope so. That girl with the wonky eye and the – what shall I call it? – under-arm problem, at the Ritz grill down the road will be sorry to see the back of you.'

'Ah, yes. The ugliest girl in London.'

'In Britain,' says Vinny indignantly. 'Don't sell her short!' I laugh again. Poor thing. It's so obvious she's got a thing for Vinny. And she hasn't got a wonky eye. Or an underarm problem. She's actually very pretty. Jane says it is Vinny's defence mechanism because he can't handle someone fancy-ing him.

'Don't worry,' I say, suddenly feeling overcome with emotion. 'I'll be back for footy and fry-ups.'

'Oh, yeah,' agrees Vinny as he heads for his room.

I've been half-heartedly stuffing things into bags for an hour or so when Chris, Marion's chauffeur, arrives with Anna Maria. He stands uncomfortably in the hallway in his uniform, looking very tall and worrying about how safe the car is, double parked outside. Anna Maria, meanwhile, thinks it is all great fun. She sniffs and turns up her pug nose. 'Berry bad smell.'

'Is it?' I say, sniffing around.

'Smell like, er, smell like old sneakers and sweat.'

She runs her finger along the radiator. Not surprisingly it comes up black. She gasps in horror and begins to giggle again. I lead her upstairs, asking what is so funny. Laughing, she follows me into the bedroom, looking anxiously around her.

I point to my shirts hanging up in the wardrobe and ask her to take them down and fold them. Still giggling inanely, she discovers she can hardly reach. I take them down for her and chuck them on the bed while I deal with my underpants. No one touches my underpants apart from me – and my mum.

Still giggling and muttering 'Oh, my God', Anna Maria begins to fold things neatly and put them into my suitcase and my Head bag.

'Is that all?' she says after an hour or so. Chris takes the boxes with my ghetto blaster, some books, CDs and tapes. We set off back to Marion's with Anna Maria still laughing at this whole ridiculous business and me worrying about what I'm doing. What am I going to tell my mum and dad? If they ring I'll have to get Vinny to say that I'm out and then ring me at Marion's and I'll ring them back and do 141 beforehand. This is getting very complicated. As for Jane – I'll have to cook something up with Vinny. Another lie.

One month. That's all. While I find . . . all right, let's face it, while I find another job but perhaps a job I can actually stand to do. Then I'll take the money – the £15,000 Marion has promised me – and get somewhere to live. Somewhere normal that Jane can deal with. Like *this* flat. I look around at my old room and listen to Vinny singing along to Elvis on the radio. What am I doing?

But I can't afford to stay here, I tell myself, picking up some socks listlessly. At least I can look back and say I went to hotels and restaurants I would never have seen any other way. I've got some nice clothes and, best of all, nearly a year's salary all at once, tax free.

When we get to Belgravia Chris takes the bag, the suitcase and the boxes upstairs and Anna Maria follows him, ready to unpack them. Marion has set aside some of her wardrobe space for me.

'Is that it?' asks Marion.

'Yes,' I say. 'I haven't got that much.'

'We'll have to do something about that.'

Yeah, yeah, yeah.

The next morning I suddenly realize I haven't seen my ghetto blaster. I ask Marion where it is.

'That old thing? With the sticky tape on the front and the aerial all bent up? Yuk! I had Anna Maria put it with the garbage. You can use mine. I've got one in almost every room. We don't need any more of them, that's for sure.'

I suppose not.

My mum and dad bought it for me on my first day at college.

CHAPTER TWENTY

AND SO THE DAYS DRIFT ALONG. I get up late, have a long, leisurely breakfast, watch a bit of TV, go for a walk, sit at the Picasso Café in the King's Road and have a cappuccino or two while I read the paper or just watch the people walk past. I meet Marion for lunch somewhere nice or Anna Maria makes me something and serves it to me, as I sit at the head of the dining table on my own. I go to the gym or swimming or even the pictures in the afternoon. Sometimes I go window shopping. Or sometimes it's back to the Picasso Café if I've got enough money. I spend quite a bit of time listening to music while I'm lying in front of the telly with the sound turned down. It makes whatever crap you're watching look like a documentary or some satirical pop video. In the evening we go out to dinner or to the theatre or to a party with people I don't know and she hasn't seen for years.

I find myself doing funny things at funny times of the day: I'm in the bath at three o'clock in the afternoon sometimes or having lunch at four. I don't always sleep very well so I sometimes wander downstairs and put the telly on at two in the morning or I take some pills Marion gave me.

She nags at me sometimes to do something but whenever I ask what she means – like getting a job? Accompanying her to lunch? To her daily treatments? – she just changes the subject and I go back to the telly or the paper or the stereo.

I ring Jonathan almost every day but either I can't get through or some woman explains that he's on the phone or out but he'll call me back. I go to visit him on a few occasions at the office in Pimlico but he is never in. Usually I get the woman's voice again, trying a bit too hard to be posh, squawking out of the entry phone that she's terribly sorry, he's out at the moment and she doesn't know when he'll be back.

Once when I walk up the street, on the opposite pavement,

277

trying to decide whether to be Mr Nasty or Mr Nice on the entryphone today I casually look up and I'm sure I see him through the Venetian blinds of a first-floor window.

I run over to the door, jam my finger into the buzzer and hold it there until I get a voice shouting, 'Hello? Hello? Could you stop that, please.' It's him, it's Jonathan.

Almost as if he's my saviour, not my tormentor, I shout, 'Jonathan, hi, Jonathan, it's me, Andrew.' There is a silence and I wait for the door to open. It doesn't move. 'Hello? Jonathan?' I push the door again, perhaps I just didn't hear it buzz.

'How can I help you?' says Jonathan through the metal grill of the entryphone.

'I just wanted to pick up my other cheques.'

'OK. Hang on, let me look at my file.'

'Can I come in?' I say but there is silence.

'I've got a record of another job but, like I said at the time, I take the earnings from the first jobs to cover my expenses.'

'What, still?'

'Things like photographs cost money.'

'But I never had a photograph and . . .' I realize I'm getting off the point here. 'Look, what about the other jobs I did?'

'Well, you didn't do many jobs because you haven't been around much. I've talked to your flatmate more than you,' he adds prissily.

'But I did do jobs for you – Marion, er the American woman, and that girl, the young girl, in Clapham—'

'Have you got dates for these jobs?'

'Dates? Look, I can't . . . erm . . . there was one a few weeks ago.'

'Andrew, I'm really sorry, I need dates.'

'The young girl, Erren. It was . . . let me think. Tuesday the eighth. Yeah, it must have been. Or the ninth. Whichever was the Tuesday.'

'What about the credit card receipt?'

'I gave it to you.'

'Did you keep a copy with the job reference number on it?'

'What copy? What job reference number? Jonathan, can you let me in for a minute?'

'I need the dates and job reference numbers, Andrew. I'm

very sorry but you'll need to be more precise. I've got a lot of guys working now – and girls. I can't just dole out cheques willy nilly.'

'Willy nilly?' I repeat, probably because it's such a daft phrase. 'Willy nilly? Listen, you owe me that money, for Christ's sake.'

'Andrew, this is getting a bit boring. I told you: I need the credit card slips and the references.'

I bang the door with my hand and take a deep breath, trying to get a grip. Then I have an idea. 'What if I asked the clients for the slips? They might still have them.' Does Jonathan laugh at that?

'I really don't want you pestering clients.'

'What about Marion, you know, the American woman in Chelsea?' She must have noticed that the amount has been debited from her card and she'll certainly remember the date. 'I can ask her tonight . . . hello?'

'Tonight? I don't have you booked to see her tonight. Laura? Do we have any bookings for Andrew Collins tonight?'

'No, but I'm seeing her anyway,' I explain desperately, almost hysterically and then it hits me.

'You mean you're seeing a client without the agency?' says Jonathan calmly.

'No . . . well, yes. We've started sort of going out, that's all.' Oh, shit! Why did I say that?

'Andrew, as I explained when you signed up, dealing with clients without the agency is strictly forbidden. I'm afraid I've no choice but to end your employment with us. Goodbye.'

'What?' I screech. The entryphone is silent. 'Jonathan! Jonathan!' I bang the door again, so hard my hand hurts but I don't care – I just wack it again. I stab the button again and yell at the small metal box in the doorway. 'Listen, you fucking bastard. You fucking owe me.' I stand back and look at the door for a moment as if it's going to give me a break and open by itself. Then I kick it as hard as I can. The force sends me staggering backwards. I lose my balance and fall down the steps, landing at the feet of two middle-aged women.

One of them cries out in fear. They back off quickly as I

struggle to stand up. 'Cunt!' I bellow above the noise of a passing motor bike at the impassive building towering above me. 'You bastard.'

'Excuse me,' says a voice from behind me.

'Oh, fuck off,' I hiss without turning.

'Now, hang on a minute, sir.' I spin round, ready to punch someone but it's a policeman. I look away from his intense, curious gaze.

'He owes me money,' I mutter.

'Well, I don't think you're going get it by swearing at him in the street,' says the policeman in the kind of calm, patronizing logic you would expect of someone in a uniform in this kind of situation. 'I'm going to have to ask you to move on.'

'I've got no money,' I hear myself saying.

'Look, you'll have to talk to a solicitor about recovering it, then. You can't stand here shouting and swearing.' There is an edge to his voice now. He is about my age. 'That's not going to get you anywhere.'

'What *will* get me anywhere?' I ask but he just watches me silently until I move off.

A few days later I also think I see Jonathan whiz past in a cab when I'm sitting at a café in Brompton Road. I leap up ready to run after the cab but whoever it is is on a mobile phone or something so I can't quite see for sure. I could really do with that money. It's also the principle of the thing. He owes it to me. Plus cab fares, plus hours of sleep, plus my job . . .

My encounter with Jonathan, or rather his entryphone, is about the only exciting event to upset the gentle rhythm of my pointless existence. Marion gives me ten or twenty pounds or so every now and then and buys me some more clothes: a really cool Dolce & Gabbana white T-shirt. If you look at it close up and you know about these things you can tell it's expensive. Unfortunately, after Anna Maria washes it it becomes a bit tight and when I catch sight of myself in it with my shades I realize I look too gay. She also buys me an off-white suit from Hugo Boss which looks pretty cool, especially with the aforementioned white T. Except that there aren't many places I can wear it and Mark says something about Richard Gere in *American Gigolo* having one. I sort of leave it at the back of the wardrobe after that.

I think about Jane a lot and ring Paperchase a few times but put the phone down before there is any answer. I can't work out what to say to her. My prepared speech or plan to meet her suddenly sounds all wrong when I get ready to say it. Sometimes I think it's pure lethargy that prevents me from arranging to see her, or the thought of having to invent some story about Marion and where I'm living now or simply not knowing what to say to someone so sensible, so organized, so together. But in fact it's probably just shame that stops me from ringing.

One of my dad's books talks about something called creative visualization – if you really see something happening you can actually bring it about. The square-jawed motivator who wrote the book was referring to a more senior position within your department, I think, or a pay rise or something else really worth having, but with me it seems to work with Jane.

I'm sitting at the Picasso Café reading the paper I used to work on for a change when I look up and see her. She is wearing Ray-Bans and a pale blue summer dress.

But it's not her.

It's just another girl walking down the street. A girl with a job and a flat who has friends she sees for a glass of white wine after work and who reads glossy magazines at the hairdressers.

So I pay for my coffee quickly, pick up my magazine and Dolce & Gabbana sunglasses and go off to find a phone box. I have to hold on for a while because Jane is serving a customer but somehow I manage not to put the phone down.

'Hello, can I help you?' she says finally. I'm slightly taken off guard by her formal greeting.

'It's me, Andrew.'

'Oh, hi,' she says, surprised but friendly. There is a pause. The phone box suddenly seems very hot and smelly.

'How are you?'

'OK, how are you?'

'Fine, thanks.'

'Great . . . how's it going?' Shit, haven't we just done this one?

'Good, yeah, busy.'

'Oh, sorry. Can you talk?'

'Yes,' she says but then she doesn't. She is obviously going to make me do all the running on this.

'I was just ringing to say hello . . . and . . .' Either she takes pity on me for my faltering conversation or she is genuinely interested.

'Where are you? It's very noisy, it sounds like a phone box.'

'It is. I . . . er . . .'

'You not at work?'

'No . . . I . . .'

'Day off?'

I may as well tell her. 'Everyday's a day off at the moment. I've been sacked.'

'Oh, God. I'm sorry.' She seems genuinely surprised, upset. It's as if I've got my slick, yuppy come-uppance. 'That's awful.'

'Oh, don't worry. I'm quite relieved, actually. Stupid bloody job.'

'Oh,' she says quietly. Perhaps I sound like I don't care at all about working, like I don't have to.

'Jane, I just wondered if you wanted to do something tonight.'

'I can't, I'm going to see at film at the NFT with my friend.'

'Oh, of course. Sure.' A huge truck thunders past. I wonder if she has said something that I didn't hear. 'Sorry, did you say something?'

'No,' she says quickly. 'No, sorry.' Why do words always get in the way when there's something important you want to say?

I try again. 'Er, tomorrow night, then?'

'OK, why not?' She sounds quite pleased, quite enthusiastic.

'Great!' I say. 'I'll see you – where? Sloane Square Tube? At what? Eight? And we'll have something to eat. You know – somewhere cheap and cheerful.'

'All right.' She seems to warm to it. 'All right, that'll be fun. See you, then.'

*

'Marion,' I say over dinner at Ciccone's that night. 'I've been thinking about this marriage thing.'

'Yes?'

I take a deep breath. 'Well, I think I'll do it.'

Yep, I will do it. I'll take the money and then get the hell out of this. No more Ciccone's perhaps but no more tight lead, no more killing time over coffee in the King's Road – oh, and no circumcision. I might get out of here in one piece.

So now I've got to escape from this mess, cut my losses, get what I can and get out of it. A bogus marriage was not what I had originally planned but it's better than carrying on like this. At least it's money – perhaps cash. Quickie wedding, quickie divorce, take the money and run. Like Mark says, everybody does it. And Marion will be getting something out of it, too. So will Anna Maria.

'OK,' says Marion coolly.

There is a pause.

'Well, you know, if it's still on, if you still haven't found anyone?'

'Mark had a friend, I think, but, as I said, I would prefer to give you the opportunity.'

'I know, thanks for that.'

'I'll speak to the lawyer in the morning and he'll tell you what to do.'

'I don't fancy talking to Mr Markby again.'

Marion spears a piece of ravioli. 'Don't worry, I've found another one.' She puts the pasta in her mouth and chews gently for a moment. 'More amenable.'

I ring Jerry, the more amenable lawyer, the next morning and he *is very* amenable – and very reassuring. Over his mobile phone in what sounds like a Coffee Republic he explains exactly how it all works. He tells me to let him sort out the forms. He's done it a hundred times. No one ever gets caught. Easiest thing in the world.

After my experiences with Jonathan I wonder whether to ask him to draw up something between me and Marion for the little matter of the £15,000 but that sounds just too tacky. Besides she'd never go for it. I'll have to trust her.

When I tell her how helpful Jerry was and remind her of

the payment we discussed, she says, 'I should hope he was helpful – the amount he's making out of me.'

Following my conversation with Jerry I've made a careful note of what we have to do and then I go into the kitchen to explain it all to Anna Maria. I realize that we haven't spoken about this before and perhaps she doesn't even know that I've agreed to do the deed. As soon as I walk into the kitchen and say her name she senses something is afoot. I suddenly feel rather nervous and realize that I am, in fact, proposing to her. It almost makes me laugh for a moment and then I realize that this is how it's going to be: a grotesque parody of what should be one of the most serious and moving events of my life.

We are going to do it 'by licence' since this means we only have to give three days' notice. We'll do it Chelsea Registry because technically I now live in the Royal Borough. We just need two witnesses. Marion will ask two discreet friends to do that, probably Charles and Victoria. Then, after a few months we will send our papers to the Home Office in Croydon and they will lift the residency restrictions on Anna Maria's passport and she can stay in Britain as long as she likes without any difficulty. Later she can apply for citizenship if she wants.

I think she takes it all in. Later that afternoon the driver takes us to the Town Hall to register. The clerk in charge with his over-used suit and brown striped shirt seems to radiate disapproval even though he doesn't say anything beyond what he is legally bound to tell us. He looks at me and then at her and then back at me again. I give our names, spelling them in an attempt to be extra helpful and curry favour. He types them into a computer and asks for our addresses. There is something about the formality, the smell of disinfectant, the polished lino floor, the faint echo of our voices and the forms on the desk that reminds me of school exams and I begin to feel slightly sick. Suddenly Anna Maria is tugging at my sleeve. I look round and realize how ridiculous we must appear – she's got to be less than five feet tall.

'What?' I say, trying to look lovingly at her.

'My name.'

'Yes, dear.' I say. It sounds ridiculous, like I'm taking the piss out of this whole thing even more. 'He's got to put them both into the computer.'

'No, my name no like that.'

'What?' I was hoping that this little tiff made the whole thing look quite convincing. What comes next doesn't.

'You no write it like that.'

'How do you mean?'

'Like this'. She reaches forward to the screen and covers up half her name with her finger.

'Sorry?' Irritably, she snatches a pen from off the desk and writes her name on one of the leaflets we've been given. 'Ana Maria' One 'n'.

'Of course, darling, I forgot.' Yeah, forgot how to spell my fiancée's name – as you do. 'Sorry, can you just delete that extra "n",' I say. The clerk looks at me for a moment and then very slowly and meticulously moves the cursor over one 'n' in Ana and presses the backspace button. He swivels round in his chair prissily and picks up a huge diary.

'When would you like to book the ceremony itself? You can do so any time from the day after tomorrow,' he asks, skimming over pages and avoiding looking at us. My stomach twists further at the thought.

'Let's do it this week, shall we, darling?' I say, looking down at the book, as if we just can't wait. Impassively, the clerk turns the page and Ana Maria and I both stare at the week spread out before us in little lines and boxes – ready for me to make the worst mistake of my life. I wait a while for the clerk to suggest something but he just shrugs his shoulders dismissively and looks up at me.

'Erm.' My heart is racing and I know I've got to get out of here. 'Friday. Shall we?' I don't wait for Ana Maria to reply. 'Yep, Friday, what's that? 10.30? OK, let's do it then.'

'Ah, my husband,' laughs *Ana* Maria hysterically as we leave. I want to tell her never to call me that but instead I smile at her.

'Where are you going?' says Marion.

'Just out for a drink with a friend.'

'Which friend?' she says from the bath. 'And don't get shaving foam and stubble all over the sink, will you, it's not very nice for Ana Maria to have to clean up. Your poor wife.'

I exchange a glance with myself in the mirror, which Marion might or might not see. Then I carefully sluice the sink and taps down with water. 'Which friend?'

'Just an old college friend.'

'This is new – what's his name?'

'Jack.'

'Jack who?' she says, soaping a shoulder.

'What does it matter? You don't know him.'

'So what am I going to do tonight on my own?'

'I thought you were going out tonight?' I lied. 'You've usually got something planned.'

'Only to entertain you.' Eh? Never mind. Marion's World. A bit like Wayne's World only slightly less anchored in reality. Marion soaks and I shave in silence for a moment. Then I rinse my face and sit on the side of the bath.

'Look, I won't be late.'

'It's not that, Andrew, it's just that I really hoped you would take up with a slightly more prestigious set now that you're dating me. You should raise your game a little, that's all.'

'Well, I could cancel.' She sighs painfully.

'No, don't worry. Luckily I've arranged to have dinner with my Personal Shopper. She's going to do a Wardrobe Audit for me so that we can plan for the Fall.'

'Oh, good,' I say. 'I mean, that's a good idea.'

Marion still manages to make me late by asking me to zip up her dress, tell her which brooch goes best with it, which chain goes best with the brooch and whether she should go darker for the winter. Her new organic colourist says that everyone is doing it. Finally, just as I'm tearing out of the front door she tells me that I must get some new shirts because mine are *so* last year but I don't bother responding to that one.

Jane is looking slightly annoyed as I stride up to her. For one awful moment I'm reminded of our first meeting outside Paperchase in Tottenham Court Road.

'Christ, sorry I'm late,' I say kissing her on the cheek. 'You look lovely.' And she does – navy blue and white summer dress, red cardigan. Her hair is up and I can see her ears properly, the smallest, whitest, most perfect ears I've ever seen.

'Thank you,' she says. 'I was a bit early.' Good on two counts: a) she is taking the blame herself and b) she is keen.

'Where shall we go?'

'I don't know. This is your manor, isn't it?'

'Right. Well, there's an Italian place right down the other end where you can sit outside.'

'Sounds lovely. It's not too expensive, though, is it?'

'This is on me.'

'Andrew, you're the one who's out of a job.'

'Yeah, but . . .' Hang on, we don't want to go down this avenue, do we? She is looking at me expectantly. 'Yeah, but I've still got my credit cards. Come on, we can get that number 22'.

We run and just catch it.

'Upstairs,' says Jane.

'At the front.'

We go to a little Italian restaurant at the end of the King's Road and the manager, a huge man with suspiciously black hair and radiant body odour, makes a great play of finding us the last table in the garden. As we wait I realize how good it feels to be like a normal couple – girlfriend and boyfriend, husband and wife, rather than being surreptitiously scrutinized by other people as they try and decide whether we're mother and son, aunt and nephew, boss and young exec, or something more exotic.

Finally seated amidst great ceremony with napkins and jolly laminated menus, we have oily, garlicky bruschetta and then pasta with tomato salad.

'It's like being on holiday,' says Jane, looking round. Then she adds, 'Christ, that's just the sort of thing my mother would say.'

'Oh, oh. That's the first sign. You'll be dressing like her next.'

'I am. This is her dress.'

'Really? Shows how much I know about women's clothes.' Actually I've learnt quite a lot recently, following Marion from shop to shop but I don't want to think about that now.

'She's got great taste,' says Jane, stabbing a piece of penne. 'Except in boyfriends.'

'Yeah?'

'Nothing outrageous like drug dealers or toy boys,' I catch my breath but she continues unaware. I hope.

'But they never seem to work out and it's so obvious why to everyone except her.'

'I think that's quite fun. My mum and dad are depressingly happily married.'

'Oh mine only got divorced . . . what was it? Five years ago? Up to then everything was blissful. I remember thinking how boring it was when everybody else's parents were splitting up and going off with other people. I used to make up stories about them having rows and throwing pots and pans around the kitchen. I told my friends they had a very tempestuous relationship – they hated each other but were yoked together by some deep-seated passion like the couple in *Private Lives* or something.'

'Bloody hell, that's a good one.'

'Mm, I might write it up as a film script.'

'In the last scene they make love and then she dies.'

'Why not? Horribly.'

'Eaten alive by their pet piranhas.'

'Accidentally shot by one of his collection of eighteenth-century muskets.'

'Strangled by her scarf as she sets off in her sports car.'

'Anyway, then what happened? To your parents, I mean,' I ask, gesturing subtly but successfully (thank God!) to the waiter for another bottle.

'I came back from my first term at university and they said they were getting a divorce. They'd only stayed together for me and my brother and now we'd both left home they were going to go their separate ways.'

'That's awful.'

'I was more surprised than upset. Anyway they seemed quite happy about it. We went out for a Chinese that night. Weird, like a celebration. They don't live far away from each other now so it doesn't make that much difference.' The waiter brings another bottle over and she watches him open it, smiling up at him when he refills her glass. I realize how nice it is to be sitting opposite someone who doesn't feel the need to treat the waiter like shit. 'My mum said she wanted to spread her wings so she moved three streets away.' We laugh and Jane shakes her head. 'She's hardly ever been away from Birkenhead in her life. She's went to Malta three years ago and didn't like the food. She's only been to London twice and once was to stay with me last Christmas. She just walked around open-mouthed and kept talking about the price of everything and how many foreigners there were.'

'Just like my mum and dad,' I say. 'It's so embarrassing.'

'I thought you *were* from London,' says Jane, eyeing me suspiciously. Why do I always feel I'm on trial with her?

'No, who told you that? Vinny again?'

'Oh, I thought you said.'

'Vinny said, didn't he?'

'No,' says Jane, opening her eyes wide. 'Anyway, he said you'd been asking questions about *me*.'

'God, he's a gossip, that boy.'

'He's had a bit to gossip *about*.' I'm not sure what she means by this so I plough on. 'No, I'm from Reading. But if you come from Birkenhead, anywhere in the south counts as London, I suppose.'

'Patronizing bastard,' says Jane gently.

'It's true. Reading's about as cool and metropolitan as—'

'Birkenhead?'

'Well . . .'

Jane has mock hysterics and then leans back in her chair and sighs contentedly. She looks around the restaurant while I look at her. Her smooth pale cheeks are slightly flushed with wine. She turns back to me.

'What you looking at?' she says, smiling slightly.

'Not much,' I say, smiling too.

'London's mad, isn't it?' she says.

'Mad?'

'Yeah, just like so different from where I grew up. It's not just those twenty million pound houses you read about in the *Standard* and seeing famous people in the street – the kind of thing my mum loves to hear about, it's, well . . .' Her voice drops to a whisper. 'Look at those girls over there.' I take a casual glance around the garden and pause to see two pretty average Sloanes sitting behind us, talking about a wedding they've both been to. I look back at Jane and shrug my shoulders. She leans over to me and I catch another whiff of her perfume again.

'If those two went into the pub at the end of our road in Birkenhead people would think they'd come from Mars,' she hisses. 'Those accents, the pearls, the Alice bands,' she looks over my shoulder again to get a proper look, frowning with curiosity, 'the stripy shirts with up-turned collars and I bet . . .' She drops her napkin on the floor and then leans down to pick it up very slowly. 'I knew it – Gucci loafers on one and navy blue pumps on the other. If you've grown up in Birkenhead and you suddenly see them they're like creatures from another planet. If they tried to order a drink I don't think the landlord would even understand them.'

'Is that why you moved to London?'

'Sloane spotting?' She freezes for a moment and then grimaces with embarrassment.

'What's the matter?' I mouth.

'Shit, how embarrassing,' whispers Jane, trying not to giggle. 'She turned round. Never mind. No, it's just what Scousers do – move to London. It's Liverpool's biggest export, isn't it? Its population.'

'So you came to London to make some money?'

She looks at me for a moment. 'Er, no! Why do you assume everyone's obsessed with money just because you are?'

'I'm not obsessed with it. I just want to—'

'Do anything you can to make a fast buck?'

'No, I'm just . . .' Yes, I suppose I do, that's exactly it. Make some money quickly while I'm young enough and free enough to enjoy it. What's wrong with that? Why is it worse than making a slow buck? But then I'm suddenly back in the Registry Office with Ana Maria. Poor Ana Maria, who just wants to stay in a country where they'll let her clean toilets and scrub floors six days a week. I'm just doing Marion a small favour and in return she's giving me a small amount of her money so that I can get a bit of leg up.

Jane is looking at me, curious, expectant. 'Well I'm just fed up with being poor,' I say, exasperated at the simple prosaic truth. 'With having to save up for things, do without things, feel guilty if I buy something, eat out, go on holiday. Work out if I've got enough to buy a new shirt. I'm fed up with watching the pennies. I want to have enough money so I don't have to think about it.' OK, fifteen grand won't do that but it's better than nothing.

'And that's the most important thing to you?' asks Jane.

'It's not money itself, it's what it can buy.'

Jane laughs loudly. 'That old one. I don't believe you just said that.'

'And perhaps like most clichés, it's true. I want the freedom money brings you.'

'And a BMW and a house in the Cotswolds is freedom?'

'Not those particular things necessarily. But I want to just be able to go out and get them if I want them.'

'A very materialistic type of freedom.'

'Not at all.' A potent mixture of passion and two bottles of Frascati means that we're both talking loudly now but I don't care. 'I might just buy a small house somewhere warm and sit under a tree all day.'

'Very ambitious.'

'Oh, right. A moment ago you were accusing me of being a shallow, materialistic yuppie and now I'm a slob.'

'You certainly sounded like it, Mr BMW. Perhaps I was wrong, though – perhaps you just aspire to being one of the idle rich. Much grander!'

'Fuck off.' She stares at me, surprised but not offended. 'It's all right for you being a woman.' At this her jaw drops in horrified amusement. 'Oh, shut up. You don't *have* to work. You don't. Even these days, it's perfectly acceptable for you to marry some bloke and let him pay for you.'

'Ha! While I lie on the settee watching *Richard and Judy* or having coffee mornings.'

'If you want to.'

'Oh, thanks.'

'Or you could concentrate on bringing up the children, or go to art classes or write a novel or do gardening or work for a charity—'

'While my husband provides for me?'

'Yeah, because at the end of the day he *has* to. Don't you see? Even now, you've got the choice. I *haven't*. I'm going to have to sell space or do something equally soul-destroying and brain-rotting in an office until I'm sixty-five and then watch telly in the afternoon and follow my wife around Sainsbury's carrying the shopping bag and telling her to hurry up.' I have to say it: 'Like my dad.' This last comment takes the wind out of her sails.

'You could look after the children while your wife works,' she says, unconvinced.

I snort cynically. 'You've been reading our features section: "Andrew and Amanda live in West London. Amanda, twenty-seven, works in PR while Andrew, twenty-eight, looks after the couple's two children, Lily aged one and, er, Lysander aged four". Picture of floppy-haired twat in Breton top with baby sling standing next to people carrier. I used to have to share the lift every day with the gormless, horse-faced Sloanes who write that shit.' I see from Jane's face that the two specimens behind me must have turned round again. 'Oh fuck off,' I mutter and we giggle like kids then we sit back in silence while I play with the remaining penne on my plate and Jane watches me.

She says, 'God, you're gorgeous when you're angry.'

'Now who's being patronizing?' We both sit back enjoying the effect of the wine and food and pondering on this little outburst.

'I'd better be going,' she says at last.

'Sure,' I say, sitting up and looking round for the waiter. 'Sorry if I was a bit aggressive there.'

'No, don't be,' she says, reaching across for my hand. 'I like it when people are honest. What do they call it? A frank exchange of views.' She smiles wickedly.

'We certainly had that.' I catch the waiter's eye. He smiles and nods and begins to make his way over.

'You're very good at that,' she says.

'Good at what?'

'The restaurant thing. Catching the waiter's eye, asking him what's good today. All that stuff. I'm crap at it.'

'You don't have to do it, you're a girlie,' I explain sweetly.

'Any coffee, dessert?' says the waiter as he takes our plates.

'What about some *zabaglione*?' I ask Jane.

'Ooh, I *love* zabaglione,' she says, pronouncing the 'g'.

I look up at the waiter and he nods and smiles.

'One? Two?'

'Just one and two spoons,' I say.

'God, I feel quite pissed after that,' I say almost to myself as we leave the restaurant.

'I don't,' says Jane immediately.

'You must be, a bit.'

'No, I'm not,' she says boldly, walking along a line in the paving stones as if to make her point. 'I could drink you under the table, you wuss.'

'I'll take your word for it.'

We continue in silence for a while.

'You're living with her now,' asks Jane.

Oh, shit! 'How do you know?'

'Well, you more or less said, and then I rang Vinny and he confirmed it.'

'Good old Vinny.'

'Don't blame him.'

I have to answer the question she hasn't asked, 'I've just got no money and it's a place to stay. She says nothing. 'It's just made me realize how wrong the whole thing is,' I say truthfully.

'Well, like I said, I'm not keen on playing the home breaker. It's your decision,' she almost whispers.

'I'm going to end it. It's crazy. I'll live at home if necessary till I get another job.'

'Vinny says your room's still free in Fulham,' she volunteers and then seems to regret it. 'At least it was when I spoke to him.'

'I don't deserve you, Jane,' I say, stopping and turning her to look at me. I touch her neck and ear.

'No, you fucking don't,' she says.

When we arrive at the Tube station I lean down to kiss her on the cheek but somehow she moves or I change my angle of approach halfway through and our mouths meet. She tastes of garlic and wine and she smells of perfume mingled with warm skin. I pull her towards me. After what could have been three quarters of an hour we disengage. She is blushing slightly and rearranging her hair. I'm just staring at her.

Then she says, 'Thanks. It's been really nice.'

'Yeah, I'll ring you at work.'

'Yes,' she says, but not enthusiastically. 'Ring me when you've sorted things out.'

It's not late when I get back – just after eleven. Marion is on the phone. All over the settee are bits of paper – sketches of dresses, photographs, pictures from magazines. She has obviously made sure her Personal Shopper earned her dinner. I take off my jacket and get a glass of mineral water from the cabinet by which time Marion has finished on the phone. She is staring at me.

'Hi, babe,' I say and make to kiss her. She offers her cheek and I know I am in trouble. Then I know why.

'How was *Jack*?'

How could she know?

'Fine. Why?' I mumble.

'Just wondered.'

'How was the Personal Shopper?'

'Don't change the subject,' she says evenly. 'We're talking about *your* evening.'

'Oh, go on, then.' And she does. She walks over to the settee, shuffles about in the papers strewn over it for a while and then brings out a handful of Polaroid pictures. For a moment I think they must be something to do with the Personal Shopper but then she holds one up triumphantly, her eyebrows raised, quizzical and triumphant.

It's a picture of Sloane Square Tube. I look at Marion. She looks down at the photo in her hand. I look at it again. It's slightly blurred and taken at an angle but there we are: Jane, with me walking towards her, smiling. Marion holds up another – us kissing hello. Then another – us talking together, smiling again. And another – me pointing past the camera down the King's Road. Finally we're walking off together, Jane laughing.

'Where the hell did these come from?'

'Never mind. Why did you lie to me?'

I actually feel slightly sick – partly at being found out and partly at the thought of being spied on. They look like something from a *News of the World* exposé except that I'm in them.

'Oh, I didn't want you to get the wrong idea.'

'What wrong idea?' snaps Marion. 'You're fooling around.'

'I am not. Jane is an old friend from college, like I said. I just said she was a bloke to stop you worrying,' I lie fluently.

'Stop me worrying?'

'Yes. You're so paranoid. I told you – she's just an old friend. We've known each other since we were at college. She's like a sister, that's all. Look, you can see – I'm just kissing her on the cheek.' I have a quick shuffle through the pictures to check that *is* all I'm doing to her. Marion seems at least halfway convinced. She snatches them off me.

'Why haven't I met her?'

'You haven't met any of my friends. You're always telling me you don't want to.' My turn to make it up as I go along.

'She's quite pretty, even though I don't know *what* she's wearing. Is it Voyage?'

'What?'

'Voyage? That looks like a Voyage number.'

'I doubt it. I expect it's a Top Shop number.'

'Where?'

'Exactly. It's where girls from Reading get their clothes.'

'Mmm. I see.' She stares so hard at Jane that her face puckers up. I wonder whether Jane is shivering on the Tube. Then she looks at it again at a distance and looks at me suspiciously. I shrug my shoulders. 'Let's just hear no more of it.'

'OK. I'm sorry I lied to you,' I lie.

Marion takes my face in her hands. 'I don't want you to lie to me, Andrew. A relationship based on lies is no relationship at all. I discovered that from my husband.' She looks up at the ceiling. 'Both of them, come to think of it.'

What about the others? I wonder.

'I know,' I say, looking at the Polaroids. What I really want to know is who took them.

After breakfast the next day Marion goes out for a cranial massage and Ana Maria goes out to Sainsbury's so I dive onto the phone and ring Paperchase in Tottenham Court Road.

'Jane?'

'Hello?'

'It's me, Andrew.'

'Hello.' She sounds pleased to hear from me.

'I just wanted to check you got home safely.'

'Fine – just the usual onslaught from muggers and rapists but I ran faster.'

'I really enjoyed last night.'

'So did I. Erm, yes, of course, we've got them in red, blue and green but not black.'

'What's the matter? Is someone there?'

'That's right.'

'Can't talk?'

'Exactly.'

'OK, so if I say I really, really like you and I love the way you put your hair behind your ear and your theories about James Bond and snuff movies and I want to see you again, you can just say, er, what can you say? "We'll have them in soon"?'

'What size did you want? A4?'

'Say it.'

'I'll have to have another look.'

'Why won't you say it?'

'We've already discussed that but we might have them in soon.'

'That's good enough for me. Shall we do something tomorrow night?'

'If that's convenient for you but you, er, know, our terms and conditions.'

'I do – very well. I'm going to tell her tonight.'

'I'm very glad to hear that, Mr Smith.'

When she comes back Marion decides to take me to get some new clothes. We go to Emporio Armani in Brompton Road. She doesn't like the black formal suit I like mainly because I picked it out and said 'I like this one'. Of course, Mark would have approached it differently but then he's a professional and I'm an amateur. Soon to be retired amateur. In the end she buys me the one she likes plus a pair of swimming trunks because apparently we're going on holiday soon. Then we go to the florist and while she is verbally assaulting the woman behind the counter I take the opportunity to talk to Chris, the chauffeur.

'Thanks,' I say.

He looks up at me in the mirror. 'What for?'

'You know.'

He almost smiles. 'Sorry, mate, don't quite follow you.'

'The pictures. Of me with that girl?'

He shrugs slightly and grins. 'Sorry, don't know what you're on about.'

'Yes, you do, you bastard.'

Still looking in the mirror he grins even more, takes off his sunglasses and says quietly, 'Don't try and get smart with me, son. I'm only making a living out of her like you are. Oh, and just remember this, you little cunt, I know plenty of people who would gladly beat the shit out of you for the price of a pint, no problem. You won't be sleeping with any more rich old women – or men – for that matter, with a glass in your face and your balls smashed into porridge.'

'You- you'd better watch it, too,' I say huskily.

He laughs. Then he leans forward, gets out of the car, walks round and opens the rear door. One of my hands goes instinctively to my balls while the other scratches around for the door handle on my side just in case I have to make a quick exit. But he's just opening the door for Marion.

'I'm *never* going in that—' she begins. Then she stares at me. 'Are you all right?'

'Yeah, fine,' I say in a voice that doesn't sound like mine. 'I think I just need some fresh air.'

'That's a good idea. Let's walk a little,' says Marion. The last thing I see as I get out of the car is Chris smiling at me in the mirror.

'Chris, we'll see you at home.'

'Certainly. Mind the traffic, madam,' he says softly.

CHAPTER TWENTY-ONE

I TELL MARION THAT I'M GOING OUT with Vinny that night. I've rung him already, given him Marion's number and told him to ring me and suggest we go out. When he does I make a big show of saying 'Hey! How are you? Yeah, I'd love to.' Of course Vinny can't resist going slightly over the top as a piss-take but he is still quite convincing, which is particularly useful because towards the end of our conversation I hear a click on the line. I've already rung Jane from a phone box and arranged to meet her at seven-thirty at the Bibendum Oyster Bar. I want to eat shell fish with her – knock back oysters and pull the salt, sweet flesh of crab and lobster out of their pink shells.

'Out again?' says Marion when I tell her.

'Yes, just for a quick drink with my old flatmate Vinny.'

'But I have a reservation for two at The Ivy tonight.'

'Oh.' I'm not sure if I believe her. 'Sorry.' She is lying on the bed watching *Oprah* on one of the cable channels and eating low-calorie pretzels.

'Well, what am I going to eat tonight?'

'Can't Ana Maria get you something? We'll go out tomorrow night.'

'Boil in the bag fish on my own in front of the TV with that peanut-brained troll to keep me company.'

I sigh. 'I'm really sorry, I know I should have told you before, only . . .'

She looks at me for a moment. Then she picks up the phone and dials a number.

'Channing? Hi, it's me. What're you doing tonight? Who? That old lush! Cancel her. I'll pick you up at eight. OK? See you then.' She hangs up and looks daggers at me again.

'There you are,' I say pleasantly. She looks back at the telly. I watch her for a moment. Women! I sit down and pick up her hand and begin to kiss it. 'Oh, Marion, it's just my old mate Vinny.' She yanks her hand back.

'Where're you meeting?'

'A pub.'

'Near here?'

'Quite near,' I say helpfully, shit-for-brains that I am.

'OK, I'm leaving at a quarter of eight. I'll give you a ride.'

'No! Don't worry.' She shoots me another glance.

'Why not?' She smiles slightly. 'Don't you want a ride?'

'I'll just walk, thanks anyway, besides I'm going a bit earlier than that'.

'OK.' She looks back to the TV again and celebrates her victory with another pretzel.

Marion does what I half-suspected she would do.

'Bye.' I say quickly, popping my head round the bedroom door. 'See you later.'

'I'm ready,' she says, getting up from the dressing table. 'I can give you that ride after all.'

'Are you?' Normally she takes forever to get dressed and put her make-up on and I end up pacing up and down or having a couple of drinks and watching the telly while she buggers about. Sometimes by the time we arrive somewhere I am already half-cut but after a while I've got used to it and, anyway, it helps me relax.

'Yes,' she says sweetly. 'Isn't that good timing?'

'I thought you were going at eight.'

'Oh, did you?' She says innocently. 'Well, seven-thirty, eight o'clock. Something like that, Channing will just have to scrape off his face mask before it's dry, that's all.' She slips on her shoes and then looks at herself in profile in the mirror. 'What do you think? Good enough to eat?' By this time the little girl voice has become quite sinister.

'Delicious,' I say quickly.

'Shame you won't be having any then, isn't it?' she says sweeping past me. I stare at the floor in disbelief for a moment and then follow her downstairs. Then she turns round and walks upstairs again.

'Where are you going?'

'I forgot my earrings.'

I pace around the living room and flick the telly on and then off. Then on again.

Marion returns.

'That's better,' she smiles. 'OK, let's – oh- oh.'

'Now what?'

'Wrong shoes – that's you hurrying me.'

Twelve minutes – *twelve minutes* – later she comes back down again with the same shoes on as far as I can see. We finally walk out to the car. I decide I'll drop her off at Channing's and then walk onto the Oyster Bar.

'Evening, madam,' says Chris as we get in. He looks at me in the mirror. 'Evening, Sir.'

'Good evening, Chris,' says the seven-year-old Marion. 'How's your mother?'

'She's much better now thank you, Madam.'

'I'm glad to hear it. I'm going to Channing's and we're dropping Mr Collins ... Where are we dropping you, Andrew?'

'Albero & Grana in Sloane Street,' I mumble.

'Where?' says Marion, innocently.

'Albero & Grana. That bar near the top of Sloane Street. I'll show you.'

'Sounds very expensive for your friends,' says Marion.

'We don't drink much,' I say.

'Very sensible,' says Chris. I shoot him a look. He grins again.

'Oh, my God. I forgot my pocket book,' says Marion, ferreting around in her handbag. 'What is the matter with me today? Won't be long, dear, you wait here.'

She gets out. I look at my watch. It's already twenty to eight. I look up and see Chris staring at me in the mirror so I get out of the car. At a quarter to I go back in to shout to Marion that I'll walk after all but she is coming out again.

'Sorry about that.'

Without saying anything I get back in the car.

'Right, Chris, to – where was it?'

'Albero & Grana.'

'Yes, to Albero & Grana and on then to Mr Charisse's please.'

'No. Well, we may as well go to Channing's first,' I suggest half-heartedly.

'But you've got to be there at seven-thirty. Oh look, it's nearly ten to eight now. Chris, step on it will you?'

We set off into the early evening traffic. As we move into Sloane Square Marion suddenly pipes up; 'Is there an office licence near here?'

Chris is as flummoxed as I am this time.

'A what?' I say.

'An office licence. Is that what they're called? Channing asked me to bring a bottle.'

'Bring a bottle?' I gasp. 'What do you mean? Your friends never bring bottles.'

'But he's run out of booze. He had a party last night.'

I sit back. It's nearly five to eight. OK, Marion, you've won. You've *so* won.

'Safeway might be the best bet, madam,' says Chris helpfully. 'They've got quite an extensive selection of wines and spirits.'

I think 'Cunt' at Chris but he just smiles helpfully.

'Safeway?' says Marion. 'There's a thought. Is there one nearby?'

'In the King's Road, madam, five minutes from here.'

'Marion, I'll just get out and walk.'

'Bit difficult to stop here, sir,' says Chris.

'I'll see you later,' I say to Marion and give her a peck on the cheek. But the door handle doesn't work.

'Better wait,' Marion says quietly, without looking round.

Minutes later we're at Safeway. Marion goes in. I debate whether to get out and run off. Instead I pick up the car phone, get the number for the Oyster Bar from directory enquiries, scribble it on a piece of paper that I've been sitting on, and begin to ring it. I don't care that Chris knows that I'm not going to Albero & Grana.

'Hello, I'm supposed to meeting someone there and I'm slightly late,' I say quietly, aware that Chris is listening to every word, probably ready to relay it all back to Marion. Above the roar and clatter of the restaurant the girl at the other end doesn't sound very hopeful.

'What do they look like?'

'She's got dark red hair, early twenties, pale complexion . . . erm . . .'

'Hold on,' says the girl. I hear her shouting something to someone else. I look up and Chris is watching me

'Oh, fuck off, will you?'

He laughs and looks away.

'I can't see anyone exactly like that, listen we're really busy, can you ring back later?'

'Oh, please, she must be there. She's got a sort of bob and—'

There is a knock of the window which makes me jump so that I bang my head on the ceiling. It's Marion with a Safeway guy struggling under a huge box. The door seems to be working now.

'Well, give me a hand, won't you?' says Marion, who is not doing anything. The boot pops open and I help the Safeway assistant who is sweating under the strain of putting a box of Veuve Cliquot into it.

'Phew,' says Marion, giving him a tip. We get in. 'Who were you calling?'

'No one.'

'OK, let's go to – where was it?' Chris moves off slowly. Then Marion grabs my arm and shouts at him: 'Stop! I forgot: Channing asked me to bring cigarettes.' I'm almost past caring. We reverse back into a place on the double yellows lines.

'Look, I'll walk,' I say firmly.

'You can't,' says Marion. 'It's going to rain.' She slams the door and immediately the central locking clicks in. Biting my lip hard, I sit back and wait. There is nothing I can do now. Marion will be ages – she'll make sure of that. It's nearly ten past eight. I consider giving the Oyster Bar another call but then decide against it because I can't stand the thought of Chris listening in and laughing at me. I look at the piece of the paper I've written the number down on. Along the top it says: 'Montague Car and Van Hire, Wimpole Street, W1 – Leasing Agreement'. It's for this car – it mentions a black BMW Seven Series and I recognize the number plate but under client it says 'Kremer Holdings Ltd' with an address in the City. Suddenly there is click and Marion gets back in again.

'Sorry about that. Right, let's go.' I slip the paper down onto the floor.

I run into the Oyster Bar at just after twenty past eight. It is busy and there is a queue.

'Can I help you, sir?' says a young waiter, assuming that I'm trying to push my way in which, of course, I am.

'I'm supposed to be meeting someone,' I say irritably, looking over his shoulder. A few people stare up at me from their tables as I look around the room for her. I push past and then wander around, wanting to believe she is still there, that I just haven't seen her yet, that I'm just looking through her. Is that her? No, it's a middle-aged bloke with a beard. Not quite. After what seems like half an hour, by which time I've disrupted the whole restaurant and made a total tit of myself, I walk out, past people in the queue who stare at me with narrowed eyes.

I look down Sloane Avenue and then the other way towards South Kensington Tube. Suddenly I see her. In the distance. It must be her. I run across the road. A taxi blows its horn and a car stops inches away from me. I can see her walking along slowly, looking up at a poster, moving out of the way to let a woman with her pushchair past, swinging her bag at one point. When I'm near enough I shout. She doesn't turn round. I get nearer and shout again and this time she does. Thank God!

'Hi,' I say, running up to her and panting slightly.

'Oh, hello,' she says flatly, her strong intelligent mouth set determinedly.

'I'm sorry,' I gasp.

'I thought I'd been stood up.'

'I know, I'm so sorry. I just couldn't get away.'

'Don't worry about it,' she says and starts walking again.

'Jane.' I walk after her, sweating now. I catch her arm. She looks round angrily and shrugs my hand off her. 'I'm really sorry.'

'Oh, Andrew, forget it,' she snaps. 'I waited over half an hour for you, sitting there like a fucking lemon in that poncey place. Five quid for a glass of wine, for Christ's sake.'

'Look, let me buy you another,' I say and immediately regret it because it doesn't come out the way I meant. It sounds like I'm offering to reimburse her, not talk to her. She looks at me for a moment, face contorted with contempt.

'Don't worry. Really, don't worry about it.'

'Look I'm so sorry, I just couldn't get away. I tried to ring.'

'I told you it doesn't matter.' She starts to walk again.

I run up to her again. I'm conscious of stopping other people walking down the street.

'Marion just screwed things up when I was trying to get out.'

Jane looks at me again. 'Is that her name?'

I realize I've never mentioned it before. 'Yes'.

'Marion. Mmm.' She carries on walking.

'Jane.'

'Wasn't that the mother in *Happy Days*?' she says casually, still walking.

'Yeah, yeah it was. She's not very like that, though,' I add helpfully, talking to keep Jane where she is while I try and think of something to say. She takes a deep breath.

'Did she know you were coming to see me?'

'No, of course not.'

She thinks about it for a moment. 'Andrew, I don't really want to talk about her.'

'Oh, no, neither do I.' I'm looking closely at her, trying to work out what she is thinking, trying to will her to forgive me. 'Shall we go and have a drink somewhere?'

She is silent for a moment. Then she looks straight ahead, avoiding my eyes. 'I can't do this. I can't be the other woman. I've just got more self respect than that.'

'Of course, I—'

'Funny thing, is,' she says, the muscles in her pale smooth neck twitching as she fights back the tears. 'Funny thing is, I'm always meeting complete . . . fucking . . . arseholes trying to be nice guys and you're basically a nice guy trying to be an arsehole.' She gives an irritable, confused laugh. 'Why? I just don't understand.'

'Jane, I—'

'Oh, never mind,' she mutters, which is quite a relief because I don't actually know how to answer this accusation. 'You know how I feel about you, Andrew, but you've got to decide. I've had enough. Like I said, I just can't do this.' She sniffs and looks around her. 'The phone's working again, you've got my number. Just, er . . .' She starts to walk away and I know she's crying. I don't go after her. It would just make it worse.

I begin to walk back home. 'Home'? Is that what it is? By the time I get to the King's Road it has become very dark and as I walk into Sloane Square the heavens open. Big warm splats of rain clear the streets and some people at a café start squealing and running inside.

I don't care, though. In fact I walk all the way round Eaton Square as well, taking in the warm, sweet-smelling air. By the time I get back I'm well and truly soaked, even my shoes are squelching. I ring the doorbell and Ana Maria opens the door very slowly. She gasps, begins to giggle and opens it properly.

'Mr Andrew, you soaked.'

I look at her for a moment. This is the woman I'm going to marry.

'I know,' I say unnecessarily. I walk in and trudge upstairs, leaving big soggy grey footprints on the white carpet. I decide to have a bath because I need to think.

By the time Marion gets back at just after eleven I'm sitting in front of the TV still in my bathrobe. She looks slightly surprised to see me.

'How was Vinny?'

'Fine,' I say looking her in the eye and realizing that I must have drunk an awful lot. I've spurned Ana Maria's kind offer of supper. To be honest, I just can't bear to look at her at the moment. Not since we've become engaged.

'Where'd you go? The pub?' she says brightly, putting her bag down on the settee. She eyes the bottle of Scotch sitting on the coffee table next to my feet, neither of which I can be bothered to move. God, Marion don't you ever give up?

'Yeah.' I don't care that she's probably had Chris following me again with his Polaroid camera. He'd have got some good shots this time, though – me charging round the restaurant glaring at the customers while the staff try to decide how much longer they'll give me before they chuck me out or call the police, me haring around outside looking for Jane, me running along the road in front of oncoming cars to catch her up, her turning her back on me and walking off. In a way I'd quite like Marion to see those pictures, I'd like her to see what I'll do for someone I really love, really care about, someone who is straightforward and honest and just wants to have a normal relationship, not play weird mind games. And I'd like her to know that I'd never bother to run after her like that.

'Andrew, would you fix me a Perrier with ice, I'm terribly

305

thirsty. I'm just going to change.' She grabs her bag and walks off.

When I get up I realize that actually I'm really pissed. I stumble over to the drinks cabinet, gashing my shin on the coffee table. I look at it for a moment and then kick it hard with the underside of my foot. The huge vase of lilies shifts very slightly but the table itself hardly moves.

CHAPTER TWENTY-TWO

I WAKE UP IN THE SPARE ROOM. I can't quite remember how I got there but I'm just so relieved I don't have to face Marion. I reach over and check my watch. Twenty past ten. I try and swallow and find that my mouth is dry. I'm horribly hungover, of course, really sick as well because I didn't eat anything last night. I take a deep breath, stand up and have to sit down on the bed again quickly. I feel hot and cold at the same time and an icy hand seems to be very slowly squeezing my brain. I lie down again, perhaps I'll fall asleep and feel better when I wake up. But I can't.

It's not Jane's words from last night that chase around my poor, damaged mind, it's her expression. Disgust. Contempt. And I can't blame her. I look around the room for a moment and think about the house I'm in. The five-million-pound house in Belgravia. I've got the clothes. I've been to the restaurants. The truth is I deserve that look of disgust and contempt. Perhaps this my reward for trying to have my cake and eat it, have Jane and my glossy, five-star, designer-clad, business-class lifestyle. Perhaps what I am actually cut out for is to be a bit of passive, brain-dead arm candy for rich old women, after all. Like Mark, except that I haven't got the guts to go that extra mile and make some real hard cash. I might be shocked at the way he earns his living but he obviously doesn't care. Better than working in an office. Two fingers to the lot of you. But I can't quite do it.

I can't help thinking about Jane, who does work for a weekly salary fix, who does travel on the Tube, trying to open her book under someone else's armpit, who does save up for cheap holidays on a Greek island and who does talk about what was on telly last night with her colleagues. Jane, who does all the things I used to do, used to think I was too good for. The kind of things that Vinny, Sami, Pete and all my old friends do every day without thinking about them. Ordinary activities that suddenly seem not just routine but comforting and normal. I used to hate them, used to think I could find something better but now I want to do them again. With Jane.

I can't believe how easily I've slipped into this role. Lost my drive, my energy, lost most of my interests, my friends, most of all my self respect. Jane said she had too much dignity to be the other woman but I've just got no dignity at all.

What do people think when they see Marion and me eating in expensive restaurants together? When they see us nosing our way up Sloane Street in that huge black BMW with the peak-capped chauffeur – immaculately turned out (as I always am now), rich and very bored? Not just a rich couple with nothing left to say to each other but a rather strange, almost laughable, couple of beautifully dressed oddballs.

I put my bathrobe on and open the door. Marion's bedroom door is open and I can see that the bed is made.

I go into the main bathroom and let the tap run cold for a while then I splash a few careless handfuls of water onto my face and round my neck. I look up at my puffy bloodshot eyes. I don't bother to dry myself, too much effort, besides my skin still feels very warm. Carefully holding onto the bannister, I ease myself down the stairs. Still no Marion. Thank God – she must have gone out for the first appointment in her busy schedule.

I have to sit for a while on the bottom step. Then I pull myself up again and walk over to the kitchen to find some cold orange juice. Just as I am approaching the door it is thrown open and Marion appears. Suddenly it's all too much: her look of surprise and then haughty disdain, the smell of her perfume, the sadistic way she is pulling on her black leather gloves, the roar of the dishwasher behind her and Ana Maria crashing pots and pans about on the draining board. I just have that overwhelming need to get down very low, where I can't fall down any further, where I belong. Somehow I sense that the floor is my only friend at the moment.

I squat for a few seconds, concentrating on not fainting or throwing up and then look up to see them both staring down at me: Marion's face a picture of loathing, Ana Maria partly intrigued, partly concerned.

'Can I have some orange juice please, Ana Maria?' I say in a very small voice.

She looks at me for a moment and then mutters 'Yes, Mr Andrew.'

Marion is still staring.

'Oh, what?' I whine.

'Can I have a word?' she says, pushing me out of the kitchen. She is surprisingly strong. Or am I just very weak?

As soon as the door closes she puts her face close to mine. 'Now you listen to me, young man, and you listen good. When I invited you to come and live with me I was making a big commitment and doing you an enormous favour, you understand?' She pauses. 'Look around this house.' I keep my eyes firmly on the floor. 'Look at it!' she hisses. I stare at her and then look around obediently, unable to take anything in. 'Everything about it is just the way I like it, designed for me, the best of its kind, absolutely perfect. Not a thing out of place. Everything arranged exactly the way I like it. Just like my life. And I've worked fucking hard for that. You, on the other hand, are beginning to bore me just a little bit. You're the one thing that's messing things up round here and that's a real shame. You understand? Do you *understand*?' I nod. 'Good.'

There is a pause during which I begin to hear that hissing sound that you get just before you faint. 'Andrew,' she says gently. 'You're a real disappointment to me. I thought you and I could have a proper relationship, that I could teach you things, show you another world, help you to grow, but now I'm not so sure. Please prove me wrong.'

She pauses again and adjusts her gloves and then adds in a jolly way, 'OK, I'm going for a cranial massage and then to the reflexologist and then my usual epidermal rehydration session. Call me on the mobile if you want to have lunch.' She strides off towards the front door, stopping briefly to rearrange a stray lily.

Getting dressed very slowly, still in the spare bedroom, I stop for a moment and hold my thumping head in my hands. That was probably one of the worst bollockings of my life but what spooked me about our encounter was the fact that when she saw me appear at the kitchen door it wasn't just revulsion on Marion's face, she seemed to be rather amused.

After a couple of glasses of orange juice and two aspirin I begin to feel a bit better and so I sit down to watch a bit of *I Love Lucy* and some American chat show in which a girl called Shanaya, who is wearing huge gold loop earrings and a hairstyle that looks like a fairground helter skelter, is telling the heavily lip-glossed hostess that she won't have sex with her boyfriend until he stops doing her mother as well. 'Go on, girl,' shouts someone from the audience and everybody whoops and claps.

Ana Maria, meanwhile, is warming to her task: 'Here you are – breakfast for bery sick baby,' she says, bringing a pot of coffee and two slices of toast dripping with butter and marmalade. As my initial nausea begins to subside I realize that I am really quite hungry. The toast is delicious.

'Thanks, Ana Maria, you're a life saver,' I say, watching her pour some coffee.

'Here – more sugar make you well,' she says, adding two spoonfuls.

'Thank you.'

'Oh, poor sick baby,' she laughs.

'God, I'll say,' I agree, holding the cup in both hands. 'Marion's furious with me, isn't she?'

'Madam is old bag.'

'Ana Maria!' I say in mock outrage. This provokes more giggles. We both laugh, glad to release the tension.

'Madam say "Don't be kind Mr Andrew, he bring it on himself. His own fault drinking whisky".'

'Don't remind me, I think I drank half that bottle.'

'Half bottle of whisky?' shrieks Ana Maria. 'You bery sick. My poor husband.'

Oh, fuck. Why did she have to say that? I'd almost forgotten. I look up at her. 'Sorry,' she says, embarrassed. She looks away for a moment, then picks up the toast plate and goes quickly back into the kitchen. I look down at my coffee in my gilt-rimmed china cup and realize how quickly I've got used to having someone make it and pour it for me. When did I last wash up a cup?

I find myself thinking about Jane walking back to the Tube station trying not to cry like a little girl. Then I imagine having this toast and coffee in bed with her. Like I used to do with Helen at college and when she came to see me at weekends in London. Would toast taste the same with Jane? I imagine going down to the kitchen in Fulham and making it. Odd mugs and chipped plates. Bringing my badly buttered slices up to her. Eating it in bed, getting into trouble for dropping crumbs everywhere – giggling and wiping the butter from her chin. Snuggling down and making love again.

Will that ever happen? I'm planning to marry someone else, someone I don't love. Someone I can't even bear to look at anymore. Would I tell Jane – or any other girl – what I'd done? I couldn't spend the rest of my life without telling her that I'd been married before, could I?

I watch a bit more telly and listen to Shanaya's sister reveal that she is also sleeping with Shanaya's boyfriend and then I get up and go into the kitchen to break the news to Ana Maria.

She is sitting at the kitchen table looking at a clothes catalogue. I sit down opposite her. She knows something is up.

'Ana Maria, this marriage thing. I've been thinking about it. I—' Her reaction catches me out – she just bursts into tears, pushes the magazine out of the way and puts her head on the table. 'Ana Maria, listen . . . I . . .'

After a few moments she looks up at me, her breath still slightly irregular. 'Please Mr Andrew . . . look what I get.' From the pocket of her uniform she extracts a folded letter. It is very flattened and the edges are well worn. I open it carefully and immediately recognize the Home Office logo. It basically tells her that she has less than a month to leave the country or give a reason why she can stay. 'I cannot go back dere,' she sobs again.

'Ana Maria, I know.' I reach across the table and take her hand with its stubby fingers and bright red nail polish. 'I'm sorry, I just don't think I'm the one . . .'

'You want more money, I have money,' she says quickly.

'Oh no, it's not the money, I don't care about the money,' I hear myself saying. Did I really say that? 'It's just that . . .' I don't actually want to explain that going through this illegal charade makes me feel sick and that I'm afraid of us both getting caught by the police and that it might rob me of the possibility of a real wedding at some point in the future. Or force me to live a lie. Ana Maria's probably more worried about food and sending money to her family than she is about issues like flowers, choral music and making my mum happy. As I watch her shoulders heaving and tears falling on the catalogue pages I ask her, 'Isn't there someone else who could do it? Mark? Don't you know someone?' All of which sounds bloody insulting but the whole situation is too weird to worry about that.

'No, we try. My friend, Maria, she might know a guy who do it, but he want too much money and madam won't pay him because she don't trust him and there is no time.' She fingers the letter as if it were a death warrant. We sit in silence as I try and think of anyone I know but then I realize that every single one of my friends, hip, urban, fun though they might be, would be just simply appalled at the idea of doing this. I've got to try and remember how normal people think, difficult though it is these days.

Then I think about the ceremony – ten minutes, horrible, a bit like going to the dentist, but then I get £15,000, yes *fifteen thousand quid*, let Jerry sort out the legal stuff, Ana Maria's dream is fulfilled and a year later the divorce thing comes through and no one is any the wiser. I'm single again. After all the hassle I've been through over the last few months, I'll finally have something to show for it. I look at Ana Maria again, she is staring up at me through huge, brown, watery eyes. Oh, God, I've come this far, raised her hopes, made plans for myself with it, let's just do it.

People do worse things for money.

I nod at her. 'OK,' I almost whisper. I try to smile.

She smiles back up at me and then begins to cry again. I squeeze her hand and wander out of the kitchen.

Back in the living room I stare out of the window for a while and think about Jane. I'm about as low in her estimation as I could be, so it's not like this marriage thing, even if she ever possibly knew about it, could make things much worse. OK, Jane, with your shared flat in a crappy old house in Holloway and your job at Paperchase, your nights in front of the telly with tea or cheap white wine and your friends who bring their own cans of lager to barbecues – you've got it made. Congratulations!

It's no good, I start envying her again. That's the life I know.

I lean forward and let the cool glass of the window soothe my aching, burning forehead. Then I reach for the phone and start to ring Mark's number but I hang up quickly before it rings, realizing that I need to talk to a real person about this, someone who would understand that you might want to spend some time with someone without crisp fifties being involved so I ring my old direct line at the office. Unsurprisingly I don't recognize the voice that answers. I ask to speak to Sami.

'Who?' says the voice.

'Sami. That is Classified Ads, isn't it?'

'Yes, but I don't think there's anyone here called Sami.'

'There must be: Sami, Asian girl with long hair, sits at the end by the photocopier.'

'Look, I'm sorry, there's no one here called Sami,' says the voice, obviously getting pretty irritated that I'm stopping him using his phone to do what God put him on earth to do – sell space. 'Can't help you, goodbye. Oh, hang on . . . What's your name?'

'Andrew. Andrew Collins. I used to work there.' I hear my name being repeated to someone else. I decide that if it's Debbie I'll just put the phone down but it isn't, it's Maria.

'Andrew, look, I can't really talk because Debbie will be back in a minute but Sami's sort of disappeared.'

'What?' I get up quickly and start to pace around the room. 'What do you mean she's disappeared?'

Maria sighs deeply. 'Oh, God. Listen, you mustn't ring here again, OK and please don't try and do anything because you'll make things worse.'

'Maria, what the hell do you mean she's disappeared?'

'She's gone away for a while,' says Maria. 'Thing is, Andrew, she was having a bit of fling with Ken Wheatley. The finance director? And anyway, her brother found out and went ballistic. He came here, beginning of last week, threatening to kill Wheatley. God, it was awful – such a mess. It was too much for security, old Ted nearly had a heart attack. They had to call the police and they calmed him down – Sami's brother that is. Seemed like a nice bloke, really, just very, very upset. Can't really blame him can you? What a shit!'

'Wheatley? I'll say, I just can't believe it. There was no clue, was there?'

'No one can believe it but it's true. So, anyway, he's on – what do they call it? Gardening leave, or something, probably going to get the sack I should think—'

'Where is Sami?' I almost shout at Maria.

'We don't know, I think she did go home in the end. She didn't even have time to clear her desk. I had to do it. Didn't take long, very neat and tidy, actually, that's Sami for you—'

'Have you got her home number?'

'Can't give it out, Andrew.'

'Oh, Maria, for fuck's sake—'

'Debbie's the only one with it and she wouldn't give it out to anyone, certainly not—'

'To me. Yeah, s'pose not.' Debbie probably thinks I'm the last person who could help her – and she's probably right. 'Poor Sami. Where does she live? Somewhere in Ealing, isn't it?'

'No, Hounslow, I think.' Christ, I can't even remember that. How little I really know about her. Poor Sami, always smiling, always good, doing all the right things and look where it got you.

Maria suddenly whispers, 'Gotta go – Debbie's back.' The phone goes dead.

I put the receiver down. Suddenly there is a tight feeling in my throat and a pressure behind my eyes and I realize I'm about to cry. Oh, Sami, perhaps if I'd been there I could have helped. You could have told me about what was happening with Wheatley. I could have calmed your brother down. I could have helped you sort out your life. Perhaps instead of your thinking about me all the time and about the mess I was slowly getting myself into I could have been there for you a bit. Poor, poor Sami.

I arrive early at Joe's and order a bottle of Badoit with lots of ice because I'm still dehydrated from the night before. Marion arrives just as I'm downing my third glass.

'Hi, sweetie.' She'd rung me an hour earlier, all love and kisses, to ask me if I would have lunch with her. The complete character U-turn had spooked me a bit. I agreed to have lunch partly because I want to get this wedding thing sorted out, well, all right, tie up the money aspect after the way Jonathan has ripped me off so royally – and partly because I'm hungry and there is no food in the fridge and, as usual, I don't have enough cash to buy any.

I smile. It must be pretty unconvincing.

'Aw, poor baby,' she says, putting her bag down.

'I feel terrible.'

'You boys. You must have been really bad last night.' I look at her for a moment, wondering how she can do this. Aren't I the one thing in her life that isn't perfect and is screwing everything else up? She's either being sweet to me as part of some sadistic mind game or she really just does not have normal emotions. I begin fingering my fork, looking at my Picassoesque reflection in it. A shattered, distorted face.

She knows perfectly well that I didn't go out with Vinny last night.

'How much did you drink in the end?' I just look at her for a moment. 'You were still at it when I came back, weren't you?' She waits for me to say something. 'Channing says "Hi".' There is another pause. 'You must feel bad. You needn't have come if you didn't feel up to it.' She reaches across and runs the back of her hand down my cheek. I turn my face away from her and tell her to get off me. Two Prada princesses on a nearby table turn to look at us and then carry on talking. Marion looks disapproving.

'Are you going to eat something? It'll make you feel better.'

'I'd better since I'm here.' I'm starving actually.

'Well, don't force yourself.'

Marion begins to chat a bit about how funny Channing was last night and about how there was a boy called Tony there who was so adorable and so funny and so cute she'd invited him to dinner next week. Then we eat just one course – bangers and mash for me, caesar salad for her – in silence.

As we wait for the bill, Marion says, 'Don't forget your wedding is on Friday.'

'I know.' Of course! So that's why she's being so nice to me, she wants to make sure it's all going ahead.

'I thought you might have forgotten.'

'No.'

'I've given Ana Maria the morning off.'

'Very kind of you.'

'Have you thought what you're going to wear?'

'Christ, no. Just a suit, I suppose. Do you want to buy me one as a wedding present?'

'We'll see. Charles and Victoria have agreed to be your witnesses.' Marion looks down at the table and smiles.

'You think this is funny, don't you?'

'No,' she says, hurt. 'This is a big commitment for me.'

'For you?'

'Yes. To make sure the Home Office believes your story, you'll be married to Ana Maria for at least a couple of years.' I look at her for a moment. Which is worse – having your lover married to another woman for two years or having your maid shackled to a no-hoper like me for that long? And, more importantly, which of us is she planning to get rid of first? She raises her eyebrows quizzically. 'Besides, I don't think you realize what kind of effect it's having on me.'

'What kind of effect *is* it having on you?'

'I'm quite cut up about it.'

'*You're* cut up about it?'

'Of course, seeing my lover marry someone else. That's a pretty bitter pill to swallow.'

I laugh. The Prada princesses and some other customers turn round.

'It's a pretty bitter pill for *me* to swallow,' I say through gritted teeth.

'I think it's the least you can do for me,' she says coldly, her dark eyes narrowed. 'I've given you a home for the last few weeks, taken you on trips and how have you repaid me? Getting drunk, abusing my staff. Cheating on me – yes, I know about that Australian slut. You're certainly making plenty of money out of it.' Her tone lightens. 'Which reminds me, I'll give you a cheque this afternoon.' I don't answer for a moment. 'If that's OK with you?' I still don't answer, wondering whether to tell her to stuff it and walk out now. 'Unless you don't want it.'

'Thank you, thank you, I'm very grateful.'

'If you want cash it will take a bit longer,' she says, looking around the room to see if there is anyone she knows.

'No, a cheque is fine.' I mutter. Cash would be safer, but

makes it all even more demeaning. But this is the last time she'll taunt me like this. And somehow it makes me all the more determined to get that money, her money. I know now what I'm going to do with it. I'm going to use it so sensibly, invest it, make every penny work for me. It's small change to her, a couple of trips to New York, a shopping trip to Paris, but it's a massive sum to me and I'm going to use it to start a business or put down a deposit on my own flat, something worthwhile, something laudable, something that will give me some security so that I never have to do this, never have to beg again. Something that even Jane couldn't disapprove of even if she would be appalled by how I got it.

The bill comes back and as Marion signs the slip for the first time in our relationship I get a close look at her credit card.

She goes off for a seaweed rub and I wander down Fulham Road, window shopping as usual, until it occurs to me that the only way I'm going to get one over on Marion, the only thing that will really spook her is if she realizes I know who she is. If she knows that I know she told me a pack of lies on our first lunch date and that I know she is not the Upper East Side aristo she pretends to be but . . . who is she? Someone else. I'm sure it won't help me get anything out of her financially but it will just make feel better. Besides, I think I deserve to know the truth: father in the discount furniture business, dodgy South American hubbies, Kremer Holdings and all. Not least I want to know why her credit card has 'Mrs J Martinez' written on it. The only person who can help me and corroborate Davina's story is Victoria. I can't go to Channing because he'll just go running back to her and besides, I can't stand the sight of him. I didn't get to ask Victoria the other night but now might be my chance.

I grab a taxi with the £20 Marion has given me.

'Where to?' asks the driver and I give him Victoria's address.

Victoria arrives back at her house just as I do.

'What a delightful surprise,' she says, taking off some huge dark sunglasses with massive gold coins on the arms and then triple-kissing me. Bending down so far makes me feel a bit queasy again but I recover myself. 'I was having lunch at the Collection with an old friend from Spain. We used to live in

Madrid, you know. Guess who she is staying with in London?'

'I've no idea,' I say quite truthfully.

'Her sister! Can you believe it?' Well, very easily actually, but I manage to look suitably surprised. 'Will you have some tea?' says Victoria as she lets us in.

'Thanks very much, I'd love to.'

Victoria says something in Spanish to her maid and then we sit down in her tiny living room. She chats about some people I don't know and then asks how things are going in the hotel business. I look at her for a moment and then realize that's supposed to be me.

'Oh, I'm not in the hotel business.'

'I thought you worked in hotels,' says Victoria, totally unembarrassed.

'No,' I say in a friendly way. 'I'm ... Well, I'm just deciding what to do next.'

'Very sensible,' she says seriously. 'It took me many years to decide what I wanted to do with my life.' We both sit in silence for a moment trying to think what she must have plumped for. A career in lunching, perhaps?

'Victoria,' I say, leaning forward in the ridiculously small seat I'm squashed into. 'I was just wondering something.' How am I going to put this? 'About Marion.'

'Oh, Marion,' says Victoria laughing and clapping her hands together. 'I love Marion, she is my best friend in all the world.'

'Yes,' I laugh as if to say 'Isn't she everybody's?' 'Well, Marion and I were teasing each other last night—'

'Oh, Marion! Always teasing, always joking.'

'Yes, always. Erm, well, we were joking about our previous lovers, you know. She was trying to guess who mine were and I was trying to guess who she had been out with or, you know, even married to before she started going out with me.'

'Oh, Marion has had lots of husbands. She love them.'

'Oh, I'm sure she did love them—'

'Yes, Marion love husbands.' That is not quite what I meant but never mind.

'There was Edward, wasn't there?'

'Oh, yes, Edward.'

'Yes.' There is a pause. 'Did you know him?'

'Oh, no, she is diborcing Edward before I know her.'

'Oh, of course. What about the South American guy?'

'My father love Marion, she's so funny, so beautiful.'

'Yes, I know. But who was the South American guy?'

Victoria looks at me. 'My father.'

'What? Marion was married to your father?'

'Yes, that's how I know her.'

'Your father's . . . what was his name? Josef?'

'Yes, they meet in a restaurant in Rio and fall in love.'

'And was your mother still alive, then?'

'Oh, yes, she was in the ladies' restroom.'

'Right.'

'Then she married British man.'

'Yes, Lord something or other.'

'Right.'

'Then she married another South American? Carlos or something?'

'Yes, Carlos. Bery nice man. Bery funny. Bery generous. Bery good shot.'

'Good shot?

'With a gun, you know.' She aims an imaginary fire arm at me.

'Right. Very useful. Do you know what her father did?'

'Her father? Oooh, what did she say her father did?'

'Was he a lawyer?'

'Lawyer, that's right. Very good.'

'It's just that someone, er, one of her friends told me that he sold furniture or something.'

'Ah yes, so they say. In Scarsdale or Queens, I think.'

'So he *wasn't* a lawyer?'

'Oh, I can't remember,' laughs Victoria.

'And she told me her second husband, your father, was so jealous that she had to divorce him, she couldn't stand it any more. And then she said she had never been married again.'

'Yes.'

'But this friend of hers told me that she married this British lord and then the other South American – Carlos.'

'Yes.'

'Victoria, sorry, it's all a bit confusing, that's all. Marion tells me one thing but then her friends tell me another.'

Victoria laughs and then looks at me sweetly. 'So the thing

is,' I carry on slowly. '*Was* she married twice or was she married *four* times? And *does* she come from the Upper East side or is she from Scarsdale?'

Victoria shrugs her shoulders.

'Do you know?'

Her expression changes, 'Why you want to know?'

'Why do I want to *know*? Well, it's obvious isn't it, I want to know who Marion is.' Just then the maid brings in the tea and Victoria concentrates on pouring it, offering lemon or milk and then handing me a tiny, china cup with a silver teaspoon. 'You understand, don't you? She's lied to me and it's all a bit weird.'

Victoria sighs and looks at me. 'You *know* who Marion is.'

'No I don't.'

'Of course you do. You see her every day, talk to her, make love to her. Why you want to know who her parents are? They are not *her*. Does it *matter* who she is married to before she meet you? It's so English. You're so, so concerned with history, always thinking in the past. All you ever want to know is where people come from, who their parents are, where they go to school. Does it matter? It's the person you know here and now that counts. Like that song: was it Ethel Merman? Do you remember Ethel Merman? No, probably too young. "It's not where you start, it's where you finish". Marion once say to me "You gotta hate where you came from and love where you're going to". Understand? Marion has made bery nice life for herself – very American really. Let her be whoever she wants to be, why shouldn't she? The important thing is she is in love with you and you are in love with her and you guys are happy at the moment. Make the most of it while it lasts.'

I set off to walk back to Marion's. Some children are coming out of a junior school in the next street. A little girl is walking along in a very busy, grown-up manner while holding her boater on with one hand and struggling to carry a painting in the other. White socks pulled right up and children's sandals – heavy and comfortable. It's a painting of a big red boat on a thickly painted wavy blue sea. The sky, hanging above, is also blue and thick and wavy. I smile at such solid childish certainties. 'Then we had music and movement with Mrs

Jackson and then we had sausages for lunch and, Mummy, Emma didn't eat all hers . . .' she is saying.

She looks up at me, sees me smiling and smiles back. Looking away, I catch her mother's eye – cold and suspicious.

I get home and ring my old Fulham flat just in case Vinny happens to be home. I'm glad to hear that my voice is still on the answer machine. I don't leave a message.

Then I find a piece of writing paper and begin to write to Jane care of Vinny. I don't mention the wedding, of course. But even though I try various versions nothing sounds right. When I look again at what I've written for a fifth time I notice Marion's address at the head of the paper.

CHAPTER TWENTY-THREE

MARION IS SITTING IN THE LIVING ROOM on the phone with a towel on her head. A woman with red hair in a messy bun and 'Miami Beach' sweat top is painting her toenails while Marion watches intensely. The woman looks up at me and says 'Hello' in a slightly uncertain way.

I nearly rang Jane on the way back but I chickened out. I'll ring her when I've got this crap out of the way. I did ring my mum and dad. Thank God I got the answer phone. I left a message saying that I had moved into a new flat and that it didn't have a phone yet but as soon as it did I'd give them the number.

'Where have you been all afternoon?' asks Marion, still staring at the woman working on her feet.

'Oh, I just went for a walk,' I say, dropping down on the settee and putting my hands behind my head.

'Where did you go?' Marion is obviously mystified why anyone would want to do such a thing since it doesn't involve people or money or expensive things.

'Just round Chelsea,' I say.

'You sure that's Mustique, Dawn? It looks much darker on the colour chart.'

The pedicurist looks up in terror at Marion, mumbles something and then shows her the bottle. Marion squints at it for a moment. 'Doesn't this look too dark? You can hardly see my tan,' she says.

I open my mouth but realize that I can't be bothered to answer so I shut it again.

'Mmm.' Marion considers it for a moment. 'It'll have to do. It's just because I'm wearing sandals at Marsha's thing tonight. Come round tomorrow morning and take it off, though, will you?' Assuming she is talking to the pedicurist and she hasn't found some new task for me, I channel surf for a moment – a woman wearing a sweatsuit, standing in a huge

American kitchen is tearfully telling a man she is going to get her daughter back whatever it takes, then there's a woman cutting up a kiwi fruit and telling us how easy something is, a woman sitting on a settee asking another woman how she felt when she heard the news. Marion is talking to me again.

'Sorry?'

'I said you'd better start getting ready.'

'What for?'

'For Marsha's.'

'What time does it start?'

'About eight.'

'It's only quarter to five,' I say.

'Well, we don't want to be late.'

'How is it going to take me three hours to get ready?'

There is a pause as Marion stares at the woman whose hands are now visibly shaking. Then she says, 'Once you get in that bath.'

'What?'

'Well, maybe you should go and rest up a little. You know how wine goes to your head when you're tired,' says Marion. 'I don't want you embarrassing me again.'

'Again?'

Marion says nothing. I look at her for a moment but she is concentrating again on the pedicurist who is literally keeping her head down. I get up and walk to the door.

'Where're you going?' says Marion. I don't answer, partly because I can't be bothered and partly because I don't know. I really don't know.

I walk around Eaton Square and up to Sloane Square where lines of traffic are gradually moving around the traffic islands and disappearing down the King's Road and Sloane Street like a knot slowly being pulled undone. The light is low and yellowy and autumnal. It feels like the end of the summer holidays.

I decide to sit at a café in the square and have a cappuccino. After half an hour of idle origami with an empty sugar sachet I order another one.

By now I feel tired and sticky and want to have a bath. Marion is actually right – I could spend a couple of hours in there. I catch the waitress's eye and do some air writing. She smiles and moments later brings me a saucer with the bill. It is £6.40. For two cappuccinos? Bloody hell! Ridiculous! God, I sound like my dad. I reach into my trouser pocket and know immediately that I haven't got enough. I find a fiver, a twenty pence piece and a penny. Fuck! The taxi fare plus a couple of magazines and a bag of Maltesers have used most of the twenty Marion gave me.

I look round and immediately the waitress, a French girl with long black hair in bunches and thick black eye make-up, is at the table.

'Hi, look, sorry, I'm a bit short of cash. I'll just dash across the road to the cashpoint shall I?' The girl looks and smiles and I realize that she hasn't understood a word I've said. I take my card out of my wallet and start thrusting it into the air.

She laughs and says,

'Oh, OK.' I laugh too and get up to leave. On the way out I walk into the manager who has been watching us.

'Can I help you?' he says, obviously meaning the opposite.

'Yeah, I'm a bit short of cash so I'm just going across the road to get some more. Won't be a minute.' He nods sullenly and turns away. By the time I get to the cashpoint a queue has mysteriously formed and I get stuck behind some daft old biddy in an anorak who, when she is asked whether she wants a receipt, tries to calculate to the nearest tree the effect it will have on the world's non-sustainable forests. I'm just about to reach over her shoulder and press 'no' on her behalf when she does it herself.

Then it's my turn. I jam in my card, stab in my PIN number, choose 'Cash' and the machine blinks back at me: 'Card retained – refer to bank'.

I have to walk round the square, down the King's Road a bit, behind Peter Jones, across Sloane Street and along to Eaton Terrace Mews to avoid the café and its justifiably suspicious manager. It's nearly seven when I ring the bell and so Marion, who opens the door to me, is furious.

'Where the *hell* have you been?'

I can't be bothered to argue.

'Just walking.'

'Walking? What is it with all this walking suddenly?'

'I dunno, I just like walking.'

The next morning I'm watching TV while Marion gets ready to go out. Our usual morning routine.

'What are you doing to today?' she asks, looking in her bag for something.

'Dunno, really.' I keep my finger on the remote so that the telly flicks through one channel after another.

'Will you turn that off while I'm talking to you?' says Marion, interrupting her ferreting. I hit the off button and we're both slightly stunned by the sudden silence.

'That's better,' say Marion after a moment. 'You watch far too much TV for a young man. You should be out doing things. How do you expect to be able to make the kind of money you need to live in this style?' Well, that's where you were supposed to come in, I think, almost laughing out loud at the idea of it. Did I ever really believe that?

Instead I say, 'I don't know.'

'Such a waste of a life,' says Marion sadly. I let her consider this tragedy for a minute. Then I switch on the telly again.

'Andrew?'

'What?'

There was a pause.

'I said what are you going to do today?'

'Oh, I don't know. The usual. I might go for a swim a bit later.' I swill the last of the coffee around my cup and wonder if it's too cold to drink.

'That's a good idea. I'm going to arrange for you to join the gym I go to down the street. It's extremely good.'

'Thanks,' I say, switching the TV on again.

'They have a very good swimming pool and someone to swim alongside you all the way.'

There is a pause as I notice a girl in a swimsuit and hope for a moment that I might have unwittingly stumbled on the porn channel. It's not – she's actually modelling some white plastic garden furniture on a quiz show.

'What's the point of that?'

'What's the point of what?' says Marion, now scraping around in a drawer in her desk. There is another pause. This time I'm sure I've found it. No, it's an American advert for 'Sports Illustrated – the Swimsuit Edition'.

'The point of having somebody to swim alongside you,' I murmur vaguely.

'Erm.' Marion apparently finds what she is looking for. 'To keep you company, take your order for the café afterwards. One of them is an astrologist – like she says, you can firm your thighs and know your future at the same time.'

Perhaps I was just rather drunk last night at Marsha's but I'm beginning to suspect that I'm becoming quite incoherent. I can't seem to finish a sentence these days, perhaps because I never have to say anything much, really. I just have to ask for things – in shops, restaurants, from Ana Maria. Sometimes I just point or raise my eyebrows. Marion's friends don't really want to hear from me and I certainly haven't got anything to say to them.

I watch the TV for a moment longer and hear the hoover start up in the other room. Then I rush upstairs into the bedroom and open the wardrobe. My two scruffy old bags have long been chucked out but there is a nice new leather and canvas holdall in their place. I pull it down and then open the drawers.

My socks and underpants are neatly folded. Who else do I know who has their undies ironed and *folded*? I pick them up and throw them into the bottom of the bag. Then I look at them – all unfurled and twisted, like bodies thrown from a car crash. I pick up a pair of socks. They are silk ones Marion had Ana Maria buy for me when I complained that all mine had holes in them. I smell them and rub them gently against my cheek. They catch slightly on day-old stubble. Poor things. I fold them neatly again and put them back in the drawer. Then I do the same with the undies. I squash down the bag again and push it back onto the top shelf of the wardrobe.

On the way to the pool I go into a call box, put ten pence in, then a twenty just in case and begin to dial Vinny's number at work. Just for a chat. Perhaps meet up for a drink. The number rings once and I hang up. I stand and look at the cards around me, offering Strict Nurse, 50DD, Asian Babe and New to London. I realize people walking past must assume I'm trying to choose which one to call so I leave quickly.

Marion and I spend a quiet evening in watching TV at opposite ends of the settee. I suppose she doesn't want to go out to dinner because she doesn't really want to talk to me. The feeling is mutual. I can hardly bear to look at her these days. I think she just wants to get this marriage thing out of the way and then dump me. I was wondering why she couldn't find an English maid but then who would want to work six and a half days a week and get treated like shit by a mad woman? Fifteen grand sounds like quite a bargain on Marion's part when I come to think about it. Every time she opens her mouth it is to say something ridiculously offensive. I've asked her a couple of times about the cheque but there is always a problem with it. Once she said it would take a while to raise it and I said, 'Oh, come on, you must have that much in your current account.' She told me not to be impertinent. I just laughed at her. Another time she started writing it but then Channing rang and next thing she had to get ready for dinner which takes her about eight hours. I can hardly stand over her and make her write it but it's just such a shag to keep pestering her. How did I choose such a wrong 'un? I don't know whether she does it to be annoying or whether she simply doesn't understand she is doing it. Which is worse?

I don't sleep much that night. Marion tuts every time I turn over or move. Eventually she says, 'What's the matter with you?'

'I'm getting married tomorrow, remember?'

'So? Just get some sleep. You want to look your best on your wedding day, don't you?' I can't be bothered to get cross with her. I change my mind about going through with it every few moments. £15,000 for nothing. I'd be divorced within a year and no one would be any the wiser. What if the police find out? What if I'm thrown into a nightmare scenario of official letters, police interviews, summonses. Would I go to prison? Or would it be just a fine? Marion would have to pay it – she got me into this mess. I look across at her, apparently asleep peacefully under her eyepads. Somehow I just know she wouldn't be around if that happened. I turn over again, away from her, and hug my pillow. No, like Jerry said – and Mark too – people do it all the time these days, no one ever finds out. No one is ever caught.

I can smell again the disinfectant and hear the squeak of shoes on those hard, polished floors in the Registry Office. Would it matter if in years to come I say to my future fiancée, 'I'd prefer a Registry Office. Why? Not very religious myself and there is something else I should mention . . . ' Almost embarrassed to think it, I find myself wondering, in case the situation ever possibly arose, about what Jane would want. I keep replaying a conversation with her over and over in my head. 'Jane, I've told Marion it's over. I've left her. I want to be with you. I love you.' 'Want to be with you'? No, that doesn't sound right.

I nod off for a moment and then wake up to find the room bathed in a pale orange light. I realize that I'll never get back to sleep again so I get out of bed very quietly and go downstairs. I get myself a glass of orange juice from the fridge and flick on the telly. It's some seventies detective thing my mum used to watch.

I suddenly have another panic – what if someone *sees* me? What if someone from work or one of my friends happens to be walking down the King's Road and sees me coming out of the Registry Office in a dark suit with a girl in a dress?

They'd just assume I'm at someone else's wedding. Besides, who cares?

My head suddenly feels heavy and my eyelids sting with lack of sleep. I rest my head on the back of the chair and close my eyes.

I wake up after what can only be ten minutes or so with a headache and the makings of a stiff neck. Literally in the cold hard light of day I've decided not to do it. I'll pack my stuff and sneak out. Poor Ana Maria – left in the lurch. Still, it won't be the first time it's happened to a bride and not many grooms could have as good a reason as I have for not turning up. I'll never have to see any of them again. I'll get out of this, out of this whole mess. I wish I had someone to talk to about it. Someone normal.

I go upstairs to have a shower and a shave and by this time Marion is awake. It's just gone eight. I can smell bacon frying downstairs. Ana Maria has obviously decided that her husband needs a hearty breakfast. Or is that the condemned man? A thought strikes me: isn't it unlucky to see your bride the day of the wedding? I look at my foamy face in the mirror and laugh. How unlucky can I get? Marion calls to me.

'Yeah?' I carry on shaving.

'You all right in there?'

'Fine.'

'Nervous?'

Am I? Not really, not any more.

'No, fine.'

'Good.' Marion comes to the bathroom door and I look at her. Is this one of the last times I'll see her? She catches sight of herself in the mirror and ruffles up her hair.

'I've arranged for Chris to take Ana Maria. He says to leave here at ten fifteen to be safe. You should leave maybe a little earlier – why not walk? You're very keen on walking at the moment.'

'I suppose so.'

'Then we can all come back here and have a glass of champagne.'

'OK. Are we having lunch after the, er, the thing?' There is a pause. Marion ruffles her hair again, still gazing at her reflection.

'Do you think I should go shorter this Fall?'

I walk downstairs and there is a scream and a giggle from the kitchen. The door slams shut and then a moment later another Ana Maria emerges.

'Hello, Mr Andrew,' she says, as if reading a script. 'I am Ramona, Ana Maria's friend. I cook you breakfast because you must not see Ana Maria this morning.'

I look at her for a moment, noticing that she is almost identical to my bride. 'I just want a cup of coffee and some Rice Krispies, please,' I tell her. I wander over to the settee and switch the telly on again. The girl goes back into the kitchen.

'Now *I'm* feeling a tad nervous,' says Marion, coming into the room. Somehow this is obviously supposed to be my fault. I carry on staring at the telly. 'Is that the suit you're going to wear? Well? Stand up and let me look at you.'

I glance up at her. Immaculate in a bright yellow suit with black brooch and necklace.

'Oh, Marion, for God's sake.'

'Stand up and let me look at you.' I do as she says. She tightens my tie and picks some imaginary fluff of my shirt. 'Where's your jacket?'

'Over there.'

'Don't leave it on the settee. It'll get crumpled. Hang it up.'

Ramona creeps into the room with a tray.

'Ana Maria, pick up Mr Andrew's jacket and hang it somewhere, will you,' says Marion to her. 'Oh, and I'll have a coffee – decaff and some of my special herbal detox pills.'

Ramona pauses, looking confused and frightened for a moment. Then she whispers, 'Yes, madam.' Leaving the tray on the coffee table she makes a dash for the kitchen.

'No, forget the coffee,' says Marion, still picking fluff off me. 'Just some of that organic Chilean honey in hot water.'

'Yes, madam,' says Ramona now in abject terror.

'Oh, and make sure it's mineral water. Not that cow piss out of the tap.' She carries on patting my shirt and adjusting my tie. 'You want to look your best even just for this wedding—' She stops and looks at me quizzically. I give a little snort of laughter.

'It's Ana Maria's friend,' I explain. 'Ana Maria doesn't want me to see her this morning.'

'Oh, OK. Sweet. Anyway, what was I saying? Oh, yes. I know it's not a real wedding but it'll be good practice anyway. I have to tell you, I was so much better at my second wedding. Everyone said so'.

'What about about your third and fourth?' I ask, looking her straight in the eye.

'There, that'll do,' she says, patting down my lapels. 'I'll see you at the Registry Office.'

Chris rings the entryphone dead on ten.

'The big day,' he says.

'Fuck off,' I tell him, not looking away from the telly. Marion has gone back upstairs to shout at the pedicurist. Ramona appears again.

'Mr Andrew, Ana Maria says you should set off.'

I'm about to tell her to get lost but then I think I'd actually quite like to get out of the house. I pick up my jacket, push past Chris in the doorway and walk out.

I'm slightly stuck for cafés so I wander into Peter Jones. Women in pearls and stripy shirts with up-turned collars are picking up crystal glasses. 'Something like this would be perfect for a casual supper party in Gloucestershire,' says one to her mother.

'But will it fit in the dishwasher?' the mother points out, triumphantly. They look up at me. I must be staring.

Finally I make it up to the computer department and so I start to play patience on one of the machines. Someone asks if they can help. I say no, thank you. After losing a couple of games and finally winning one I check my watch. It's nearly ten twenty-five. I'm not surprised. I follow a woman with a pushchair into the lift and go down to the ground floor.

Outside it's started to rain. There is a taxi coming down the other side of the road so I dash across and grab it. Funny how you can always get a taxi when you don't want one. I tell the driver 'Chelsea Town Hall, please' and reach into my pocket. Five quid. That'll do. The traffic inches along in a dismal line. Ahead there is nothing but rain-blurred rear lights. It takes us ten minutes but finally I see the Town Hall coming up on the left. The driver slides back the glass and twists his head round.

'Wanna geddout 'ere, mate? Might be quicker.'

I think about it for a moment.

'No, just carry on.'

'Suit yourself.'

By nearly twenty to eleven we are just yards away and there is Ana Maria wearing a bright orange suit, peeping out anxiously from the doorway. She is carrying a little bunch of flowers. Oh, God, Ana Maria, why are you making this worse? Or do you just think that you're never going to get a chance to do it properly? With a real husband who really loves you? You deserve better than this.

Chris is standing next to her, looking around furiously. Then, behind them I notice Charles and Victoria. The witnesses, Marion said. Very kind of them. But there is Channing, wearing a Tartan suit, orange shirt and a black tie. And beside him are Farah and her new boyfriend who looks very uncomfortable. What the hell *is* this? I notice Marion's friend Renata and another couple we met recently from Hong Kong or somewhere. Daria is looking madder than ever with thick black, pencilled-on eyebrows and the two French boys are lighting cigarettes. A woman we were introduced to at Aspinalls is checking her face in her compact while another woman I recognize from New York is talking to her and adjusting her hat. Even the couple we bumped into after our first date are there. Scattered around them are other rich, glamorous oddballs I've met over the last few weeks. I see

Christopher Maurice-Jackson looking at his watch and the woman talking to him is Marsha whose house we went to the other night. Standing behind them, smiling that 1000-watt smile and listening intently to a Middle Eastern-looking woman I don't recognize, is Mark.

The whole fucking world is here.

Marion has invited everyone she knows. They're all here to witness my humiliation, to take part in this ridiculous pantomime. 'Look,' she is saying. 'Look at what I can make my toyboy do. Much funnier than jumping through a hoop, don't you think?'

I lean forward. 'Just . . . '

'Yeah?' says the cab driver, watching the traffic anxiously.

I take a deep breath. Chris has spotted us and is moving forward hesitantly, looking down into the cab window to check it is me. He says something to Ana Maria and she looks straight across at me.

'Just keep on.'

'What?'

'I said, just keep going.'

'I thought you wanted—'

'Well, I don't now. I've changed my mind. Drive on. And lock the doors, please.'

'What?' says the driver, looking round.

'Please will you just lock the doors and drive on.'

Chris has dashed down the steps, through the shoppers with their umbrellas and across the pavement to the cab. His hand reaches the door just as it clicks locked. The other side of the steamy, rainy glass, his face is a mixture of surprise and anger. We stare at each other then I throw myself back into the seat.

He pulls at the handle again and shouts something. The cab driver is also shouting. He moves forward and Chris is dragged along with us a few yards. He starts to bang on the glass.

'What the fuck's going on?' says the driver looking round. 'Oi, fuck off.'

'Look, just drive, will you.'

Chris's hand hits the glass again, leaving a perfect hand print. The driver stops again.

'He a friend of yours?'

'No, no. Please, let's just get out of here.'

'You'll be lucky. Have you seen this traffic? What the fuck you want me to do? Drive over it?'

Chris knocks on the glass hard and his face, streaked with rain, contorted with fury, appears inches away from the window, shouting for me to stop.

'Look, I don't want no trouble,' says the cab driver, beginning to sound nervous now. 'What's the matter with him?'

'Nothing. Let's just get out of here. Can't you overtake or something?'

'If he smashes that window—'

'He won't. Please! Just get going. Look, let's turn off here.'

I look round again and there is a flash of orange. It's Ana Maria. Her hair is flattened and scraggly with the rain and her mascara is running down her cheeks. She looks at me mystified for a moment and then starts pleading and crying, her fingers trying to push down the window.

'I'm sorry,' I shout. But it sounds like I'm sneering.

'Who's she?' says the cab driver, trying to keep his eyes on the road. 'Look, what the hell's going on here?'

'Take this right,' I yell. 'Look here, we can go now.'

I look round again and Chris has his arm round Ana Maria a few yards behind us. The driver sees this as well and seems relieved. But just then Chris and Ana Maria move aside. I know what is coming next.

Marion's face appears, miraculously dry because someone is holding an umbrella over her. She is calm and says loudly but without shouting, 'What *are* you doing?'

I look her full in the face, realizing that it is probably the last time I'll ever see it.

'I said, what are you doing, you pathetic little piece of shit?'

Is she smiling?

It's very faint, but she's definitely smiling. And then it comes to me. Marion and me: it's not about arm candy, a blank canvas for her to draw on or even sex with someone less than half her age.

It's about sadism. And I've fallen for it. There are no whips or nipple clamps, here, no, it's much weirder than that. Marion just loves torturing me: making me run around after her, poor and lonely and bored to death. She loves the thought of my making a fool of myself with her outrageous camp friend in a restaurant, looking like her lap dog in posh shops, cutting a bit of my dick off for her and now taking part in a grotesque farce in front of her friends. No wonder she is prepared to pay so much for *me* rather than anyone else to marry Ana Maria.

The cage I've been in for the last two months or so isn't a gilded one, it's one of those accessories for bondage you see on late-night television shows about kinky sex. The tight lead I've been on is the leather-studded one you see a corset-wearing woman in a black, plastic-lined cell using on a bank manager or a civil servant.

"Kin' 'ell" mutters the driver and does a sharp right. I keep staring ahead, not daring to look round. A few hundred yards down the street we stop.

'Right, get out,' says the driver.

'I'm sorry, can we go on?'

'I've had enough of you, mate.'

'Look, please. It'll be fine now.' I apologize some more and tell him where to take me. He curses again under his breath and we set off.

When we finally arrive, the rain is hammering down harder than ever but I hardly feel it as I get out. I reach into my pocket and pull out the single fiver. The meter says £11.80. I look at it and then at the driver and dumbly hand over my only note. It takes a second for him to realize that he is not getting anything else.

'I don't fuckin' believe it.'

I turn round and walk through the traffic with the driver shouting after me.

She is nowhere to be seen and I'm just about to ask someone when I spot her at a till at the back of the shop, handing over some change. The customer, an old woman, says something to her and she smiles.

'Jane.'

She looks up at me and then freezes.

'Andrew.'

'Can we talk?'

She looks down at the counter.

'Not here. Ring me tonight if you want. Vinny's got the number.'

'Jane, I've finished with Marion.' It feels good to say it finally.

'Andrew, please, not here.' Something is wrong. I try to catch her eye, hoping that my news just hasn't sunk in, that she hasn't understood yet. I reach across the counter and try to touch her hand but she moves back.

'Jane, I've left her.' I take a deep breath and say it. 'Look, I love you. I want to talk.' She winces and looks away.

'Oh shit, Andrew.'

'What's the matter?'

'Please, not here, not now. Can we talk about it later?'

'All right, all right.' I try to look her in the face but she is still staring down at the counter. 'Just tell me everything's all right, that you're pleased and . . .'

But she doesn't. Then she looks up, but not at me.

'Are you all right, Jane?' A woman is now standing next to me at the counter.

'Yes, I'm fine. Sorry. Can I just have a few minutes off the floor?'

'Of course, I'll get Belinda to cover for you,' says the woman, looking at me. I'm still staring at Jane, trying to work out what she is thinking. Silently she leads me across the shop and we go out through the fire exit into a long, dimly lit corridor. Jane stands against the wall opposite me.

'Andrew . . . oh, Christ, how can I say this?' Finally she looks me in the eye and begins to shake her head very slowly.

'Oh, no, please.' I realize it's me speaking.

'Well, what did you expect? I thought you might try and ring me the next morning. I don't know what's going on. You're *living* with another woman, for God's sake—'

'I know but like I said, I had no money—'

'Let me finish.' She stares at the wall next to me. Then she laughs bitterly. 'I was going to say I thought it was over but it was never really on, was it?' I can't answer that. 'Was it? Andrew, if you really cared about me you'd have rung me the day after we had that – we *didn't* have that stupid drink in that stupid bar. You just went back to her. What did you expect me to do?'

'I had to get things sorted out.' No, I don't really believe that.

'Sorted out?' She laughs again. 'All you had to do was to end it with her – if you really wanted to.' She looks at me. Now I'm looking down, trying to avoid her eyes. 'I told you I wasn't the sort of girl who'd be the other woman and I meant it.'

'I know you did.' I take a deep breath. 'Jane, look, I'm sorry, I've been so stupid.'

'It's not that,' she says softly. 'You've been so weak. That's what got me. Andrew, I really liked you, I think I still do, but you've been so pathetically weak.'

I open my mouth to speak but I can't think of anything to say. Jane is silent. The fire door bursts open again and a woman walks into the corridor and looks slightly startled. She mutters something apologetic and then carries on.

'I told you, it's too late. Look, this is my last day here. I'm going to South America tomorrow.'

'What?'

'I'm flying to Buenos Aires tomorrow afternoon.'

'Why? Who with?'

'A friend from university. I handed in my notice here the day after we met and they let me go early. Remember we talked about South America in the pub that night? Well, I'm doing it.'

'What about when you get back?'

'Andrew, I've told you. Please don't make this worse. Look, I've got to get back to work.' She sniffs back a tear. 'Goodbye.' She walks back towards the door and pauses for a moment. 'I'm sorry,' she says, without looking round.

The sun is breaking through the clouds as I leave the shop. I begin to walk down Tottenham Court Road towards Oxford Street. As I approach the Tube station a girl comes up to me, looks me in the eye and says something to me in a sad, soft voice. She has long blonde hair and pale blue eyes. But it's her skin – so clear and so pale you can almost see the veins underneath it. Her eyes open wider, almost in fear, and she speaks to me again.

'What did you say?' I ask. I've got no money if she's begging or looking for business. She seems so vulnerable, so

unworldly that I wonder whether perhaps I've found someone who's in worse shit than I am, somebody who has
managed with great skill and determination to fuck up their
life more badly than I have.

She fixes me with a desperate look and touches my arm
'I say you want learn English?' I look down. She has a flyer
in her hand.

'No,' I tell her. 'No, thank you.'

I never went back to Marion's. Slowly I walked all the way
from Tottenham Court Road to Fulham. I'd probably have
walked even if I'd had the Tube fare. I rehearsed all the things
I should have said to Jane, trying to cap her arguments as if
winning these little battles would help me win the war I had
so hopelessly lost. At the beginning of Knightsbridge I nearly
started back again at one point. Then I stopped at Hyde Park
Corner, watched the traffic for a while from the safety of the
pavement and carried on walking west again.

By the time I got back to Vinny's it was gone four o'clock. I
sat down on the step to wait. It rained again, I think, and at
one point a woman walked past with a pushchair and a
Walkman, telling the little boy running alongside her 'No! I
said no. You've already had one – don't be greedy.'

'Andrew?' says Vinny. I look up at him.

'Hi,' I say, my voice surprising me with its huskiness.

'What you doing here?' he says, apparently only slightly
surprised to see me.

'Fuck knows.'

He lets me in and we have a long game of One A Side
Indoor Football, silent and intense. Both gasping and gleam-
ing with sweat, we come to a sort of natural full time and
Vinny takes a couple of my remaining beers out of the fridge.
He chucks me one. I open it on the side of the kitchen table
and drink.

'Well?' says Vinny after he has done the same.

'My room still free?'

Vinny smiles. 'Yep.'

'Good.'

'Wanna talk about it?'

'No.' I take another swig of beer. 'Well, not yet, anyway.'

I found a job in a pub round the corner the next day. My mum and dad were horrified when I told them I'd left the media sales business (OK, I couldn't bring myself to say 'sacked') to go and work in a pub. Later though, my dad was quite impressed when I told him how much I got cash in hand with overtime. I had visions of him trying to find a reference to this in one of his self-help books. ('Don't be a service industry wuss! Implement multi-directional manual glass-stacking procedures to suit your personal dynamic opening time schedule!').

The flat's landlord still had my deposit and I calculated that I could actually make my rent quite easily with my new income – and I didn't have to start work until ten. Yes, Marion did ring for me – three or four times. Each time she just left a tight-lipped message asking me to call her as if she was chasing up a debt or ringing to enquire why I'd missed a dental appointment. I never returned her calls.

I got into the habit of letting the answer machine click in rather than answer the phone just in case it was Marion again, or Mark or Jonathan or a dozen other people I didn't want to speak to. But one evening when I was at home between shifts drinking tea and reading the paper in the living room I picked it up without thinking. It was Sami.

'Sami?' I gasped.

'The one and only,' she giggled. 'The notorious.'

'What, what? Where are you? Are you all right? I've been trying to get hold of you but I didn't have your—are you all right?' I was cradling the receiver as if the connection might break at any moment.

'All right, all right,' she laughed. 'I'm staying with a friend at the moment. I'm OK.'

'Thank God. I rang the office and they wouldn't give me your number.'

'I bet they wouldn't – probably Debbie's attempt to punish *both* of us.' Her voice sounded different – deeper, more self-assured.

'So what happened? You and Wheatley? I can't believe it.'

She laughed. 'Neither can I. Neither could anyone else.'

'How . . . when?' There were so many questions.

She told me their affair had started about six months ago

when he called down to our office for some figures. Sami was working late and she happened to know where the relevant papers were kept so she brought them up to him.

'We spent some time going through them in his office and by that time it was gone ten o'clock so he offered me a lift home. We stopped for a drink in a wine bar nearby,' she said, sounding rather well rehearsed. No doubt she had told this story to quite a few people already. 'After that we had a drink or dinner together a few times, very discreetly, of course, and then—'

My mind was racing for more clues. I remembered Sami's strange reaction – more than simple embarrassment – when we bumped into him that morning in the lobby.

'But he's such a creep,' I blurted out.

'Don't laugh, but he's actually quite charming when you get to know him and quite funny actually.' She giggled at my stunned, sceptical silence. 'Really. Anyway, I suppose he made me feel good, special. Suddenly a rich, successful . . . I don't know . . . powerful man takes an interest in you, someone who knows how the world works, someone older and more sophisticated who takes you to expensive restaurants . . .' Sounding less practised, she drifted off for a second. 'Do you see what I mean?'

'I know exactly what you mean,' I said quietly.

'And it wasn't just sex – it was more than that. We only slept together a few times, at weekends away and things.'

'I think I can understand.'

'Not many people can. My parents don't know why I left such a good job, they're always going on at me. I told my sister a while ago and she just couldn't believe it, kept asking how I could do a thing like that. Then my brother, Jat, overheard us talking about it one evening and the next morning he went round to the office and just blew up. He won't speak to me but apparently it was awful.'

'So Maria told me.'

Sami said, 'Then I realised that you were doing something similar . . . I mean, going out with an older woman.'

'Sort of,' I said, comparing Ken Wheatley to Marion for a moment but then feeling slightly disgusted at the thought of both of them. 'I don't think I was as much a victim as you were, though. I asked for it.'

'Victim? It takes two to tango.' Sami and her phrases.

'I suppose so. But that's all over now.'

'You split up?'

'Yep.' Then I said, 'Sami, why didn't you tell me?'

'I couldn't believe it was happening at first and and then, well, you had troubles of your own, didn't you? How could I?'

I swallowed hard. 'Oh, fuck, I'm so sorry. If only I hadn't been so wrapped up in my own problems, so—'

'Half asleep at your desk?'

'Well, yeah, I suppose so. Otherwise perhaps I would have noticed something.'

'Andrew, men *never* notice these things.'

I laughed. We made a date to meet for a drink, the first evening out I'd planned for a long time and I hadn't been so excited about a date since Jane.

One weird thing I noticed was that although my biggest work concerns were checking that we weren't running out of clean glasses during opening times and my greatest challenge was trying to understand how the till worked, I was actually enjoying the experience of working again.

When I was with Marion at first I thought that if a day off work was enjoyable and a week off was even nicer then, by simple arithmetic, a lifetime off must be better still. Every day a holiday! Just what I always wanted. Like winning the Lottery.

But it's not. It's like being unemployed except that you're not even aiming towards something. You fill your days but in the same way you kill time on a rainy Sunday afternoon. 'A task fills the time allocated to it' or something like that, says Parkinson's Law, according to what we learnt at college and it's amazing how long you can spin out going to the shop to buy a newspaper if you work at it.

While I was serving one evening some men in suits came in shouting about bonuses and it occurred to me that you can place the various different ways you can get money on a sort of ladder of merit. You can earn it (which is pretty high up), you can make it yourself (also quite high up – unless, perhaps, you're poor, sad Errin's dad), you can earn cash in hand (like I'm doing now and that is slightly lower down), you can inherit it (quite far down), you can steal it (further down) or you can beg for it (just a bit higher up, perhaps?).

I'd probably put Marion, a serial alimony beneficiary, quite low down and the same with Jonathan the pimp, Viv the hooker and Mark the rent boy. I don't quite know where Channing, Charles and Victoria and lots of the other people I met would come because I still don't know how they made their millions but I'd put the scheming, desperate little shit I became somewhere beneath all of them. I was right when I was at Errin's that night – the way you get money can bugger you up. Like I said: make it and it can turn you mean and bitter, inherit and it can make you soft and decadent. Beg it from someone you're living off, leaching off, and it makes you both.

I do miss the expensive restaurants and the holidays but not the stress that went with them. I realise now that I never felt comfortable travelling or eating out with Marion – I knew people were staring at us discreetly in those restaurants, shops and business-class lounges. Going out with Vinny and Malc the other night for a curry just felt so easy and natural.

However shocked I was to discover that I was playing slave to Marion's sadistic master, the truth is I can hardly I blame her, of course. Like Chris said, I was just trying to earn a living off her and so perhaps she was right to expect something back – although it wasn't quite what I could ever have imagined. I was doing better out of her than Chris in many ways and Mark, if I'd bothered to ask him, would probably have given me seven out of ten for a first go.

Except that there'll never be a second go.

I bumped into Mark in the King's Road one day. He didn't seem particularly pissed off or surprised that I'd left him and the others in the lurch that rainy Thursday but Marion, he said, was furious. When she got home she physically attacked Ana Maria and blamed her for frightening me off. That's a good one, I thought, when he told me. Then she went off to Mauritius or somewhere with Channing. When I asked Mark whether she was angry and upset because I had dumped her or let her down in front of her friends and inconvenienced her domestic arrangements, or whether it was because she really loved me, he looked surprised by the question.

'Oh, I think she was just generally pretty narked. It *was* a bit embarrassing for her and Marion hates to be embarrassed. Hey, listen, there's a South African woman I met the other night, late forties, newly divorced, absolutely loaded, horny as hell . . .'

Looking at his handsome face and into his smiling, vacant eyes, I said, 'No thanks, mate. Seeya,' and slapped him on the arm affectionately.

Other than not wanting to meet Mark's South African, or anyone else he knew, I wasn't sure what I wanted to do with my life until one Saturday morning, a postcard arrived. It had a picture of the opera house in Buenos Aires on one side and an address in the city on the other.

It was all I needed.